S0-ADA-183

Mates, Dates Simply Fabulous

BOOKS 1–4

Mates, Dates Simply Fabulous

BOOKS 1–4

Cathy Hopkins

Simon Pulse

New York   London   Toronto   Sydney

This book is a work of fiction. Any references to historical events, real people, or real locales are used fictitiously. Other names, characters, places, and incidents are the product of the author's imagination, and any resemblance to actual events or locales or persons, living or dead, is entirely coincidental.

SIMON PULSE
An imprint of Simon & Schuster
Children's Publishing Division
1230 Avenue of the Americas
New York, NY 10020

Mates, Dates, and Inflatable Bras
copyright © 2001 by Cathy Hopkins
Mates, Dates, and Cosmic Kisses
copyright © 2001 by Cathy Hopkins
Mates, Dates, and Designer Divas
copyright © 2001 by Cathy Hopkins
Mates, Dates, and Sleepover Secrets
copyright © 2002 by Cathy Hopkins

Originally published in Great Britain in 2001, 2002 by Piccadilly Press Ltd.

Published by arrangement with Piccadilly Press Ltd.

Designed by Debbie Sfetsios
The text of this book was set in Bembo.
Manufactured in the United States of America
This Simon Pulse edition January 2006
2 4 6 8 10 9 7 5 3 1

Library of Congress Control Number 2005935236
ISBN-13: 978-1-4169-1829-5
ISBN-10: 1-4169-1829-9
These titles were published individually by Simon Pulse

Mates, Dates Simply Fabulous

BOOKS 1-4

Mates, Dates, and Inflatable Bras

Chapter 1

What Makes Me "Me"?

If she picks me out in class again, I shall scream.

Wacko Watkins. That's what I call her. Our new teacher. We've got her for PE first period this morning, worse luck.

"I wonder what kind of weird project she's got lined up to torture us with this week," I said as we hurried down the corridor to get to our classroom before second bell.

"She's okay as teachers go," said Izzie. "She makes you think about stuff. And she seems really interested in what we feel. I like her lessons."

1

"Well I don't," I said. "It's bad enough having a mum who's a shrink without getting it at school as well. I get that 'let's all share our feelings' stuff at home. I wish Watkins would give me a break here. She always singles me out."

"Probably because you're quiet in class. She's trying to find out what's going on in that daft head of yours. You're lucky. At least your mum and dad bother to ask what's going on. All mine care about are my marks. Whether I get A, B, or C. I think I'd faint from shock if either of them ever asked how I actually *felt* about anything."

Izzie's my best mate. Or was. I'm not sure anymore. Not since Nesta Williams arrived at the end of last term. Izzie and I have hung out together since middle school. It's always been me and Izzie. Izzie and me. Sharing everything. Clothes. Makeup. CDs. Secrets. And then along comes Nesta, and I reckon it's two's company, three's a crowd. But I seem to be the only one who sees it that way. I'm going to have to tackle Izzie about it, but I rarely get her on her own these days.

"Hurry along and take your places, girls," called

Miss Watkins, coming up behind us.

I hope she hadn't heard what I said about her.

Miss Watkins is a bit odd looking. Make that very odd looking. She looks like she put a finger in an electric socket. Her expression is always startled, like a cartoon character who's seen something shocking and their eyes pop out. She's as thin as a wire, and her hair's frizzy grey, coiling out at all angles.

"Okay, girls, now settle down," she said. "We've got a lot to talk about today."

Here we go. Talk. Talk. Let's talk. I wish we could read today. Quietly. Or write. Quietly. Why do we have to talk? Doesn't anyone realize I'm going through a quiet-but-mysterious phase? Like Geri when she split from the Spice Girls.

As Wacko perched on the corner of her desk and hitched her skirt up, we all got an eyeful of her pale legs above knee-high stockings. She has skin like Saran Wrap. Transparent. You can see all the veins underneath it. Enough to bring up your breakfast first thing in the morning, I can tell you.

3

"There's a few things I want you to start thinking about for the rest of the term," she continued. "As you probably know, it's soon going to be time to choose your subjects for next year. Which ones you want to do."

Inwardly I groaned. I've been dreading this. See, I don't know. Haven't a clue. Not the faintest.

"I know it's a lot to think about and I don't want any of you to panic or feel pressurised. We've plenty of time, that's why I want you to give it some attention now so it doesn't come as a big rush later on."

Too late, I thought. I'm already in major panic mode.

"I want you to think about your future. Your goals. Ambitions. What you want to be when you're older. Right, anybody got any ideas?"

She started to look round the class so I put my head down and tried to become invisible.

"Lucy?"

I knew. See. I knew it would be me she asked first.

"Yes, miss?"

"Let's get the ball rolling. Any idea what you'd like to do?"

4

I could feel myself going red as everyone turned to look at me.

Duhhh? I dunno. Doctor. Nah. Too much blood. Dentist. Nah. Fiddling about in people's mouths all day. Yuk. Vet? *Yes*. Vet. I love animals. After Izzie, Ben and Jerry, our Labradors, are my next best friends. So, vet? I could be on all those animal rescue programs on telly, looking glam as I save poor animals. Maybe not. Ben stood on a piece of glass last week. I almost fainted when the vet said he'd have to have a few stitches in his paw. I couldn't watch. Had to leave the room like a right sissy. He was fine after but I can't bear to see an animal in pain. So probably not the best career choice. So what else? What?

"Don't know, miss," I blurted out, wishing she'd choose someone else.

"No idea at all?" she asked.

I shook my head.

Candice Carter put her hand up. She was bursting.

Thankfully Wacko turned to her.

"Candice?"

"Lifeguard, Miss Watkins."

5

"Lifeguard. Now that's an original one. And why do you want to be a lifeguard?"

"So I can give all the boys the kiss of life, miss."

Everyone cracked up laughing. She's such a tart, Candice Carter.

"Anyone got any more sensible suggestions?" asked Miss Watkins, looking round.

By now, half the class had their hands up.

"Writer," said Mary O'Connor.

"Nurse," said Joanne Richards.

"Air hostess," said Gabby Jones.

"TV presenter," said Jade Wilcocks.

"Hairdresser," said Mo Harrison.

"Rich and famous," said Nesta, and everyone laughed again.

Everyone knows what they want to do. Everyone. But me.

I'm fourteen. Everyone's always saying, "Oh don't grow up too fast" and "Enjoy your youth," now suddenly it's, "What're you going to do with the rest of your life?"

"Excellent," said Miss Watkins. "Those who know what they want to do are lucky. And those who don't," she looked pointedly at me, "don't

6

worry. You don't have to decide today. But it does help to have some inkling of what direction you might like to go in when it comes to choosing your subjects later. For those of you who don't know, we'll have a look at it all over the next few weeks. In fact a good starting point is to take a look at who you are now. Identify your strengths and weaknesses. The seeds of today are the fruits of tomorrow. The thoughts of today are the actions of tomorrow. So, to start with, I'm going to give you an essay to be handed in at the end of term. Doesn't have to be too long. A page or so."

She picked up her chalk and turned to the blackboard.

What makes me "me"? she wrote.

"That's your title. I'll give you fifteen minutes now to make a few notes."

She wrote a few more questions up on the board.

Who am I?

What are my interests?

What do I want? What are my goals in life?

What are my strengths and weaknesses?

What would I like to do as a career?

7

For the last part of the lesson, I could see everyone scribbling madly.

I knew what Izzie would be writing. She wants to be a singer. Has since we were nine. She writes all her own songs and plays guitar. She wants to be the next Alanis Morissette. She even looks like her now. She's got the same long dark hair and she wears the same hippie dippie clothes. Not my taste, but they suit Iz.

I glanced across at Nesta. She was writing frantically as well. Typical. She's so sure of herself and where she's going. She wants to be a model and will probably get there. She's totally gorgeous-looking. Her dad's Italian so she's got his straight black hair, like silk right down to her waist, and her mum's Jamaican so she's got her dark skin and eyes. She could easily be Naomi Campbell's younger sister. Tall and skinny with an amazing pixie face.

I wish I were black. They have the best skin, even when they're old. Like Nesta's mum. I've seen her on television. She reads the news on cable. She's ancient, at least forty, but she only looks about twenty. I'm the typical "English rose," pale, blond, and boring. I'd rather be a tropical flower, like Nesta, all exotic and colorful.

I stared at the blank piece of paper in front of me. What makes me "me"? I began to write.

I'm small and don't look my age. People always think I'm in Year Seven or Eight.

I stared out of the window hoping for inspiration. Jobs for little people. Maybe I could audition to be one of the Munchkins if they ever remake *The Wizard of Oz*? They're tiny. Or Mini Me in the next Austin Powers movie.

And what are you going to be when you grow up, Nesta? Model.

And you, Izzie? Singer-songwriter.

Lucy? Mini Me.

Yeah. Right. Now I'm being plain stupid. I must have some decent ideas locked in my brain somewhere.

I made myself concentrate. What makes me "me"?

I'm the youngest in my family.

Fifteen minutes later and that was all I'd written.

"Just before the bell goes," said Miss Watkins, "I'd like to give you all a profile sheet to fill out.

Purely for yourselves to help get you started if you're stuck. Nobody needs to see them, they're only for you, to get you thinking along different lines."

I looked at the sheet of paper she handed me.

Help. I'm usually good at essays and stuff. But this time I haven't a clue. I don't know who I am. Or what makes me "me."

Or what I'm going to do when I grow up.

Or where I fit.

Profile Sheet

Name: Lucy Lovering

Physical
Age: 14 but I look about 12.
Height/build: 4 foot 8 and a *HALF*. Slim,
   30 minus A chest. My brothers call me Nancy
   no tits. Not funny.
Coloring: blond hair, blue eyes.

Sociology
Parents' occupations: Mum's a shrink
   (psychotherapist), Dad runs the local health
   shop and is a part-time musician.
Education: favorite subjects: Art, English
                worst subjects: anything else.
Home life: two elder brothers: Steve (17) he's
   a computer whiz, Lal (15) he's sad, spotty,
   and humungously gross but thinks he's God's
   gift. Two dogs: Ben and Jerry.
Race/nationality: English/Scottish. Possibly alien.
Hobbies: reading, magazines, old movies, TV,
   sewing.

Psychology

Ambitions: good question.

Frustrations/disappointments:

- my parents, who are a pair of old hippies.
- Mum and Dad always ramming herbal teas and health products down my neck when I'm quite happy with chips and burgers.
- Mum's obsession with recycling and buying clothes from charity shops.
- the fact I'm so small.
- the fact my best friend now appears to be Nesta Williams's best friend.

Temperament: I think I may be going mental.

Qualities: sense of humor, a good best friend when allowed to be.

Abilities/talents: good listener, good at drawing.

Chapter 2

Angel Cards

When I got home after school I did what I always do. Headed for the fridge.

"When the going gets tough . . ." I said.

"The tough eat ice cream," finished Izzie, swooping in and taking the tub from the freezer.

"Diet again on Monday," said Nesta.

I can't believe she diets. She's as thin as a rake.

By five o'clock our kitchen was packed. Me, Izzie, and Nesta tucking into bowls of pecan nut fudge. Brothers Steve and Laurence plus two of their schoolmates, Matthew and Tom, all busy

13

cutting mammoth hunks of bread then slapping on peanut butter and honey. Yuk. Mum making a cup of tea. Herbal of course. And Dad attempting to feed Ben and Jerry who are more interested in my ice cream than dog food.

It's chaos in here.

"Why did you call them Ben and Jerry?" asked Nesta, pointing at the dogs—Ben, who had his paws up on my knees trying to get his nose in my bowl, and Jerry, looking longingly at Izzie in the hope she'd take pity and give him a taste. I gave Ben the last spoonful to lick; I'm a sucker for his great sad eyes and that pathetic "no one ever feeds me" look of his, plus he's still got his paw in a bandage, poor thing.

"We named them after they ate a whole tub of Ben and Jerry's Chunky Monkey when they were puppies," said Lal through a mouthful of bread. "They love ice cream."

I think Lal fancies Nesta, he's gone all creepy and over-friendly since she walked in. He keeps flicking his hair back and giving her meaningful looks. I don't think she's even noticed. He likes to imagine himself as a ladies' man. Ever since Tracy

Marcuson next door let him snog her last Christmas. He's not bad-looking in a kind of Matt Damon way, but I don't think Nesta would be interested. She likes older boys or so she says. And not that she'd fancy my eldest brother Steve either. He's seventeen and a bit too swotty-looking for her, though he's quite nice looking when he takes his glasses off and has a decent haircut. But he's not bothered about girls, unlike Casanova Lal; Steve prefers computers and books.

"It's like Waterloo station in here," sighed Mum, clearing a space at the table. She doesn't mind though. Our house is always full of people, usually all piled in the kitchen, which is the largest room in the house. Dad knocked a wall through last year to open it up a bit, and though we do have more space now, he ran out of money so couldn't finish the job.

"What are those marks on the wall?" asked Nesta, pointing to some pencil marks by the fridge.

"Our heights as we were growing up," said Lal, getting up and going to stand against the wall to show her how it worked. "See, on every birthday we measure how much we've grown with a pencil mark." He pointed to the highest. "Those are Steve's."

"And these must be Lucy's," said Nesta, looking at the shortest marks. She stood at least six inches higher than I had last birthday.

She then had a close look at our "original" wallpaper. To cover up for the lack of it, Steve, Lal, and I have plastered our artwork from school all over one wall. And Mum, who's convinced that one day Dad will actually get round to decorating, has used another area to try out different color paint samples.

"Very *Vogue* interior," Nesta smiled as she examined Mum's wall, which looks like a patchwork quilt of misshapen daubs in various shades of yellow, blue, terra-cotta, and green.

"Not," I said.

I haven't been to Nesta's house yet, but Izzie has and says it's amazing. Straight out of an interior design mag. Still, Nesta doesn't seem bothered by our lack of decor style. In fact she appears to like it here, as she comes back most nights after school now. Her mum works different shifts as a newsreader on the telly and her dad's a film director so he's often away shooting. Nesta has an older brother as well but she says he's hardly ever at home either.

Izzie has always come home with me, ever since I've known her. Her mum and stepdad don't get home from work until after seven so it was arranged ages ago that she'd come here until one of them picks her up.

Izzie says I have to give Nesta a chance and get to know her properly, but I'm not sure how I feel about her being here all the time. It's like, first she moves in on my best friend, and now she's moving in on my family. I'm trying to be friends and I do sort of like her—it's hard not to, she's great fun—but I can't help feeling pushed out. Everyone loves Nesta when they meet her. She's so confident and pretty.

It all started a few weeks ago when Izzie came to find me after school. She looked out of breath as if she had been running.

"Can Nesta come back with us to yours?" she asked, looking behind her as though someone was following.

She saw me hesitate.

"She needs friends," she said. "She's not as sure of herself as she makes out. I know she acts all tough, like she doesn't need anyone or care what anyone thinks of her but I just found her at the bus

17

stop, crying. That creep Josie Riley and her mates have been calling her names, and she doesn't want to go home until her mum's back. I don't want to leave her there on her own.'

I'd have felt mean refusing and I did feel sorry for her. I know what those bullies in Year Eleven can be like.

"Yeah. Tell her to come," I said. "That is if she doesn't mind my mad family."

Course Mum and Dad made her welcome straight away. They always do with people. They may not have enough money to paint the kitchen walls but they don't seem to mind feeding the neighborhood. Love, peace, and have a chunk of organic bread. That's what they live by. Share what you have. The world is just a great big family.

Because Dad runs the local health shop we're fed all sorts of weird stuff. All organic, preservative free. Tastes okay though. But some nights I don't know what I'm eating. Tahini. Gomasio. Miso. And herbal teas. Disgusting. Especially chamomile. Smells like cats' pee. What I'd give for a McDonald's followed by a big fat chocolate milkshake. But no, Mum and Dad are veggies so the only burger you get round here is the tofu variety and milkshakes are made of soy.

Izzie says it's one of the things she likes best about Mum and Dad, but then she's into all that stuff as well. New Age, alternative.

"I wish my parents were cool like yours," she said once. "They really care about stuff. The environment. What we put in our bodies. They're not like usual boring parents."

"Exactly," I said. "I used to love the way they were when I was younger, but I wish Mum would look a bit, well, a bit more bland these days."

"Why?" said Izzie. "I think she looks brilliant."

"Brilliant?" I said. Not a word that would spring to my mind when describing Mum's style. Peculiar more like.

"I love a bargain," Mum's always saying. "Which is why I shop at all the charity shops. You get a good class of cast-off in North London."

Mostly I don't mind, but last month's parents' meeting was the worst. I wanted her to look normal for once, but she came down the stairs ready to go, wearing red-and-white-striped tights, a purply tweed skirt, *and* a green checked jacket. She has no sense of color coordination at all and slings it all together with total disregard for what mixes and matches.

"What do you think?" she asked, giving me a twirl.

"Er, very colorful," I said, thinking fast. "But why not try your green jacket with some navy trousers? Or maybe the purple skirt with a grey or blue shirt? That would look nice."

"But I love the tights," said Mum. "I have to wear them."

"Well how about with a plain black dress?" I suggested. "And you could accessorize the red and white stripes with red and white bracelets?"

She sort of listened. *Sort of.* She went upstairs and changed into a black dress. Then threw a multi-colored poncho that looks like an old blanket over it. And, of course, she was *still* wearing the red-and-white tights. I give up. Everyone was staring at her when we got to school. She stood out among all the other mums in their Marks and Spencer's navy and white. Even her hair is different. Most mums have the standard short haircut, but Mum's is really long, halfway down her back. Too long for her age, I think, though it does look okay when she puts it back in a plait.

Then again it could have been the car that people were looking at that evening. We've had the same one for years. I think Mum and Dad bought it at university, which is where they first met. It's a Volkswagon Beetle. And for some reason Dad painted it bright turquoise. No, you definitely can't miss it amongst the Range Rovers and BMWs.

Dad dresses pretty normally. Cords and jumpers. I mean, he doesn't exactly have to dress smart to dole out people's muesli at the shop, but I wish he'd get rid of the ponytail. Does he listen? No. According to a mag I read, balding men compensate by having a ponytail. Poor Dad. It must be awful losing his hair, but it would look so much better if he had what little he has left cropped short.

"So how was school today?" he asked the assorted chomping faces in the kitchen.

"Mmphhh, okay, fine," came the reply.

"What have you been doing?" he asked, turning to me.

"Career choices, course choices," said Nesta, butting in. "Making decisions."

And that set them all off again. Even Lal, Steve, Matthew, and Tom joined in.

"I want to be a record producer," said Lal.

"I want to play in a band," said Tom, getting up and playing air guitar.

"I want to be an inventor," said Steve.

It was a repeat of the morning at school with everyone knowing what they want to be except me. I could see Mum looking at me as everyone babbled away.

"What about you, Lucy?" she asked. "What do you want to be?"

I shrugged. "Dunno."

Izzie and Nesta burst in with their brilliant career plans, and I could see Mum was watching me with concern as they enthused away. She doesn't miss a trick. She winked at me when no one was looking.

"The longest journey starts with the first step," she said.

Steve, Lal, and I groaned. We're used to her coming out with her "quote for the day." In her work as a psychotherapist she spends loads of time with people who are fed up with their lives in one way or another so she's always looking for new things to say to them to cheer them up a bit. She

22

reads all the latest self-help books and likes to pass on words of wisdom to the rest of us.

"Okay, who wants an Angel Card?" she asked.

"Oh, *Mum*," I said, feeling embarrassed, "I'm *sure* no one's interested."

"What's an Angel Card?" asked Izzie enthusiastically.

"A box of cards I bought last week to use in my counselling sessions," said Mum. "I haven't got round to taking them into work yet. Each card has a quote written on it."

She got up and found her pack.

"You pick one," she said, shuffling the cards and selecting one, "and let it speak to you."

"*The darkest hour is just before dawn*," she read, then handed the cards to Izzie. "Your turn, Iz."

Izzie loves stuff like this. Tarot cards, astrology, I Ching. She took a card and read out, "*Choice not chance determines destiny.*"

"Very sensible," said Dad. "Better to choose what you want than let it all drift by you and end up doing something you don't really want to do."

I started to feel panicky again. Was that going to happen to me because I didn't know what to

23

choose? I'd just drift along in a haze of confusion?

Suddenly I felt a cold, wet nose pushing against my hand. Ben's dopey face gazed up at me from under the table as if to say he understood. Sometimes I think dogs are psychic.

Izzie handed the pack to Nesta. "You choose one."

Nesta picked and read, "*The tragedy in life doesn't lie in not reaching your goal. The tragedy lies in having no goal.*"

Arggghhhh. It was getting worse. I have no goal. It's a tragedy.

"That's okay," continued Nesta. "I've got a goal. Clothes Show in a few weeks. I get spotted by talent scout and become a super-duper supermodel"

Lal's jaw dropped even more as he goggled at Nesta. "A supermodel? You'll get picked easy." The creep.

Nesta handed the cards to me and I let my hand hover, then shuffled. Let it be a good one, I prayed, let it be a good one.

I picked one out. "*Don't wait for your ship to come in,*" I read. "*Swim out to it.*"

"Good one," said Dad.

24

Psychic Ben clearly liked the card as well. He tried to jump up on my knee to lick my face. Seeing as he's an enormous thing, he almost knocked me flying, making everyone laugh.

"Down, Ben," I said. "You know I love you but you're too heavy."

Reluctantly he got down but sank his head on to my lap and refused to budge it.

I read my card again. Right, I thought. I'll be positive. I'll swim out to the ship. Right. I will. But how?

Once again Mum clocked my anxious expression. She squeezed my hand. "There's no hurry, you know. You don't have to decide what you want to be this minute."

I knew she meant well, but I thought the sooner I swam out to my ship the better.

The darkest hour
is just before dawn.

ANGEL CARD

Choice not chance
determines destiny.

ANGEL CARD

The tragedy in life doesn't lie in
not reaching your goal. The tragedy lies in
having no goal.

ANGEL CARD

Don't wait for your ship to come in.
Swim out to it.

ANGEL CARD

Chapter 3

Girls' Night Out

Saturday night. Girls' night out.

We're going to go to the Hollywood Bowl in Finchley. Dad calls it teen paradise. Everyone from our school hangs out there. It's a huge complex with a bowling alley, cafés, and a cinema, all built round a square where you can park if you have a car or stand about looking cool if you want to be seen. At the weekend, this is most of the teenage population of North London.

Speaking of which, what am I going to wear? Nesta and Izzie always look fab so I'd better make an effort.

27

I rifled through my wardrobe, but all that stared back at me were last year's oddments, worn out, boring, or babyish. I had a pink phase for a while but it looks too girlie girlie now. I really need some new clothes.

Suddenly I had an idea.

"Mum," I called down the stairs. "Where did you put that pile of stuff from Oxfam?"

"In the hall cupboard," she called from the kitchen. "I thought you didn't want any of it."

Mum had arrived back this morning from her weekly shop with the usual carrier bag of Oxfam bargains. I wouldn't be seen dead in most of it, too big or too patterned, but there was one shirt: size twenty. I don't know who Mum thought was going to wear it and initially I cast it aside. But it was nice fabric, silver and silky.

I pulled it out of the bag, got a large pair of scissors and went to the sewing machine in the sitting room. I cut off the sleeves and the front panels, leaving me with the back. I cut it down, hemmed the bottom then set about shaping the top and sides.

In under an hour, I'd finished. Posh Spice, eat

your heart out, I thought as I tried on my new handkerchief halter top. It didn't look half bad either. I could wear it with my black jeans.

"You're not going out in that," said Dad as I modeled my top for the family. "It's October, you'll freeze to death."

"I'll take a jacket," I promised.

"It's far too revealing for someone your age," he frowned.

"I'm not a baby any more, Dad," I said.

"I think you look cool," said Lal, looking up from *Xena: Warrior Princess.*

"What do you think, Steve?" I asked.

He gave me a cursory glance up and down. "Not bad."

That's praise coming from him.

"You've done a really good job," said Mum, examining my stitching, "that silver brings out your blue eyes beautifully. Oh, let her wear it, Peter."

"Can't you sew some sleeves in?" said Dad, still not convinced.

"This is the look; it's not meant to have sleeves."

"Well, all right but make sure you keep your jacket on. And I'll pick you up at nine thirty. No later. I don't want you staying out late looking like that."

"Oh, Dad, please, ten at least. I'll be with Nesta and Izzie. They can stay out later. Please. *Pleeease*."

"Ten o'clock, no later," said Mum. "And Dad will be there waiting for you."

"And don't do anything I wouldn't," smirked Lal.

Permission from a fifteen-year-old to snog anyone, I thought.

I began to get ready in plenty of time. First I had a bath, but unluckily for me Steve and Lal had been in after their football practice. The soap was all slimy from where one of them had left it in a puddle of water in the soap dish, and the towels were on the floor and dripping wet. The joys of elder brothers. Not.

I went into Mum's room to get clean towels from the cupboard and that's when I noticed the jar. Wax for removing unwanted hair. Just the thing. I had a fuzz of hair growing under my arms and didn't want to get caught like that time the press saw Julia Roberts on her way to a film premiere. When she waved at them, they all photographed her hairy armpits. Not that the paparazzi are going to be at the Hollywood Bowl tonight but you never know who else might be. One day my prince will come.

Mum was out visiting next door so I snuck the jar into my room and read the instructions. Heat up, apply to the area, then pull off. Sounded simple enough so I went into the kitchen and warmed the wax up in a pan of water on the stove. I waited until it began to bubble.

"What you doing?" said Steve, coming in and sticking his nose in the pan. "Toffee?"

"Waxing," I said and showed him my underarms.

"Erlack," he said, backing away. "Girlie stuff."

"I'll do your chest if you like," I offered. His "chest hair" was a family joke. He has just the one. We all saw it in the garden this summer when he stripped off. We sang "macho macho macho man" to him. He was dead embarrassed.

"Won't it hurt?" he asked.

"Nah," I said. "It'll be easy. And so cheap. Izzie went for a leg wax last month and it cost her twelve quid. This is costing nothing."

Steve looked doubtful. Ben and Jerry looked up

31

from their sleeping spot under the table. Even they looked doubtful.

When the wax had cooled slightly, Jerry followed me upstairs and watched with interest as I took the spatula and smoothed it on liberally under both my arms.

Rip it off, in one firm upward motion, the packet directed.

I lifted my left arm, eased a bit of the now hard wax and began to tug.

Ohmigod. OHMIGOD. *Argggghhhhh!!!* Agony. My eyes began to water and my face flushed red. I tugged again. No way. Absolutely no way. It wouldn't come off. What was I going to do?

I took a deep breath and ripped. *ARGGGHH-HHHH!* I fell back on the bed, sweating in agony. Jerry immediately pounced up and gave my face a great wet lick.

Fending him off, I gasped, "Why does nobody tell you it's torture? Izzie never said."

Then I realized; I'd plastered the horrible stuff under both arms. But I couldn't go through that again. I just couldn't. But it would show if I didn't get it off. There was no way out.

I lay on the bed with my right arm above my head and timidly began to pull at the wax. The pain was indescribable. Jerry began to bark as I heard Mum come in through the front door.

"Mum," I called. "MuuUUM, I need you!"

I could hear her running up the stairs. "What is it?" she said, bursting through the door. "Has something happened?"

I nodded and pointed at my arm. "I used your wax to do my underarms."

Mum sat on the bed and started shaking with laughter. "Serves you right for snooping in my things," she said.

"I didn't want to do a Julia Roberts," I said.

Mum looked at me as though I was mad.

"It's not too bad when you use it on your legs," she said. "But your underarms," she started laughing again, "your poor underarms are a bit more sensitive."

"Have you got something that will dissolve it?" I asked hopefully.

She shook her head. "'Fraid not. Come on, let's get it over with. Arm up. Come ON. Arm up."

Tentatively I lifted my arm.

"Eyes closed, deep breath," said Mum.

I took a deep breath and she ripped.

"*ARGGGHHH!*" I screamed and Jerry howled in sympathy. It was like someone had sliced my skin off.

Mum leaned over and looked under my arm. "Bit of talc on there and no harm done." Then she grinned. "Welcome to the world of you have to suffer to be beautiful."

"Is she with you?" asked the ticket lady at the cinema.

Nesta nodded and tried to brave it out. "Three, please."

I turned away and tried to make myself disappear as everybody in the cinema queue stared at me.

"You do know that you have to be fifteen to see this film?"

Nesta nodded. "Yeah. Course."

"Do you have proof of your age?" said the lady, looking pointedly at me.

Nesta shook her head. "Not on me."

Izzie tugged Nesta's sleeve. "Come on, let's go."

As we made our way out of the foyer, I could hear the ticket lady tutting as she took money

34

from the people next in line. "Honestly, kids these days," she said. "They're always trying it on."

I tried not to meet anyone's eyes as we snuck out. I felt awful. It was my fault. Izzie and Nesta could both easily pass for sixteen. It's me. Even though I've put some kohl on my eyes and am wearing lipstick. I've ruined their evening.

"Bad luck," said a voice from the queue.

We all turned back and saw Michael Brenman standing with a bunch of his mates waiting to get in. He was smiling at Nesta.

"Anyone can see the midget's underage," sneered Josie Riley, looking at me. She's a snotty Barbie lookalike from Year Eleven and well-known as a bully in our school, always picking on younger or smaller kids like me. She linked her arm through Michael's and pulled him away then looked back at us to say, "Stick to Disney in future, kids."

Nesta glared at her.

"What are you staring at?" said Josie.

"I'm just trying to visualise you with duct tape over your mouth," said Nesta.

I gulped. Ow. Move over Scary Spice, I thought.

Nesta Williams has come to town. I made for the exit. I didn't want any trouble. I knew what Josie could be like. Once she and her scabby mates had got me in the school loos and put my books in the sink and turned on the taps. Took me ages to get the pages dry.

Michael moved away from Josie and came up to Nesta. "You're new in school, aren't you?"

Nesta nodded, not taking her eyes from Josie who was still gobsmacked at her comment and was looking more than a bit unhappy. I don't think anyone had ever talked back to her before.

"We could get tickets for you," he said.

Izzie pulled Nesta's arm. "I don't think it's worth risking," she said to Michael. "If the ticket lady sees us going in, you'll only get in trouble as well."

"Come on, Mickie, leave the children to play," called Josie, moving up the queue. "It's almost our turn."

Michael turned back to the queue. "Well I'll see you around," he said and smiled again at Nesta.

"Wow!" said Nesta when we got outside. "Who is he? He's gorgeous, easily an eight out of ten."

"He's Michael Brenman, he goes to the sixth form college in Finchley," Izzie said.

"And he smelled amazing, lemony and clean, could you smell it?"

Actually I could. It had almost knocked me out. Never mind splash it on. He smelled as if he'd marinaded himself in it.

"Yes, er, lemony," I said diplomatically.

"What's he doing with that bullying creepoid? What's her name, anyway?" said Nesta.

"Josie Riley," I said. "Isn't she one of the girls who was calling you names that day at the bus stop?"

"Yeah. I wonder if she's his girlfriend" said Nesta.

"One of the many. I wouldn't bother if I were you," said Izzie. "Everybody fancies him."

"But he did smile at me and say I'll see you around. What do you think he meant?"

"I think he meant he'll see you around," said Izzie.

"Yeah but, see you around like I want to get to know you better? Or see you around, just see you around?" insisted Nesta.

"See you around, like join the list of girls I've already got gagging for me. He's cute and he knows it. Best play hard to get with someone like him."

37

"You reckon?" said Nesta, looking back at the cinema. "Mmm, very interesting."

She did look stunning tonight. Her hair was loose down her back and she was dressed in a denim jacket, tight jeans, and high-heeled ankle boots that made her legs look endless. It wasn't surprising that Michael had noticed her. All the boys were staring at her. She looks so sophisticated. Izzie looked good too in a tiny white cut-off top and combat jeans and trainers. I caught our reflections in the burger bar window. They both look like grown-ups who'd let their kid sister tag along.

"I'm really sorry," I said. "You'd have got in if it hadn't been for me."

"Don't be silly," said Izzie. "You look great tonight and I love your top. Where did you get it from?"

"I made it," I said. "Do you really like it?"

"It's fantastic," said Nesta, feeling the material. "I've got one just like it from Morgan. But mine's real silk."

Izzie saw my face drop. "But this is lovely," she said quickly. "It does look like real silk, Lucy."

"So what shall we do?" I said, trying to draw the

attention away from my top. "No point in going home now, and we're all being picked up from here later."

"Let's go and practice flirting," said Nesta, flicking her hair back as a group of lads walked past and looked appreciatively at her.

"Okay," I said, "but much good it'll do me. Boys never notice me even when I'm doing my best flirtie gertie act."

"Rubbish," said Izzie. "You're better with boys than anyone I know. Probably because you've got big brothers. Boys always find it easy to talk to you."

I winced when she said this as I remembered last summer. Izzie and I had been to watch Lal play football and we'd met this boy, and, for a change, he'd really chatted me up. I didn't really fancy him, but I was flattered by the attention. Then Izzie went off to get us some hot dogs, and he asked if I thought she liked him and would go on a date with him.

"Yeah, but only so as a way to get talking to you," I said. "Or Nesta. It's like I'm everyone's kid sister. One of the boys. They never take me seriously."

Suddenly I realized I sounded like a right saddo

so decided I'd make them laugh with my Madonna impersonation. My party piece at Christmas. It always makes Izzie crack up. I danced along behind them singing "Like a Virgin" at the top of my voice.

"Lucy," said Iz, giggling despite herself. "People are staring at you."

"It's one way to get noticed," I said. "Okay. Maybe not. So what shall we do, then?"

We looked around at the various alternatives.

"I suppose we could go bowling," said Nesta.

I felt my heart sink. Dad had given me my pocket money, but it was only enough for the movie, popcorn and a Coke. Bowling cost lots more and, of course, there'd be drinks.

"No point," said Izzie. "All the lanes will be booked on a Saturday night. Why don't we go and get some chips in the café and just hang out? They play good music over there." She pointed in the direction of one of the restaurants.

I sighed with relief. That would be okay, I thought. I could afford that.

"I feel rotten you didn't get in because of me," I whispered to Izzie as we made our way over.

"It's okay, honestly," she insisted. "I didn't really want to see the film that much anyway."

I knew she was trying to make me feel better. She'd been dying to see the film ever since it came out. Ewan McGregor was in it and he's one of Izzie's pin-ups.

On Sunday evening, I phoned Izzie to see if she wanted to come over and watch a video with Steve and Lal and me. Mum and Dad were going out, so we were going to get a couple of horrors in and scare ourselves stupid.

"Oh Izzie's not here," said Mrs Foster when I called. "She's gone to see that film. You know, the one with Ewan McGregor."

"Who's she gone with?" I asked, as though I couldn't guess.

"Nesta. She called for her half an hour ago. Er . . . are you not going with them?"

No. I wasn't going with them. And I know exactly why I hadn't been asked.

41

Chapter 4

Love
at
First Sight

School was awful. I was avoiding Izzie and Nesta. I'd been really hurt last night. But I'd got the message. Izzie'd moved on and didn't want me around any more.

I ignored them both in English though I could see Izzie was trying to catch my eye. I kept my head down and pretended I was fascinated by Shakespeare's sonnets.

Mr. Johnson was substituting the class, and I usually like his lessons. He's big and jolly with a red

42

beard like a Viking. He chalked a load of stuff up on the board then said, "Now, watch the blackboard while I go through it."

Everyone cracked up and when he realized what he'd said, he started laughing as well. But not me. Me and Hamlet. We got things to think about. "To be friends with Iz and Nesta or not to be? That is the question."

After English, we had a special lesson with Mrs. Allen all about third world countries and their need for help. Mrs. Allen is our headmistress so everyone was on their best behavior and really quiet. But it wasn't just because she was taking the class. It was depressing hearing about the hunger and wars in some areas.

We had to get into groups to discuss the lesson so I made sure I was in Mo Harrison and Candice Carter's group so I didn't have to speak to Izzie or Nesta.

"I don't understand why people fight," I said, feeling guilty that I was having my own conflict with Izzie, "and over something stupid like land. I reckon it's like, if you look at the sky there aren't any fences or boundaries. It should be the same on the ground."

43

"Yeah," said Mo. "Why can't we all just share everything?"

"Same sun, same air, same earth," I said. "It hardly makes sense that there's famine in the world when you see all the shops with food spilling out the doors. And people over here on diets all the time when on the other side of the world, other people haven't even got enough to eat."

The lesson made me feel very sad. I mean, Mum's been going on about poor people and the starving for years. Like when one of us wouldn't eat dinner or something. But I never took much notice. Watching the slides Mrs. Allen showed and seeing the real people was different. I could see it made us all think. I'd got all freaked out about not having a best friend any more but in some places, some people have just lost their parents or their kids.

I don't know what to do about Izzie and Nesta. It seems so petty to fall out, especially after today's lesson. I feel really confused now and don't know what to think.

Maybe I could go and be a volunteer in the third world when I grow up. But then what could I volunteer to do? My only special talent is making

44

cheese omelettes, so it's probably best I learn a skill first. But what?

At lunchtime, I was out of class before Nesta and Izzie could catch up and made my way to the library. I needed time to think and decided I'd go and look through books about courses and careers and stuff and see if there was anything I fancied or might be good at.

It all seemed a bit daunting as I leafed through the pages; there's so much to choose from.

"Hey, Luce," said Izzie, coming up behind where I was sitting at a desk. "What're you doing in here? Me and Nesta have been looking everywhere for you."

I pointed at the books. "Trying to decide on my brilliant career."

I carried on reading as if she wasn't there, but the silence felt uncomfortable and the words were swimming on the page in front of me.

"You've been very quiet lately, Luce. Is everything okay?"

I felt as if I'd swallowed a wad of chewing gum and it had got stuck in my throat.

"Luce?"

"How was the film?" I finally said.

Izzie looked embarrassed. "I know. Mum said you called." She slid into the chair next to mine. "Nesta's got drama tonight so why don't you come back to mine? Just us. We'll have a laugh. Tell you what, I'll do your birth chart. I've found this fab site on the Net and we'll see what the future holds."

It did sound tempting, but I didn't say anything. I still felt confused and pushed out.

"Oh pleeease, Lucy. We could do the Tarot cards as well. It might help you get some more ideas about what you want to do."

"I promised I'd help Dad do his shopping at the wholesaler's," I lied.

"You could come after. It won't take long with your dad. Look. I'm sorry about last night. I suppose I didn't think. Nesta was on her own and the wicked stepsisters were visiting round at ours. I had to get out. I knew you'd be okay. At least you've got a normal family."

I had to laugh at that. "Normal? Us? What planet are you on?"

46

I have to say I know what she means though. Her set-up is pretty complicated.

1 Her mum and dad got divorced about seven years ago, when Izzie was little, then her mum remarried.

2 Her stepdad's a lot older than Izzie's mum and he has two grown-up daughters from his first marriage, both accountants like their father. Izzie calls them the wicked stepsisters.

3 Oh. And her dad remarried as well. He married someone a lot younger. Anna. At least Izzie likes her.

She had a little boy, Tom, who's two now, and Izzie completely dotes on him.

So, see what I mean? Stepsisters, a stepdad, and a stepmum *and* a stepbrother, as well as her real mum and dad.

Pretty complicated.

Izzie wasn't giving up on me. "Oh, please come over, we haven't had time on our own for ages."

Understatement, I thought, but I couldn't stay mad at her. We've been friends for too long and I don't want to lose her.

"Okay," I said, realizing that now I was going to

47

have to help Dad. "After I've finished with Dad, I'll get him to drop me off at yours."

It was on the way to Izzie's that I saw Him. We were driving through Highgate past St. Michael's school, and he was coming out of the gates with another boy. We were stuck in traffic coming up to the roundabout and as the car slowed down, he darted across in front of us. A ten-out-of-ten, a face like Leonardo DiCaprio's, but he was taller with olive skin and dark hair. Absolutely drop dead goooorgeousissimo.

I watched him walk away down the pavement on the other side. It was like time stood still, and suddenly I understood what all the fuss is about. Usually I never see boys I like. Not really. Even at Hollywood Bowl, I've never seen anyone who's caught my eye. Not like him. I wonder if he goes there to the movies? I wonder who he is? I must find out. I'll persuade Izzie to come up to Highgate and hang out. There are loads of cafés there. He must go into one of them sometimes after school, all the St. Michael's boys do. My heart was racing.

It had happened. At last. Love at first sight.

48

As we drove on, I felt elated. I had a goal: Meet that boy.

Izzie lives a few roads away from me on the Finchley borders. Their house is one of those mock Tudor jobs, detached, with gardens at the front and back. It's very neat inside and so quiet compared to the bedlam at ours. The kitchen looks like an operating theater, all white and steel. I always feel I have to talk quietly even when there's no one there.

Izzie's mum likes things just so. Izzie says it's because she's a Virgo and they're perfectionists. Even though they have a cleaner come every day, Mrs. Foster still likes to clear around us if we're there. I'm a bit scared of her—like once I was eating an apple in the hall when I was waiting for Iz.

"Where are you going with that apple?" she said, coming up behind me.

"Er, nowhere," I said.

"Well, don't drop bits on my clean carpet, will you?"

And she went into the kitchen and brought me out a knife and a plate. Eek. She wouldn't last ten minutes in our house.

I'm glad she's not back tonight so Iz and I have the place to ourselves. Izzie's room is different from the rest of the house. It's the only room that has any color as Mrs. Foster favors neutral shades, on the carpets, curtains, and walls. And she only wears black. Black with pearls. Always immaculate and expensive-looking. Her dark hair cut into a severe bob to match her personality.

Izzie painted her room herself and she's done it a deep turquoise. "A very healing color," she told me. And she's got purple curtains and cushions. It looks vibrant and interesting. Like Izzie.

She lit one of her nice smelly candles then cranked up the computer. I looked at her posters. Ewan, of course, Suzanne Vega, who's one of Izzie's heroines, and a dolphin. Izzie's big on them. She wants to go swimming with them one day. Honestly, she's more like my mum than I am.

I flopped on the bed, and Izzie sat at her desk and starting pressing keys.

"Right, I've been dying to try this. I got some new software and it works out a personalized horoscope for you," she said. "You were born May twenty-fourth, Gemini, right? What time?"

"Five past midnight," I said. I remember because it's Dad's birthday as well and Mum says I was his birthday present. Only just made it by five minutes though.

Izzie punched in the information. "Give it a few minutes and it will tell us all about you. While we're waiting for it, we'll do the Tarot cards."

She gave me the pack and I started shuffling.

"Have you done your chart yet?" I said.

"Yep," grinned Izzie. "Aquarius, sign of the genius, humanitarian, eccentric . . ."

"Barking mad, you mean," I said. "And I dunno about the genius bit, but the rest sounds like you. I suppose you are humanitarian most of the time when you're not swanning off to see films without me."

Izzie threw a pillow at me. She knew I was teasing.

"What did you think of that lesson with Mrs. Allen?" I asked. "Sad, wasn't it?"

Izzie nodded. "I'm going to write a song about it."

"Why?" I asked. "It's a bit of a depressing subject for people to listen to."

"Ah, but songwriters have as much power, if not more than some politicians."

51

"How can they?" I laughed. She was always coming out with mad stuff like this.

"Well look at Bob Geldoff. He did loads, didn't he, when he did that Band Aid concert? Raised more money than anyone in years. And look at Comic Relief. Millions in a night. And John Lennon. 'All we are saying is give peace a chance.' I reckon if you can write a song or a book or make a film, sometimes you can touch more people that way than boring politicians droning on. Music makes people think. They listen to lyrics. Better than lecturing them or dropping a leaflet through the door that only gets put in the wastepaper bin."

This is one of the things I like best about Izzie. She makes *me* think. She's so wise. Mum says Izzie's an old soul. When I asked if I was, Mum looked at me strangely and said, "No, love, I think it's your first time on the planet." I don't know if that was a compliment or an insult.

And Izzie's right. I'd only thought about being a volunteer and going wherever needed and doing some cooking or clearing up or something. But if you could reach people and touch them, there'd be more people to help. If only I had a skill like she has with her songwriting.

"I was talking to Nesta about it at break," continued Iz. "She wasn't into going and being a volunteer and sleeping in a tent and having no MTV. She says her plan is to be mega mega rich when she's a model then she can give some of her money away."

"What, Nesta? I wouldn't have thought she ever thought about anybody but herself."

"You've got to give her a chance, Lucy, she's okay. And I think it's a good plan. I mean, you could give your time and be a volunteer, or you could become mega rich like Nesta wants to be and give your money instead and pay to train volunteers. You know, actually do something with your money as well as having a good time with it. Best of both worlds."

"I guess," I said. I didn't want to admit that Nesta's idea was pretty smart. Nesta. Nesta. Nesta.

"Finished shuffling?"

I nodded, and she took the pack, sat on the floor, and split the cards into three piles. Then she consulted her book.

"This is a Grand Cross," she said, laying the cards out. "It tells you the Past, the Present, and the Future."

I flopped on the beanbag next to her. I felt

happy. Iz and me. Me and Iz talking about stuff, and Iz predicting my future.

"What does it say, Madam Rose?"

"Oh, interesting," Iz murmured. "Very interesting. The card that crosses you is the Wheel of Fortune. It signifies a new chapter. A turning point."

"Tell me about it," I said. "Decisions, decisions, decisions."

"The influence passing over you is the High Priestess. She indicates potential unfulfilled, but it will be revealed."

"Oh, I hope so," I said. "It's been awful lately with everyone knowing what they want to do but me." I pointed to the next card. "This looks *très* interesting."

"The Lovers. In your future, it indicates a love affair."

"Oh, fantastic. . . ." I was dying to tell her about the boy I'd seen.

"But there's some kind of trial or choice involved. Lucy, why are you blushing? You've gone scarlet."

"Izzie," I couldn't hold it in any longer. "I've seen someone. . . ."

"Someone?"

"A boy. I think he goes to St. Michael's. . . ."

54

Izzie grinned. "And . . . ?"

"Well I've only just seen him. When I was driving here with Dad. He was coming out of the school gates and was absolutely gorgeous. Could that be what the Lovers means? Maybe I'm going to meet him. Does it say anything about him?"

Izzie looked at the card spread. "Maybe. Here. There's the Page of Swords card in your future. That could be him."

I looked at the card, a young man with a sword held high.

"That *must* be him. Who else could it be? It's amazing. He's so gorgeous. I thought maybe we could hang out in Highgate after school one day . . ."

"Well if it's in the cards, you'll meet him anyway." Izzie looked concerned as she read her book. "But he could be ruthless. The Page of Swords is sometimes deceitful. Not to be trusted. So go carefully, Lucy. You don't even know what he's like yet."

Nothing could dampen my enthusiasm. "Oh, I could see he's not like that. He had a really nice face."

Izzie continued looking at the cards. "Well let's see what the outcome is."

"I don't like the look of the last card," I said.

55

It had a picture of a tower on fire with a body falling out of the window.

"Oh, that's the Tower," said Izzie. "I know it looks a bit scary, but actually it's a good card to get. It represents the influences around you and means in order to move forward, old ways must be broken down, but in their place comes greater freedom. See, the card after it is the World, the outcome of the reading. That's a fantastic card to get. It means happiness, strength, and success. The realization of a goal. Wow. Lucy, this is a really positive reading. I mean, it says there will be a bit of confrontation, change, and adjustment, but the outcome is very good."

I left Izzie's that night feeling on top of the world. Even my personalized horoscope was good. And she was going to do one for Nesta as well. Astrology's one of Izzie's career choices. She might do it as well as being a songwriter. Lucky thing. It must be great, having not only one idea of what you want to be, but two. And I still haven't decided on anything. Still, when Izzie printed my horoscope, it said pretty much the same as the cards. It was all going to be all right. Break down to break through, it said. It was all a process. I was going through a time of change and mustn't resist. The outcome was good.

Things were looking up. It was going to be okay. Success. Achievement. Me and Izzie were all right with each other again. But best of all, the Page of Swords. I couldn't wait to meet him.

Horoscopes

Lucy: May 24th. Gemini. Cancer rising. Moon in Taurus.

Saturn the taskmaster is forcing you to look deeper into your goals. It's only by experiencing testing circumstances that we learn where our destiny lies. Don't resist.

With Neptune and Venus so close, romance is in the air, but tread warily as things may not be as they appear.

Nesta: August 18th. Leo. Aries rising. Moon in Gemini.

Mercury is moving retrograde at the moment so causing you to misread signals. Misunderstandings are likely to occur. Around the New Moon, you're more positive and productive as new opportunities present themselves.

Izzie: January 26th. Aquarius. Gemini rising. Moon in Scorpio.

The relationship between the Sun and Neptune means that you may misjudge a situation which needs careful handling. Don't be surprised if people overreact. Close relationships may be tense until this phase is over.

Chapter 5

Disaster
Strikes

I don't believe it. I just don't believe it. What started out as a brilliant week has just ended in complete, total, and utter disaster.

Course Izzie told Nesta I'd seen someone I liked. That part was okay, in fact Nesta was really enthusiastic, though I did feel a prat when I had to admit that I hadn't even spoken to him.

"So how do you know what he's like?" she said.

"I don't. I just know we'll get on," I replied.

"Then first of all, we have to get him to notice you," she said.

"I know," I replied.

I'd been thinking about it a lot. Is he going to be another in a long line of people who think I'm twelve and don't even register me? No. I was being positive. I'd find a way.

Don't wait for your ship to come in, swim out to it.

I had a plan.

Luckily I had Izzie to myself for the week. Nesta's in the school play and has rehearsals every night, and, I have to say, I was relieved. Not wanting to be mean or anything, but she's what Lal calls a Top Babe, and the chances were if He saw her, I wouldn't even get a look-at.

So. The plan was that Izzie and I'd get the bus up to Highgate and hopefully bump into him, sort of accidentally on purpose.

Tuesday P.M.: went to Highgate. I like it up there. Tall, white Georgian houses set back behind wrought iron railings around the square. *Très* posh. And the village isn't like the rest of London with big supermarkets and chain stores. The shops up there are all individual and interesting. Little jewelery shops and nick-nacky places. We got so absorbed in looking in the windows at first that we almost forgot to look for Mr. MC. Mystery Contestant. (That's Izzie's nickname for him.)

We tore ourselves away from the shops and walked past the school about twenty times. We hung around at the bus stop. Boys of every shape and size were pouring out. But did He appear? No.

Wednesday P.M.: Highgate. This time we went to the cafés. Café Uno. Café Rouge. Costa's. I was getting cappuccinoed out by the time we'd finished. Everywhere was full of St. Michael's boys. But Mr. Top Totty? (My nickname for him.) No.

"Maybe he's off with flu or something," said Izzie.

"Maybe I imagined him," I said. His image was already starting to fade in my mind.

Thursday P.M.: Walked past the school *and* did the cafés. I was running out of pocket money. It's an expensive business looking for the Mystery Contestant. Still no show.

Friday: Izzie was convinced he's off with a bug.

"But you don't know for definite," I said. "And if he was, he might be better by now."

We did our usual walk past the school, but, once again, he didn't appear.

"Let's go to Costa's," said Izzie. "That's where most of them go."

Just at that moment, we saw Nesta crossing the road and waving. She looked amazing. Although we don't have to wear school uniform, she sometimes wears her own version and puts on a shirt, tie, skirt, and three-quarter stockings. Very Britney Spears. She'd hitched her skirt up and her legs looked fantastic. Cars were almost driving into lampposts as male drivers did double-takes.

"Rehearsal was canceled so I thought I'd come and join the boy-chasing troops," she grinned.

My heart sank as Izzie told her our plan and we set off for Costa's.

"I'll meet you in there," she said, "I'm just going to get a copy of *Bliss*. There's a piece in there on the Clothes Show I want to read."

Izzie and I went to the café and settled ourselves at a table by the window so we could look out as well as in. I did a quick check of the customers. No, he wasn't there.

That's when my brilliant plan took on a life of its own.

Izzie went to get the cappuccinos and I looked out at the passersby.

Suddenly my mouth dropped open. Nesta was coming out of the shop and down the road. And guess who she was with? Him. MC. Two minutes in the shop and she'd got talking to him. Talk about fast worker. He was even laughing at something she said. I *knew* this would happen if Nesta came along.

Oh no. Even worse, she was coming over the road. With him. Coming into the café. She couldn't possibly know that he was my He and I decided not to let on. But I felt myself going red and prayed no one would notice.

She burst in with him in tow and came up to us just as Izzie came back with the coffees.

"Iz, Lucy. This is Tony," she said.

Close up he was even better-looking than I remembered. Sleepy brown velvet eyes, thick black eyelashes, and a gorgeous mouth with a full bottom lip.

"Tony's my brother," said Nesta.

My jaw dropped and Nesta started laughing.

"I know what you're thinking," she said. "How can that be?"

I was thinking exactly that. I mean, Nesta's half Jamaican. Skin like coffee ice cream. Tony's complexion is more Mediterranean. Luckily no one had noticed my face which by this time was bright scarlet. Everyone was too busy looking at Tony.

"He's my half brother," she explained. "My mum is his dad's second wife. A year after he married my mum they had me. So same dad, different mums."

She'd told us she had a brother, but I didn't expect this! No wonder she and Izzie have so much in common. But *brother*. He's Nesta's brother. Half, step, or whatever. Oh NO. Now I can never tell anyone, not Izzie, not Nesta. With Nesta's big mouth, she's bound to blab to him that I fancy him and have been up here looking for him. I'd end up looking really desperate. Can life possibly get any worse?

"Hi," he smiled at us. "Which one of you is Lucy?"

I felt all wobbly and faint when he looked at me.

"I am," I said weakly and blushing even more furiously.

"Nesta tells me you've got your eye on one of the St. Michael's kids. I go there so I might know him. What year is he in? What does he look like?"

"Er, tall, er . . . hair," I stuttered, trying my best not to describe the vision standing in front of me. "He was too far away for me to get a really close look."

Izzie and Nesta cracked up laughing.

"Gorgeous, apparently," said Izzie, coming to my rescue. "We know that much at least. Just find us the best-looking boy at your school. He'll do."

"Well you're looking at him," boasted Tony. "But I'll try and look out for the next best thing."

"Big-head," said Nesta.

I wanted to die.

Thankfully Tony didn't stay around too long, and after a while I got up to go as well. I wanted to run away and hide.

All the St. Michael's boys were oggling Nesta and one even sent her over a coffee and a Danish. Izzie got chatting to some strange-looking boy with long hair in the corner who was reading *Mojo* magazine. She went over to him and soon they were busy discussing music and the charts. I felt like a spare part. No one noticed me. It's like I'm invisible. It's weird: When I feel good, I can make people laugh, but when I'm down, I disappear. And Tony's gone home. Not only is he Nesta's brother, but he was right about him being the best-looking boy at the school. I can't believe Izzie didn't clock that he was the One.

"I'm off," I said.

"Don't you want to stay and see if Mr. Right appears?" said Nesta, spooning the froth from her cappuccino. "See I reckon the reason you haven't seen him is that he's been doing some class after school. They do all sorts of extra curricular stuff— fencing, music, drama. Tony told me. He's often late because he's been doing something or other. Hang around another half hour or so and another lot of guys will be out."

How could I tell her that He *was* out? That *He* was Tony. Tony, who was now, thanks to Big Gob Nesta, only too happy to help me find my mystery boy.

I didn't want her to suspect so I sat down again and went along with the pretence that I was still looking for Mr. Right. Luckily Nesta changed the subject. She's too excited about the up-and-coming Clothes Show to think about anything else at the moment.

"Premier, Storm, and Select are all sending talent scouts to the show," she read from her magazine, "and both Erin O'Connor and Vernon were discovered at shows in the past. And we could get a makeover. There will be people there giving a whole new look."

Izzie came back to sit with us, and her and Nesta spent the next half hour gabbing about what they were going to wear and what they were going to do there. Makeovers, accessories, manicures.

"What are you going to wear, Lucy?" asked Nesta.

"I haven't thought about it," I said. I'd been miles away, thinking about Tony. I had a million questions I wanted to ask Nesta.

What birth sign is he? Izzie could do his chart to see if we were a good match.

What does he like doing?

What sort of girls does he like?

What did Nesta and Izzie think he thought of

66

me? He had smiled at me very warmly.

And why doesn't he live with his mum? Usually when a couple split up, the children stay with their mum. So how come Tony lives with his dad but Nesta's mum? Where's his mum?

And oh! Worst of all. What if *Izzie* fancies Tony? She's bound to. He's so cute. Irresistible. *Magnifique*. How can I find out without her guessing that he's the MC?

But I couldn't ask anything. It had to be my secret.

That ship I was going to swim out to? I think it just sunk.

Chapter 6

The New Me

Izzie's just phoned. Apparently Tony told Nesta he thought I was a sweet kid. What kind of word is that? Sweet? It's like being told you're nice. Pleasant. Agreeable. *Urggghhh.*

What makes me "me"? I'm sweet. Yuk.

I don't want to be sweet. I want to be a Babe. A Boy Magnet.

But no. I'm *sweet.*

Sweeeeet. A sweet kid. Kid.

But at least he noticed me. And said something to Nesta.

68

I look at myself in the bedroom mirror. I suppose I do look kind of sweet. Small, flat-chested, not the slightest evidence of a bust. And that's another thing. Izzie and Nesta both have breasts, in fact Izzie says hers have taken on a life of their own lately. But me, nothing. Pinpricks. Pimples. I have the body of a nine-year-old boy.

I could have my hair cut. It's been long for years. I could have it done spiky. And highlighted. Although it's blond, I could have white blond streaked through it. Yeah, I thought. Like how? On my pocket money?

I look around my bedroom. It was last painted when I was ten. Pink. The beginning of my pink phase. And fluffy toys everywhere, on the window ledge, the wardrobe, the bed. I picked up Mr. Mackety, my favorite teddy. He's fat and grumpy-looking and I've had him since I was five. I thought about chucking him out. Nope. Mr. Mackety in a bin liner? Too awful. No way. Can't. We've been through too much together. Still, I can't deny the overall effect of my room is sweet. Sweeeeet.

I went downstairs to see what everyone was

doing, but the house was quiet for a change. Mum was out doing her Saturday shopping, Dad was at the health shop, and the boys were out at football.

I spied Mum's Angel Cards in a bowl on the kitchen table. I took the pack and shuffled them.

"Okay, oh clever clogs cards, let's see what words of wisdom you have for me today." I picked a card and read.

"'*The people who get on in the world are the people who get up and look for the circumstances they want. And if they can't find them, make them.' George Bernard Shaw.*"

Well, that's telling me! If they can't find them, make them.

Okay. I will, Mr. Shaw. I'll do my own makeover. I've had enough of mooching about feeling miserable. Feeling like second best. I'm not like that normally. It's only lately I've been feeling peculiar. But I'm going to fight back. I'll show them all who's a sweet kid.

I sat at the table and made a list of all the changes I want to make.

1 My hair.

2 My bedroom.

3 My clothes.

4 My life.

Mum came in the back door laden with bags of groceries.

"What're you doing?" she asked.

"Changing," I said, then read her my Angel Card.

"But you're lovely the way you are," she said and hugged me. "My lovely sweet Lucy."

Arggggghhhh. That word again.

"I don't want to be sweet anymore."

"Well what do you want to be?"

"I don't knOWWWW."

Mum sat down and looked at me with concern. "Are you happy, Lucy? That's the main thing."

"Yes. No. Sort of. Sometimes."

Mum laughed, then saw my paper with the list.

"Things I want to change," I said.

"Oh but not your hair, your lovely hair!" She read down the list. "Tell you what, though. You can decorate your bedroom if you like. It's needed doing for a while now."

"Really? Can I?"

"Pick some paint colors and the boys can give you a hand painting. Then we'll look in the

71

Curtain Exchange for curtains. They won't be new, but they have a great selection there and we're bound to find something you like. Or we could go to the market and get some fabric and make them ourselves."

Fantastic. It's a start.

Then I looked at the patchwork of colors on the wall opposite me. "But, Mum, what about the kitchen? You've been wanting to do that for ages."

"Oh, that can wait," she said. "I've got used to it in a funny sort of way. No. It's decided. Lucy gets a new bedroom."

I couldn't wait to get started. "I'll call Izzie and she can help me choose colors," I said. "If you can't find the circumstances you want, make them. I like that."

I ran into the hallway to phone Iz.

"Don't try to change everything in one go!" called Mum. "Remember, he who would climb the ladder must begin at the bottom."

I stuck my head back round the door. "I know. And Rome wasn't built in a day. See, Mum, you're not the only one round here who knows quotes. By the way, where did all that Oxfam stuff go?"

"Back in the cupboard under the stairs. Why? What are you up to?"

"This is the new me. I'm going to make myself some new gear. Just you wait. That halter neck top was just the beginning.'"

Mum laughed as I ran off to the phone.

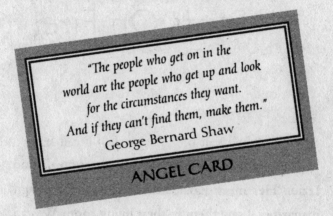

"The people who get on in the world are the people who get up and look for the circumstances they want. And if they can't find them, make them."
George Bernard Shaw

ANGEL CARD

Chapter 7

Liar, Liar,
Pants On Fire

"Let's go over to Nesta's this afternoon," said Izzie. "Her mum has loads of fab interior design magazines. I saw them in their living room. We can browse through . . . Lucy, Lucy? Are you there?"

"Yes, yes, I'm here," I said. "Sorry. I dropped the phone."

Ohmigod. Nesta's. I know I've got to go some time, now that we seem to be officially a threesome. But Nesta's? What if Tony's there? Part of me is dying to see him again. Part of me is dreading it. What if Nesta and Izzie suss me out? I'm bound to go pink if he's there and I never was much good at hiding anything from Iz. But then again, he might not be there. Either way, I can find out a bit more about him. Oh decisions, decisions, decisions.

"Izzie?" I said seriously.

"Yes, Lucy?" she said seriously then laughed.

"Do you fancy Tony?"

"God no. Not my type at all. Too pretty pretty boy. And he's a bit too sure of himself, you know what I mean?"

"Yeah," I sighed with relief.

"Why, do you fancy him?" she asked.

"Course not," I lied. "Too pretty pretty boy."

Liar, liar, pants on fire, said a voice in my head.

"So, shall we go over to Nesta's?" Izzie asked again.

"Okay," I said. "I'll come to your house later and we can go together." Eek. Er. The new brave me. If I plaster on a load of foundation, perhaps no one'll notice if I blush.

Nesta's flat is amazing. She lives on the ground floor of a detached Victorian property near Highgate. One of those places you hear estate agents describe as having character and original

75

features. Lovely old cornicing in the hallway and stained-glass windows.

"Are you okay, Lucy?" Nesta asked, taking our coats. "You're looking a bit pale."

"Oh, I'm fine," I said, immediately reddening under my matte factor 16. "I like your flat."

"Wait until you see the rest of it," Nesta said proudly. "I'll give you the tour. You've already seen it, Izzie, so make yourself at home."

She led us into a large room with French windows at the back. It looked warm and welcoming with deep red walls and curtains and plush brown velvet sofas. The overall look was a mix of Eastern and old, stylish, and comfortable.

Izzie helped herself to a pile of magazines by the fireplace and flopped down on a sofa while Nesta led me into a country style kitchen-diner at the side.

"It's huge in here," I said, staring around. "You don't often find flats this big."

"I know," said Nesta. "Dad likes the big old rooms with high ceilings, and the houses like that were out of his price range. He says we were lucky to find a flat like this with three bedrooms."

She led me out of the kitchen and down the corridor and opened a door. "Mum and Dad's room."

I peeked in. "Are they here?"

"No," said Nesta. "Dad's in America and Mum's on late shift."

"Nice," I said as I looked at their bedroom. A big square room done in honey golds with soft muslin at a bay window overlooking the garden.

Back out in the corridor hung black and white photographs of bleak landscapes—mountains and sea against dramatic skies, each one beautifully framed.

"Who took these?" I asked. "They're great."

"Dad. It's one of his hobbies," said Nesta, opening the next door. "Tony's room."

I trooped in after her feeling like I was spying. The room was done in grays and blues and he was very tidy for a boy. His books and papers were neatly stacked on his computer desk. Steve and Lal's rooms always look like a bomb has hit them. Then I saw the posters on his wall. Jennifer Lopez. The Corrs. Buffy the Vampire Slayer.

"Tony likes girls," laughed Nesta when she saw me staring.

"Did your mum decorate?" I asked.

77

Nesta nodded. "She did an interior design course before she was a newsreader. Says it's always good to have something to fall back on. She reckons you have a limited time working as a presenter on television. They keep hiring younger and younger presenters and she says oldies like her can get thrown on the scrap heap at any time."

"You're so lucky to live somewhere like this," I said. I was really impressed. "She's got a great eye for color, your mum."

"You've got a good eye as well, Lucy," said Nesta. "You always dress in colors that suit you and that halter neck you made was fabulous."

I felt really chuffed. That was the nicest thing Nesta had ever said to me. I suddenly warmed to her and decided it would be all right to ask the question I'd been dying to ask ever since I met Tony. Where is his mum?

Just as I plucked up the courage, we heard the front door open. My heart began to race. Oh, please don't let it be him. Please don't let it be him and he find me standing in his bedroom.

We heard footsteps coming down the corridor

and a moment later, Tony appeared. He looked startled to see us.

"Just giving Lucy the tour," said Nesta.

Tony grinned. "Only too happy to come home to find a pretty girl in my bedroom. Hi, Lucy."

He remembered my name. Oh, God. And he gets better-looking every time I see him.

"Hi." I could feel myself going puce and prayed my makeup was doing its job.

"So how's the search for the mystery man going?" he asked. "The one with the, er . . . hair."

"Er . . . I haven't seen him again . . ." I muttered.

"He'll turn up," said Nesta. "But we need a plan. To get Lucy noticed. You like girls, Tone. What do you look for? What do you find attractive?"

Tony looked deep into my eyes as he thought about his answer. "First I like girls who are funny. Who can make me laugh. And girls who know who they are," he said finally, "you know, who know what they want and where they're going. Confidence, I suppose. It's a real turn-on."

Girls who know who they are. Confidence. That's the last thing I needed to hear. I glanced over at Nesta, hoping she'd shut up or change the

79

subject or something, and I could swear she was laughing. I bet she's guessed that it's Tony I like and she's told him. He's probably having a laugh as well.

Izzie came in to join us and the three of them spent ages blabbing on about how to get noticed by boys. I felt like I'd frozen inside.

Suddenly I wanted to go home. To our mismatched walls and my baby pink bedroom. And my mum.

Tips for getting noticed by the opposite sex

Nesta's

➤ Be blindingly beautiful. There's no such thing as a plain girl, only one who can't be bothered. Lipstick, sunglasses and anyone can be a Babe.
➤ Wear heels to make your legs look longer.
➤ Get a Wonderbra.
➤ Always have clean shiny hair.
➤ Stand up straight. Don't slouch. It's the first thing they teach at model school. Good posture makes you look more confident and makes your body look slimmer.

Izzie's

- Relax. Boys hate clingy or desperate.
- Make eye contact, then smile.
- Find out his interests then ask him about them.
- Laugh at his jokes.
- Don't be too available. Play hard to get for a while as boys like a challenge.

Tony's

- Be confident. Don't carry on about what you don't like about yourself.
- Look fit. Boys respond when they like what they see.
- Flirt outrageously, then go home, it will leave him wanting more.
- Don't smoke. It makes your breath stink as well as your clothes and hair.

Lucy's

- Pray for a miracle.
- Grow another six inches.

Chapter 8

Giving Nesta a Second Chance

"I'm sure she wouldn't do anything like that," said Mum after I'd blurted out all my worst fears about Tony when I got home later that day. "Nesta seems like a really nice girl."

Mums are a peculiar species. Sympathetic when you don't expect it and unsupportive when you do.

"She was laughing at me, Mum, I swear she was. And she kept asking him what he liked about girls. Then Izzie joined in. And they were all going on about how to get a boy. It was so embarrassing."

"So you really like this Tony, do you?"

I nodded, turning my usual bright purple.

"How old is he?"

"Seventeen," I said.

"Well, if he's got any sense at all, he'll like you too."

"Yeah but it's like, I'm Nesta's friend. His kid sister's friend. How am I ever going to get him to take me seriously?"

Suddenly I felt awkward talking about it all to Mum. I should be discussing this with Izzie. But that was out of the question.

"You won't ever say, will you, Mum? You know, that I like Tony. Not to anyone. Not Steve or Lal or Nesta or Izzie or anyone."

"Course not if you don't want me to. But I don't really understand why Nesta and Izzie can't know. They are your friends."

I pulled a face.

"Why the face?" asked Mum.

I shrugged. "Since Nesta came, it's like her and Izzie are friends and I'm the odd one out."

"And how do you feel about that?" she asked, going into shrink mode. I felt like one of her patients. I've heard her come out with the "and how do you feel?" line a hundred times when she's been on the phone to one of them.

"I *feel* left out," I said.

"I'm sure you're imagining it," said Mum. "Izzie will always be your friend. And I think Nesta wants to be too if you'll let her."

"You don't understand," I said.

I felt cross. How could she know what it had been like lately?

I wasn't going to say any more.

"Well how do you think Nesta feels?" asked Mum. "It can't have been easy for her, starting a new school, new area, and everything."

"Oh, she's fine. Her life is completely together. She lives in an amazing flat. All the boys fancy her. And now she has Izzie."

I felt as if I was going to cry. Everyone cared more about Nesta Williams than they did about me. I bit my bottom lip. I wasn't going to blub. Not in front of Mum. No one understands. And Tony likes girls who know who they are and what they want, and I still don't have a clue. And there's no one to talk to anymore.

84

I picked up Mum's *Good Housekeeping* magazine and started leafing through it. She got the message. Counseling session over.

She started tidying up around me, and as she moved things off the kitchen table, she put her hand on her cards.

"Angel Card?" she asked with a grin. Now even *she* was laughing at me. It wasn't funny.

"No thanks," I grumbled. "Those stupid cards have got me into enough trouble as it is."

"Suit yourself," said Mum and went upstairs.

When she'd gone, I noticed she'd left the cards on the table. I stuck my tongue out at them. But then I couldn't resist. Just one more to see what it said. I picked them up, shuffled and chose one.

If you want a friend, be a friend, it said.

Arggghhhh. I threw the card down. This was getting spooky. They always seemed to say just the right thing. If you want a friend, be a friend. That was it. I hadn't exactly gone out of my way to be Nesta's friend. I'd been so busy thinking that she'd stolen Izzie from me that I hadn't even thought about how I'd come across to her.

And I suppose Mum was right. It can't have

85

been easy for her starting a new school where everyone already knows each other.

Okay, Nesta Williams, I thought. One more chance. I will be a friend to you.

And see what happens.

I went up to my room and had a good think about what I could do to be more of a friend to Nesta.

Make her a cake. No, that's silly. Anyway she's always on a diet.

Invite her over for a video night with Steve and Lal. No. Lal will only drool over her.

I know. I'll organize a girlie night. Izzie and I often have them, well used to have them, we haven't done one for ages. We can put on face masks and do manicures and do each other's hair. Nesta'll like that with the Clothes Show coming up. And I'll be really really nice. In fact, I'll even be sweet, seeing as I seem to be so good at it.

I looked into my purse to see how much money I had left then popped out to the local chemist so I had everything in.

I got an avocado face mask, some purple nail polish as Nesta likes that, hair conditioner, and last of all some Häagen-Dazs pecan as I know it's Nesta's favorite. And some Flakes because they're Izzie's favorite and I can't forget her in all this. And Mum said we can send out for pizza. Excellent.

When I got home from the shops, I went to my computer and designed an invite on e-mail to send to both of them.

```
Dear Izzie/Nesta
   You are invited to a girls' night
at Lucy's house tomorrow night at six
o'clock. Bring: makeup bags, nail
polish, hair stuff, favorite CDs, and
yourselves. I've got the pizza and
ice cream.
   Love Lucy
```

I pressed the send button and waited for their replies.

*If you want a friend,
be a friend.*

ANGEL CARD

Chapter 9

Bor-ing
Sundays

I got up the next day and went to check my incoming mail.

Nothing. That's strange. I know for a fact that Izzie always looks to see if she's got any e-mails first thing in the morning. What's going on?

At eleven o'clock, I phoned Izzie's house. No reply. Only Mrs. Foster's message on the machine: "I'm afraid we're unable to take your call at present. Please call later."

I called Nesta.

"Hi, is that little Lucy?" said Tony.

Gulp. "Yes. No. Sorry. I mean yes but I'm *not* little," I said.

He laughed at the other end, "Okay. *Lovely Lucy*, then. You want Nesta?"

"Yes, please."

"Not here. She went off somewhere with some guy from your school. Michael I think he was called."

"Was Izzie with them?"

"Don't think so. Shall I tell her you called?"

"Please," I said. "Thank you."

"And, Lucy?"

"Yes?"

"I think small girls are cute," he said, then he hung up.

When did I get so polite? Please. Thank you. Sorry. So much for my dazzling conversation. He must think I'm stupid. Why didn't I think of something brilliant to say? He likes girls who are funny. I could have told him my Scottish joke.

What's the difference between Bing Crosby and Walt Disney?

Bing sings but Walt disn'y.

But he did call me lovely Lucy. And he thinks small girls are cute. Maybe there's hope after all.

Sundays. What to do? It's such a *boring* day. *And* it's raining.

I had a quick look at my homework. My project for Miss Watkins stared back at me from my desk.

What makes me "me"?

What are my interests? Tony Williams.

What do I want? To snog Tony Williams.

What are my goals in life? To snog Tony Williams.

What am I? Shallow I suppose, since those are my main goals. Probably not ones that will impress Miss Watkins or Mrs. Allen either.

Okay. Snog Tony Williams and bring about world peace. That sounds better.

What would I like to do as a career? Still dunno.

Never mind, we've got a week or so left yet. I'll think about it later.

I went downstairs and flopped on the sofa in front of the television. Steve and Lal were squabbling over the channel changer. Steve wanted to watch a video of *The Matrix* and Lal wanted to watch *another* repeat of *Star Trek*.

I couldn't be bothered to join in and stake my claim. There was nothing on I wanted to watch anyway. Where was Izzie? I hope she hadn't gone off doing something with Nesta without me again.

"What can I do?" I asked, going into the kitchen where Mum was busy preparing some sort of weird nutloaf thing for lunch.

"Homework?" said Mum.

"Done it," I lied.

"Tidy your bedroom?"

"Boring . . . I've got *nothing* to do. . . ."

"Well I don't know," she said. "Just don't mope about under my feet. Anyway, I thought you were going to make some clothes. Why not make a start?"

I spent the rest of the morning rooting through bags of assorted jumble from the cupboard under the stairs. Most of it rubbish by the look of it, all sorts of stuff that Mum's collected over the years. Izzie says it's because she's Cancerian and they hate to throw stuff away. She's certainly right in Mum's case. There are clothes in here from when I was a baby.

91

Dad got up from reading his papers in the living room. "Time for a cup of tea!" he declared. He always says it like it's a really exciting thing. A sensational world event. TIME FOR A CUP OF TEA.

On his way to the kitchen, he spotted the baby clothes lying on the carpet. "Oh. Ahhhh," he said and picked them up and took them in to show Mum. They stood in the kitchen like a couple of dopes, all misty-eyed, looking at the tiny pink cardigans and miniscule blue booties.

"Our little baby," said Mum, gazing softly at me.

"It seems like only yesterday," said Dad, looking at me, "when you were still in nappies."

"*Errgh*," I said. "Stop it."

"Maybe we should have another," said Dad.

I put my fingers in my ears. Yuk. I don't even like to think about it.

Suddenly I spied a box jammed in at the back of the cupboard and hauled it out.

I couldn't believe my eyes when I opened it. It was full of old dresses. I don't mean old like worn out, I mean old in that they looked like they'd been kept for decades. Fabulous fabrics, a velvet wrap, crêpe blouses with tiny little tucks and

92

pleats, beautifully sewn, an evening gown with exquisite beading, a top with sequins. Satin, silks. I felt like I'd hit the jackpot.

"Mum," I called. "Whose are these clothes?"

Mum came to look at the heap of clothing I'd piled out on the hall floor.

"Oh, those. Those were your grandmother's. I used to wear them in the Sixties." She picked up a gorgeous pale lilac crêpe jacket. "I haven't looked at these in years. . . ."

"What are you going to do with them?" I asked.

"I don't like to throw them out . . ." she said.

"Supposed to be good Feng Shui, isn't it?" called Dad. "Clear your clutter and all that."

"I don't suppose I'll ever wear them again," Mum laughed. "But they're not exactly your style, are they? Maybe I could take them down to the secondhand shop or even to a costume shop for people to use in the theater."

I held my breath and asked, "Can I have them?"

"What on earth for? Are you doing a production at school?"

"Not exactly," I said. "It's just, I *think* I can do something with them."

❤ ❤ ❤

I piled the contents of the box and bags out on to the floor and started sifting through. Some of it was junk. Cable knit sweaters that had gone hard. T-shirts with paint all over them. But Grandma's stuff was a treasure trove.

I made a heap of the clothes I wanted and carted them upstairs with the sewing machine. Then I leafed through a couple of magazines for good designs and set about cutting, chopping bits off, hemming, and reshaping.

After a few hours, Mum appeared at my door. "What are you doing? We're all wondering where you've disappeared to."

"Creating," I said with a flourish, showing her what I'd done so far. "A short black velvet cross-over skirt and . . . my *pièce de résistance* for special occasions."

"Lovely," said Mum, feeling the material. It was powder blue lined chiffon with tiny pearls sewn all over it. "Isn't this from one of the evening gowns?"

"Yes. It was so easy to make, as it's only a sheath dress and got no sleeves, just the back and front sewn up at the sides. It's like one I saw Jennifer Aniston wearing in one of the mags."

"Oh, try it on, let me have a look," said Mum.

It fit like a glove.

"Very pretty," said Mum. "And it looks really professional."

"I doubt if anyone makes material like this any more. And I bet Nesta won't have anything like it from Morgan this time."

"Are you still worried about Nesta?" asked Mum.

"Not really. I've decided to make more of an effort with her. In fact, I'm making presents for both her and Izzie. I want to surprise them when they come over later."

I'd showed Mum the bandero top I'd started out of red sequin material for Nesta, then I was going to do a halter neck for Izzie with the leftover black velvet from the skirt.

Mum pulled a black ostrich feather out of the bag. "Why don't you use this to trim Izzie's top?"

"Good idea," I said. "I could hem it along the bottom."

By the time I'd finished, both tops looked so

good I was tempted to keep them for myself. But no, I wanted to give them something to show I can be a good friend.

"Lucy, phone!" called Steve from downstairs.

I was so absorbed in my sewing I hadn't even heard it ringing.

"Lucy," said Izzie's voice as I picked up the receiver. "I'm so sorry, I just called home and Mum said that you'd left a message."

"Oh right. And I sent you an e-mail too. I wanted to know if you and Nesta wanted to come over tonight for a girlie session."

"What, now?" said Izzie. "Isn't it a bit late?"

I looked at my watch. I couldn't believe it. It was nine thirty. I'd been sewing all day.

"Where have you been?" I asked. "In fact, where are you?"

I could hear music and voices in the background. It didn't sound like she was at home.

"Hold on," she said. "I'm going into the bathroom. I'm on the mobile."

"Where are you?"

"Lucy, please don't be mad when I tell you."

I immediately felt apprehensive.

96

"See Nesta went into Hampstead this morning and . . ."

Nesta again. I might have known she was with her.

"Yes, and?"

"Well she bumped into Michael Brenman and one of his mates and he asked her if she wanted to do something."

"Right . . ."

"Well she didn't want to be hanging around with two of them. She really likes Michael and wanted a bit of time on her own with him so she called me on her mobile and *begged*, begged me to go and meet them. Please understand, Lucy, we didn't mean to exclude you, but we couldn't ask you as well. I mean, we'd have looked like a right load of twerps if we'd all turned up."

"I know," I said grimly. "Two's company, three's a crowd."

"No. It's not like that, not exactly," said Izzie. "In fact, I wish you had come as well. I've got lumbered with Michael's mate. We're back at his house and he's a right Kevin. I'm going home in a minute if I can drag Nesta away from snogging

Michael. I'd rather have spent the day with you honest, *honest,* Lucy. You're not mad, are you? I had to meet Nesta. As a friend. And I did spend all last week with you trying to meet the Mystery Contestant. I didn't want to let Nesta down. . . ."

"Yeah, if you want a friend, you have to be a friend," I said, looking at the presents I had waiting for them and the face masks and makeup all laid out ready for the girls' evening.

"Yeah," said Izzie. "Oh, hold on a minute, Nesta's just come in. She says, come over to her house tomorrow after school. And oh, she says Michael is the worst snogger she's ever met. I suppose that means we can go home now."

Chapter 10

First
Kiss

Monday morning I overslept. I'd been up so late chopping up fab fabrics for future use, I was late for school and didn't get a chance to see Izzie or Nesta before lessons. I was feeling a bit wary of them both after Sunday.

Izzie gave me a little wave as I scrambled into my place in class, then in came Miss Watkins with a large shopping bag.

"I have a little homework for you all," she smiled mysteriously as she took what looked like three dozen eggs out of her bag. I could tell by her face it was going to be one of her mad ideas.

"Now then, Candice," she said. "I want you to hand out the eggs. One to each girl."

Candice did as she was told as we all looked at each other, mystified.

"I've been thinking about your career prospects," Miss Watkins said as she perched in her usual position on the desk corner. "There's one choice that none of you mentioned. It's full-time. It's demanding as well as rewarding. It means total, and I mean total, commitment. It's days, nights, and weekends. And sometimes no time off. Can any of you guess what I'm talking about?"

She looked around hopefully.

"Doctor," said Tracy Ford. "They're on call day and night sometimes."

"Okay, good," said Miss Watkins. "But they get holidays. No holidays with this."

"God," said Candice.

Miss Watkins laughed. "Not a job available to most of us," she said. "Any other suggestions?"

No one had a better idea.

"I'm talking about being a mother," she said. "And it's something you should all think about carefully."

Blimey, I thought. I'm only fourteen. Give me

a break. I haven't even got a boyfriend yet.

"Everyone always says it won't happen to me, but it only takes one time," Miss Watkins continued as half the class went scarlet and the other half went giggly, "and it can change your life for ever. I know you've all had classes about contraception, but this little exercise I want you to do will help you realize the responsibility you're undertaking if you don't use it."

My mind was boggling. Contraception? One night that can change your life for ever? Responsibility? What is she going to make us do with the eggs? I thought we were trying to decide our subjects.

"I want each of you to take the egg home," she continued as Candice placed one in front of each of us. "That's your baby for the week. I want you to bring it back next week in one piece, not broken."

Easy, I thought. I'll put it in the fridge.

"I want you to take it everywhere with you," said Wacko. "To the shops. To your friends' houses. To the bathroom."

What? Mad, she's completely mad.

She hadn't finished.

101

"And while we're at it, there's some leaflets on all the types of birth control available. I want you to pick one up from my desk at the end of the class so you can read through it at home. Any questions, ask your parents, or please come to me whenever you like."

Does she think we're sex mad in this class?

Clearly the answer is yes.

Nesta, Izzie, and I met up after school. With our egg babies. And our leaflets.

We read them on the bus to Nesta's house.

"It's weird, isn't it?" said Izzie. "One minute everyone's telling you not to grow up," she put on her snotty cow accent, "*to enjoy our youth.* Next minute, it's all grow up, decide what you want to be, and think about babies."

"I know," said Nesta. "But she must think we're a right load of plonkers if we don't know all about contraception by now."

"So what's oral contraception, then?" I asked.

"Talking your way out of it," said Nesta.

"You only have to say one word," said Izzie. "No."

I got the feeling neither of them had a clue. Best

to ask Mum. She's always too happy to fill me in on all the gory details.

"This coil thing sounds painful," I said, scanning the leaflet. "It goes in your womb. *Urgggh*."

"More painful for him more like," giggled Izzie. "Imagine, what if his thingy touches it, bd*OING . . . argghhhh!*"

Once we started laughing we couldn't stop.

"My brothers found Mum's maxi pads once. Of course they didn't know what they were," I said. "Lal put one on over his head then pretended that he was a brain surgeon."

"When I was little I found my mum's. I used them as hammocks for my dolls," said Izzie. "She hid them after that."

"My mum uses a diaphragm," said Nesta, reading her leaflet. "I found it in her bedside drawer when I was about eight and thought it was a toy frisbee. So we had *the conversation,* you know, when they get all embarrassed and tell you the facts of life."

"The whole business sounds very messy to me," I said.

"Not as messy as having a baby," said Izzie, getting up suddenly and screeching. "I've just sat on mine."

Egg yolk dribbled off the bus seat on to the floor and that set us off laughing again.

"Egg on your face," sang Nesta, "egg on your face . . ."

"Not my face," grimaced Izzie, wiping yolk from her skirt. "Oh, my poor baby."

"Can't make an omelette without breaking eggs," I said.

"Oh, oh," moaned Izzie. "I'm a terrible mother. Look at you two. You've still got yours."

"I know," I said, looking at Nesta. "And I know exactly what we should do with them."

"What?" said Nesta.

"Let's go home and boil them."

"Great idea," said Nesta.

Somehow I don't think any of us are ready to be mothers just yet.

When we got to Nesta's, she made us big cups of frothy coffee on her dad's cappuccino maker and we went into their gorgeous living room. No sign of Tony.

"So why was Michael such a rotten snogger?" I asked Nesta. I was intrigued to know what a rotten snog was, not having being snogged at all so to speak.

"Onions," she said. "He'd had a hot dog. And it was all sloppy. Wet."

Sounded awful. "Have you snogged many boys?" I asked.

"Not really," she said. "About seven."

Seven? She's so experienced!

"The best was Alessandro," continued Nesta dreamily. "I met him last year when we were in Tuscany. He did it fabulously. Soft. Tender. Why? How many have you snogged?"

True to form, I went red. "None," I said. "I've never seen anyone I liked."

"Except Mystery Boy," said Izzie. "Don't forget him."

"How many have you snogged?" asked Nesta, turning to Izzie.

"Two," she answered. "Peter Richards when I was seven, so I don't suppose that counts. And I can't really remember how it was. And Stuart Cameron last year. He was okay, but he kept trying to grope me as well and I didn't really fancy him. No, I'm waiting for someone special. Not one of the local nerds, thank you very much."

Just at that moment, Tony appeared with a huge grin on his face. Oh, God. He'd been in the house all the time. How much had he heard?

He came in and flopped on the sofa next to me. "The art of kissing," he said. "My speciality."

"You wish," said Nesta. "What do you know? Nothing."

"More than you think, actually." He turned to me. "Never been kissed, eh?"

Red turned to scarlet turned to purple.

"Leave her alone," said Izzie.

"I was just going to offer to show her how it's done," said Tony. "Then she'll have something to measure it against in the future."

Aaarghhhh. I didn't know what to do. What to say. He was sitting so close. His long gorgeous legs in jeans stretched out in front of me. And he smelled nice, clean, not like Michael Brenman's overpowering pong. My breathing went all funny like someone had just pulled a belt across my chest.

"Yeah, she'll know what it means to be kissed by a huge show-off big-head . . . ," started Nesta.

106

"You want to try?" he said, turning to Izzie.

She tossed her hair. "In your dreams."

So he turned back to me.

"Lucy. Do you want to learn from the Master?"

"The Master . . . ," guffawed Nesta.

This only seemed to egg him on. He tucked a strand of hair behind my ear, tilted my face up to his, and looked into my eyes. My insides melted into warm honey.

"Tony . . . ," warned Nesta.

"Close your eyes . . . ," he whispered.

"TONY . . . ," Nesta again.

Too late. He was kissing me. I didn't care that Nesta and Izzie were there. My first kiss. Little firecrackers were exploding inside me. Nice. Very nice.

Suddenly a hand grabbed him by the back of his shirt. "In the kitchen," said Nesta harshly. "NOW."

He laughed and got up to follow her.

Izzie looked at me as they disappeared. "You okay?"

I nodded. I giggled stupidly. Okay? I was in heaven.

"The cheek of him," said Izzie. "Who does he think he is?"

"Just going to the loo," I said and crept out into the hall.

I could hear Nesta's voice in the kitchen. "You stay away from her, do you hear?"

My heart sank. *Why* was she saying that to him? He'd kissed me, surely that meant he liked me, and now she was ruining everything again. Why should he stay away from me? I didn't want him to. Not now.

There was only one thing for it. I'd tell Izzie and Nesta that he was my Mystery Contestant. And I was very happy to kiss him.

The doorbell rang and Tony came out of the kitchen. As he went to answer it, he gave me a wink.

Nesta obviously thought I wasn't good enough for him. But he did like me. I knew he did. He couldn't have kissed me like that if he didn't. Why did she always have to spoil everything?

Standing at the door was one of the prettiest girls I've ever seen, tall with long auburn hair and all dressed in black.

She pecked Tony's cheek, gave me a hands-off look, and followed him down the hall into his bedroom.

Just before he went in he turned back and grinned. "Homework," he said, then disappeared.

"His girlfriend," said Nesta, appearing at the kitchen door.

And more kissing lessons, if you ask me.

"Come on," said Nesta. "Let's go and make a plan for meeting that boy you like."

"Lucy, you look awful," said Izzie as I went back in.

I felt awful.

"It's Tony's fault. I could kill him," said Nesta.

"She's very pretty, that girl," I said.

"She must be completely thick," said Nesta, "to be going out with him."

"I know he's your brother," said Izzie, "but he *is* a bit big-headed."

"Understatement," said Nesta. "Nobody in their right mind could possibly fancy him."

Something told me this wasn't the best moment to tell them that Tony was the MC.

Has life ever, ever been worse? Just as I thought me and Nesta were getting on better, she tells her brother to stay away. And now I don't know what to think. Anyway, he has a girlfriend. A gorgeous girlfriend. What chance would I ever have against her?

How to be the Master Snogger,
by Tony Williams

Do
Have clean teeth and fresh breath
Vary the intensity of your kisses
Close your eyes
Leave her wanting more

Don't
Give gooey, wet, sloppy open-mouthed kisses
Kiss when you've been eating garlic, onions,
or tuna
Pin her down so she can't breathe
Kiss with your mouth shut tight

Chapter 11

Haircut From Hell

"I'm going to get my hair cut," I told Izzie on the bus to school the next morning. "What do you think?"

I showed her all the pics I'd cut out of a mag last night showing different styles.

"Good idea," said Iz, pointing to one photo of a girl with cropped hair. "That would suit you. When are you going to get it done?"

"Tonight," I said.

"Wow, you move fast. Where?"

"The mall. Remember Candice had her hair cut last month? She told me if you go to the Aura school, where hairdressers go to get trained, they do it for free. They're always looking for volunteers to go along in the evenings."

"Great, me and Nesta will come as well. It's late-night shopping so we can get your hair cut then we'll have a mooch round. But what's brought this on? You've had your hair long for years."

"Angel Card," I admitted.

"An Angel Card told you to get your hair cut?"

"They were waiting for me when I got back from Nesta's last night. On the kitchen table. Waiting. Calling me. *Luuuucy, pick one.* I tried to resist but I couldn't help myself. In fact, I'm going to have to ask Mum to take them out of the house. I think I've become an addict. No resistance no matter what I tell myself or what kind of trouble they get me into. I see the pack and I *have* to pick one."

Izzie laughed. "They could start a group for addicts. ACA. Angel Cards Anonymous."

"Yeah, I'd get up and say, 'Hello. My name's Lucy Lovering and I'm an Angel Card addict. Let me tell you my sad story.'"

Izzie laughed again. "I'm a bit like that with the Net. Specially now I've found such a fab astrology

112

site. So what did it say? The card last night?"

"No one can make you feel inferior without your permission."

"Wow. That's a good one," said Izzie. "I'll have to try it when I tell Wacko that I sat on my egg baby. But why did that make you want to get your hair cut?"

I wasn't sure how much to tell Iz. I'd gone home from Nesta's last night feeling like a complete failure. I didn't want to bore her to death with the list of things that make me feel inferior lately:

- Everyone knows what they want to be when they grow up but me.
- My lack of kissing experience.
- I only look twelve.
- Josie Riley's right. I am a midget.
- I'm as flat-chested as my brothers.
- I've never had a proper boyfriend. And now probably never will as the only one I like belongs to another.
- I can't even decide what color to paint my bedroom.

Inferior. Definitely.

"Time for a change," I said. "Remember that

113

horoscope you did for me that said it was time for a new me so don't resist? I thought what better place to start than with my appearance? I've been so busy thinking about inside stuff like who I am, strengths, weaknesses, all that sort of thing Wacko told us to think about, and it's got me nowhere. So I'm going to change the outside. Hair. My room. My clothes."

"Watch out world," grinned Izzie. "Sounds good to me."

After school we went straight to the mall. I sat in the hairdressing college reception with ten other volunteers. Girls behind an enormous glass desk registered everyone then told us to wait. It all looked very swanky. A vast marbled reception with the most enormous bouquet of white lilies in a vase. Everywhere were posters of Aura products and TVs up on the walls showing demonstrations. I've definitely come to the right place, I thought. I am going to look fantabuloso.

Nesta immediately started chatting to the girls on reception about where they got their models and how could she apply.

"Aries rising," said Izzie, watching Nesta flicking her hair about as she charmed them all.

"That's the leap before you look sign, isn't it?"

"Yeah. They have fantastic energy. Go for it is their motto, and never mind the consequences."

"But Nesta's a Leo," I said. "How can she be Aries as well?"

"That's what I've been discovering. Our individual horoscopes are far more complex than just having a Sun sign. Like Nesta. Leo is her Sun sign. Like yours is Gemini and mine is Aquarius. That's determined by the month you're born. Your rising sign is worked out by the *time* and place you're born. It changes every two hours."

"So people with the same Sun sign can be quite different personalities?"

"Exactly," said Izzie. "There's all sorts of factors— where your Moon is . . ."

"Moon? I thought you said Sun?"

"Astrology's a real science when you get into it. Everyone has a different Moon they were born under as well. That changes every two days. You have your Moon in Taurus."

"Is that good?"

"Fantastic. It's exalted there. The Moon rules how you are emotionally. And means you're very romantic. Taurus is ruled by Venus. It means you appreciate beautiful things."

"Have you worked out my rising sign?"

"Yeah. Cancer," said Izzie. "That means you're very sensitive. Emotional even, sometimes. Cancer is the sign of the crab and they can be a bit prickly on the outside but as soft as mush on the inside."

"So what does your Sun sign mean?"

"How you look, your general characteristics," said Izzie.

"Gemini's an air sign, the sign of the twins, isn't it?"

Izzie grinned. "Yep. So you have two sides to you. The public and the private."

"Schizophrenic, you mean? That explains how I've been feeling lately."

Izzie laughed. "Geminis are good at communication. Creative."

I stared at her with admiration. She really knows her stuff and I don't know why I ever worried about what makes me "me." I should just ask Izzie. She seems to know exactly.

"Lucy Lovering," called the girl at reception.

I got up and followed her, suddenly feeling apprehensive.

Izzie gave me the thumbs-up. "Meet you afterward."

I was ushered down a maze of corridors and into a small salon with a row of mirrors and chairs.

A girl with bright red hair and even brighter red lipstick came forward. She looked very young. She can't have been training that long. "Hi, I'm Kate and I'll be cutting your hair," she said. "Take a seat."

After that I might as well not have been there.

An older lady with long curly blond hair came in and they both stared at me for a while then played with my hair, tilting my head from side to side, frowning and tutting.

"Splits ends," said Kate with disdain. "Who cut it last?"

"Er, my mum," I said, feeling smaller by the minute.

Kate and her supervisor looked at each other knowingly. "Ah. That explains it."

"Take a seat at the basin," ordered Kate.

"Er, what are you going to do?" I asked as Kate shampooed me. "I've brought some pictures of how I'd like it to look. I've got them in my bag."

"We won't need those," said Kate. "Don't you worry, I know what I'm doing."

She led me away from the basin back to a chair then started snipping. I told myself to relax. Kate's hair looked fab and so did her supervisor's. I sat back, crossed my fingers, and closed my eyes.

A minute later, Kate's mobile rang. She had a quick look round to see if her supervisor was around, then seeing she wasn't, took the call. It went on like this for twenty minutes. Snip, snip, then she'd take a call. Some drama about a boy called Elliot. I could see she was getting in a panic about something he said, and didn't seem to be concentrating on my hair at all.

"Where were we?" she asked, coming back to me after the third interruption.

"You were on the back," I said. Then the phone went again.

"Won't be a mo," she said and disappeared again.

When she came back she was more flustered than ever, whatever was upsetting her, she seemed to be taking it out on my hair. Snip, snip, chop, chop.

I stared at my reflection in horror. My hair was gone. Cut or rather hacked bluntly to my neck and it didn't look even. It was *awful*. I felt myself go red and I wanted to cry.

By now, Kate was busy with the hairdryer, blowing and pulling.

"Ouch, that hurts," I said as she yanked a piece of hair then almost burned my scalp with the dryer.

"Got to get a move on," she said. "Got to get out quick. *Major* drama."

I didn't care about her major drama. I had one of my own. She'd totally ruined my hair.

When she'd finished blowing, she stood back to look at her work. I looked younger than ever. Nine. Eight. A baby. Oh no. What has she done?

By the look on her face, she didn't like what she'd done either.

"Are you pleased?" she asked, while shoving her things in her bag.

"It, er, looks a bit uneven," I said.

"That's the look," she said. "Very Meg Ryan. And those split ends had to go. It can be a bit of a shock if you've had long hair for a while. You'll get used to it."

Then she put on her coat and scarpered.

A moment later, the supervisor came back in and looked surprised that Kate had gone. "Where's your cutter?" she asked.

"Dunno," I said. "Gone."

"That girl is dizzy," she said crossly then she examined my hair. As she looked the frown on her forehead deepened. "If you don't like it," she sighed and looked at her watch, "come back another night and we'll restyle it for you."

No way, I thought. I'm not coming back here. Why did I have to get the cutter who was having some sort of relationship crisis? If only she'd looked at my pics. I looked a disaster.

Izzie was waiting for me in reception. I could tell by her face that she hated it too.

"I know," I said, feeling my eyes fill up again. "It's awful, isn't it?"

"It's different," she said, then saw my stricken face. She put her arm round me. "It'll grow back."

What? In five years. How could I have been so

stupid? Thinking that if I chopped my hair off suddenly I'd grow confidence. Look amazing. Now I looked worse than ever.

Izzie sighed. "I *am* sorry, Lucy. Look, Nesta's waiting for us so let's get out of here. Come on, we'll go and meet her then get a cappuccino."

"I can't go anywhere looking like this," I said. I wanted to get on the bus and go home and hide under the duvet until my hair had grown back.

"I said we'd meet her in the John Lewis lingerie department," said Izzie. "She's trying on Wonderbras."

"On no, please. I want to go home."

"Five minutes," said Iz. "Then we'll go."

We made our way into John Lewis and up to the first floor. Everywhere I looked I saw girls with lovely long hair and in mirrors that seemed to be on every wall, I saw me looking like a bird had built a straw nest on my head.

Nesta was waiting for us waving three bras in her hand.

"Oh," she said when she saw my hair.

"Yeah. Oh," I said.

"I like it," she lied.

"I have to go home for ten years," I said.

"But I've got a bra for you to try. I've picked one for each of us."

"I can't," I said. "I have no chest. And no hair."

"That's what's so wonderful about the bras," said Nesta. "No matter what size you are they make you look fab." She looked me up and down. "They give everyone an amazing cleavage."

"Come on, Lucy," said Izzie. "It'll be fun. You need cheering up."

They dragged me into the changing room and Nesta handed us our bras.

Reluctantly I took mine and went into a cubicle. A strange face looked back at me from the mirror. If I didn't know who I was before, I certainly didn't know who this was staring back at me. And the back of my neck felt cold.

"Wow," screeched a voice from next door. "It makes me look enormous." I popped my head round Izzie's curtain and, despite my hair, I couldn't help laughing.

"Hello, boys," she giggled.

"Aruba, aruba," I said. "Those things look like lethal weapons. *The Guns of Navarone*."

Izzie pulled a face. "My mum'd never let me wear it. You know what she's like."

"Ready!" called Nesta from the other side. We stuck our heads into Nesta's cubicle. She'd chosen a red satin one and though her bust is nothing like as big as Izzie's, the bra gave her a great cleavage. I decided I *would* try mine on. If they had this effect on Izzie and Nesta, it was bound to help me.

I went back to my cubicle and, avoiding looking at my hair, I stripped off and put on the bra. Outside I could hear Izzie and Nesta laughing their heads off about something.

"You ready?" called Izzie, then stuck her head in.

Tears were welling up in my eyes again.

"Oh, Lucy, don't cry . . . ," said Izzie.

I couldn't help it and now I'd started I couldn't stop. The dam burst and all the tears I'd been fighting back for weeks suddenly came pouring out. The more I looked at my reflection, the more I sobbed. I looked like a little girl in her mother's bra. A little girl with a really bad haircut.

Nesta put her head round the cubicle curtain and when she saw my face came in. "Lucy, whatever's the matter?"

I sat on the stool in the cubicle. "My bra doesn't fit," I sobbed.

"It's only a bra," said Nesta softly.

That made it even worse. "I know, it's not really that," I said, quickly putting my clothes back on. "It just seems nothing fits. Nothing. I don't fit. And this stupid bra is just the last straw."

I looked worse than ever now as my nose had gone red and my eyes were all swollen and puffy.

"I'm pathetic," I said.

Izzie and Nesta exchanged worried looks.

"I don't fit here. I don't fit at school. I don't know what I want to be when I grow up."

I looked at the two of them, both gorgeous with long glossy hair and fabulous cleavages. "And now you two are best friends and there's no room for me anymore."

Before they could say anything or get dressed, I ran out of the store and caught the bus home.

No one makes you feel inferior without your permission.

ANGEL CARD

Chapter 12

Inflatable
Bras

When I got home, everyone was eating supper.

Four faces stared open-mouthed at me from the kitchen.

"What've you done to your hair?" cried Lal.

Wrong response, I thought. But I knew there wasn't a right one.

I ran upstairs and hid under my duvet. Minutes later, Mum knocked.

"Come and have something to eat, love'" she said.

"Not hungry," I called.

Five minutes later, Dad knocked. "It's not so bad, love. We don't care what you look like. Come down and have your supper."

"You've got more hair than I have," I cried. "It's not fair!"

Then Steve tried. "Lucy, come down. *Buffy's* on."

"Go away," I said. I didn't want to watch "*Buffy the Vampire Slayer*". All the girls in it had long fabulous hair.

Then Lal knocked. "I've got something for you," he said, then pushed his Beatles wig under the door. Ha ha, very funny. Not.

The clothes I'd made were lying on the chair at the end of my bed. I put them straight in the wastepaper bin. What had I been thinking of? They were rubbish. It doesn't work to try and change the outside if the inside isn't right. And my inside feels definitely not right.

I looked at my awful hair in the mirror again. I pulled at the roots, willing it to grow like the doll I had when I was five. You just tugged the hair and it came straight out right down to her waist. Why wouldn't mine do that? I couldn't even tie it up any more so that no one would notice what a strange style it was. So sticky-outee. I felt miserable.

And Izzie was right: I did have two sides as a Gemini. There were definitely two in me, both driving me nuts.

One part was completely freaked. My hair, my hair, I can never go out again. The other side was saying you selfish, petty, pathetic thing. Think about all the starving people in Africa. What does your stupid hair matter when there are war and famines?

Where did *that* voice come from? I know. Our headmistress Mrs. Allen. How did *she* get in my head?

I think I may be going mad. Completely. What makes me "me"? I am a nutter. Completely and utterly barking mad. And ugly.

At eight thirty, the doorbell rang.

"Lucy, it's for you," called Mum.

"Not in," I called back.

I heard a knock on the door.

"Lucy," said Izzie's voice. "It's me and Nesta."

I hid even further under the duvet as the door opened and they both trooped in.

"Luce, come out. Nesta has an idea."

I stuck my face out of the covers as both of them sat on the end of the bed.

"I spoke to Mum," said Nesta. "She has someone come to the house to do her hair every other week. She's coming tomorrow. She's really good, Lucy. She could fix yours."

"But I haven't got any money," I said. It was hopeless.

"Me and Iz have thought about that. We know you get less pocket money than us and we'll club together and we'll pay."

Both of them were looking at me with such kindness, it set me off again. Blub, blub. What *is* the matter with me these days?

"We thought you'd be pleased," said Nesta, looking puzzled.

"You're being nice to me," I sobbed. "Don't be nice to me. And I'm so selfish when there are wars and everything."

They both laughed.

"You're not responsible for the whole human race," said Iz. "Not yet anyway."

"I wanted to say something else," said Nesta,

looking embarrassed suddenly. "I never meant to take Izzie from you. It's just, I thought you didn't like *me*."

"But you always seem to want to be with Izzie . . . ," I began. "And I know I don't look old enough for some things you want to do like the cinema and hanging out with Sixth Formers and . . ."

"Those things don't matter. And I realize we shouldn't have gone without you that time. I really like you, Lucy. I want to be friends with Izzie *and* you. If you'll let me."

"But what about your brother? I thought you told him to stay away from me because you didn't like me."

"NoOO. Only to protect you, Lucy. Not because I don't *like* you. You don't know my brother. He thinks he's Casanova. A different girl every week. Once the challenge is over, he dumps them. We've only been in London a few months and already he's left a trail of broken hearts. I didn't want him to hurt you. That's all, honest."

"Really?"

"Yeah. I really *do* like you, Lucy, and want to be friends."

Tears filled my eyes again. "I'm so sorry," I said. "I don't seem to be able to stop crying. Just lately, I've felt I don't fit anywhere."

"My mum says it's our hormones running riot," said Izzie.

"I went through a time," said Nesta, "where we lived before. I was the only dark-skinned kid in our school. I *really* felt I didn't fit. . . ."

"So how did you handle it?"

"Decided I'd be proud I was different even if some days I didn't feel it. I toughed it out. I know sometimes that's all people see and they think I'm stuck up. But here in London, it's all been so different. Meeting you and Izzie. I feel I've got really good friends for once. And your mum and dad. You're so lucky. . . ."

"But yours are so glamorous . . . ," I began.

"Yeah, they're okay, but they're never there. Always working. That's why I love coming back to yours. It's so comfy and your brothers are great. I feel at home here. Everyone's made me feel so welcome."

"Except me," I said. I was beginning to see I'd misjudged her. She'd been trying to be my friend all along and I hadn't let her near.

Nesta grinned. "I was hoping I'd win you round in the end. I don't give up easily."

Suddenly Izzie spotted the clothes spilling out of the wastepaper bin. "What are these?" she said, pulling them out.

"Actually those are some presents I had for you, but . . ."

"Wow," said Nesta, seeing the red sequin top. "Where have you been hiding these? Why haven't you ever worn them?"

"Do you really like them?" I asked, getting out from under my duvet.

"They're fantastic," said Izzie, holding the clothes up and examining them. "Where did you get them?"

"I made them."

"You're kidding," said Nesta. "They look really expensive. Like designer stuff."

"Actually," I said. "I made that red one for you. And the black one's for you, Izzie."

In a second they had stripped off and put their presents on.

"Ohmigod," said Nesta, admiring her reflection in the mirror. "This is absolutely brilliant. I can't believe it. It's perfect."

It did look good, the red against her dark skin.

"This is the best thing I've got," said Izzie, twirling around in the halter neck. "Can we really have them? I just love it—and the ostrich feather trim. Mucho sexy."

I was glowing with pleasure. "I was going to chuck it all out. After today . . ."

"NoOOO, you mustn't," said Iz, seizing the blue dress I'd made for myself. "God, this fabric is amazing. All the little pearls. Put it on."

I put on the dress and both of them ooh-ed and aah-ed. It did look good as long as I didn't look above my neck.

"It fits like a glove," said Izzie, then laughed. "See, *something* fits!"

"Might look better if I had boobs," I said, thinking back to the lingerie department.

"Don't be mad," said Nesta. "They'll grow soon enough. And if they don't, you can always have silicone."

"Silicone! I'm four*teen*."

"Well what I mean is, at least you can do something about having no chest. Bras, uplifts. Not like my feet." She pulled off her trainers. "Look. Massive. Horrible. I can never get shoes to fit."

I couldn't believe it. Nesta wasn't perfect after all.

"That's nothing," said Izzie. "Try having my thighs. Both of you have such slim legs and I've got great whoppers. And short stubby ones at that. I can never get jeans to fit."

I felt so happy. Nesta and Izzie both had complexes. Why had we never talked about it before? I thought I was the only one who felt the way I did.

Hurrah. We're all mad.

Suddenly Izzie and Nesta started grinning like maniacs.

"What?" I said, suspicious. "What are you two up to?"

"Are you feeling better, Lucy?" asked Nesta, producing a package from her bag.

I nodded warily.

"Good, because we got you a little present as well," said Izzie.

"Something you really want," said Nesta.

Something I really want? My mind filled with

images of CDs, books, makeup I've had my eye on. What great friends.

Nesta giggled as she handed me the package in a carrier bag.

I put my hand in the bag and pulled out "the present."

Izzie and Nesta collapsed on the bed laughing as I looked at what looked like a bit of wrinkled pink plastic. "It's for your, er, your chest problem."

An inflatable bra. I started laughing and Izzie blew into the hole in the bra to inflate it. A perfect 34C.

"Put it on, put it on," she said.

I had to comply and shoved the bra up under my dress then stood in front of the mirror and turned to profile.

Nesta and Izzie made long wolf whistles.

"Pamela Anderson eat your heart out," I said, strutting and wiggling round the room. "*Baywatch* here I come. Yeah, thanks girls, like *very* funny."

Chapter 13

Pop Star
Names

We are the Three Musketeers. One for all and all for one.

Izzie brought her wet-look gel with her on the bus the next morning and Nesta plastered it on to my head.

"There, that's better," said Nesta, slicking my hair away from my face. "It's stopped it sticking out and you can't see it's all uneven any more. Then tonight, we'll get you sorted at home."

When we got off the bus, we headed straight for the corner shop. We had Wacko first lesson and it was hand in the egg baby day. Half our class were in the store. All buying free range eggs.

"Well done, girls," she said, when we all put the eggs on her desk. "I hadn't expected half of you to bring them back in one piece."

Everyone looked at the floor so we wouldn't catch each other's eyes and start laughing. Then Wacko said she wanted us to get into groups and discuss how far we'd got with our What-makes-me-"me"? project.

Just as things were going well, she had to bring *that* up again.

Izzie, Nesta, and me got into a group and stared at our files.

"Let's put in our pop star names," said Nesta.

"Pop star name?" I asked.

"Yeah, like a stage name. You take the name of your first female pet and your mother's maiden name and *voilà*, your pop star name. Boys pick the name of their first male pet."

I thought for a second. "Our first cat was

Smokey," I said. "And my mum's maiden name is Kinsler. So Smokey Kinsler."

"Takes all sorts, darlin'," said Nesta huskily.

"Hubba hubba," said Izzie. "Here's Smokey an' she's smo-oking tonight. Mine's Zizi. Zizi Malone."

"Mine's Sooty Costello," laughed Nesta.

"But Williams is your name," I said.

"I know, my mum kept her name and I use that instead of Dad's. So I'm using *his* maiden name. Sooty Costello. I like that."

"Perfect," I said.

"Let's put in our Mills and Boon writer names too," said Izzie.

"How do you do that?" I asked.

"You take your middle name and the name of the street where you first ever lived," said Iz.

"Suzanne Lindann," said Nesta.

"That works," said Izzie. "Mine's Joanna Redington."

"Mine's Charlotte Leister," I said, getting into it. "And we could put our death meals in too. It might come in handy if the aliens ever arrive and we have twenty-four hours before the world blows up."

137

"A death meal being?" asked Nesta.

"Your last meal ever on earth, stupid, like, if you know you've only got a few hours left."

That set us off dreaming for a while. All the lovely things we could eat and not have to worry about the calories or dieting.

"Chips, a burger, and Häagen-Dazs pecan," said Nesta.

"Roast chicken and roastie tatoes and banoffi pie," said Izzie.

"Spaghetti bolognese and treacle pudding and custard," I said. "And chocolate. Lots of it."

Nesta sent a note round class when Wacko wasn't looking. By the end of the lesson we had everyone's pop star names.

A good lesson methinks. And I suppose I'm getting clearer on the What-makes-me-"me" front. I'm Gemini with Cancer rising and the Moon in Taurus. I am an air sign, the sign of the twins. I am Smokey Kinsler, pop star queen or possibly Charlotte Leister, romantic novel writer.

Well, it's a start.

I looked up at Wacko and wondered if she would be impressed with our hard work.

"Lucy Lovering," she said, seeing me staring at her. "Stop sniggering."

She's picking on me. Do I care? No.

In the afternoon we all had to pile on to the school bus for an outing to the Tate Modern. Worse luck, some of the Year Eleven girls had come along to help "look after us."

As we took our seats at the back of the bus, Josie Riley came down the aisle and stood threateningly over Nesta.

"Hear you've been trying to cop off with Michael Brenman," she said.

Nesta immediately stood up. "It sounds like English but I can't understand a word you're saying," she said, going into her Scary Spice persona.

Now Nesta is definitely someone who doesn't give *anyone* permission to make her feel inferior. She's five foot five and Josie's at least three inches smaller.

Josie backed away then saw me giggling and turned to me. "What happened to your hair? Whatever look you're going for, you missed."

Izzie stood up next to Nesta. "If I throw a stick, will you leave?"

Josie turned on Nesta again. "You think you're it, don't you? Well let me tell you something. Michael Brenman is mine and I'd appreciate it if you'd stay away."

"Thank you, I will," said Nesta. "And as for Michael being *yours*, may I say we're all refreshed and challenged by your unique point of view. Anyway you can have Michael Brenman, I'm not interested, he kisses like a whelk."

Josie's mouth dropped open. "He *kissed* you? What does he see in a kid like you?"

Nesta stuck her nose in the air. "I'm really easy to get along with once you lesser people learn to worship me," she said.

Josie's mouth shrank to resemble a cat's bottom and by this time, I was on the floor laughing.

"One for all and all for one," I said as she sloped off.

There are a million things to look at in the Tate Modern. On the bank of the river Thames, it's an enormous warehouse type building with loads of different floors, each one with room after room of remarkable oddities, some beautiful, some seriously deranged.

As far as our class was concerned though, there was only one room worth looking at. After an hour of trooping around and trying to make sense of it all, we all jammed ourselves into a tiny dark space where there was music playing. On the wall a film was playing of a man with a beard. A naked man, sort of hippie dancing in slow motion. His willy was flopping up and down in time to the music. Everyone was falling about laughing and Candice Carter went up to the wall and started dancing along with him. That made us laugh even more.

"Is this art?" said Mo Harrison.

"Well it beats *The Hay Wain*," said Nesta.

"I thought you had to be able to draw to be an artist," I said.

"Not any more," said Nesta. "My dad said anything can be art if you say it is."

Then Mr. Johnson came in and caught us. He took one look at the film and said, "Move along, girls, come on, move along. Plenty more to see."

"Oh, I don't think so," said Izzie, trying not to laugh. "I think we've seen it all."

Sometimes school is great.

Year Nine

	Pop star name	Mills and Boon name
Lucy Lovering:	Smokey Kinsler	Charlotte Leister
Izzie Foster:	Zizi Malone	Joanna Redington
Nesta Williams:	Sooty Costello	Suzanne Lindann
Candice Carter:	Duchess Black	Rebecca Park Mead
Joanne Richards:	Muffin O'Casey	Emily Belmont
Gabby Jones:	Lucky Nolan	Lavinia Rosemount
Jade Wilcocks:	Roxanne Bennie	Rosemary Milton
Mo Harrison:	Flossy Cable	Gabriel Westerly

And: Nesta went up to Miss Watkins and said she was doing some research into old names for her history project so we also have:

Miss Watkins:	Mango Malloy	Violet Laurier

A class full of potential pop stars and Mills and Boon writers. Excellent. Most excellent.

Chapter 14

The Mystery Contestant Revealed

My hair is fantabuloso. At last. Can life get any better?

Betty, that's the hairdresser, is my new best friend. She looked more like a mum than a trendy hairdresser, and at first I had my doubts as to whether she could repair the damage.

Nesta's mum was just off to do her newsreading shift having had her hair done. She looked ever so smart in a navy suit and silver jewelery, and I thought I'd be intimidated by her like I am by Izzie's mum, but she was really friendly. She took one look at what Kate had done and said to Betty, "Oh no, she wants it softer, feathered, layered, don't you think?"

I nodded, but just to be on the safe side I showed them the picture I'd cut out of the magazine.

"Exactly," said Mrs. Williams, looking at the photo. "Something to show off your lovely bone structure. And, Betty, run a few highlights through." She turned to me before going out of the door. "My present, Lucy. I know what it's like when your hair gets ruined."

Nesta's family is fab.

And off Betty went. This time I didn't look in the mirror until she'd finished, then when I did . . . Wow. It was fantastic. Spiky and short at the front and layered all over. Then she put some white blond highlights through the top. Even I had to admit that this time the cut really suited me.

"You look gorgeous," said Izzie. "It really shows off your cheekbones. Amazing."

"You look elfin," said Nesta. "Very Winona Ryder."

After Betty had gone, we had another look

through Mrs. Williams's interior design mags and I saw the room I wanted. Pale lilac. With powder blue paintwork.

"*Très chic*," said Izzie.

It was all coming together. My hair, my room, my friends.

It was time to ask Nesta my burning question.

"Nesta," I said gravely.

"Yes, oh gorgeous one?" she replied.

"You know Tony?"

"Yes," she laughed. "He's my brother."

"Why doesn't he live with his mum?"

Nesta went quiet. "She died. In a road accident when he was six months old. He never knew her. A year later, his dad met Mum, and, well, my mum's the only mum he's ever known, even though she's not really his mum physically."

"Where is he tonight?" I asked. I wanted him to see me with my new haircut. Looking fantabuloso.

"Some class after school, I expect," said Nesta. "He often stays late for one thing or another."

Suddenly Izzie clapped her hand over her mouth and gave me a strange look, "Ohmigod," she said. "OhmiGOD."

145

"What?" chorused Nesta and I.

"Tony," said Izzie. "*Tony*."

She knew. I *knew* she knew. I went purple and now she definitely knew.

"What?" said Nesta.

Izzie crossed her arms and looked at me as if to say, I'm not saying, are you going to?

I glanced at Nesta and decided I could trust her.

"What?" she said.

"Tony," I said.

"I know," she said. "Tony, Tony. *Tony* what?"

"A boy that we didn't see in Highgate because he stays late for classes after school?" said Izzie, waiting for the penny to drop.

Nesta thumped her forehead. "Except we *did* see him, didn't we? Obvious. Obviouso. Tony is the MC."

I nodded.

"And he made you kiss him," said Izzie.

"And I told him to stay away from you," said Nesta. "No wonder you hated me. Why didn't you say, Lucy?"

"I thought you'd tell him I fancied him and then I'd, I'd look stupid. If he knew I'd been

146

waiting for him to come out of school, I'd look like a real desperado."

At that moment, we heard someone coming in the front door.

Oh, let it be her dad back from America, I prayed, but of course, Murphy's law, it was Tony.

"Hiya, everybody," said Tony. "Wow. Is that little Lucy? Hey, you look great. Gorgeous."

He came and sat next to me. "Want another kissing session?"

Nesta and Izzie just sat there gaping.

"*What?*" said Tony. "Why are you all staring at me? What? What's happened?"

Suddenly I got the giggles and couldn't stop. That set Izzie off then Nesta and soon the three of us were holding our sides laughing.

Tony got up and stomped to the door. "Girls. Sometimes you lot can be really juvenile."

"I thought he liked girls with a sense of humor," I said, still laughing.

"Not when it's directed at him," said Nesta. "And I won't say anything, about, you know, him being the MC, if you don't want."

"Thanks," I said. "I *don't* want."

147

"Anyway," said Izzie. "I reckon you could get anyone you want looking like you do now. Play the field a while."

"Ah, but I have been kissed by the Master," I said, giggling again.

"Then you owe it to yourself," said Izzie, "to see if anyone else can match up."

Chapter 15

Decisions, Decisions . . .

"So girls," said Wacko a fortnight later. "Next week I want your subject choices in. You've all had plenty of time to think about it, so I expect your papers on my desk on Monday."

Eek. Double eek. I hadn't thought about it at all. Not for ages. I'd been too busy having a good time with Nesta and Izzie and making clothes and doing my bedroom.

We'd spent the last two weekends painting. Lal and Steve had helped and it looked fantastic. I chose lilac mist for the walls and, as I'd seen in the interior magazine, we painted the woodwork pale powdery blue. The room was transformed and looked much bigger, as well as cleaner and brighter.

Mum took me down to a market in the East End to look for fabrics for the curtains and cushions, but we didn't see any I liked at any of the stalls. Then we passed an Indian shop. Rolls of beautiful materials were spilling out on to the pavement. I had to stop. Lovely shimmering jewel colors with silver and gold borders.

"Mum, let's look in there," I said, pulling her in.

I found a roll of sky blue *sari* fabric with a silver embroidered border. It would look stunning against the lilac walls and it wasn't too expensive. We made our purchase then bought some lining and some curtain rails.

When I got home, Mum helped me do the curtains and we made them so that the lovely silver border was at the bottom. We even had enough to swathe some at the top. It was the finishing touch and made the room look floaty and soft.

The overall effect was lovely but had taken up all my spare time. Subject choices hadn't even got a look-at.

❤ ❤ ❤

Things were looking up on the boy front, too. When I go out with Izzie and Nesta now, boys look at me as well. And not just the nerdy ones that no one else wants. Some quite cute ones have given me the eye. But to my mind, no one came close to Tony.

I saw him a couple of times at Nesta's, but he ignored me. I don't think he had recovered from us all laughing at him. Then one evening, he came out of his room when I was going to the bathroom.

"*Psst*," he said. "Lucy, in here."

I followed him in and he shut the door. I stood there nervously wondering what he wanted. Then before I could say anything, he pushed me back against a wall, put my arms around his neck and kissed me. A long deep sensual kiss that went right down to my toes and back again.

Then he stood back. "So, do you want to go out some time?"

I remembered everything that Nesta had said about him. He likes a challenge then dumps the girl. Nesta said he'd even chucked the girl I saw there a couple of weeks ago. Izzie's words also went through my head. Don't be too easy. Boys like a challenge. Although it was very tempting, I took a deep breath and moved away from him.

"I don't know," I said. "I'll think about it."

He looked taken aback then shrugged. "Suit yourself."

Then he opened the door to let me out. "You're probably too young for me anyway."

But he was smiling as he said it.

Time was running out. Monday was D-day for Wacko and Saturday was the Clothes Show. When was I going to have time to choose my subjects? I got my file out and sat at the kitchen table with what I had done so far in front of me. Three lines.

"Lucy, shouldn't you be in bed?" said Mum. "It's almost eleven o'clock."

"We have to hand this in on Monday and I still haven't a clue what I want to do when I grow up. Too many choices. It's driving me mad."

Mum sat down at the table next to me. "I remember feeling the same," she said. "In fact even now I don't know what I want to be when I grow up."

"But you *are* grown up. And you have a job."

"Yes, but I still feel nineteen sometimes. There're always choices, aren't there? I mean, I know I have a job. I'm a psychotherapist. But that's not what I am. It's only what I do. Who I am is changing all the time and I could change my job any time I want."

"I wish I could decide on just one thing, never mind think of changing. It's such a nuisance."

"Choice isn't a curse, Lucy. It's a blessing. And there will always be choices. Every day, every week. They'll keep coming."

I groaned.

"There are easy choices, like do I want tuna pizza or four cheeses? Shall I paint my nails pink or purple? And there are the bigger choices, more serious stuff like career or relationships. And those choices will seem to keep changing depending on how you're feeling inside as well as how outside influences affect you."

"It all sounds so complicated,' I sighed. "Oh for an easy life."

"I'll drink to that," said Mum. "How are you getting on with that boy you like?"

153

"He says I'm too young for him. But it's not that. One of the girls he went out with, I thought she was sixteen but turns out she's the same age as me. I just look young for my age."

"You'll see that as a gift one day," smiled Mum. "It's a family gene; none of our family looks their age. Believe me, when you're thirty or forty you'll be glad you look younger. But for now, come on, up to bed. Sleep on it. You never know, it might all become clear in the morning."

Fat chance. I'll never be able to sleep. What if I pick the wrong subjects and regret it? I wish, I *wish* I knew what to do. Decisions, decisions, decisions.

Chapter 16

The Way is Clear

I made a special outfit for the Clothes Show. Halter tops are turning out to be my speciality and I ran one off out of some of the leftover *sari* material using the silver to make crisscross straps at the back. Then I made a gray crêpe wrap skirt to go with it.

I met up with Nesta and Izzie at the tube station. Nesta looked sensational wearing her black leather trousers and a short jacket. And I was so pleased to see that she had my red top on underneath.

Izzie was wearing a long hippie dippie outfit in purple with some amethyst jewelery she found at a stall in Camden.

The hall was heaving with people when we got there. We paid for our tickets then went to join the crowds wandering around the many stalls and shopping areas. Izzie was soon absorbed in a stall selling New Age lotions and crystals. Nesta was busy craning her head looking for talent scouts.

"Aren't they supposed to spot you, not the other way round?" I asked. "Just relax, Nesta. Enjoy yourself. The talent scouts will be doing just that: scouting."

We were wandering into one of the shops when I stopped in my tracks.

"What? Who have you seen?" asked Nesta.

I pulled Nesta behind a rail of clothes and pointed. There was Josie Riley and a bunch of her mates. Josie was flirting with a boy who was standing in the middle of them lapping up the attention. She was flicking her hair about and doing all that touchy feely stuff, brushing the boy's arm and looking deeply into his eyes.

It was Tony.

"Oh, don't worry, Lucy," said Nesta. "He may be a big-head, but he's not stupid."

I wasn't so sure. He'd said how much he liked

confident girls and Josie was certainly that. Plus he looked like he was really enjoying himself.

Suddenly Josie spotted us and gave us a sick smile and a wave.

"Want to go over?" said Nesta.

"Oh no," I said, darting behind another clothes rail. "I couldn't bear it if he likes her."

"Suit yourself," said Nesta. "Anyway he hasn't seen us."

There was so much to take in. Hours flew by as we tried clothes on, experimented with new eye colors and plastered ourselves with free samples of moisturizer and perfume.

Izzie wanted to return to one stall to have a toe ring fitted, so Nesta and I decided to go and watch one of the catwalk shows. We turned a corner and I walked smack into Josie.

"Ah, the midget," she said, then looked me up and down and laughed. "What have you got on? The Eastern look was out years ago. You look like an advert for curry in a hurry."

All her friends started laughing and suddenly my new found confidence failed me.

"She made those clothes herself and I think she looks fantastic," said Nesta, coming to my defence. "I don't suppose someone with your IQ could even sew on a button."

"Ahhhh," said Josie. "Made them yourself, did you? Poor thing. Can't afford new clothes." She did a twirl. "My mum brought my outfit back from Milan."

"There's a big difference between buying expensive labels and having style," said Nesta. "Lucy has style. Something you'll never, ever know about."

"And I suppose you do," said Josie, then smiled smugly. "Oh and Michael Brenman, you can have him. I've met someone much better."

Nesta shrugged. "Oh clear off, Josie, I'm not in the mood," she said, and tried to get away. But as she walked to the right, Josie and gang walked with her. She tried to walk to the left, but again they blocked her way. It was starting to feel uncomfortable as there were four of them and only the two of us, then Josie stepped forward and trod on Nesta's foot.

"Ow!"she cried. I winced even though it wasn't

my foot. Josie was wearing high, spiky-heeled shoes.

"Oh *sorry*," said Josie insincerely. "Did that hurt?"

"Need a hand?' said a male voice.

We all turned. It was Tony. Josie and her mates sprang back straight away.

"No, I'm fine," said Josie, going all coy and girlie.

"Not you," he said, brushing her aside and putting his arm round Nesta. "You all right, Nesta?"

Josie looked shocked. Of course she couldn't know that he was Nesta's brother, and he was clearly the best-looking boy in the hall.

"We were just admiring Lucy's outfit," lied Josie, and her friends started sniggering again.

Tony turned to me. "Looking good, kiddo," he said. "Come on, girls, I'll buy you a cappuccino."

Josie obviously thought he meant her as well, as she trooped along after us.

He put his arms round Nesta and me and turned back to Josie. "Sorry, three's company. Four's a crowd."

Ha ha. That showed her.

"I thought you liked girls who are sure of themselves," I said as we walked towards the coffee bar.

"Do me a favor," he said. "Yeah, I like confident

girls, but I don't like the music turned up *quite* that loud if you get my meaning."

Tony. I think I'm in love.

As Tony went to find a table, Nesta and I queued up to get our drinks. As we stood waiting, I noticed the redheaded lady in front of us staring. I felt embarrassed and wondered if my homemade stitching was so obvious.

"Nice top," the woman said.

I blushed. "Thanks."

"Where did you get it?" she asked.

"I made it myself," I said.

The woman looked me up and down thoroughly. "I'm impressed."

"She made this top as well," said Nesta, doing a twirl for her.

"Really?" the woman said. "You've got a good eye. Simple designs always look the best."

Then she put her hand in her bag and pulled out a card. "Here. Remember me when you've finished college."

"College?" I said.

"I presume you are going to do fashion. Design?"

160

I was taken aback. I'd never thought of it. Then it felt like the clouds lifted. The way was clear.

"Yes," I grinned back at her. "Course I am."

"Well good luck and get in touch when you finish. I'm always on the lookout for fresh talent and innovative design."

Then she bought her drink and moved away.

Nesta took the card. "Ohmigod," she said.

"What?"

"That was Viv Purcell."

The name meant nothing to me.

"*The* Viv Purcell. She's one of the hippest designers around. Anyone who's anyone is fighting to wear one of her outfits."

I felt myself glowing with pleasure. She'd picked me out and told me to keep her card. And, best of all, she'd put her finger on the spot. What I want to be when I grow up. A designer. Of course, of *course*.

I spent the next hour cruising round in a rosy glow of happiness. Tony hung round with us for most of the morning and every time we spotted Josie and crew, she looked sick with jealousy. Especially when at one point, Tony put his arm round me.

When he was leaving, he winked and smiled at me. Maybe. I thought. Maybe one day. It wasn't over yet.

Of course Nesta got spotted by her talent scout. She stood out from the crowd like she always does and was approached by not one but two talent scouts who asked her to get in touch with them.

We went home, over the moon. Nesta, her head in the clouds with dreams about being a model. Me, over the moon because now I knew what made me "me." I knew what I wanted to be when I grew up. I'd be able to choose my subjects.

Later that evening, I sat working on my What-makes-me-"me"? project when the phone rang.

"Lucy, it's me," said Nesta. She sounded as if she'd been crying.

"What's the matter?"

"My mum," sobbed Nesta. "She won't let me phone the agencies."

"Why not?"

"She says I have to focus on my studies. My life is over. My one chance and she's ruining it all."

"Does she have to know?"

"Yes. That's just it. Both the scouts said if I go in to see them I have to take Mum with me."

"What does your dad say?"

"Same. I rang him in LA and he said I shouldn't even think about it yet. My life is over. What else can I do? You're so lucky you know what you're doing. And your mum and dad aren't likely to object."

I knew how she felt. Wow. Did I know how she felt.

"Nesta," I said, remembering what Mum had said. "There will always be choices. Always. Anyway, being a model isn't your only one. You can be an actress as well. And if you don't want to do that, you can join a model agency later. You're not going to lose your looks."

We chatted on for about half an hour and at the end Nesta said, "Thanks, Lucy. You're a really good friend."

As she put the phone down, I realized she was right. I am.

Lucy Lovering. What Makes Me "Me"?

My name is Lucy Lovering. I am a person that makes choices.

They change. I change. That's life.

Who am I? Astrologically, I'm Gemini with Cancer rising and the Moon in Taurus. That makes me the individual I am, but how I feel can change according to the stars and the sun and moon depending where they are in the sky.

At the moment I am four foot eight. And a half. That will change.

I like pepperoni pizza. That *might* change.

My favorite color is blue. That also might change.

My pop star name is Smokey Kinsler and my Mills and Boon name is Charlotte Leister. But I doubt if I will take up either of those names as I have other plans.

What are my interests? Art, design, fashion. I hate math and I hate science. I doubt if that will change, but you never know.

What are my strengths and weaknesses?

Strengths are making clothes, and design. And being a good friend.

Weaknesses, ice cream, Tony Williams, and any animal with sad eyes.

What would I like to do as a career? Easy. Design. Maybe fashion, maybe interiors. I'm told I have "the eye."

Best of all, I have two best friends. Izzie Foster and Nesta Williams.

That will never change.

Mates, Dates, and Cosmic Kisses

Chapter 1

The Bridesmaid of Frankenstein

Lucy's jaw dropped when I came out of the bathroom.

"Izzie! What on *earth* have you done?" she cried.

"It's different," said Nesta.

Both of them stared at me like I'd stepped out of a horror movie.

"Do you like it?" I asked, giving them a twirl.

It was the day of the wedding of my boring stepsister Amelia to the equally boring Jeremy, and I had to be bridesmaid with my other stepsister Claudia. Typically Amelia chose a disgusting dress for me. Emerald green satin. Empire waist. Awful.

But then I'd had an idea.

"I had to do something," I said. "I looked like I had a starring role in a Jane Austen costume drama."

"Yes," said Nesta, still gawping, "but *green* hair?"

"It matches perfectly," I grinned. "Don't you like it?"

"I think it looks fab," said Lucy. "But what about school? Mrs. Allen will kill you."

"Oh it washes out after a week. It's only mousse. But I'm not going to tell Mum that."

I looked at my reflection in my bedroom mirror. "I like it and I think I might keep it in until Monday at least."

"Won't your mum make you wash it out?" asked Nesta.

"She's been dashing about all morning and the car will be here any minute so by the time she sees me, it'll be too late."

Lucy giggled. "You look like an Irish colleen. All that emerald makes your eyes look even greener than normal."

"Then my grandma would have been proud—

Irish roots and all that. Geddit? Emerald green roots?"

They were staring at me as if I'd gone mad.

"*Hair* roots, dummies."

"More like she'll turn in her grave," said Nesta. "I don't think wearing green stretched as far as hair."

"Maybe her ghost will show up at the wedding," I said, "and when they get to that part where the priest says, 'Anyone here got any objection?' her ghost will rise up to the ceiling groaning, 'Yes I do, I *do*. My granddaughter has dyed her lovely long brown hair green.'"

Lucy and Nesta laughed.

"Seriously though," I continued, "I wish you two were coming. It's not fair. Everyone else was allowed to bring friends, at least to the reception. But then, I suppose because they're all grown up it's one rule for them, another for us."

"Well there might be some decent boys there," said Nesta. "You can practice my flirting tips."

"Fat chance. It'll be deadly dull. There's not even a disco. Jeremy's an accountant and, like Amelia, is from a family of accountants. They even had the wedding cake made into the shape of a calculator."

"What's her dress like?" asked Lucy, interested as always in the styles of things. She's thinking about going to art college and being a dress designer when she leaves school.

"Big meringue. Makes her look enormous even though she's skinny. In fact, I don't know how she'll fit into the wedding car."

"If I got married," said Nesta, lying back on the cushions like Cleopatra, "I'd look fantabulous. Of course I'll be famous by then and there will be lots of press there as all the mags will want to buy the wedding photos."

"What would you wear?" asked Lucy.

"Something slinky. Figure-hugging. Maybe ivory silk with no back. And I'd have my hair loose, like it is now, right down to my waist. Not stuck up in one of those awful styles a lot of women choose for their wedding day, you know, beehives, all stuck up on top. And I'd just carry a simple bouquet, a couple of lilies or something. Elegant. And I'll have the ceremony in the grounds of my mansion and there'll be

170

loads of rock stars and celebrities there."

"You'd look stunning whatever you wore," I said, looking at her stretched out on my bed. Nesta's easily the best-looking girl in our class, if not our school. She's half-Jamaican and half-Italian and has drop-dead gorgissimo looks. She could be a model if she wanted but lately has decided that she'd prefer to be an actress instead.

Lucy's pretty too but in a different way from Nesta. She's petite with spiky blond hair, and looked like an elf, sitting cross-legged in her favorite place on the beanbag on my floor.

"What would you wear, Lucy?" I asked.

Lucy looked out of the window dreamily. "I think I'd like to get married in winter, in the snow. In velvet, with a cloak. And little white rosebuds in my hair. I'd arrive at the church in a horse-drawn carriage and the church would be covered in flowers and ivy. . . ."

"You're such a romantic, Luce," I laughed. "As long as you don't subject your bridesmaids to anything like this awful monstrosity I have to wear."

"We would be the bridesmaids, wouldn't we?" asked Nesta. "Being your best mates an' all?"

"Course, but I'd like to have Ben and Jerry as well, as they are my other best friends," said Lucy.

"What?" exclaimed Nesta. "Dogs at a wedding?"

"Yeah, they could be page boys."

Nesta and I had to hold our sides laughing. The idea of two fat Labradors waddling up the aisle with flowers round their necks was too much.

"Well I'm never getting married," I said. "What's the point? So many people split up a couple of years later. Like my mum and dad. Once I overheard my dad on the phone saying he thought divorce was nature's way of saying 'I told you so.'"

"But you might fall in love one day," said Lucy. "And then you'll feel differently."

"Nah. Look, I'm already fourteen and still not had a proper boyfriend. I've never met anyone who's come even close to what I want."

"But if you did?" insisted Lucy.

"Okay. If I did. Which I *won't*. I'd wear a red rubber minidress and rollerskate up the aisle with an all-singing, all-dancing gospel choir in the background."

"But I can't rollerskate," said Lucy. "And I *have* to be one of the bridesmaids."

"Don't worry. It's not going to happen. I can't see me ever falling in love. Especially not if I stay round here. All the boys round here are total Kevins."

"Well I wouldn't want to get married for ages," said Nesta. "I want to play the field for as long as possible. Why settle for one fruit when you can try the whole basket?"

"You're such a tart," said Lucy. "Anyway, it's easy for you, being the boy magnet of North London. But what if you meet someone really special?"

"What, like Tony?" teased Nesta.

Poor Lucy went bright red. Tony is Nesta's older brother and Lucy has an almighty crush on him.

"He's asked me out on a date next week," said Lucy shyly.

Nesta looked concerned. "And are you going to go?"

"Course. But I know, I *know*, don't get too serious. I know what he's like. A different girl every week."

"Don't you forget it," warned Nesta. "It's me and Iz who'd have to pick up the pieces."

"I can look after myself," said Lucy. "But what about you, Iz? What do you want in a boy?"

"How long have you got?" I asked. "Can I ask the audience? Go fifty-fifty? Phone a friend?"

"Final answer," said Nesta. "Give us your final answer."

I had to think about this. The perfect boy?

"Okay. Good sense of humor. GSOH. Has to be able to make me laugh. Er, intelligent. I don't want some thick idiot. Someone I can talk to and have lots in common with."

"Good-looking, surely?" asked Nesta.

"Yeah. A bit. I mean, I don't want a pin-up as I think a lot of boys that are way handsome are too cocky. . . ."

"Like Tony," said Nesta, looking pointedly at Lucy, who ignored her.

"Er, excuse me," I interrupted. "I haven't finished. Final answer for the million dollar boy. GSOH. Intelligent. Generous. Decent looks. A nice bum. Genuinely likes girls' company. Clean fingernails and last but not least . . ."

"Rich," said Nesta.

"Cute," said Lucy.

"No," I said, "last but not least . . . able to stand on his head and sing 'God Save the Queen.'"

Lucy cracked up. "You're mad, Izzie."

"Good luck to you," said Nesta. "I mean, most of it sounds okay, but *clean* fingernails? I think you're pushing it, girl."

"Izzie," called Mum frantically from downstairs. "The car's here."

I took a deep breath. "Here I go! So. Final final question. Do I look all right? Green and all. Do you think I need more kohl on my eyes?"

"You look great," said Lucy. "And let us know how it all goes."

"Okay, Nesta?" I asked.

Nesta laughed. "Well put it like this. When Amelia sees you, let's hope love really is blind."

"If love is blind," I said, "then marriage will be an eye-opener."

"Yeah, right," said Nesta, getting up off my bed and heading for the door. "Come on, Luce, I suggest we get out before Mrs. Foster sees her and all hell breaks loose."

175

Lucy grinned. "Yeah. Nice knowing ya, Izzie."

And with that, the two of them ran for it.

So much for my plan to freak out our head-mistress with my green hair on Monday. As soon as we got back from the wedding, Mum marched me upstairs and into the bathroom.

"Right," she said through gritted teeth. "Start scrubbing and don't stop until your hair is back to normal."

She handed me the shampoo and I waited for her to leave, but she stood there glaring at me.

"It's not enough that you shame me in front of all our family and friends," she continued, "but you ruined Amelia's special day. And *how* are we going to explain the fact that one of the bridesmaids is missing from most of the wedding photographs?"

"I wouldn't have minded being in the pictures," I began.

"Well Amelia minded. She was furious. Honestly, Isobel, fancy upstaging the bride on her wedding day."

"I didn't mean to . . ."

"You never think, do you? You'd have stood out a mile in every photograph."

"Sorry," I said for the millionth time that day.

"And I won't have you going into school looking like that either. Lord knows what the teachers would think of us and what kind of home you come from."

I was going to tell her loads of girls have colored hair and highlights but I know defeat when I see it, so I bent over the taps and began washing.

Mum was still hovering as streams of green dye filled the bath. I could hear her sighing above the gushing water. I decided silence was the best policy so I continued washing, then reached for a towel.

"NOT THAT ONE!" cried Mum. "For heaven's sake, Isobel!" (She always calls me by my full name when she's mad at me.) "Not a white towel. It'll leave stains. I'll get you a dark one."

Mum's very big on white towels. Once, after I'd been washing my face, she came into my room holding the towel I'd used.

"Is it you who's marked my towel?" she asked, pointing to mascara blotches. "Towels are for drying with, not for using to remove makeup."

Honestly. I wish she'd get some normal colored ones so I could use the bathroom without worrying, but then she's like that about everything. Our house is immaculate. Mum's immaculate. Always dressed in neat black suits for work and neat black trousers and cashmere sweaters for home. Dark hair in a neat bob. I don't know how she does it. Never a hair out of place. Never a scuff on her shoes. Never a mark on her clothing. Her star sign is Virgo, the perfectionist. She even cleans up before the cleaner comes in as she doesn't want her thinking we're a dirty family. What *is* the point of having a cleaner if you can't make a mess to clean up?

I wished she'd go away and let me finish doing my hair in peace, but no, she plonked herself on the side of the bath and looked at me sternly. "Now are you going to give me some kind of explanation?"

"Er, I . . . I thought it looked nice."

Sigh. Bigger sigh.

"I didn't mean to upset anyone . . . ," I began.

I didn't. But I did get quite a reaction. We were going up the aisle and everyone was oohing and aahing at the bride when suddenly the guests all spotted me and the place went quiet. Then people looked away. But not Amelia. I could see the moment I caught her eye that there was going to be trouble. Big trouble. I swear I could see steam coming out from under her veil. I kept my eyes on the altar and prayed she'd mellow out a bit at the reception after a few drinks. She didn't. She went completely ballistic.

Mum was still glaring at me from the side of the bath. I didn't know what else to say.

"Um, sorry," I said. "Sorry, sorry."

"Sorry? You don't know the meaning of the word. Go to your room. I can't bear to look at you."

I crept into my room. Definitely in the doghouse. Definitely *persona non grata*. Again.

Chapter 2

A Strange-looking Parasite

"And where do you think you're going?" asked Mum the next day as I tried to sneak out the front door. I was hoping to escape before I was grounded.

"Out with Nesta and Lucy."

"Have you had breakfast?"

"Not hungry," I said, stuffing my gloves in my coat pocket.

"It's cold and raining out there. You can't go out without anything inside you. Come back."

I followed her back into the kitchen and she started putting bread in the toaster.

"Er, no thanks, Mum, I'll just have some fruit. I don't eat white bread anymore."

"Since when?"

"Since now."

"And why's that?" she asked. She was looking quite cheerful considering the events of the day before. Was I forgiven?

"Er, no reason. I just don't fancy any."

"Then I'll do you some eggs."

"No thanks, I don't fancy eggs. I'll take some fruit."

How can I tell her I only eat free-range now? I read how they keep the battery hens all cooped up in tiny spaces. Awful, poor little chicks. But I don't want to go there with Mum today. It would only start an argument.

"Izzie, what is it with you lately? Can't eat this, won't eat that!"

I took a deep breath. "Well, see, we did a class on nutrition at school and I was wondering if, er, maybe we could have more healthy food."

"What do you mean, more healthy food?"

"Like maybe fresh food rather than frozen, free-range eggs, maybe organic . . ."

"And what's wrong with what I give you?"

"Er, nothing wrong with it, but we could be eating better."

"Nonsense. We eat very well here. There's always plenty of food in the cupboards."

"But Mum . . . I'm not talking about quantity, I'm talking about quality. . . ."

"Are you saying my food isn't good quality?"

"No, NO . . ."

This wasn't going well.

I decided to try another angle. "You know how you like everything to be immaculate in the house?"

"Yes."

"Well, see, that's all external. What I'm talking about is what's inside. You are what you eat and the more fresh and healthy the food is that you eat, the better you feel and the more immaculate you are on the inside. You'd like that, wouldn't you?"

It was worth a try. She seemed to be considering what I'd said.

My stepfather Angus looked up over his *Financial Times*. "What Izzie's saying is she wants to go green!"

Very funny. Not.

Thanks, Angus, I thought. Last thing I need is someone reminding Mum of yesterday.

"No. Not green. I'm not talking about the environment. Although that's important too. I'm talking about not eating rubbish."

Oops. Me and my big mouth. Didn't mean it to come out like that. Mum's stern expression returned in a flash.

"Why can't you be like normal teenagers, Izzie? Most girls your age want nothing but pasta and chips. Why do you always have to be different?"

"You can get organic pasta. Lucy's mum and dad buy all organic food. In fact, Mr. Lovering sells it at his shop."

"Well they're welcome to it. We don't live like them."

Wish I did, I thought. Lucy's house is so different from mine. It's lived-in, cozy. *And* they have colored towels in their bathroom so you can get them as dirty as you like.

"But Mum . . . it's a well-known fact that fresh produce is better for you than all that stuff you eat.

Out of the freezer and into the microwave, full of preservatives . . ."

"Don't speak to your mother like that," said Angus.

I can't win. I wasn't speaking to Mum like *that*. I thought we'd all benefit from my health suggestions, but I'd wanted to pick my time for bringing it up. Escape seemed the best plan.

"Can I go now?" I asked, getting up.

"Not before you eat that toast," said Mum.

"Whatever. I'll take it with me. I'll eat it. Promise."

I wrapped the toast in a napkin and made a dash for the door. I'll feed it to the birds, I thought.

But I bet even they prefer wholemeal.

Lucy and Nesta were waiting for me at Camden tube station, standing by the ticket machines, munching on Snickers bars.

"We match," I said, seeing we were all dressed in black.

"When in Camden," said Nesta, "do as the Camdens do . . . or something like that."

Everyone in Camden seems to wear black or

gray. Maybe it's to fit in with the December weather which, as usual, is dull and rainy.

"So how was the wedding?" asked Nesta as we fought our way through the Sunday crowds to the indoor market at the Lock. "I see your hair's back to normal."

"I know. Mum went ballistic and made me wash the green out as soon as we got home. Amelia was furious when she saw me. She banned me from most of the wedding photos and said she'll never speak to me again."

"Good result, then," grinned Nesta. "She was never your favorite person, was she?"

"Not really," I laughed. "And I don't think I ruined the day as much as everyone made out. The wedding was quite sweet in the end. Specially when one of the page boys read out The Lord's Prayer. He was so cute, only six. 'Our Father who are in Devon,' he said. 'Harold be Thy name.' It was hysterical."

"Any boys?" asked Lucy.

"Don't even go there. Nah. Well, one; he tried to chat me up. But he's Jeremy's younger brother so he must be a total nerd."

"What did he look like?" asked Nesta.

"About seventeen. Quite nice-looking. Little John Lennon glasses. But wearing an awful suit that didn't fit him properly. Jeremy made him get up on the stage at the reception and play the piano. It was awful. Songs from the shows. All the oldies were singing along to *The Sound of Music*, *Singing in the Rain*, *South Pacific*, *Kismet*. All that "Take my hand/I'm a stranger in paradise/All lost in a wonderland" stuff is so naff. . . ."

"My dad's got the video of *Kismet*. My brothers do their own version of that song," said Lucy, then began singing: "Take my hand, I'm a strange-looking parasite, all wrapped in a wonderloaf . . ."

"A much better version," I said as we made our way through the market. "So to the serious business of shopping. What do we want to look at?"

"Boys," said Nesta.

"I'd like to get some earrings for my date with Tony," said Lucy.

"And we must get something new for the end-of-term disco," said Nesta. "You never know who might be there."

"I heard King Noz are playing," said Lucy.

186

"Who are they?" I asked.

"Oh they're fantastic. They're in the Sixth Form at my brother's school. Lal's got a tape of theirs and said they may even have a recording deal."

"Well, anything's got to be better than songs from the shows," I said.

Camden Lock sells all sorts of paraphernalia: books, frames, joss sticks, essential oils, crystals, jewelry, mirrors, clothes, hats, pottery, music. You name it, they sell it. The place was heaving with people browsing, buying, or meeting friends.

I wanted to do a bit of pre-Christmas shopping so I steered the girls upstairs to the New Age stalls. I thought I'd buy everyone aromatherapy oils this year.

Lucy was soon stuck in at a stall selling jewelry and Nesta was trying on sunglasses so I wandered over to a corner stall selling essential oils. I picked out the rose and jasmine bottles and had a good sniff. They're my favorite scents but also the most expensive so I haven't been able to afford them yet for my collection at home.

"Hi," said a voice. "Can I help?"

I glanced up and found myself staring into a pair of chocolate-brown eyes. Something very peculiar happened to my insides, like someone had tied a knot in my stomach and tightened it. This boy was gorgeous. I mean *seriously* gorgeous. A wide smiley mouth and silky black hair flopping over his face.

"Er, no thanks, just looking," I blustered, then turned and ran.

I pulled Lucy and Nesta into a corner behind a dress stall. "I've just fallen in love," I said breathlessly, leaning back against the wall.

"Who with?" said Nesta, sticking her head round the wall.

I pulled her back. "Don't! He'll see."

Lucy immediately stuck her head round the corner. "There's a boy looking over here. Is he the one by the stairs? In a white T-shirt and jeans?"

I stuck my head out and the boy at the stall grinned and waved.

"Oh no," I groaned, darting out of sight. "He's seen us. He'll think I'm a complete dork. Come on, we have to go. *Now*. Downstairs. He'll think I fancy him."

"But you do," said Nesta. "What are you going to do about it?"

"Nothing," I said, and walked back into the crowds, studiously avoiding looking back at the oil stall.

When I got downstairs, Nesta and Lucy came charging after me.

"If you like him," said Lucy, "go and talk to him."

"I can't. I don't know what to say. Oh God. I'm so stupid. He'll think I'm stupid."

"No he won't," said Nesta. "Tell you what, we'll have a look round down here then we'll go back up, and Lucy and I will go and look at the stall then kind of casually call you over to look at something."

"Good plan," I said. "But you browse. I'm going to the loo to comb my hair."

Lucy laughed. "I told you it would happen one day, Izzie. Never say never."

After an excruciating fifteen minutes of pretending to be interested in stalls on the ground floor, we made our way back up to the top level. I peered over the crowds and could see the boy serving someone so I went and stood with my back to him at a neighboring stall.

Nesta and Lucy made their way over toward him.

"Lucy," said Nesta in a mega-loud voice, "I want to look at some aromatherapy oils."

God. She's *so* obvious.

Lucy and Nesta were soon occupied sniffing bottles. Then Nesta said, again in her stupid loud voice, "Izzie, come over here. Isn't one of these oils supposed to be an aphrodisiac?"

OhmyGod. Subtle is not a word in Nesta's dictionary. I turned toward them and made my way over, trying to look as cool as I could.

The boy looked up and grinned. "Ylang-ylang," he said, offering me a bottle of oil. "It's supposed to be a real turn-on."

"And what do you do with it?" asked Nesta.

The boy smiled suggestively. "Whatever you like."

"You put a few drops in the bath," I said sternly and sounding embarrassingly like my mother.

Nesta pulled on Lucy's arm. "Come on, I want to look . . . er . . . over there."

She hauled Lucy away to another stall, but not before turning back and giving me the thumbs up. Remind me to kill her later.

I looked back at the boy and grinned stupidly.

"I'm Mark," he said, then looked in Nesta's direction and shrugged. "Mates, huh?"

"Yeah, mates," I said. "I think she forgot to take her medication today. Or I forgot to take mine."

Mark laughed. "So you know about all this stuff, do you? Oils and that?"

"A bit. I use some of them at home, like lavender for relaxation. And eucalyptus when I've got a cold. Do you know a lot about them?"

"Not really. A bit I've picked up from my mum. I help her out here sometimes."

"It must be great working here," I said.

"It's okay," shrugged Mark, then looked right into my eyes. "You get to meet some *interesting* people sometimes."

Gulp. Did he mean me? I think he did because he did that flirting thing that Nesta is always on about—holding eye contact then smiling. I felt my stomach tighten again as I looked back into his eyes.

"Look," continued Mark, "if you like all this stuff, there's a fair on at Alexandra Palace next week. Mind, Body, and Spirit. Mum's got a stall there. Give me your number and I'll call you with the details."

I handed him one of the cards I made in Art last term. I'm quite proud of it. I did it on turquoise paper with silver writing.

"Izzie Foster," he said, reading the card. "Cool. So I'll phone you later."

Result! A date with wonderboy.

Nesta's Flirting Tips

Look into his eyes, keep contact a moment too long to show you're interested, then look away.

Smile.

Study body language: Does he lean toward you, knees pointing in your direction? If he does, he's interested.

Mirror his body language.

Lean slightly toward him.

Laugh at his jokes no matter how bad they are.

Keep it fun, make small talk.

Don't get heavy.

Listen to what he's saying and look interested, fascinated even.

Don't go on about other boyfriends.

Don't be too easy.

Don't act desperate.

Don't be too available.

Don't get serious or over-emotional.

Don't be clingy.

Don't overstay your welcome. Leave when things are buzzing. That way he'll want to come back to you for more.

To check if he's interested: Make eye contact that moment too long as in tip 1, then hide behind a pillar where you can see him. Watch to see if he looks to where you were last standing and, seeing you gone, looks round for you. If he does, he's interested.

As I wandered back to the tube station with Nesta and Lucy, Christmas lights were coming on in the street and in the shops and Camden looked colorful and strangely magical. I felt like I was walking through a film set. Dusk in a perfect street in a Walt Disney world.

We linked arms and sang at the top of our voices. "Take my hand, I'm a strange-looking parasite, all wrapped in a wonderloaf . . . thinking of yoooooou!"

Chapter 3

Boy
Speak

"When a boy says he'll phone you later, what does that mean?" I asked Nesta and Lucy as we made our way to class the following Wednesday.

"Ah," said Nesta, "tricky one."

"It means later, *much* later, not like a girl," said Lucy. "When a girl says I'll phone you later, she means later, like that night. But boys have a language all of their own."

"I take it Mark hasn't phoned yet?" said Nesta. I shook my head.

"Early days," said Lucy, looking at me sympathetically. "He'll phone. He said he would."

Nesta shook her head. "That means nothing in

boy speak. 'I'll phone you' could mean anything. I'll phone you in a week, in two weeks, next month. If I remember.'

I groaned. "Oh no. It's agony and it's only been three days. I stayed up late every night hoping he'd call, but zilch."

"He'd never phone that soon," said Nesta, "not if he's cool. It would make him look too keen. Give it a day or so and even then don't hold your breath."

I do love Nesta but sometimes I wish she wouldn't say *exactly* what she means all the time.

"A watched phone never rings," said Lucy sagely.

"Tell me about it," I said as I took my place at my desk. "But he has to phone in the next couple of days as the fair at Ally Pally is on Saturday."

School has been a riot this week and a welcome distraction from waiting for the phone call. We have a student teacher called Miss Hartley standing in for our regular PE and RE teacher, Miss Watkins. As usual, poor thing, she's live bait for some of our class who like nothing better than to give trainee teachers a hard time.

First class she substituted was religious education. I usually enjoy RE, as we've been doing all the different belief systems from all over the world. I find it fascinating finding out what different cultures think. Last term I was a Hindu. They believe that you have many lives, not just one, that our souls change bodies when we die and we come back as someone else.

I made a badge saying *Reincarnation's making a comeback*, which I wore to school until Mrs. Allen saw it and told me to take it off. It was nice though, thinking I might have known people in another life. One day I asked Nesta if she thought we had known each other before.

"Oh definitely," she said.

"What, as your sister or something?" I asked.

"No," she said, "you were my pet frog."

Then Lucy piped up in her daft Scottish accent, "What does a Hindu?" She waited for our answer. "Lays eggs," she giggled. "Geddit? *Hen*-du?"

Nesta and Lucy think it's all one big joke and don't seem to realize that I really want to know about stuff like why we're here and what it's all

197

about. Though I have decided to stop being a Hindu and be an agnostic until I decide for definite.

Miss Hartley coughed to get our attention then began. "Okay, class, today we're going to talk about God. What do we know about him?"

"Omnipresent, omnipotent, omniscient," said Jade Wilcocks.

"Very good," said Miss Hartley.

"Best-selling author," said Mary O'Connor. "He wrote the Bible."

The class started sniggering so I put my hand up.

"Izzie?"

"Well actually, miss, I have a question about God."

I'd been thinking about it ever since the wedding on Saturday when the priest had said, "Here we are gathered in the presence of God . . ."

"If God is omnipresent, that means God is everywhere, doesn't it?"

"Yes," said Miss Hartley.

"Then why do people go to church to pray? If he's omnipresent, wouldn't we be in his presence everywhere? In the cinema, at home? Everywhere? Why go to a church?"

"Good point, Izzie," said Miss Hartley. "Anyone else like to comment?"

"Miss, if he's everywhere, does that mean he's watching you when you go to the toilet?" asked Candice Carter.

Oh no. They were off. Wind-up time and I was hoping to get some answers to my questions.

"Why do people pray to the ceiling if he's everywhere?" said Joanne Richards. "You could just as well pray under the sink."

Quite right, I thought. I put my hand up again.

"Miss, if he's omnipresent and people are always praying to him, how does he hear everyone at the same time? Does he have an exchange system? It must be hard with all the millions of prayers coming in in all the different languages. He may speak only Swahili for all we know."

Miss Hartley was beginning to look a bit flustered.

"Anyone else got anything to say?"

I put my hand up again. I had loads to say as I think a lot about things like this.

"Do you think maybe God is in a bit of a bad mood because being omnipresent isn't as much fun as it used to be when the world was new and fresh? Like, being everywhere all the time, he has to watch *all* the repeats of *Neighbours* every day, plus all the repeats, in all the languages, in all the different countries, for eternity. It must get very boring."

"Is eternity like a Sunday when it's raining?" asked Lucy.

"Good questions," said Miss Hartley, avoiding the answers. "Maybe you could write an essay for next week on how you see God. Now get out your Bibles."

I was still wondering how God answered prayers. But maybe he's like Mark. Doesn't call back. Now that got me thinking again.

I stuck my hand up again. "Miss, why do we call God a he? Why not a she? Or an it?"

"I think we'll call you Izzie Why Foster from now on," said Miss Hartley. "Why why why?"

She obviously doesn't know as she didn't bother to try to answer. "Now, class, who can name some of the famous characters in the hymns we sing in assembly?"

"Gabriel," said Mary.

"Lucifer," said Jade.

"Er, no," said Miss Hartley, "that's another name for the devil. He was a fallen angel."

"Fallen from where?" I asked before she could tell me to shut up.

"Heaven," she said.

"Devon," whispered Lucy behind me. "And Harold is his name."

I got the giggles then and decided to give up on my next question which was, "And where exactly is heaven?"

"I've got a character out of a hymn," said Candice Carter.

"Okay," said Miss Hartley.

"Hark, miss."

"And in which hymn is there a reference to a character called Hark, Candice?"

"Hark, the Herald Angel, miss."

There was no stopping the class after that. Even Nesta joined in.

"I've got one, miss."

"Okay, Nesta, go ahead."

"Gladly, miss."

By now poor Miss Hartley was looking as

though she wished she could be anywhere else but that classroom.

"Gladly," she said wearily. "Who was he?"

"Gladly the cross-eyed bear, miss."

The whole class fell about laughing as we all know Gladly well, but being new to the school, Miss Hartley didn't get the joke.

Candice put her hand up. "It's one of the ancient hymns we sing in assembly, miss. It starts, 'Gladly the cross I bear.'"

Miss Hartley still didn't laugh. The bell for break went a moment later and she was out of the class and down the corridor before any of us.

At lunchtime I checked my mobile. No messages, so I called home and punched in the code numbers to check the answering machine. Nothing. Then an *awful* thought struck me. Mum got me a new mobile a month ago and I made the cards *two* months ago. *Oh no*. The mobile number on the card I gave Mark was the old one.

"He won't call in the day," said Lucy. "He'll be at school."

"You're right, though he might have a mobile," I sighed. "But he'll probably call tonight."

"But tonight you're coming back to our house with Nesta, aren't you? Mum and Dad are going to a movie and we're going to watch a video."

"Sorry, Lucy, I don't want to miss the call."

Lucy looked disappointed. "You haven't been back one night this week. Oh, come on, Izzie, the machine will keep any messages."

I thought Lucy of all people would understand, being so in love with Tony. But she didn't.

Boy Speak

Call you later:	Sometime in the next century
Commitment:	A word only applied to a football team
I need space:	For all my other girlfriends
Let's just see how it goes:	Back off, I'm feeling pressured
Would you like a back rub?:	I want to try my luck
Isn't it warm in here?:	Take your clothes off
Hi. Your friend looks nice:	I fancy her and am using you to get to her
Don't get heavy:	I don't feel the same way about you
She's ugly/a lesbian:	She didn't fancy me
I'm not ready for a relationship:	Not with you, anyway
I'm very independent:	I like to do things my own way, on my own terms
We can still be friends:	It's over and this is probably the last time you'll ever see me

Chapter 4

Consulting the Stars

Wednesday night: no call.

Thursday lunchtime: no call.

Thursday night: no call.

Friday morning: no call.

I'm going out of my mind. Perhaps he lost my number? Perhaps he put the card in his jeans and his mum washed them and it got soaked? Perhaps he didn't mean to call at all and saying he would was a way of getting rid of me? Perhaps, perhaps, perhaps.

It's time to consult the oracles.

I sent Lucy a note in English.

Will you come back to my house tonight? I want to look at my horoscope and do the tarot cards to see what they have to say about Mark. I know Nesta's busy with Drama but can you come?

Sure, Lucy wrote back. *But it's my turn to feed the dogs. We can do it on the way. I won't be long.*

"Izzie Foster, Lucy Lovering, pay attention," said Mr. Johnson, "and get out your folders. Today I want you to write something about school. How you feel about it. It can be in any form you like: an essay, a poem, whatever. You've got twenty minutes. And no talking."

I spent the first ten minutes gazing out of the window, hoping for inspiration, but all I could think about was Mark. I was trying to picture what he looked like, as already his face had gone blurry in my mind. Maybe he wasn't as good-looking as I remembered. Maybe I'd see him again and it would be like, Yuk, what did I ever see in you? I wondered what he's really like. What kind of music he's into.

"Izzie Foster, have you written anything yet?" asked Mr. Johnson.

"Er, no, sir."

I looked at the blank sheet in front of me and put my mind to the exercise in hand. An essay about school. How boring. Then I remembered he'd said it could be any form at all. I want to be a songwriter when I leave school—well, either that or an astrologer, and maybe both. I've written loads of songs at home so I decided I'd do one here. I put my head down and started writing.

After another ten minutes, Mr. Johnson clapped his hands.

"Okay, time's up. And seeing as it took you so long to get going, Izzie, let's hear what you've come up with."

Oh NO. *NO*. I never show anyone my lyrics. Ever. They're completely private. He never said we had to read them out loud.

"We're waiting," said Mr. Johnson, tapping his fingers on his desk.

I stood up. "It's a rap song. Called 'Education Rap,'" I said, then began reading:

"*Now I'm walkin' down the street with my feet on the beat, An' I look real cool cos I ain't no fool, I go to school . . .*"

Immediately Mary O'Connor and Joanne

Richards started sniggering. I felt myself freeze and stopped reading immediately.

"Er, that's all I've written, sir," I muttered to the floor. It wasn't. I'd written a whole verse but I didn't want to read more if people were going to laugh at me.

I looked up at Mr. Johnson. He seemed to be laughing as well. "Hmmm, an interesting start," he said.

I sat down feeling miserable. Never again. Never ever ever again. No one's ever going to see my lyrics, not if they're going to make fun.

"I thought your song was great," said Lucy as we let ourselves in the back door at her house.

"Thanks," I said as one of the dogs pounced forward to lick my face, almost knocking me over. "Down, Ben, down."

"I won't be long," said Lucy as she took off her coat and started rummaging in a cupboard for tins of dog food. "Put the kettle on."

"But we're not staying long, are we? Got to get home, remember?"

"Oh right," said Lucy. "Mark."

"Yeah. Mark," I said. I was getting seriously concerned by now. It was Friday night and the fair was Saturday and Mark still hadn't phoned. "Who's playing the guitar?"

Music was coming from the living room so I followed the direction of the sounds and found Lucy's brother Lal lying on the sofa listening to a CD.

"Who's this?" I asked.

"King Noz," said Lal.

"Oh yeah, Lucy mentioned them, they're playing at our end-of-term disco."

"Yeah," said Lal. "They go to our school. Top band."

"Can I listen?"

"Sure."

A boy was singing with an acoustic guitar and piano accompaniment. I sat back on the sofa, closed my eyes, and listened to the lyrics.

> *"If you were a wheel*
> *I'd follow your highway.*
> *If you were a raindrop*
> *I wish you'd fall my way.*

If you were a gypsy
I'd give a fortune to tell
That whenever I'm with you
I see heaven, not hell. . . ."

"Wow," I said when he'd finished. "He's really good. I really like it."

"Not all of it is quiet like that," said Lal. "I prefer the heavier numbers."

"Ready," called Lucy.

"Got to go," I said, getting up. The stars were calling.

When we got back home, I checked the machine for messages. Nothing. *Nothing.*

"Never mind," said Lucy. "I have a surprise for you."

We went up to my bedroom and she handed me an envelope.

"What is it?" I asked.

"Look and see."

I ripped open the envelope and there were three tickets to the Mind, Body and Spirit fair the next day.

"Fabola!" I said. "Where did you get these?"

"Dad," said Lucy. "He has a stall there selling his health foods. He gave them to us so we can all get in for free. So even if Mark doesn't phone tonight, we can go anyway, check out where his mum's stall is, then accidentally-on-purpose bump into him."

I gave Lucy a huge hug. So she *did* understand how much it meant to me after all. "Excellent. Lucy, you really are a pal."

Lucy beamed. "Well, come on, let's see what our horoscopes are. I'm dying to know, as I'm seeing Tony tomorrow night and want to know if it's going to go well."

I switched on my computer and went to my favorite Web site. I typed in my and Lucy's birth dates and waited for the horoscopes to print out.

"Where are you going with him?" I asked.

"Hollywood Bowl," Lucy replied. "We're going to see a movie then going to get a burger or something after."

"You really like him, don't you?" I asked.

Lucy grinned. "Oh yeah, oh *yeah*."

"But you'll be careful, won't you? Nesta's not the only one worried that he might hurt you."

"Gimme a break," said Lucy. "I know what he's like. Nesta's told me enough times."

I picked up the sheets of paper from the printer and began to read.

"What does it say?" asked Lucy.

"This is amazing," I said. "This explains *everything*. It says that Mercury has been retrograde but moves direct on the sixth of December. That's tomorrow."

"What does that mean?" asked Lucy.

"Well Mercury's the planet of communication. Whenever it turns retrograde, it slows down all kinds of things. Misunderstandings happen, appointments get double booked, you can't get through to people you need to talk to, all that kind of stuff. Then when it turns direct, it all starts flowing again. So don't you see? That's why Mark didn't phone. Because Mercury was retrograde."

"Do you really think the stars influence us that much?" asked Lucy doubtfully.

"Oh absolutely," I said, reading on. "Oh this is

fantastic, for both of us. Venus is well aspected tomorrow with a full Moon in Taurus . . ."

"Izzie," said Lucy, "you're talking gobbledygook to me. Explain."

"Venus is the planet of love. It rules the star sign of Taurus. It couldn't be better placed tomorrow. It looks like we're both in for a good time. Top. I can't wait. I'm going to mark all the dates on my diary when the stars are well aspected. I don't know why I've put myself through such hell this week. I should have consulted the site in the beginning then I wouldn't have been through such misery."

Lucy was still looking doubtful. "I'm sure there's more to it than that," she said.

"Nonsense," I said, feeling better than I had for days. "Astrology rules, okay?"

"Oh," laughed Lucy. "Okay."

At that moment, the bedroom door opened.

"Supper's on the table," said Mum. "Would you like some, Lucy?"

"Oh, yes please," said Lucy. "I'd love some."

"Can we have ours up here?" I asked. "Please, Mum?"

"Okay," said Mum. "Seeing as Lucy's here. I'll

bring a tray up. But be sure to eat at the desk and not off your laps."

When she'd gone, I got up and shut the door. "Honestly, it drives me mad. She won't let me have a lock on my door. She doesn't even knock. I have no privacy. She's always bursting in when I'm doing things. Nesta's allowed a lock on her door. Why shouldn't I be?"

"I know," Lucy said. "I've asked for a lock on my door too but Mum and Dad said no way. What if something happened to me? Durrh, like what exactly? Sometimes parents have overactive imaginations."

Mum came back a few minutes later carrying a tray with two plates of shepherd's pie. "There you are, Izzie, your favorite."

I pulled a face. "Mum, you know I don't eat meat anymore."

Mum put the tray down. "Oh for heaven's sake, Isobel. I can't keep up." She turned on Lucy. "And have you stopped eating meat as well, Lucy?"

"Er, no," said Lucy, taking the plate. "I love shepherd's pie. Thank you very much, Mrs. Foster."

Mum turned to leave. "Well, see if you can talk

some sense into Little Miss Contrary here. Because, Izzie, I've had enough. I made it specially. So if you don't eat that, you don't eat anything."

Lucy pulled a silly face when she'd gone. "Little Miss Contrary. Don't worry, I'll eat yours."

"I'll eat the potato and vegetables. And you can have the meat. I don't know why she won't give me a break. Honestly. It's not like I'm being difficult or anything. I just believe you are what you eat."

"Mooo," giggled Lucy through a mouthful of minced beef.

"God you're daft at times," I said, but I couldn't help laughing. "Now let's plan what we're going to wear for the fair."

Education Rap
by Izzie Foster

Now I'm walking down the street with my feet on the
    beat,
An' I look real cool cos I ain't no fool, I go to school.
Don't wanna be a loser, a street corner boozer, a bum for
    rum or a no-hope dope.
Now I'm really going places, I'm holdin' all aces,
I got smart cos I know in my heart I got a real good
    start,
I'm ahead of the pack, no lookin' back, I'm goin' up
    don't need no luck,
Cos I ain't no fool, I go to school.

Chapter 5

Ready for Action

I woke up feeling like it was Christmas day already. I felt so excited—today was the big day. But first I needed breakfast. I was ravenous after not having had much dinner the night before. Sometimes it's hard being healthy, as there's one thing I do like and that's my food. I'd been dreaming of it all night—deep pan pizza with pepperoni topping, roast chicken, and stodgy treacle pudding. Lovely.

I went down to the kitchen and searched the cupboards to see what I could find that was

217

nutritious. Before I knew it, I'd woolfed down three slices of white toast with mashed banana. At least the banana bit was healthy. I'd have to buy some whole wheat bread at the fair. They'd be bound to have stalls selling it. And maybe Mum'd get the message if I brought some back and left it for her in the bread-bin. In the meantime, I'd have to compromise. Another piece of toast. With maybe a dollop of that lovely chocolate spread on it.

After breakfast I took a long bath with my special bubble bath for relaxation, then went to change into the clothes that Lucy and I had picked out last night—my zip-up black top, black micromini, red tights and a red cloche hat. With bright scarlet lips as the final touch, I thought the whole effect looked pretty cool.

I hope my bum doesn't look too big in this skirt, I thought as I put on my ankle boots. I took a last check in the mirror and thankfully the boots made my legs look a bit longer so I guessed I'd have to do.

I grabbed my leather jacket and was ready. Get ready, Mark, because here I come!

"I'm off to Ally Pally," I called to Mum as I came down the stairs.

"Okay, love, have a good time," she said, coming out into the hall. "Have you got enough money?"

"Yes, thanks. I've got my Christmas savings."

And then she saw me and her face dropped.

"Where do you think you're going dressed like that?"

"I told you. Ally Pally." I prayed she wasn't going to make a fuss. I was meeting Lucy and Nesta outside the Woolworths in Muswell Hill at ten thirty.

"Back up those stairs this instant."

"But *why*?"

"You're not going anywhere in that skirt. You're showing everything you've got."

"But Mum . . ."

"*Now*, Izzie. And wipe that lipstick off. It's far too bright for someone your age. And put some warmer tights on, those are too thin for this weather."

I sighed and turned back upstairs. I took off the tights and miniskirt and put on my usual long black skirt. She couldn't object to that. It comes right down to the floor. But before leaving, I stuffed the miniskirt and red tights into a carrier bag and shoved them in my bag.

"Okay now?" I said to Mum as I went back downstairs.

"Much better," Mum smiled. "Have a nice time."

When we got up to Alexandra Palace we stood and admired the view for a moment. It was a rare clear day and you could see for miles over London, right out to Docklands.

"This place is really cool," said Nesta as we walked up the steps and into the vast reception hall. It was a huge conservatory with a glass ceiling and the most enormous palm plants I'd ever seen. In the middle of the hall there was a choir singing Christmas carols.

Lucy and Nesta listened to the choir while I went into the ladies', put my microskirt and tights on, and reapplied my lipstick.

"Wow," said Nesta when I went out to join her and Lucy. "You look hot."

I grinned. "Ready for action."

"Ready for action!" echoed the girls.

★ ★ ★

The main hall was heaving with people. First stop was Mr. L.'s stall to thank him for the tickets. Mr. L. is our nickname for Lucy's dad; he doesn't seem to mind.

"Hi, Izzie," he said. "You're looking . . . striking."

"Thanks, Mr. L. And thanks for the tickets."

"Pleasure," he said. "And how's the guitar playing coming along?"

"Good," I said. "I've been practicing hard."

Lucy's dad looks like an old hippie with his ponytail. He used to be in a band back in the seventies and still plays a bit at some jazz club in Crouch End but he also gives people lessons. I go every other week and he's really helped me improve.

"Lucy tells me that you've opted to follow a more healthy diet," he said.

"Yeah."

"Well I hope you're doing it properly, Izzie. A lot of people change their diet but don't eat the right sorts of foods. You need plenty of grains, lentils, that sort of thing. . . ."

Yurgh, I thought, no way I'm eating lentils. But I wasn't really listening as Mr. L. carried on about nutrients and soy products. I wanted to get going and cruise the hall to look for Mark.

"Do you know where the stalls selling essential oils are?" I asked.

"Over by the back wall," said Mr. L. "I think they've put all that sort of thing together so people can find them easily."

"Brill, thanks," I said. "See you later."

We made our way over to the area he'd said and I made sure that Lucy, Nesta, and I were laughing so that if Mark saw me, he'd see what a good time I was having and realize what a fun person I am.

"What did Good King Wenceslas say when he phoned the Pizza Hut and they asked what he wanted?" I asked.

"What?" said Lucy.

"The usual—deep pan, crisp and even," I replied, throwing my head back in what I thought was an attractive manner and laughing.

Nesta and Lucy looked at me a bit oddly.

"You okay, Izzie?" asked Lucy.

"Oh yes," I said, laughing hysterically. "It's just *sooo* funny."

Lucy and Nesta exchanged worried looks.

"She's cracking up," said Nesta.

"Literally," said Lucy.

When we got to the aromatherapy area, I suddenly got the most awful attack of butterflies.

"What if he didn't phone on purpose? Didn't want to see me?"

"Oh come on," said Nesta, dragging me into the aisle. "There's only one way to find out."

We started looking at the first stall. The man behind it was bald and in his fifties. The second stall was run by a couple of middle-aged ladies. Third stall, another man. Fourth stall, two young girls.

"Can you remember what brand of oils Mark's mum sold?" asked Lucy. "Any of these could be his stall and he hasn't arrived yet."

"No," I groaned as I looked up the aisle. "And any one of these people could be his mum or his dad."

By the time we got to the end of the aisle, we'd seen about twelve stalls, some selling oils, some

223

bath lotions, some burners, some books. But there was no sign of Mark.

"We're going to have to do the whole hall," sighed Nesta. "Maybe his mum's stall has been put somewhere else."

I looked around. The hall was enormous; there had to be about three hundred, if not more, different stalls.

"It's going to take ages," I said. "Look, why don't we split up? We've all got our mobiles. If you see him, call. If not, meet at the big clock at about one o'clock.'

"Okay," said Lucy. "Let's synchronize watches."

We all checked our watches.

"Right, let's go," said Nesta.

This wasn't part of my plan. Now the chances were he'd spot me on my own like some desperate saddo, wandering about looking for him. I began to think perhaps I shouldn't have gone at all.

As I searched my area, I couldn't help but be drawn into what was on sale. Really good stuff. I bought some organic bread and muesli, then a rose quartz pendulum for my mum. I decided I'd wear it just for the afternoon as the lady selling them told me that the stones soothe the nervous system and dispel fear. Just what I need at the moment, I thought, as each time I turned a corner the butterflies came back. I also bought a book on Feng Shui and thought I could do my bedroom when I got home.

I was just talking to a man about some detox potion when my phone rang. My heart lurched. Lucy or Nesta must have spotted Mark.

"I'm going to the clock," said Nesta. "I've looked everywhere and there's no sign of the culprit."

My heart sank. I looked at my watch. An hour had gone by already.

"No show," said Lucy when I got to the clock. "Why don't we go and get a hot chocolate?"

We wandered to the snack bar where I bought the girls chocolates to thank them for their efforts and got myself a herb tea.

"Ergh," said Nesta, smelling the cup. "How can you drink that stuff? It smells like washing-up water."

225

I took a sip and had to agree, but I was determined to stay with my new regime no matter what.

"I don't think he's coming," I said. "So much for Venus being well aspected today."

"It's not over yet," said Lucy. "Don't give up on him just yet."

"No," said Nesta. "*Do* give up. I reckon it's when you give up that things happen."

"Thanks a lot! Give up, don't give up . . ." I laughed. "Rotten pair of agony aunts you two would make."

"Let's just enjoy being here for a while," said Nesta. "Forget all about Mark for now."

"Don't have much choice, do I?" I said.

We spent the next couple of hours having a good wander and trying out all the different things on offer. Nesta had an Indian head massage, and Lucy and I had a reflexology session which was really nice but Lucy ended up giggling as she said it tickled. Best was a massage chair which you sat in and it massaged up and down your back with rollers. It was wonderful and any other day I would have loved being at the fair, but I couldn't help feeling disappointed.

Mark hadn't phoned and he hadn't come. The first time I see a boy I like and I don't even get the chance to get to know him and dazzle him with my brilliant personality.

"Maybe something's happened to him," I said. "Perhaps he's had an accident."

"Perhaps he's just a boy," said Nesta. "Unreliable. Forget him."

"And I have to go soon," said Lucy. "I have to get ready for tonight."

"Me too," grinned Nesta.

"Why? Where are you going?" I asked.

"Baby-sitting."

"You baby-sitting? Why?" I asked. I knew Nesta didn't need to earn extra pocket money as her parents gave her a very generous allowance. There had to be an ulterior motive.

"Yeah, me baby-sitting," she said. "For our next-door neighbor."

"And?" I asked.

"And," said Nesta, "it just happens that their oldest son Nathan will be back for the weekend from university."

"Why can't he baby-sit?" asked Lucy.

227

"He's going to some concert in town," explained Nesta. "That's why I said I'd do it. I want to see him before he goes."

"Why? Do you fancy him?" asked Lucy.

"Nah," said Nesta. "But he does go to university in Scotland. And a young man I have my eye on will be studying there. I'm hoping Nathan'll get to know him and introduce me."

"This is the first you've told us," I said. "What young man?"

"Prince William," said Nesta.

"Prince William!"

"Yeah," said Nesta. "Why not? You have to aim high."

"Yeah, you and Britney Spears," I said. "Wasn't she e-mailing him at one time?"

Nesta nodded. "Yeah, but I think I'm much more his type."

Despite my disappointment at not seeing Mark, I had to laugh. If there's one thing Nesta's not short of, that's confidence.

After the girls had gone, I mooched around for a while by myself, looking for Christmas presents for Lucy and Nesta. With still an hour to kill before the end of the fair, I had a henna tattoo done on my ankle. A delicate bracelet of leaves, it looked really cool.

"I hope my mum doesn't freak out too much," I said to the woman painting it on.

"Oh don't worry. They only last a few weeks, then if you want it done again, you can come to our shop in Kentish Town and have it redone. Or pick another design."

"Fab," I said, then had an idea. I could buy Nesta and Lucy one for Christmas. They'd love them.

"I don't understand why people have permanent ones done," continued the woman, "when they can get one of these instead. They look just as good. And tastes change. If it's permanent, you can't do much about it except laser it off, which can be painful and expensive."

After my tattoo I bought a toe ring and some organic chocolate, then some love charms from a rather strange woman on another stall. By now most of the stallholders were packing up and the crowds were beginning to disperse.

229

He's not coming, I thought. I might as well go.

Feeling let down and dejected, I changed back into my long skirt and made my way out of the hall and down the hill to the bus stop.

Get a grip, I told myself as I sat on the bus. It's not like you even know Mark. In fact, to tell the truth, I couldn't even remember what he looked like very clearly. I'd got myself in a state about nothing. I decided to think about a new song. Making up lyrics always makes me feel better and I decided I'd think about a subject far removed from boys and love and heartache. At the beginning of term, we had a class about all the countries in the world that didn't have enough to eat. I told Lucy I was going to write a song for Africa, and as I sat on the bus thinking about it, words started buzzing round my head.

By the time the bus reached my stop, I was feeling more like my old self. I'd finish my song when I got home, I decided, then watch *Blind Date* with my bar of organic chocolate. Perfecto. Boys! Phfff! Who needs 'em?

★　★　★

230

As I walked past the shops toward our road, I noticed a bunch of lads walking toward me. They were all dressed in muddy football gear and I decided I'd cross the road to avoid them. I knew what boys could be like in a group when they see a girl on her own and I wasn't in the mood for any comments, even nice ones. Then my heart stopped. One of the boys was Mark.

What should I do? Oh God. They were getting closer. I couldn't resist. I'd stay on that side of the road and see what he did.

The gang of lads walked past all engrossed in some conversation about the game they'd just played. I looked straight at Mark, waiting to see how he'd respond.

I couldn't believe it. He *blanked* me.

I carried on walking, feeling numb. He'd blanked me. Oh God. I couldn't wait to get home to my bedroom where I could hide.

As I turned the corner into our road, I heard footsteps running behind me.

I hurried my own pace. It was dark, and by now I was desperate to get home. I leaped as a hand grabbed my shoulder.

I swung round, ready to kick as hard as I could. It was Mark.

"Hey," he said. "Don't I know you from somewhere?"

From *somewhere*? I thought. He doesn't even know who I am, the creep.

"The Lock, last Saturday," I said.

"Sorry about back then on the road," he said. "I didn't want to let on I knew you as all my mates would start asking questions and, well, you know how it can be. . . ."

I didn't, but I was beginning to soften. He was even better-looking than I remembered, even though he was splattered in mud and his hair was all over the place. Gorgeous eyes with silky long lashes.

He grinned sheepishly. "I was supposed to phone you, wasn't I? About the fair."

"Were you?" I said. "I don't remember."

"Yeah. You gave me your card. Pretty turquoise one with silver writing."

So he did remember.

He dived in his sports bag and pulled out a wallet.

"See? I've got it here."

"Got a pen?" I said, trying to stay as cool as possible.

"No."

"No matter, I've got one," I said, quickly rooting round in my bag. I took my card back from him and scribbled my new number on it. "One of the numbers has changed. I got a new mobile since I made those cards."

"Oh, right," he said, taking the card and putting it back in his wallet. "Anyway, did you go? To Ally Pally?"

"No," I lied. I wasn't about to let on I'd spent the day looking for him. "Did you go?" I asked.

"Nah," he said. "My sister said she'd do the stall with Mum for me. She loves all that kind of thing." He shifted awkwardly then smiled widely. "Look. Sorry I didn't call. This week's been mad. How about I give you a call next week and we go out sometime?'

My heart leaped. He *was* interested. I shrugged, not wanting to appear too easy. "Yeah, maybe," I said.

At that moment, his mates appeared at the end

of the road, "Oi, Mark, you coming or what?" one of them yelled.

"Look, Izzie Foster, got to go. I'll call you. Promise." And with that he ran off.

I felt stunned. He even remembered my name. So my horoscope was right after all. Venus was well aspected, even if it took its time to get going. And Nesta was right too. When you give up, things do start happening.

Song for Africa
by Izzie Foster

Cracked lips, parched land,
Dusty promises of help at hand.
Hungry children on Christmas cards
Won't help a world that's growing too fast.

I just wish it would rain on Africa.

But storm clouds gathering won't bring relief,
Just darker days with no hope of peace in Africa.

I just wish it would rain on Africa.
Wash out the pain of Africa.

Guns and bombs, tears and mud,
Luxury limos race through blood.
But bound by debt to hopelessness
Can we ever clean this mess?

I just wish it would rain on Africa.
Wash out the pain of Africa.

Chapter 6

Love
Spells

Cool. I am the queen of it. I consulted my horoscope and it said the week would get off to a slow start but things would start moving again on Friday. And Venus was in a good place for a romantic weekend. Top. Sounded like Mark would phone at the end of the week and I'd see him on Saturday or Sunday.

The week at school flew by and it was such a relief not to be in a flap about waiting for the phone. He'd promised he'd ring, and as Nesta said, you have to give them time.

However, by Friday the same old feelings were beginning to creep back.

"So what exactly did he say?" asked Lucy.

"That he'd call next week."

"Well that could be any day till Sunday," said Nesta. "Chill."

It was all right for her, she didn't fancy anyone special. And whenever she did have her eye on someone, they always seemed to call. Lucy, on the other hand, was anything but chilled. Her date with Tony had gone really well and she was seeing him again that evening after school. She was *so* excited.

"Though he still keeps saying I might be a bit young for him," she said.

"Probably because he wants to grope you," said Nesta. "And knows I'll kill him if he does."

"No," insisted Lucy. "He's not like that, honest."

Nesta looked at me and raised an eyebrow. She clearly had her doubts, and I have to say, I shared her concern.

I dashed home on Friday night and waited for the call. I kept busy watching *EastEnders* then *Friends,* but by nine thirty I was beginning to think Mark wasn't going to call.

I rang Lucy and asked her to phone both our home phone and my mobile to check that both were working.

The downstairs phone rang a minute later.

"Home phone working," said Lucy. "I'll try the mobile now."

A moment later my mobile rang. "Lucy again," she said. "It looks like it's all in order. And Izzie, have you got a minute? I need to talk to you."

It suddenly occurred to me that Mark might be trying to get through at just that moment so I didn't want to have a long conversation.

"Can it wait?" I asked. "Mark might be trying to get through."

"Okay," she said, sounding disappointed. "I'll talk to you tomorrow but not when Nesta's around. Okay?"

After she put the phone down I felt a bit rotten as I remembered she was supposed to have seen Tony after school. She probably wanted to talk about that and didn't feel she could open up with Nesta there seeing as he's her brother. I hoped she was okay and made a mental note to make it up to her tomorrow.

There was nothing else on TV I wanted to watch so I got out my love charms from the fair and decided to try one out to see if that would help the phone to ring.

"Charm to make a boy sweet on you," I read. "Write your love's name on a piece of paper, then sprinkle it with sugar and put it under your pillow and sleep on it."

I found a piece of purple writing paper and thought that would be the best to use, as purple is a magical color. I wrote Mark's name on it in a heart then went down to the kitchen and rooted in the cupboards for sugar.

Brown or white? I wondered. Does it matter? I settled for the brown and sprinkled it liberally on my paper. Luckily Mum and Angus were next door watching TV, as they would think I was barking if they'd caught me.

I took my charm back upstairs and put it under my pillow. Immediately the phone rang. Amazing. It worked! I dashed down to the hall to answer it.

"Is Dad there?" said Claudia's voice.

"Yes," I said. "I'll get him. But don't be long, I'm expecting an important phone call."

I hovered on the upstairs landing as Angus took his call. *Ten minutes!* Mark could have been trying to get through and Claudia would have ruined everything. What we clearly needed in our house was call-waiting, so that you could tell if someone was trying to get through when you were on the line. I must put it on my Christmas list, I thought, along with a lock for my bedroom door.

After they'd finished talking I went back into my bedroom to read but I couldn't really concentrate as my mind spiraled into maybes again. Maybe this time he really had lost my number. Maybe, maybe, maybe, zzzzz.

I must have dozed off at some point because the next thing I knew, it was Saturday morning and my mobile was ringing.

Oh thank God, I thought as I picked it up.

"Izzie, it's me," said Nesta. "Has Mark called yet?"

"No," I replied. "Do you think I should go to the Lock to see if he's working there today?"

"NO!" wailed Nesta. "No, no, *no*. Anyway, Lucy and I had a long talk about you this morning. We're both worried. What would you say if he's at the Lock?"

"Well I could say I was Christmas shopping again."

"No, Izzie. I won't let you. It'll be really obvious. You'd look desperate and if there's one things boys hate, it's desperate. Honest, Izzie, you're losing the plot. What's come over you? It's usually you telling Lucy this stuff."

"I know. I hope she's going to be okay with your brother."

"*Don't* try to change the subject," said Nesta. "We're talking about you and how you're not going to the Lock today."

"Oh come on, Nesta, come with me. I'd do it for you."

"No. You'd be all weird if you did see him, wondering if he was going to call or not. You won't be yourself. He'll pick up on it. And what if he wasn't there like the fair last week? You'll only feel down."

"So what should we do, then?" I asked. I knew better than to argue with Miss Know-It-All when she's in a mood like this.

"Lucy and I are going to meet in Hampstead. See you there in half an hour."

"Okay," I said. "But I can't stay long. I have to go to my dad's later."

Nesta and Lucy did their best to cheer me up, but I was sure that I'd blown it with Mark. I'd gone over everything I'd said to him a million times.

"I just know he's not going to phone. I think I was a bit off with him when I saw him last Saturday. He probably thinks I'm not interested."

"Relax, Izzie," said Nesta. "You're over-analyzing."

We were sitting in a café on Hampstead High Street and Nesta and Lucy were drinking cappuccinos while I sipped on a camomile tea.

"My life is over," I said. "I will never have a boyfriend. I will be alone all my life. And I've got a big bum."

Lucy started laughing. We always played a game when one of us was having a moan. Who could outdo the others with the worst life. "Ah," she said, "but I look twelve when I'm fourteen."

"Not since you had your hair cut," said Nesta. "You look at least twelve and a half now. . . ."

Lucy pinched her. "Excuse me! I haven't finished my tale of woe. My parents are mad hippies."

"I think your parents are cool," I said. "I wish they were mine. That's another thing to add to my list. I have the most boring mother and stepfather in the world."

"Okay, my turn," said Nesta. "I'm five feet seven and all the local boys are midgets."

242

"Well, what does that matter if you're going to marry Prince William? He's tall!"

When Nesta went downstairs to go to the loo, Lucy suddenly looked really serious.

"Izzie, I have to talk to you," she said. "About Tony."

"What?"

She shifted uncomfortably. "Well, you know what I was saying about him thinking I was too young for him? Well Nesta was right."

"What, about him wanting to grope you?"

Lucy nodded. "I don't know what to do. I mean, up till now we've just snogged but last night he said he wants to take it further."

"Oh God," I said. "What are you going to do?"

"Dunno. I don't want to take it further. I'm not ready. But if I don't, I reckon he'll dump me for someone who will. It's awful because I really like him. But you shouldn't just do it because you want to keep the boy, should you?"

"That's the trouble when you go out with older boys," I said. "Wandering hands."

"What should I do?"

"I've got just the thing," I said, as Lucy looked hopeful. "Have you got a photo of him?"

"Yes. We had some done in one of those photo booths."

"Okay," I said. "You do a spell. You cut the side of the photo with him on it and put it into the freezer and it will cool him down."

Lucy laughed out loud. "Oh come on. Get serious."

At that moment, Nesta came back. "What's so funny?"

"Nothing," said Lucy, clamming up.

"Lucy was just telling me something one of the dogs did," I said, trying to change the subject.

"Yeah, whatever," said Nesta, sitting back down. "Now what was I saying about Prince William and me?"

Lucy looked relieved that she hadn't caught on.

After I left the girls, I took the tube to Chalk Farm, where Dad lives now with his new wife Anna and their little boy Tom. Tom's gorgeous. He's only three. I like going to Dad's, as it's so much more relaxed than Mum's house. I reckon she drove him out with all her constant cleaning and stuff.

Dad is an English professor at a university, and

the house is always cluttered with books and journals and papers. I feel at home there, as at least his house looks lived-in, unlike ours which is a cross between a hotel and a hospital clinic.

I was really heartbroken when Dad first left. I was seven at the time and for ages was convinced it was my fault and that I'd done something wrong.

One day Mum and Dad sat me down and explained that sometimes people can still like each other but can't live together anymore and that's what had happened to them. Then they both said that no matter what happened, they both loved me and always would.

I felt better after that—that is until Angus moved in with my mum a couple of years later. I didn't like him at all at first. I asked if I could go and live with Dad, but he was living in a tiny flat at the time and there was no room for me.

Eventually I decided that there was only one way to deal with Angus, and that's to pretend he's our lodger and be polite but nothing else. I mean, he's not my dad, is he? A lodger that just happens to sleep in the same bed as my mum, but I shut those kind of thoughts out of my head straight away. Yuk. I don't want to even go there.

★ ★ ★

I was looking forward to spending some time at Dad's and thought I'd spend the afternoon working on my songs.

"Excuse the mess," said Dad as he opened the door, paintbrush in hand. "We're doing up the study."

"You've got paint all over your hair," I laughed, looking at the white streaks in his normally dark hair. "Did you actually manage to get *any* on the walls?"

"Hi, Izzie," said Anna, appearing behind Dad. "Welcome to the madhouse."

Anna was one of Dad's students when they met five years ago. A mature student, he told me, in case I thought he was cradle-snatching. But mature or not, she's still twelve years younger than he, round, and pretty with long auburn hair. She and Dad look right together. Dad always dresses in typical lecturer gear—jeans and leather jackets, looking most days like he's just got out of bed, and Anna still looks like a student, in jeans and sloppy jumpers. I don't think I've ever seen her in a skirt or dress.

I was glad when Dad met her, as I used to

worry about him all alone in his small flat when I went to visit. I got on with her immediately and always found her easy to talk to. When they decided to get married I was the first to congratulate them, secretly hoping that they'd find a bigger house and then I could move in with them. But when they moved to this flat Tom came along and it's clear there's no room for me unless I sleep under the kitchen table.

I stepped over the various paint cans and boxes strewn in the hallway and made my way into their kitchen. Somehow I didn't think I was going to get any work done on my songs that afternoon.

"Izzie, love . . . ," Dad began.

"Yeees?" I said. I knew that tone of voice. He wanted something.

"First," he said, "I've got a book for you."

I laughed to myself. Another for the box at the bottom of my cupboard, I thought. He was always giving me books to read—has since I was tiny. I got *War and Peace* for my ninth birthday. I don't think he's quite tuned into books for teenagers these days.

He handed me a book from the shelf in the kitchen. "Dorothy Parker. I think you'll like her."

"Thanks, Dad," I said unconvincingly.

247

"No really," said Anna, who was sympathetic to some of the heavy-going books he gave me to read. "I really think you will."

"Okay, I'll take a look at it," I said.

Then Dad smiled his "I want something" smile. "Would you do us the most enormous favor and take Tom out for a while? Anna and I want to finish the painting and it will be best if Tom's out of the way."

"Sure, Dad," I said as Tom paddled in and hugged my knees. "No problem."

"Izzie, you're an angel," said Anna. "I'll get his coat."

"What, right now?" I asked. I'd hardly got there.

That's one of the minuses of having two sets of parents. You get two sets of chores.

I set off for the park with Tom and tried to distract him at the shops in Primrose Hill. I spotted an amazing black velvet dress in one of the displays and made a mental note to put it on my Christmas list.

Tom pulled on my coat. "Swings," he said, pointing to the end of the road.

"Shops," I said hopefully, pointing to the windows which were bright with Christmas lights and tinsel. Sadly, Tom wasn't impressed. Like most males, he wasn't interested in shopping.

"Okay, swings," I said.

When we got to the play area there were a number of mothers there with their children and all the swings were full.

I sat on a park bench and wondered how best to keep a three-year-old entertained. Just at that moment, my mobile rang.

As I fished about in my bag to find my phone, I was vaguely aware of someone walking toward us with a toddler. Whoever he was, he was on his mobile phone.

Just as I was about to answer my phone, the boy stopped in front of me. He gawped at the phone in his hand, then gawped at me.

"I've just called you!" said Mark.

My mouth dropped open. "I don't believe it!"

"Neither do I. I call you, and here you are in front of me! It's so weird."

I switched off my phone. "Synchronicity," I said.

"Right," he said. "What's that?"

I laughed. "It's when something you're thinking about happens, or something to do with it does. I read about it. I'm not explaining it very well."

"You're not a witch, are you?" asked Mark.

I thought about the love charm under my pillow. "Might be," I grinned.

After that we had the most brilliant time. I might not be a witch, I thought, but the afternoon was magic.

Mark had been landed with his little sister like I'd been landed with Tom. We spent hours playing on the swings and slides, joining in like kids ourselves. Then we had a go on the roundabouts. Mark was fantastic and knew loads of games that had Tom laughing and giggling.

We didn't have a lot of time to talk to each other but it didn't matter, I thought, as I watched Mark rolling on the grass as his sister and Tom jumped all over him. Just being with him was fantastic.

After a few hours, my mobile rang.

"We thought you'd be back ages ago," said Dad. "Where on earth are you?"

I laughed. I wasn't on earth. I was somewhere up in the clouds.

Chapter 7

Big-mouth Nesta

"So are you going out with Mark now?" asked Lucy at break-time the following Monday.

"Not exactly, not yet," I said. "But he said he'd phone this week to arrange something. And this time I *know* he will because there he was, in front of me, phoning me. You should have been there. It was *amazing*. Like it was meant to be. And it was another day when my horoscope *said* that it was a good time for romance."

Nesta looked doubtful. "How do you know he really was phoning you? He could have seen you then felt guilty and *said* he was phoning you. I mean, you didn't answer the call, did you? Did you phone

1471 to check it wasn't a number you knew?"

I shook my head. What was she on about? "I couldn't do 1471 as Dad phoned after, so his was the last number."

Nesta's such a killjoy. I think she's jealous just because she's not in love with anyone at the moment.

Nesta shifted awkwardly. "It's just that I tried to phone you on Saturday afternoon and no one picked up."

Lucy saw my face drop. "But it doesn't matter. You saw him. That's what matters."

It was too late. The rosy glow I'd been feeling turned into a black cloud. As the bell rang, I turned to go back into class. I wasn't going to speak to Nesta anymore. Now she'd ruined everything.

"Oh Izzie," said Nesta, catching up with me. "I'm sorry. I didn't mean to . . ."

"You and your big mouth," said Lucy to Nesta. "Now you've put your foot in it."

After school each night, I went home alone. I felt such an idiot. Pathetic. I couldn't face going back to Lucy's with her and Nesta like normal. I felt mad at Nesta, even though she might have been right. And I didn't want them being all nice and feeling sorry for me. I didn't know what to think, and wanted some time on my own to sort my head out. I felt really confused.

Each night, I had to walk past the pizza shop on my way home. I could really do with one of those right now, I thought—deep pan, four cheese, and I wouldn't care if it all went straight to my bum. It's hard staying healthy at times like this when I've been feeling so mixed up. I was beginning to think what does it matter? So I am what I eat. A limp lettuce? Pooh.

Every evening seemed *soo loooong*, like each minute was eternal as I sat in my room, willing the phone to ring. And it didn't. I wished I had his number so I could call him but I didn't even know his last name.

One night I decided to distract myself by reading my Feng Shui book: *Each room is divided into different areas, each area representing a different part of your life: creativity, wealth, knowledge, family, friends, relationships. Each area falls in a positive or negative*

253

space depending on whether the room faces north, south, east, or west.

I got my compass out and did some calculations. That's what was wrong, I realized. I'd got my wastepaper bin in my relationship corner! *Disastrous.* It meant I was putting rubbish into my relationships. Durrh. No wonder Mark hadn't phoned.

I rearranged my room according to the book then started on the bathroom.

"What on earth are you doing?" said Angus, finding me kneeling in the corner trying to tack the rose quartz crystal I bought for Mum for Christmas to the sewer pipe.

"Nothing," I said.

"Nothing," he said, then stood hovering at the doorway. He looked as though he wanted to say something but eventually just shrugged. "Okay, suit yourself."

I wasn't going to waste my breath explaining that in the bathroom, our loo was in the relationship corner in a negative zone so we were flushing all the good relationship energy away. The book said a crystal on the plumbing would help direct the energy back up again. But Angus would never understand that. All he understands is the *Financial Times* and insurance policies.

Another night, for want of anything else to do— or eat (Mum *still* hadn't got the message about buying more healthy stuff)—I munched my way through half a packet of choc chip cookies. Before I ate the other half, I decided to use my time more positively and do an exercise tape. It's called *Bums, Tums, and Thighs*, and promises you a whole new body in four weeks.

What it doesn't tell you is that the next day you'll be so stiff you probably won't be able to walk.

Another night and there was still *nothing* to do. I'd done my homework and there was nothing on the TV so I had a quick look at the book Dad gave me about Dorothy Parker. She sounded pretty cool. She was a writer who lived in New York around the 1920s and it sounded like she had a rotten time with some of her boyfriends, but she managed to be really funny about it. She used to meet up with other writers of the day at a round table in a place called the Alonquin Hotel and would have them all rolling in the aisles with her poems and sayings about love going wrong and stuff. It sounded like a brilliant time and I thought I'd like to be like her when I grow up. We've got a round table downstairs in our dining room so Nesta, Lucy, and me could have meetings like she did. There was a photo of her at the back of the book and it gave me an idea.

I went into the kitchen, got the scissors, then went into the bathroom, the one room in this house where I could lock the door. My hair is all one length and I thought it might look more interesting if I cut a fringe like Dorothy Parker's. I pulled a short section up at the front and snip, off it came. I combed it out and it looked pretty good. Except it was a bit uneven on one side. So I snipped a bit more off. Oops, a bit too much. I'd better even it out. Oops. OOOOPS. Oh *no*. Now *that* was uneven. I chopped off a bit more then stood back to look at my reflection. Tears filled my eyes. I'd managed to cut it down to a stubble. I tried to comb it under the long bits. But it kept sticking out again.

Oh God, what had I done? Stupid. Stupid. I'd just

ruined my hair. Now I knew how Lucy had felt when she had a bad haircut earlier that term. What on earth had possessed me? Now I couldn't go out. It'd takes weeks to grow back. It was all Mark's fault. If he had phoned none of it would have happened. Could life get any worse? I could hardly walk from doing all those exercises and now I looked like a mad person. All because of a boy. I was seriously beginning to wonder if they're worth the trouble.

And I was getting a huge spot. On the end of my *nose.*

"Izzie, what are you doing in there?" said Mum's voice on the other side of the door. "You've been in there ages."

There was nothing else for it. She was bound to see sooner or later. I opened the door and waited for the telling off. I didn't care. I felt numb. Sometimes I can be *so* stupid.

"Oh Izzie," said Mum. "What have you done?"

"Only ruined my hair!" I wailed. "Now I can never go out again."

She gently pushed me back into the bathroom and took a closer look. "Got a bit carried away, didn't you?"

257

I nodded miserably. "Aren't you going to yell at me?"

Mum shook her head. "Do you want me to see if I can fix it?"

"No, I don't think so."

Mum pulled a bit more hair over my face. "I think I could. If I cut a bit more fringe then cut into it, then you wouldn't see the short bits underneath. Want to give it a go?"

Mum used to cut my hair when I was little. My gran used to be a hairdresser and Mum had picked up the basics from her so I knew I could trust her not to make it any worse.

"Okay." I quickly showed her the photo of Dorothy Parker at the back of my book. "I was trying to cut a fringe like hers."

"Dorothy Parker! I thought most girls your age wanted to look like that girl in *Friends*. What's her name?"

"Jennifer Aniston."

"But that's my Izzie," Mum smiled at me. "Always has to be different."

"Will you get me a wig for Christmas if it doesn't work out?"

258

"Sure," laughed Mum. "But I don't think it will come to that. Okay. Wet it a bit then it will cut better."

I did as I was told and Mum carefully snipped a bit more fringe then began to cut into it. "It's looking better already. And I'll take some off the length so it doesn't look top-heavy."

"Whatever," I said.

She finished cutting and combing and then took me into her bedroom, got the hairdryer out, and blew it dry.

"Can I look now?" I asked.

Mum nodded and I went and stood in front of her mirror. I was shocked. It looked really good. Just past my shoulders. More modern. And if I pushed it back it fell in a really nice layer.

"Not bad, eh?" said Mum, looking pleased with herself.

"Mum, you're a genius," I said and hugged her.

Now Mark just had to phone. He'd be bound to fancy me more with my new haircut.

At school the next day, Lucy and Nesta seemed agitated about something. In fact I don't think

259

Nesta even noticed my hair until Lucy said she liked it.

Nesta cornered me in the corridor at lunchtime. "Izzie, I know I put my foot in it the other day and I think we need to clear the air. Plus we have to talk about Lucy and Tony. I . . ."

Then Lucy came round the corner and Nesta clammed up.

Then Nesta went to get a drink from the machine in the hall, and Lucy started up. "Izzie, I need to talk to you."

"About Tony?" I said.

"Yes. No. Yeah. About Tony but about you as well. I've hardly seen you lately and . . ."

Then *she* clammed up when Nesta came back.

"What's going on?" said Nesta, eyeing us suspiciously.

Then *I* clammed up. Honestly. It's supposed to be *me* who's going slowly bonkers. Now they're acting all weird and I've lost track of who's not talking to who about what and why. I don't know what Lucy's problem is—at least she *knows* Tony likes her. All I know is Mark still hasn't called and I don't know where I stand with him at all.

260

As we went back into class for the afternoon, I could see Lucy was looking miserable and I wondered if it was my fault. I suppose I have been a bit wrapped up in myself lately. What a mess.

When I got home on Friday night, *finally*, my mobile rang.

Let it be Mark, let it be Mark, I prayed as I leaped to answer it.

But it was only Lucy.

"Izzie, it's me," she said. "If you're mad at Nesta, why aren't you speaking to me?"

"I *am* speaking to you, Lucy. And Nesta. It's just I feel like being on my own lately," I said.

"Well I miss you," she said. "Has Mark phoned?"

"Not yet. But I don't care anymore," I lied.

"Maybe Mercury's gone retrograde again?" she said.

"Nah. I've checked. It's supposed to be a good week for me according to my horoscope. In fact, the printout I've just done says I'll hear from someone I want to."

"*Meeee*," said Lucy. "That's me. One of your best mates. Remember?"

"Yeah," I said unconvincingly.

"I *am* sorry he's not phoned," said Lucy. "But I think you're letting it get to you."

"No I'm not," I said. "I'm perfectly cool with it all."

"Then come over for a bit. We could watch the soaps and *Friends*."

"Can't," I said. "I'm having an early night."

I could hear Lucy sigh at the other end. "Okay. I'll call Nesta and see if *she* wants to come over."

I felt a bit rotten after I put the phone down, and hoped that Lucy would understand.

I waited in all night. But the phone stayed silent.

On Saturday morning I checked my horoscope and it said it was a good day for confrontations so I decided I'd go to the Lock and if Mark was there, I'd have it out with him. Ask him why he hadn't called this week and if he *really* was phoning me last week when we met.

Unfortunately Big-Mouth phoned just as I was ready to leave.

"I'm so sorry about Monday, Izzie," said Nesta. "I can't bear it when you're mad with me. Come to Hampstead. Lucy and I both want to see you. We think you need a break from thinking about Mark."

"Can't," I said. "Busy."

Nesta went quiet on the other end of the phone. "I hope you're not thinking of going to the Lock."

"No. Anyway, why?" I asked.

"Because you *mustn't*," said Nesta. "You *know* boys don't like it if you chase them or get heavy. They don't like hassle, especially when it's early days."

"What makes you think I'm going to get heavy with him?"

Nesta paused at the other end of the phone. "Well, you have been kind of intense lately, even with me and Lucy."

"No I haven't."

"Okay," Nesta sighed. "But you haven't been your usual self. You might think I don't understand but I do. And I can see that Mark has really got to you. Trust me, Iz. It's really not a good idea to go to the Lock. You need to chill out a bit before you see him again."

"Fine," I said.

"Fine," said Nesta.

Then I hung up. I wasn't going to listen to her. Killjoy.

I made my way to the Lock, praying that Mark was working that day. I went over and over in my head what I planned to say but Nesta had got me worried. I didn't want to be "heavy" but I really wanted to know where I stood. We'd had such a good time last week. I couldn't have imagined it. Oh, I *wished* I could feel normal again.

I was feeling really nervous as I went into the market. Was this a good idea? Should I turn back now?

"Izzie!" called Mark. He was there at the stall and had seen me coming up the stairs.

"Oh, hi," I said, forcing my voice to sound casual. "I forgot you worked here."

He looked at me strangely. "Really?" he said. He looked hurt.

We both stood there looking awkward. All my

carefully prepared words deserted me. I didn't know *what* to say.

"Er, better be going then . . . ," I said finally.

"Oh." He looked disappointed. "I was just going to take a break. Can't you stay a mo? We could get a cappuccino."

I felt as if someone had poured concrete in my brain and I'd turned to stone. I was torn. Should I go, should I stay? Perhaps he'd explain. Perhaps I could ask my questions. Either way, I wanted to know what he had to say.

"Okay," I said.

We made our way downstairs and Mark bought two cappuccinos at a take-away stall.

"Sugar?" he asked.

I shook my head. Perhaps this wasn't the best time to say I wasn't drinking coffee. He might think I was a weirdo.

We sat by the canal sipping our drinks. Lovely. Bliss. Oh I'd forgotten how nice and creamy and frothy these could be. Perhaps I could do my healthy eating but have the occasional treat. Balance, I told myself, that's what it's all about.

265

"Er, Mark . . . ," I began.

"Yeah," he smiled back at me.

"You know when you said you'd phone me . . ."

"Oh yeah. I was going to tell you. My mobile got nicked. I was going to phone you."

Suddenly he looked uncomfortable. Had I gone too far? But if his mobile had been stolen maybe that explained it. Not really, I thought. There are other phones. I decided to jump right in. I didn't want to spend another week agonising over whether he was interested or playing games. I had nothing to lose.

"You know when we saw each other last Saturday and you were phoning me?"

"Yeah," he smiled and put his hand over mine on the table. "That was amazing, wasn't it? Synchronicity, like you said."

A lovely tingling feeling went right through me. I cast about in my head for how I could ask him without sounding like I didn't trust him.

"Was that your dad who answered the phone?" said Mark, interrupting my confusion.

"What do you mean? My dad?"

"When I phoned you."

266

I was more confused than ever. "What do you mean?"

"When I saw you, remember? I'd just called you when there you were in front of me."

"Yeah. And I was just about to pick up."

"Yeah. But I wasn't phoning your mobile. There were two numbers on your card. I called the first one and some bloke answered."

He must have phoned my home number. And *Angus*. Angus must have picked up.

"So you didn't phone me on my mobile? You called my *house*."

"Yeah, was that your dad? He sounded very posh."

"No," I said. "It must have been the lodger that picked up."

"Anyway," said Mark, playing with my fingers, "there you were in front of me."

Suddenly the rosy glow came back. Nesta had been right. It must have been her on my mobile and that's why she said no one picked up. But he had phoned. Hurrah. It was going to be all right after all.

★ ★ ★

When I got home later that day I stormed into the kitchen to find Angus. He was sitting with my mum at the table, drinking a cup of tea.

"Hi, Izzie," they chorused.

"Why didn't you tell me someone called last Saturday?" I demanded, turning to Angus.

Angus looked startled. "What? When? What are you talking about?"

"Don't you even remember?" I said. "It's *really* important."

Angus scratched his head. "When did you say?"

"Last Saturday?" I had to know if Mark was telling the truth.

"I don't know. Did someone leave a message and I forgot to pass it on? Let me think."

"They might not have left a message. A boy. A boy's voice."

Mum and Angus gave each other a knowing look.

"Oh yes, I think the phone did go at some point," said Angus. "But no one was on the other end. I presumed it was a wrong number."

I wanted to kill him. "You should have *told* me!" I cried.

"Izzie, don't speak to Angus like that. He wasn't to know it wasn't a wrong number, especially if no one even spoke! He's not psychic."

Tears pricked the back of my eyes. "You don't understand, do you?" I turned back to Angus. "You almost ruined *everything*."

"Sit down and have some lunch with us, Izzie," said Mum softly. "Tell us what you've been up to."

"You wouldn't understand!" I wailed. "And anyway, there's never anything I can eat in this house. Nobody cares about me. . . ."

Mum's expression clouded. "I'm getting *really* tired of your selfish attitude, Isobel. Go to your room. And don't come down until you're ready to apologize."

I stormed out and slammed the door. Go to your room. That's all I ever heard these days. I couldn't do anything right. Mums. I give up.

Song For Mum
by Izzie Foster

Hey Mum, I want you to know,
So sit down and listen,
No please don't go.
Things are different since you were a girl,
Pressures today put my head in a whirl.
Life's moving faster, we're all in the race
That's accelerated to a damaging pace.
Sometimes it's too much to bear,
So when I come home and seem in despair
Don't ask what's wrong, leave me alone.

I'm good, I'm bad,
You're nice, you're mad.
I love, I hate,
But it's never too late
To say sorry.

It's tough to say about your man,
So please forgive me if I'm not a fan
But he's not my dad and that's a fact.
Yes I know, I know I'm lacking tact,
Blame my ignorance, my stupid youth.
You always said to speak the truth.
I share your guilt and feel your pain,
I just hide mine in a secret place.

Chapter 8

Mobile Madness

I don't *believe* what's just happened.

When I left Mark on Saturday, my plan to ask him for his number went out of the window, as once again he promised to call me. I told him not to phone my home number as Mum and the lodger were hopeless at passing on messages. So he said he'd call on my mobile. Simple.

Or so I thought.

I checked my weekly horoscope and it said a slow start to the week but things would liven up around Thursday when Pluto was square to Mars, causing some confusion. Hah! Understatement.

On Thursday evening Mum took me to Lucy's

house to have my guitar lesson with Lucy's dad. She said she'd wait for me, and as she got settled with a magazine in the kitchen, Mr. L. and I went through to the sitting room. We'd just got started on some chord exercises when my mobile rang.

"Turn that off for the lesson," said Mr. L.

"Can I please take this call, just this one?" I begged. It might be Mark and I didn't want to miss him.

"Well, just this one," said Mr. L. "Then I want your full concentration."

"Izzie, it's me," said Nesta's croaky voice. "I really need to talk to you."

"Can't at the moment," I said. "I'm in the middle of a guitar lesson. Speak later."

I was feeling a bit rotten about Nesta. She'd been off with flu all week and I hadn't even called her. And I knew she hadn't meant to be mean about Mark and I *knew* I owed her an apology but I wanted to pick my time. Not when Mr. L. was listening in.

I put my mobile on the table where I could see it.

"Off," said Mr. L. "Switch it *off* for the lesson."

"Ohhh, do I have to?"

"You do. I know what you girls are like on your phones and I've got another pupil straight after you so I don't want us wasting time."

I could see he meant it, so reluctantly I switched the phone off and turned my mind to the guitar.

"You're getting better," said Mr. L. at the end of our hour. "Now did you bring me some of your songs to look at? Next time, we could start putting them to music."

"Er, yes, no," I squirmed.

"Er, yes, no. Did you or didn't you?"

I had brought my lyrics with me but I didn't want to show them. Not since that class when everyone laughed at my rap song.

"I did bring them," I said. "But I don't want to show them."

"Ah, a songwriter who doesn't want anyone to hear her songs?"

"I read a few lines of one of them in class and everyone laughed," I said.

Mr. L. looked at me kindly. "It's hard, Izzie, when you do anything creatively. There will

273

always be people who like what you do and those who don't. You mustn't take it personally. But if you're going to succeed, and I'm sure you will, you've got to be ready to take constructive criticism. Don't be afraid to stick your neck out. Just be careful who you show your work to in the beginning. Some people will criticize because they're jealous, but others can give you feedback that you can learn from."

"Well, will you read them when I'm not here? Then I don't have to see your face if you don't like them."

Mr. L. laughed. "Sure. Leave them on top of the piano there. You needn't be afraid, I'm sure I *will* like them."

"Well promise you won't show them to anyone. Promise, not Lal or Steve or even Lucy. I've never shown them to anyone."

"Promise."

As I left the room, I noticed my mum chatting to a boy in the kitchen. She looked up as she saw us coming in.

"Er, can I have a word?" she said to Mr. L.

"Sure," he said.

"In private," she said and went off into the living room with him. What's all that about? I thought.

I looked across at the boy. He looked familiar. "Hey, don't I know you?" I asked.

The boy nodded and smiled. "Yeah, Ben. From your sister's wedding."

"Stepsister," I corrected.

He looked really different from the way he'd looked at the wedding, cute almost, and in the same school uniform as Lucy's brothers.

"You go to the same school as Lal and Steve?"

"Yeah," he said. "That's how I heard about the lessons."

"Where are they all? Lucy and Steve and Lal?"

"Gone to the vid shop, I think," he said.

"So you're the next pupil?"

"Yeah," he said.

At that moment, Mum came back out. "Ready?" she asked.

"Who was that?" she asked as we drove away.

"No one," I said. "He was at the wedding playing those awful songs."

"I *thought* I recognized him," said Mum. "Of course, he's Jeremy's younger brother. He was rather good on the piano, wasn't he?"

"Oh Mum, the music he played was totally naff. I'm surprised he's bothering to have lessons. He clearly hasn't a clue about decent music."

"What were you talking about?" she asked.

"Nothing," I replied. "Why, what were you talking to Mr. L. about?"

Mum got a really cheeky look on her face. "Oh nothing," she mimicked, then we both burst out laughing.

It was only when we got home that I realized I'd left my mobile on the table at Lucy's. And it was switched off.

"I *have* to go back," I said to Mum. "I've left my mobile."

"You can live without it for one night," said Mum. "Call Lucy and ask her to take it into school in the morning."

I went to the phone to call Lucy and saw that the answering machine was flashing two messages.

I pressed the playback button.

"Hi, it's Mark," said the first message. "I tried calling your mobile but it's switched off so I thought I'd try your home number. Anyway, you're not there either so I'll try your mobile again later."

"Oh *no*," I groaned.

Then there was a beep and a message from Angus for Mum saying he was working late. Oh pants. Now I couldn't do 1471 to get Mark's number as Angus had called in between and got in the way. *Again*.

I quickly called Lucy, explained the situation and asked her to check if anyone had rung.

A few minutes later, she came back to the phone. "Only a message from Nesta about five minutes ago."

"Oh *no*," I said. "Mark said he'd try and call. Now I can't do 1471 on that phone *either* as Nesta's will be the last number. Promise you'll answer it if it goes again?"

"Course I will," she said. "And have you phoned Nesta?"

"Not yet. Why?"

"She really wants to talk to you," said Lucy.

Oh dear. She was mad at me. I'd better phone

soon and make it up with her. But first, I had to get my mobile back.

I went into the sitting room where Mum had settled on the sofa in front of the TV with a glass of wine.

"Mum. Please will you take me back to Lucy's to get my mobile?"

"Izzie. It's eight o'clock."

"It'll only take twenty minutes."

She sighed. Never a good sign. "I've had a long day at work, I took you to your music lesson, I waited for you and I'm *not* going back there now. We have a phone here."

"Well I'll go on the bus."

"You will not, not on your own at this time of night."

"Then I'll get a taxi."

"Izzie. Watch my lips. N. O. *No.* Anyway, who was that boy on the answering machine?"

"No one."

"Well what did he want?"

"Nothing," I said.

This time, neither of us laughed.

Chapter 9

Murphy's Law

At school on Friday things really came to a head.

I know Mum's mad at me. Nothing unusual there. But now Lucy is too.

"Have you called Nesta yet?" she said when she handed over my mobile phone in the break.

"Not yet," I said. "I did mean to . . . but . . ."

"But *what*?" said Lucy crossly. "She's phoned you a few times. And she's not well. What's the excuse this time? Mercury gone retrograde again so you can't pick up a phone?"

I was stunned. This wasn't like Lucy. She was all stiff and looked really upset.

"I will phone her. I've had a lot going on. And *actually*, it's not Mercury, it's Pluto. It's going through a really intense phase in my chart and . . ."

"Tell me about it," said Lucy, looking skyward. "Not only Pluto. *You*, Izzie. You're so . . . so serious about everything these days. And you can't keep blaming the stars. In fact I'm getting sick of you using your stupid horoscope as an excuse for everything anyone does, doesn't do, or thinks. You know what? You're no fun anymore. *And* you've been neglecting me. And Nesta. You're not the only one going through stuff. But lately it's all been about you. And Mark. And if he's phoned or not. And Mercury or Venus . . ."

She broke off. She looked near to tears. She turned away but I went and stood in front of her and put my hand on her arm.

"Oh don't cry, Lucy. You're right. I'm sorry. I've been a pain, haven't I?"

"Yes. You *have*."

"Look, I'll phone Nesta this instant," I said and began dialling Nesta's number. "And I'll make it up to you. Honest I will. Lucy. Lucy? Still mates? Please?"

Lucy sighed. "Course," she said. "Still mates. Just lighten up a bit, will you?"

At that moment the bell went for class.

"I'll phone Nesta at lunch. I will. I *will*. Promise."

"You better," said Lucy and punched my arm.

But at least she was smiling.

When I got home that evening, I had a good think about everything Lucy had said. I knew she was right. I had lost myself somewhere along the way in the last few weeks. And to tell the truth, I was beginning to get tired of staying in waiting for the phone and going slowly mental. I'd done everything I could think of to keep myself occupied. I'd color coordinated my wardrobe, I'd tidied all my books and CDs, I'd done all my homework, painted my nails, conditioned my hair, written my Christmas cards. I realized that I had to stop waiting around for Mark to phone. It was ridiculous. I had to get myself a life again. I'd been neglecting my friends. And I was starting to miss them.

When Lucy phoned and asked if I wanted to go to Nesta's, I didn't think twice.

"See you there at seven," I said.

"I'm not infectious anymore," said Nesta as Lucy and I sat as far away as we could from her in their sitting room. "In fact Mum says I can go out again tomorrow. Hurrah."

Lucy laughed, then went and plonked herself on the floor by the sofa where Nesta was lying like the Queen of Sheba, covered in a huge duvet and surrounded by boxes of tissues and cough drops.

I'd phoned Nesta at lunchtime as promised and, before she could say anything, I apologized for being a total pain. We talked for about an hour and I didn't even get in a state about Mark maybe trying to get through. She was great about everything and said she really values me as a friend. I felt really close to her. She said she was sorry for putting the damper on my day in the park with Mark and I said I'd been a complete prat. She agreed. We had a laugh and here we were like nothing ever happened.

"How do you handle it, Lucy?" I asked. "If Tony doesn't phone?"

282

"Easy," said Nesta. "I stand over him to make sure he does. I told him from the start that he'd better not mess her around and he knows better than to get me mad."

Lucy and I laughed. We both knew what Nesta could be like when she turned into Scary Spice mode. Not to be argued with.

"Anyway," I said, joining Lucy on the floor. "I've had enough of boys. Too much trouble. Up. Down. Happy. Depressed. I can't take it anymore. I was okay before I met Mark. And I've been mental ever since."

"Did he call this evening?" asked Lucy.

"What do you think?"

"Maybe?" said Lucy.

"Nah," I said. "And I've had enough. *Enough*. I don't know what game he's playing but I don't want to join in. First he says he had a mad week, then, last Saturday, he says his mobile was nicked . . ."

Nesta's face dropped.

"What?" I asked. "What is it?"

"Nothing," she said. But I could tell that there was something she wasn't saying. And I could tell

Lucy knew whatever it was as she looked really worried too.

"Nesta. Spill."

She shook her head. "No, honestly, nothing. It doesn't matter."

We sat awkwardly for a few minutes.

"Nesta, you *have* to tell me. I *know* you know something. If you don't tell me I will imagine the worst possible thing in the world."

"Like what?" she asked.

"Er, like secretly you've been dating Mark all this time?"

She laughed. "No, it's not *that* bad. Besides, you know I wouldn't do that."

"So what, then?"

She shifted uncomfortably. "Well, promise you won't stop speaking to me again."

"Promise," I said, starting to feel pretty uncomfortable myself. "Look, I know I've been a useless mate lately but I promise I won't go funny, whatever you tell me."

I *had* to know. There's *nothing* I hate more than when someone says they know something, then won't tell you.

284

"Well, last Saturday, remember you wouldn't come out with us to the Hollywood Bowl?"

"Yes," I nodded.

"Well, we saw Mark there."

"Really?"

"Yeah. He was with a bunch of mates."

"Well that's not so bad. I mean, we didn't have a date or anything."

"Yeah. But he was posing about. On his mobile phone."

"Oh," I said. "The creep. Why didn't he just say he'd forgotten to ring or something? Why come up with a whole story about his phone being nicked?"

"Boys do that when they feel confronted," said Lucy. "Believe me, I know, with two stupid brothers. Rather than tell the truth they'll make up some daft story so they don't look bad."

"Well that's it, then," I said. "No more boys. No matter how cute."

"Until you meet the next one you like," said Nesta.

"No," I said. I really meant it this time. "Boys are bad for your mental health."

"Some are okay," said Nesta. "They don't all mess you around. But friends are best. It's not worth losing your friends over any boy."

"Absolutely," I agreed. "I mean, boys will come and go. But we'll always be friends and be there for each other. Won't we? Let's make a pact that we'll never ever let a boy come between us again."

"Yeah," said Nesta. "And we'll always tell the truth to each other, no matter how much we think it might hurt."

"Yeah," said Lucy. "A pact. If you can't trust your mates, then who can you trust?"

I felt happier than I had for weeks. Sane again. It felt good to be back with my pals. Easy company. Uncomplicated.

"To no boys," I said.

Lucy and Nesta looked doubtful.

"How about to friends?" said Nesta.

"Okay," I said. "To friends."

When I got home later that night, Mum called me into the sitting room. She was curled up on the sofa reading a vegetarian recipe book and Angus was at the desk in the bay window, looking at some photographs in an album. Oh no, I thought. *Please* don't let those be the wedding pictures come back. That was an episode I was hoping had been forgiven and forgotten.

"What are you reading a vegetarian recipe book for?" I said, edging out of the room just in case the photos *were* from the wedding and it all blew up again.

"Just looking at a few recipes for Christmas dinner," said Mum. "We can't have you eating nothing but sprouts. How does a nut roast sound?"

"Great," I said. What was going on? She didn't seem too mad. Perhaps it wasn't Amelia's wedding album.

"Want to see yourself as bridesmaid, Izzie?" asked Angus.

I looked nervously at Mum, thinking, Uh-oh, here we go. But she didn't even look up from her book.

I went to look over Angus's shoulder. "Wow!" I said. "They look fantastic."

Angus turned and smiled. "Yes. Good solution, eh?"

287

"Yeah," I said, breathing a sigh of relief. "Excellent solution."

He'd had the photos done in black and white. In the few photos I was in, I looked completely normal. No wonder Mum was sitting there so cool about it all. In black and white no one need ever know her mad daughter had green hair on the day.

"Some boy called when you were out," said Mum. "Mark. He said he'd phone back."

"Oh *no*," I said. "Murphy's Law."

Mum looked at me quizzically. "Oh no? I thought he was the one that all the fuss was about?"

I sighed. "He was. But I just decided I'm through with boys."

Mum and Angus laughed.

"I can't keep up, Izzie," said Mum.

"Neither can I," I said. "I'm going to bed."

As I went up the stairs, I had an idea.

"Has anyone called since?"

"No," said Mum. "I don't think so."

Great! I went into the hall and dialled 1471.

I scribbled down the number then went up to

288

my room. At last! I thought. Now I could call him if I wanted.

But I was through with boys. Wasn't I?

Staying Together
by Izzie Foster

Hey there, don't you know that boys just come
    and boys just go,
But friends stay together for ever and ever.
Hey there, follow the noise and you'll soon find
    a gang of boys.

Had enough of football chants?
Smelly trainers, mindless rants?
Boys are stupid, boys are vain,
A dozen boys just share one brain.
No boys!

Yes, girlfriend, it's the truth, we're not going
    to waste our youth.
Friends stay together for ever and ever.
We're too pretty, we're too smart
to let any boyfriend break us apart.

Boys are stupid, boys are vain,
A dozen boys just share one brain.
No boys!

Chapter 10

Cosmic Kisses

"I have a date," I said to Lucy on the phone the following morning. "A proper date. With Mark."

He'd phoned back five minutes after I got home from Nesta's, so I hadn't had to think about whether to phone him or not.

"We're going to hang out this afternoon. Don't be mad with me."

"I'm not mad at you," she said. "But I thought you were through with boys."

"I know, I *know*. But a girl can change her mind, can't she?"

Talking about changing her mind, I must have

tried on every outfit in my wardrobe. Nothing looked right. I wanted to look my best but didn't want to look like I'd made too much effort.

By twelve o'clock I had every item I owned out on the bed and I was meeting Mark in an hour. Help.

"Having a clear-out?" asked Mum, coming into my bedroom and surveying the mess everywhere.

"*Mum,*" I said. "You didn't knock."

Mum raised her eyes to the ceiling. "You never used to mind, Izzie."

"Well I do now. I'm fourteen."

"Anyway," said Mum, ignoring me. "What are you doing?"

"*Trying* to get dressed. But I've got nothing to wear."

Mum looked at the heaps of clothes piled on the bed. "Nothing to wear?" she laughed. "There's loads of clothes here. Anyway, what's the occasion?"

I shrugged. I didn't want to tell her I was going out with Mark as she'd want to know everything. Who he was. What school he went to. Then she'd be inviting him round to give him the once-over. No thanks.

"I'm going to the Hollywood Bowl," I said. She didn't need to know who with. But she had a silly grin on her face. I think she knew.

"Then just wear your jeans."

"My bum looks big in them."

"Then wear a skirt."

"I can't decide," I sighed, looking pointedly at my watch.

"Okay. *Okay*. I know when I'm not wanted," Mum said, turning to leave. "And Izzie?"

"Yes?" Please don't let her ask too many questions, I prayed.

"Have a good time." She winked.

Sometimes I don't get parents.

In the end, I grabbed my black ribbed sweater, my black jeans, and black PVC coat. Black and mysterious, that's me.

The weather looked freezing outside so I added a red scarf and gloves, then a bit of lipstick, a bit of kohl, a spray of Mum's Chanel No. 19, and I was out the door.

Mark was waiting for me outside Café Original when I got to North Finchley. I was glad I hadn't dressed up too much as besides his jacket, he had on a navy fleece, jeans, and trainers. I tried my best to look cool as I walked toward him but my heart was beating madly. He looked gorgeous.

Gorgeous and waiting for me.

Gorgeous, waiting for me, and waving.

My breath felt tight in my chest as I waved back.

"Hi," he said, taking my hand and leading me into the café. "Let's go and get a drink to warm us up."

As we walked into the café all my anxieties from the last few weeks melted away. What did any of it matter now? I could see a few girls eyeing him up as we got drinks and took our seats.

Ha ha, I thought, he's with me. On a date. With *me*.

We spent the next few hours jibber-jabbering about everything. I found out he lives in Primrose Hill not far from Dad. He goes to school there as well and, most excellent, it's one of the five local schools invited to our end-of-term disco. He's seventeen and a Libra (which is an air sign like me, so we're really compatible). His favorite films are *The Matrix* and *American Pie* and *The Sixth Sense* (which is my favorite film). He's got one older brother and a younger sister. Best subjects are math and biology and he wants to be a doctor when he grows up.

We'd just ordered two blueberry muffins (my weekend treat) and got on to our favorite foods, when a phone rang. He reached into his pocket and pulled out his mobile.

After he'd finished his call, he grinned at me. "Sorry about that. One of my mates. I'm seeing him later," he said.

I put on my most innocent look. "I thought you said your phone had been nicked."

He shifted awkwardly and I could have sworn he blushed a bit. "Oh yeah," he said. "That. My dad got me a new one yesterday."

We ate our muffins in silence then he looked right into my eyes and did a kind of slow smile. Then he stared at my mouth for a moment and my insides went all tingly.

"Shall we go and have a walk before we go home?" he asked.

Suddenly I felt really nervous. It was our first date. Would he want to kiss me? I'd only ever kissed two other boys and neither of them were important. One boy when I was a kid and then some creepoid last year who had a nasty case of wandering hands. It was horrible and he poked his tongue in my mouth. All I could think was wet fish, wet fish! Sloppy, slimy. Blaghh.

This time it would be for real.

I tried to remember what Nesta's brother had told us about kissing. Tony fancies himself as the Master Snogger, and one time, before he was going out with Lucy, he offered to show me how it was done. I laughed at him but now I wished I'd taken him up on it. I mean, how do you know if you're a good kisser? I cast my mind back and desperately tried to remember what his snogging tips were. I should have asked Lucy or Nesta before I came out. I know, I thought, I'll phone them.

"Sure, a walk sounds good," I said. "But just got to go to the ladies'. Won't be a mo."

I dashed into the ladies', waited until all the cubicles were empty, then dialled Lucy's number.

"Lucy," I said. "I'm with Mark. What do I do if he wants to kiss me?"

Lucy laughed. "Durrh. Snog him back, dummy."

"But how?" I wailed. "I'm really worried I'll be useless at it and he'll never want to see me again."

"Relax," said Lucy. "Just take your lead from him."

"What if he puts his tongue in my mouth? What do I do?"

"Just do what feels natural," said Lucy.

"Thanks," I said, feeling none the wiser. I phoned Nesta for a second opinion.

"Fresh breath," she said. "V. important. Otherwise, keep the pressure varied. Soft, medium, hard, and run your fingers through his hair. Boys like that."

"What do I do with my tongue?"

"Stick it up his nostril," she giggled.

"Ergh, *Nesta*!"

"Izzie, relax. You'll be fine. Ring me later with all the details."

Thanks for nothing, Nesta, I thought as I switched off my phone. Just because she's snogged loads of boys she thinks it's really funny.

I rooted round in my bag and found some chewing gum, then put on some lipstick. Oh. Was that a good idea? If he kissed me he'd get it all over him. Maybe I should wipe it off again? God, it was so complicated. We ought to have lessons in this sort of thing at school instead of all that stuff we never needed about how many crops are grown in some remote country I'd never heard of.

I rubbed my lipstick into my lips so that it wasn't too shiny then went back out to meet him. Gulp! He was chewing gum as well. Snogging was definitely on the cards. I pushed my gum behind my teeth so he wouldn't see I was chewing as well. I didn't want him to think I was expecting it or anything.

When we got outside, we had a look at what was on at the movies then it started raining so we made a dash for the bus stop. We were the only people there and I wondered if he was going to make a move. Or should I? Or would that seem forward? I was shivering like mad though I wasn't sure if that was from the cold or nerves.

After an agonizing two minutes, Mark stepped forward and put his arms round me. He felt gorgeous, all warm, solid, and safe.

"Freezing, isn't it?" he said. "Let's keep each other warm."

I went rigid. This is it, I thought. Get ready to pucker.

He leaned his face toward me and I moved toward him and we banged noses.

"Oops," he laughed. Then he leaned in again and kissed me.

At first it was a shock, feeling soft lips on mine, and all I could think was what do I do with my hands? Run your fingers through his hair, I thought, remembering Nesta's advice. I reached up to the back of his head but my fingers got stuck. Gel. His hair was like glue. Oh no. And I still had my gum in my mouth. Gulp. I swallowed it.

Then I wondered what he'd done with his. He wasn't chewing anymore.

Then I got an attack of the giggles.

"What are you laughing at?" he said, looking taken aback.

"Er, I just swallowed my gum."

He looked at me mischievously. "So did I."

Then he did that staring at my mouth thing again and a thrill of anticipation ran through me. It's the strangest feeling in the world, like a sweet pain but just lovely.

"Come here," he said, pulling me close to him again and putting my arms round his waist. Then he kissed me properly. A lovely soft, deep kiss and this time our noses didn't bang. It felt perfect. Cosmic. And I wanted it to go on for ever.

"You're a good kisser," he said, pulling back after a few minutes.

"Thanks," I said, thinking Yippee! I'm a natural! Then I kissed him again. Practice makes perfect. That's going to be my new motto.

We must have stood there for ages. About half a dozen buses came and went and we were still snuggled up to each other, snogging away.

"So we should do this again, huh?" Mark asked, as another bus arrived at the stop.

I nodded.

"Oi! You getting on or not?" called the bus driver as the doors opened.

"Better had," I said to Mark, after checking my watch.

"I'll call you, then, Izzie Foster," he grinned, and off he went.

Cosmic Kisses
by Izzie Foster

I'm sending you cosmic kisses straight from my heart;
A planet collision won't tear us apart.
The distance between us is never too far;
I'll hitch a ride on a comet to get where you are.

In a moment a glance became a kiss,
In a heartbeat I knew my world had changed
For better, forever there is no other.
You're one in a million, of that I'm sure,
One in a million and I'm feeling so secure.

Cos I'm sending you cosmic kisses straight from my heart;
A planet collision won't tear us apart.
The distance between us is never too far;
I'll hitch a ride on a comet to get where you are.

Chapter 11

What Fresh Hell is This?

Last week of term. Teachers are relaxed, school is decorated for Christmas, with a huge tree in the hall, and generally everyone's in a good mood.

Except me. I'm Scrooge. Bah. Humbug. Pooh.

For our last English class, Mr. Johnson asked us all to take in our favorite book of the year and pick out a quote from it to read to the class.

Half the class brought in the Harry Potters, a few brought in one of Philip Pullman's trilogy, and Mary O'Connor brought a book called *Angus, Thongs, and Full-frontal Snogging* by someone called Louise Rennison. It's the confessions of a fourteen-year-old girl and it made everyone laugh (even me, despite my current mood) when Mary read out a section. I took my book by Dorothy Parker as I'd read all of it now.

"Izzie, let's hear your quote," said Mr. Johnson.

"It's only a short one," I said, "by Dorothy Parker."

Mr. Johnson raised an eyebrow. "Fine. Short is good," he said. "Go ahead."

"What fresh hell is this?" I read from my book.

Mr. Johnson looked taken aback. "Why did you choose that, Izzie?"

"Seemed appropriate," I said.

Mr. Johnson cracked up laughing. "Trust you to be different, Izzie."

It really did seem appropriate. Just as things were going swimmingly and I thought I was Snog Queen of North London, I'm into a whole new layer of torture in the boy/girl thing. Mark said he'd phone. And I was *so* sure he would this time. Positive. I mean, after all that fab snogging, how could he resist?

But he did. Resist, that is.

I'd wanted to phone him the minute I got home from our date just to hear his voice, but when I reported back to Nesta and Lucy, both of them said I mustn't. I have to give him space.

"But I have his number now," I said.

"I spoke to Tony about it," said Nesta, "and he agrees. Let Mark phone you."

Tony? She'd been discussing me with Tony?

"But surely now, now that we've *snogged* and everything. Surely it would be okay to get in touch?" I said to Lucy on my next call.

"Not really," she said. "I've been reading all about it in my *Men Are From Mars, Women Are From Venus* book. It says men fear intimacy and you mustn't pressure them or they run away into a cave or somewhere. You have to pretend that they're like a rubber band. Let them expand as far as they want, then thwang, they come back to you. Nesta agrees with me. Don't call him."

I couldn't *believe* it. Everyone's been discussing me. They've probably posted a site on the Internet: www.whatdoyouthinkIzzieshoulddonext?.com.

My *private* business.

What. Fresh. Hell. Is. This?

303

★ ★ ★

As the days went by and no call came, the temptation of having his home number was too much to resist.

One night, I rang his number (but not before dialling 141 first, so he wouldn't know it was me, I'm not *that* stupid) but all I got was an answering machine. I put the phone down quick.

The next night, I phoned again but chickened out before anyone picked up. Maybe Lucy and Nesta were right. I must be patient.

Patient. Patient. Patient. Not.

I rang again the next night. This time he picked up. I panicked when I heard his voice and slammed the phone down. He *was* there. He *could* have phoned me. What was he doing that was more important?

Maybe I'd said something that had annoyed him. I went over every bit of our conversation in my head, trying to see what it might have been. Was it because I'd caught him out about his mobile phone? What was it? Didn't he fancy me anymore? Or was it because now we'd snogged, he'd made the conquest and there was no more challenge?

Maybe, *oh no*, maybe he's met someone else.

The next night I planned exactly what I was going to say. Bright, breezy, casual.

I got the answering machine again.

"Er, hi . . . ," I said. "It's me. Just wondering what's happening."

I put the phone down. Just wondering what's happening? What's *that* supposed to mean? Happening as in on the planet? Or he might think I'm doing a heavy, like what's happening with *us*? I didn't mean it like *that*. It was meant to be cool, like durrh, what's happening, dude? He'll think I'm a dork. Then I remembered I'd said, "It's me." He might wonder who *me* is.

I called again.

"In case you're wondering who me is, it's me, Izzie."

Oh pants. My brilliant speech had gone. I put the phone down. Now he'd definitely think I'm desperate. Too eager. Oh why didn't he call me? What's *wrong* with me?

In RE on Friday, we had poor Miss Hartley again. It was our last day before the Christmas break and

305

everyone was in a giddier mood than usual.

By now I think she'd had enough of us and had come up with a way of making us shut up. Or so she thought.

"Okay, class, as we've been taking a look at religions and God over the last few weeks, I thought we'd do something practical for a change. We're going to look at prayer and meditation."

Brill, I thought. Just what I need. Something to still my mind and all the voices in my head driving me mad. Phone. Don't phone. Phone. Don't phone.

"First you have twenty minutes to write a prayer," she said. "Don't worry, we won't be reading them out loud. They're just for you."

Good, I thought. I have a few things I want to say to God. I got out my paper and started writing.

Dear God,

I know you're busy doing a million things, spinning planets, keeping it all in balance and all, but please could you spare me a moment?

But then, you're omniscient, so you probably know what I'm going to say anyway. So maybe I shouldn't waste your time.

306

But then again you live in eternity, so you have all the time in the world. God, it's confusing.

Anyway. Could you . . . ? Of course you could, you're omnipotent as well. Maybe I shouldn't ask for anything. You know best really. Maybe you should let me know what to pray for because sometimes I don't know.

PS Please could you make Mark phone me or else stop me feeling as mad as I do lately.

PPS Please could my bum stop growing now. I think it's big enough.

PPS Let there be peace and everybody be happy with no wars.

That is if that's all okay with you and doesn't interfere with your plans. Amen.

With love, Izzie Foster

After twenty minutes, Miss Hartley started up again.

"See, we are called human beings," she said, "but when do we ever *be*? We're always human *doings*, dashing about doing this and that. We never stop to just be."

I liked the sound of that. To be a human *being*. Cool.

307

"Anyway, as prayer is talking to God," she continued, "so meditation is listening. The idea is to find a quiet place within yourself and let the silence speak to you. Try to imagine that your mind is like the sea. On the surface are all the waves of thoughts, up and down they go. But if you go deep, deep, fathom deep into the sea, you'll find stillness no matter what's happening on the surface. It's the same with our minds—thoughts, feelings, all bounce about on the top, but if you go deeper, then there's stillness."

Perfect, I thought. It's a shame everyone gave Miss Hartley such a hard time. She talked a lot of sense to me. I couldn't wait to try it.

"Now different methods work for different people," said Miss Hartley. "I want you all to make yourselves comfortable and then close your eyes and focus inside. Some people find it helps to have something to concentrate on, like a mantra. Does anyone know what that is?"

I put up my hand. "It's a word, miss."

"That's right, Izzie, a popular one is *Om*. What you do is think about the word Om and say it over and over again, silently in your head. Right, let's begin. Eyes closed. Let your mind go still. Meditate."

I did as I was told and tried to make my mind go blank.

Thought 1: My mind is blank.

Thought 2: It can't be. You just thought that thought.

Thought 3: What thought?

Thought 4: The one about being blank. If you were really blank, you wouldn't think anything.

Thought 5: Okay. Try again.

Thought 6: I could kill Nesta for telling Tony my business.

Thought 7: Why oh *why* hasn't Mark phoned?

Thought 8: I've been an *idiot*. I shouldn't have called him.

Thought 9: But why *can't* a girl phone a boy?

Thought 10: This isn't helping at all. Okay. Be quiet again. Try the mantra. Om. Om. Om. Om. Om. Oh pooh. Pooh. Pooh. Got an itch.

Thought 11: How many people are there in my head? I think I may be going mad. Om, om, ommmmmmmm.

Thought 12: I think I'll just have a peek to

see how Lucy and Nesta are getting on.

I opened one eye and had a quick look around the room.

Most people were sitting quietly with their eyes shut. Candice Carter looked as though she was asleep as she was nodding forward and any minute now her head would crash into her desk.

I glanced over at Lucy. She had one eye open as well. Our eyes met and we giggled.

Then someone started at the back of the class.

"Kneedeep." A frog sound.

"Tweet twoo." Someone did an owl sound.

"Meeow." I did a cat.

"Mooooo." That was Lucy.

The whole class joined in with animal sounds until it sounded like a farmyard.

"Girls, *girls*!" cried Miss Hartley. "What on earth do you think you're doing?"

By now we were all laughing our heads off.

So much for Christmas meaning goodwill to all men and schoolgirls. We all got detention and had to stay in at lunch. *Detention.* On the last day of term? Bah. Humbug. But I was feeling marginally better. Perhaps prayer and meditation do work after all.

310

Then maybe so does a good laugh.

In detention, Miss Hartley gave us instructions to write out hymns.

"Now I'm going next door to the staff room," she said. "And if anyone speaks, there'll be another fifteen minutes' detention."

We all did a few lines, then I got bored so I wrote a song about boys not phoning. Then I had an idea. Miss Hartley said if anyone speaks we'd get another fifteen minutes. She didn't say anything about singing.

It is Christmas after all. I started up a hymn and soon everyone joined in.

> "*We Three Kings of Orient are,*
> *One in a taxi, one in a car,*
> *One on his scooter,*
> *Tooting his hooter,*
> *Following yonder star.*"

At last, term was over. A merry Christmas one and all.

Cut the Connection
by Izzie Foster

You think you're going out tonight, but you'll be
    staying in,
You'll sigh, you'll cry, you'll wonder why the phone will
    never ring.

You know he's playing games like every other boy,
But you don't care though you're aware he treats you
    like a toy.

He says he'll be there for you when all the chips are down,
But he's said the same to every girl in town.

He doesn't care you're in despair as tears burn in your
    eyes.
You'll sigh, you'll cry, you'll wonder why all he says is lies.

Cut the connection, turn off the phone, grab hold of life
    and you won't be alone.
Believe in yourself and no one else and you'll find that
    you have grown.
So cut the connection, turn off the phone, grab hold of
    life and you won't be alone.

Chapter 12

Happy
Eater

The next morning, Mum was up early and decorating our Christmas tree in her usual immaculate manner. White and silver, each bauble placed with precision and each necklace of tinsel making a perfect circle round the branches. What a contrast to the tree at Lucy's, I thought. Theirs looks like someone got out a box of colored balls and tinsel and threw it at the tree. Mum's does look nice though—elegant, very *Homes and Gardens*.

"Want to help?" asked Mum.

"Not really," I said, flopping on one of the sofas. I knew from past experience there wasn't much point. She had it very clear in her head what she wanted it to look like and I'd be bound to put a star or something in the wrong place.

"What's up, Izzie?" asked Mum, putting down the tinsel and sitting on the sofa opposite me.

"Nothing," I said.

"Oh, that again," she smiled. "Nothing always gets me down as well."

"It's just, I dunno, end of term and everything. . . ."

"You're usually ecstatic at the end of term."

"Yeah, but you know, I dunno. . . ."

Mum sat, looking at me with concern. "I do wish you'd talk to me, Izzie. Perhaps I can help."

No chance, I thought. No one can help.

"I just feel I think one thing then go and do another. Like I've been trying to eat healthily then I decided I could have the odd treat. Then found I was having *loads* of treats and only the odd healthy thing. I can't even get that right. I'm hopeless."

"You're only human, Iz," said Mum. "But it's not just that, is it?"

I shrugged.

"Is it that boy who called?" Mum asked.

"Who *didn't* call, you mean," I said. "And I don't know what I've done wrong."

"Probably nothing. Boys can be strange creatures. Call when you don't expect but never when you do."

"Tell me about it," I said. "There should be classes in all that *Men Are From Mars, Women Are From Venus* stuff. You know, we do all these classes in school but none of it really helps. Not with real life."

"I know," said Mum. "I remember when I was your age, or perhaps a little older, and just getting interested in boys. All the Latin, math, and literature wasn't much use when I had a crush on someone."

"That's just it. No one teaches you how to handle it. What to do if he phones, or doesn't? I seem to have got it all wrong."

Mum smiled. "Our school wasn't much help either. It was a very strict convent school. At least you get some sex education these days. I remember when I was about sixteen, we were all called into see the Mother Superior who explained about periods: 'It happens to everyone, even the Virgin Mary,' she said, as if that was supposed to make us feel better. Bit late, we all

315

thought—some girls had started years earlier."

I smiled. It was hard to imagine my mum as an innocent teenager, she always seemed so sure of herself.

"And another time," Mum continued, "we had to go and see Mother Superior again. This time it was handy hints for parties. 'If you're at a party,' she said, 'and the lights go out, stand in a corner and shout at the top of your voice, I'm a Catholic!'"

"How was that supposed to help?" I laughed.

"Exactly," said Mum. "Convent girls had a bit of a reputation back then so we all thought it was hilarious. Like every boy in the room would think, *Right lads, the convent girls are in the corner.* And then she told us that it was permissible to sit on a boy's knee but only if a book the thickness of a telephone directory was put on his lap."

By now, I had the giggles. "Poor you," I said.

At that moment, the doorbell rang. "I'll get that," grinned Mum.

She was back a few moments later with what looked like a large box of groceries.

All the yummy Christmas food, I thought to myself. How will I ever resist?

"Come into the kitchen," said Mum.

I followed her in, hoping she wasn't going to give me a lecture on eating what I was given.

"Ta-da!" said Mum with a flourish as she pulled out a pizza box. "Look what I've got."

What had come over her? She was acting really strange.

"Look," she beamed. "Organic pizza." She carried on pulling out a range of goodies from the box. "Muesli, you like that, don't you? Free-range eggs. Brown rice. Wholemeal bread. Mince pies *without* beef suet. Ingredients for a nut roast for Christmas day. But best of all, ice cream made with organic chocolate, no added preservatives. Get a spoon. Let's try it."

I looked in the box. She'd bought loads of fresh fruit and vegetables as well. "Mum, this is amazing!"

"I know. I never knew there was such a fantastic range of organic food around now. See in my day, healthy meant tasteless. Boring. But all the shops sell organic now. And it looks great. And after my little talk with Mr. Lovering . . ."

"Ah . . . so that's what it was about?"

Mum nodded and sat down at the kitchen table. "I've been so worried about you, Izzie, and your strange eating fads. Mr. Lovering gave me a few tips. And it's probably about time I changed my eating habits too. You were right. I do tend to eat on the go and grab whatever's to hand. From now on, we eat healthy in this house."

I went over to her and gave her a huge hug. "Thanks, Mum."

"No problem," she smiled and hugged me back. "Between us, we'll find a balance we're *both* happy with. We have fresh and healthy with our fruit and veg. But we can still have our treats."

"Great," I said. "So where's that organic ice cream you mentioned?"

Chapter 13

Sleepover Secrets

Later that day I went over to Nesta's. We were having a sleepover and were going to decide what to wear for the disco the next night.

I hadn't told them yet that I'd decided not to go.

Lucy was already there when I arrived. She was looking gorgeous in a short black skirt and a lilac crop top that she'd made. Plus she was wearing eye makeup *and* lipstick. A lot of effort for a night in, I thought, but of course to Lucy it was more than that. It was a sleepover in the same house as her boyfriend. Mmm. Should be interesting.

319

Nesta's mum and dad were going to a concert somewhere in town and popped in to say goodnight before they left.

"There's plenty of clean bedding in the spare bedroom for you and Lucy," said Mrs. Williams. "Anything you need Nesta will find for you."

"Thanks, Mrs. Williams," I said.

She looked great, all dressed up for the evening in a black velvet top and trousers. She's very glamorous, Nesta's mum.

"Don't stay up too late," said Mr. Williams, coming in behind her. He's Italian and very handsome, like a movie star. With parents as good-looking as they are, it's no wonder Nesta's such a stunner.

When they'd gone, Nesta brought up the important business of choosing our outfits.

"Fashion show, fashion show," said Nesta. "Mum got me a new dress. I can't wait to show you."

She disappeared for a few minutes then came back wearing a short silky silver dress with sequins round the neck. She looked fantastic, legs right up to her armpits, lucky thing.

"You look gorgeous," I said. "Shoes?"

"Dunno," said Nesta, holding up two pairs. "Black and strappy or these silver ones? Do you think they're a bit summery?"

"No, perfect for the dress," said Lucy. "Anyway, it'll be boiling once we start dancing. What about you, Iz? What are you going to wear?"

"Not going," I said.

Nesta and Lucy looked appalled.

"What do mean, not going?" said Nesta.

I shrugged. "Not in the mood."

"But I thought Mark said he was going," said Lucy.

"He did. But he hasn't phoned to ask if we can go together and I don't want to bump into him and go through all that stuff again. I realized that I've been doing all the running. No, if he wants to see me, he can make an effort."

"Quite right," said Nesta. "But I don't see why you should miss the disco because of him."

"You've got to come, Iz," said Lucy. "I thought you wanted to see King Noz play. You can ignore Mark if he's there. And we'll be there. Me and Nesta."

I wasn't convinced. "Anyway, I've got nothing to wear. What are you wearing, Lucy?"

"I made something specially," she said. Lucy is a real whiz on the sewing machine. She's made me and Nesta tops in the past and they're really fantastic and professional-looking. "You'll see tomorrow—it's a surprise."

"Please come, Izzie," begged Nesta. "It won't be the same without you and remember what we said about not letting a boy come between us."

I did remember. And she was right. I was letting it all get to me again. Running around, trying to bump into him accidentally-on-purpose hadn't worked. Neither had all that waiting by the phone. Maybe cutting off and hiding away wouldn't work either. Oh why couldn't it be simple? Then I thought, why *should* I let Mark ruin my Christmas? So he didn't phone. I'd had enough of letting him affect my moods.

"I suppose I could come for an hour or so," I said.

"Fantastic," said Lucy, then grinned mysteriously. "Anyway, I brought something for us to try tonight. Just up your street, Izzie, to get you in the party mood."

Half an hour later I found myself standing in front of the mirror in Nesta's bedroom while she and Lucy coached me from Nesta's bed.

"Again," demanded Lucy. "Again, but try to make it more convincing. Try and *feel* the words."

The mystery "something" was one of her mum's self-help books on affirmations.

"Just what you need," said Lucy before we got started. "You say the affirmations over and over again until your mind starts to believe what you're saying and it becomes real for you."

She and Nesta had pored through the book until finally they picked one for me.

"Say it again," said Lucy.

I straightened my shoulders. "I am full of joy," I intoned to the gloomy face looking back out at me. "I *am* full of joy."

Nesta shook her head. "Yeah, looks like it."

I slumped back on to the bed next to her. "Sorry, girls, I did try."

"Maybe it's not the right affirmation for you," said Lucy, going back to her book. It was called *Change Your Life by Changing Your Thoughts*.

"Okay, read me some of the others," I said. I knew she was trying to be helpful. The least I could do was go along with it.

"'I'm light, I'm bright, I've got it right.' Nah, that's not appropriate." She flicked the pages.

"Try another," said Nesta.

"'I'm slim and healthy, successful and wealthy,'" read Lucy.

"You do that one, Nesta," I said.

Nesta stood up and went to the mirror. "'I'm slim and healthy, successful and wealthy. I'm slim and healthy, successful and wealthy'. Is there one for what to do with big feet?"

I found a new page. "How about this one? 'To find repose I relax to my toes.' No? Okay. Pooh to that. Try 'I am feeling warm and mild, cradling my inner child.'"

"Oh yerghhhh. No thanks," cried Nesta. "Vomitous!"

"No, no, don't give up," I said, getting into it. "Oh, here's one for me. Perfect, in the self-esteem section. 'I am a perfect size, I have beautiful thighs.' Or 'Everyone knows, I love my nose.'"

Nesta and I cracked up laughing.

Lucy grabbed the book from me and flicked through the pages again. "How do you expect to change your lives when you keep laughing? Here, try this, Iz: 'I affirm that now I can, attract the perfect man.' Come on, stand up and say it to your reflection."

"Do I have to?"

"Yes."

I stood up. "'I affirm that now I can, attract the perfect man. I affirm that now I can, attract the perfect man. I affirm that now I can, attract the perfect man.'"

At that moment, Tony walked in.

"And here I am," he grinned, then went over to Lucy and gave her a peck on the cheek. "Coming into my room, Luce?"

Lucy went bright red like she always does when Tony's around, then stood up and meekly followed him out of the room.

"Hmmm," I said. "Should be interesting."

325

"He'd better not try anything," said Nesta. "Or I'll kill him."

Nesta and I spent the rest of the evening doing our nails and trying out makeup. Nesta painted her nails her usual dark purple and I did mine blue then put a layer of glitter on top.

"I affirm that now I can, attract the perfect man," we said over and over as we waited for our nails to dry. Then we did the affirmations again in all the accents we knew. Scottish, American, Indian, Irish, Cockney.

After that Nesta showed me a dance routine that she'd worked out for the disco tomorrow. Not to be outdone, I showed her a routine I used to do in Irish dancing when I was in middle school.

We collapsed on the sofa after fifteen minutes of mad Riverdancing and watched Nesta's video collection of *Friends* and soon it was half past eleven. There was still no sign of Lucy or Tony.

Nesta made up beds for me and Lucy in their spare room then went and banged on Tony's door. It was locked.

"Bedtime, Lucy. What are you doing in there?"

We heard stifled giggles then Tony's voice. "Nothing," he said.

"Well me and Izzie are going to bed and you'd better be out of there before Mum and Dad get home," said Nesta.

More stifled giggles.

"I hope she's all right in there," said Nesta, looking concerned.

"So do I," I said, then knocked again. "Lucy. *Lucy*. Sure you're okay?"

"Yeah, fine," called Lucy. "Be out in a minute."

"Or two," said Tony.

I settled down in my bed in the spare room and snuggled in to go to sleep. What a few weeks, I thought. At least things are better with Mum now. We had a really good time this morning and it reminded me she can be okay sometimes. And I suppose I have been a bit of a pain lately. Not my fault totally though, as Pluto *has* been going through an intense phase in my horoscope and it made everything seem complicated. I still think there's something to astrology no matter what

Lucy thinks. But I'll make it my New Year's resolution not to be so obsessive. And to be nicer to Mum. And I'll *even* try being nicer to Angus. He was really cool about the wedding photos the other night. It was his daughter's wedding album I'd supposedly ruined but he'd made it okay in the end.

As I went through my list of resolutions I started to nod off.

I was almost asleep when I heard the door open and Lucy crept in. I switched the light on and looked at my watch. It was past twelve.

"Sorry, did I wake you?" said Lucy.

"S'okay," I said sleepily, "You okay?"

Lucy sat on her bed and sighed. "Not really."

"What is it?" I said, sitting up. She looked close to tears.

"Promise you won't tell Nesta?"

"Promise," I said.

"Because if you do, she's bound to have a go at Tony and then he really will dump me."

"Why, what's he done?"

Lucy hesitated. "Wandering hands," she said finally.

"Oh."

"I don't know what to do, Iz. I'm happy just kissing. But he always wants to take it further. And I don't. I'm just not ready. He says it's because I'm too young for him and he knew this would happen. He says maybe it's best we don't see each other and then he can go out with someone more his own age."

"Oh, Lucy. . . ," I began.

"What he means is someone who won't say no to him. So what do I do? If I don't play along, I'll lose him and he's the first boy I've ever really liked. But if I do play along, who knows what will happen? Maybe he'll dump me anyway. Nesta's always said he loses interest when there's no challenge left."

"It's not fair," I said, suddenly feeling angry about Tony and about Mark. "Why should boys always be the ones who call the shots? It should be us. Tony's acting like a spoiled kid who can't have what he wants, and threatening you. Don't let him get away with it, Luce."

"You think?"

"Yeah. Take control. Dump *him*. He's making

you feel bad. Tell him *you* think it's not working out and you'll see how you feel about it all later but right now, you're not ready. You should feel you can trust Tony and you obviously don't. It should feel really special. You should be the one that chooses. You shouldn't feel forced into anything you don't want to do."

"Maybe we should see what my horoscope says about it," said Lucy.

"I thought you said you didn't believe in astrology," I said.

"I never," said Lucy. "I just thought you were taking it all too seriously, that's all."

"Well, I've realized a lot about all that in the last few weeks. Astrology can give you *some* clues as to what's happening, but you were right; you can't let it rule your life. It's what you make of it all in the end. You have to take control, make things happen or not. Choose."

"Even if I lose Tony?" said Lucy sadly.

"What are you losing?" I said, growing more and more sure as I spoke. "We have each other. You, me and Nesta. We should be the ones that choose or else we're all going to go through hell, up and down and round and round, trying to please boys but losing ourselves in the process."

I was only too aware that all I was saying applied to me as well as Lucy.

Lucy smiled weakly. "I suppose you're right. Boys, huh? Can't live with them, can't live without them."

"No, *can* live with them, *can* live without them. From now on, we call the shots."

Damaged Beauty
by Izzie Foster

He's frequently flawless but often unkind,
This fallen angel drives you out of your mind.
He's the devil beneath you and you ought to know,
He has to go, you really should know.

The gift you are given is kindness and grace
But each time you fall for a handsome young face.
Stop looking for light in love's gloomy rooms,
Throw open the windows
Let in the sun, you're number one.

Look into your heart, just make a start.
You really know, he has to go.

Put your damaged beauty in a silent place,
There's new love just waiting, get back in the race.
Shout out you're ready, cast into the pool,
This time remember, don't land a fool.

Look into your heart, make a brand new start.
Look into your heart, it's up to you.

Chapter 14

Girl Power

Mum dropped me off at the disco at about eight thirty the following night and already the place was buzzing with a party atmosphere. People were up and dancing, Robbie Williams was blaring out through large speakers on either side of the hall, and Mrs. Allen and Mr. Johnson, wearing daft Santa hats, were standing by the drinks table. Probably on the lookout for boys adding vodka like they did last year. Half the school was out of their skulls by midnight and the other half was sick all over the place. It was a riot when parents arrived to pick people up, with the teachers getting the tellings off for a change.

I had a quick glance round the hall before taking my coat to the cloakroom. The place was unrecognizable as the usual hall where we had assembly. The Christmas tree had been moved up on to the stage where equipment had been set up for the band, and fairy lights were strung all along the walls.

I put my coat away then went into a cubicle to change. I'd been over to see Dad and Anna this morning and was having a moan about having nothing to wear for the disco.

"Well, I was going to give you this for Christmas, but if you really want, you could have it now," said Dad. "Probably best you pick something you want yourself."

Then he handed me a fifty-pound note.

I gave him a huge hug then dashed out to Primrose Hill. The black velvet dress I'd seen weeks ago was still in the window and had been reduced in a Christmas sale. It fit perfectly, really tight and made me look tall and slim. I was a bit worried Mum wouldn't let me wear it tonight as it's backless and a bit low at the front, but she agreed on condition I wore a little top underneath. Which of course I did.

In the cubicle, I took off the little top and put it in my bag, then I put on a black choker I'd borrowed from Mum's jewelry box. I went and checked my appearance in the mirror and applied a bit of red lipstick then made my way into the main hall and soon found Nesta.

"This place is poser's heaven," I said, looking at all our class swanning about in their posh party frocks.

"I know," said Nesta. "Great, isn't it? Hey, you look gorgeous. Great dress. Really sophisticated."

"Thanks," I said. "So do you."

Nesta looked beautiful in her sparkly silver dress and her hair like black silk right down to her waist. She'd soon get off with someone and Lucy, of course, would be with Tony. I hoped I wasn't going to be the only one on my own.

"Have you seen Jade Wilcocks?" said Nesta. "She's got a ton of makeup on. I saw her just now in the corridor, all over some boy."

"She's not the only one. On the way from the cloakroom, I saw half a dozen couples having snogathons."

"It's going to be a good party," grinned Nesta. "What time's the band on?"

"Soon I think," I said, looking at my watch. "Where's Lucy?"

"Putting some silver glitter through her hair in the cloakroom," she said. "She looks amazing. And you know she's dumped Tony?"

"You're kidding. When?"

"This morning after you'd gone."

"Is she okay?"

"Yeah," said Nesta. "She's fine. Great. It's hysterical. It's Tony who's not. He couldn't believe it even though she did it really nicely. She spent ages talking to him. But he's never been dumped before. He's always been the dumper. He's gone into shock, I think. He was lolling about all morning, saying Lucy was special, not like other girls. He's phoned her about ten times today."

"Hiya," said Lucy, coming to join us.

"Wow," I said. "You look fab. Like a Christmas fairy."

Lucy had a short white hipster skirt on with a thin diamante belt round her waist and a short white top with tiny bootlace straps that criss-crossed round her back.

"Did you make the top?" I asked.

Lucy nodded. "Like it? I made it last week. I read in a mag that if you show off your back no one will notice you haven't got any boobs."

I laughed. Having a flat chest was Lucy's big hang-up, but she needn't worry. She looked fantastic.

"It looks great," said Nesta.

"But tell me about Tony," I said. "What happened?"

Lucy grinned. "It didn't feel right anymore."

I couldn't believe it. She was being so cool.

"But you really liked him!"

"I know, but after last night, I realized you were right. I was getting more and more miserable trying to be and do what he wanted. I want it to feel really special and I'm just not sure of him yet. Anyway, it *should* be us girls that call the shots. And I decided I just wasn't ready." She looked anxiously at Nesta, but she was busy giving some boy the eye. "After last night, I thought, I don't want to be poor little Lucy, dumped

337

because she's too young. I decided to turn the tables."

"Good for you, Luce," I said. "I think you're really brave. And looking like this, you'll get off with someone else really easily."

Just at that moment, the lights went down and a hush fell over the hall. I looked up at the stage and saw a boy go over to the main mike and pick up a guitar.

He looked familiar. Oh no. It was Ben. Oh *no*, I thought, he's going to play more of his appalling songs from the shows. He'll look a right prat in front of this lot. He must be the warm-up act to King Noz. I wondered what idiot booked him.

At that moment, he looked down and caught my eye and gave me a wave. I waved back nervously. Oh dear. Now everyone would know that I know him and it's going to be so embarrassing when he starts playing.

"And now," said the DJ. "Let's hear a big round of applause for King Noz."

What? I thought. It *can't* be.

Three other boys walked out on the stage to

join Ben and took their places, one at the keyboards, and the other two on guitar. Then they started playing and Ben started singing. He was amazing. *They* were amazing. Totally amazing. Everyone went mad, clapping and cheering then manic dancing in time to the music.

My jaw must have dropped open because Lucy turned to me.

"What's the matter, Iz?"

"I *know* him," I stuttered. "That's Ben up there."

"I know. He comes to Dad for lessons. He's brilliant, isn't he?"

"But he's the guy from the wedding . . . ," I said. I couldn't get my head round it. The same Ben that had looked so awkward playing at the wedding was now up on stage giving it all he'd got and looking mucho cute. Everyone was up on their feet, dancing away. The audience loved them.

After a couple of fast numbers, Ben took the mike. "And now we're going to slow it down a bit," he said. He swapped places with the keyboard player and they began to play again.

Girls paired off with boys to slow dance as Ben

sang a lovely ballad. He was really good. A strong clear voice. I couldn't believe I'd been such a nerd. I should have realized. But how was I to know that *he* was King Noz?

As the band upped the pace again Nesta disappeared into the throng with some boy who'd asked her to dance. I watched her doing the routine she'd shown me the night before. Everyone was watching her but some of the girls didn't seem too happy about the way their boyfriends were ogling.

Lucy put her hand on my arm. "Don't look now. Mark's just arrived."

I quickly turned away but too late, he'd seen me and was walking toward me, smiling.

"Izzie," he said, putting his arm round me. "You look fantastic. I was hoping you'd be here. Wanna dance?"

I couldn't believe his cheek. Hoping I'd be there. Why didn't he phone and make sure?

"No, thanks," I said. "I want to listen to the band."

He looked taken aback. Actually I did want

to listen to the band but I also wasn't going to fall into his arms the minute he arrived.

"Maybe later," I said.

"Oh, okay," he said. "I'll go and get a drink, then. Want anything?"

"No, thanks," I said, turning back to the stage as he walked off looking puzzled.

"Good for you, Iz," said Lucy.

I took a deep breath. I wasn't feeling as confident as I may have looked. Mark was still cute but I had made a promise to myself that I wasn't going to be such a pushover in future.

"Anyway, I think Ben likes you," said Lucy, pointing at the stage.

I turned to look at him and sure enough, he was looking at me as he sang the words of a song.

"Do you think?"

"I do," said Lucy. "He's really nice, you know. I've talked to him when he's been waiting for lessons at home sometimes. He thinks about stuff like you do. I reckon you'd get on."

I spent the next half hour standing by the wall, listening to the set King Noz played.

"*There's a secret there for learning,*" Ben sang. "*A journey to be taken in my search for truth. Krishna, Buddha, Gandhi, Christ, all bid me follow but which road offers proof? While I seek the smiles of angels, darkness calls my soul, Jesus help me fight the fight, Buddha lead me to the light.*"

Then he went into a rap chorus, "*Omnipresent, omni-where? I look for God but is he there? Heaven, hell, a state of mind. The way is lost for our mankind.*"

As I listened to the lyrics I thought, Lucy's right, I would get on with Ben. He seems to be asking all the same questions as me. Even if we didn't get off with each other, we obviously had a lot we could talk about. I'd never even given him a second glance. Not considered him for a moment. But watching him up there playing, I had to admit I was impressed. Very impressed.

When the band had finished playing, the DJ started up the disco again and I could see Ben heading toward me.

"You were fantastic," I said. "Really brilliant."

He looked pleased. "Thanks. Bit of a change from songs from the shows."

342

"A bit," I smiled, thinking he had really nice blue eyes with thick black lashes behind his little round glasses.

"My brother made me get up at that wedding. I felt a right prat. But it was his wedding and that's what he wanted."

"Right," I said, not wanting to admit that I'd put him in a box and labeled it naff.

"Have you been playing long?" I asked.

"About four years. Lot to learn still, that's why I'm taking lessons. In fact there was something I wanted to ask you about."

Suddenly he looked embarrassed.

"What?" I asked.

"Well, I know I shouldn't have looked and I know I should have asked . . ."

"What are you on about?" I asked.

"Well, you know that day I saw you at Lucy's house? When I was there for my lesson?"

"Yeah?"

"Well, after the lesson Mr. Lovering went off to find some CDs for me and I was just sat there waiting . . ."

"And?"

"And I saw this book on the piano. It had your name on it."

"Oh no," I said. "Oh *no*. You didn't look, did you?"

He nodded, "I did. I didn't mean to. . . ."

"I never show anybody my lyrics, not *anybody*." I felt awful. He'd laugh at me just as I've decided I like him. And his songs are so good, he must think mine are awful.

"I'm sorry," he continued. "As I said, I didn't mean to look, not for long, but I really liked what I read. Did you write all those songs yourself?"

I nodded.

"They're really good, Izzie. In fact, I wanted to ask you . . . have you put any of them to music yet?"

I shook my head.

"Well, what do you think about us getting together sometime and working on them?"

"Honestly?" I asked. I couldn't think of anything I'd like better.

We spent the next half-hour talking about bands we liked and who we didn't, when we were interrupted by Mark.

"Dance?" he said, giving Ben a filthy look.

I was feeling so pleased with the way everything was turning out, I accepted. As I danced with Mark I could see Ben watching me.

Mmm, I thought. Could be interesting.

"So," said Mark. "Want to go out next week?"

I shrugged. "Maybe. I don't know what I'm doing yet."

Again, he looked totally taken aback. "Oh well, phone me when you do," he said.

"Yeah," I said, enjoying the effect I was having on him.

He leaned close to me and whispered, "Because I really like you, Izzie."

"Yeah," I said. "Whatever."

He looked completely bemused. It was hysterical.

"Anyway, maybe catch you later," I said. "Got to go. I came with my friends. Got to find them."

I left him standing in the middle of the dance floor with his mouth hanging open. That'll teach you, I thought. You could have come with me, *if* you'd bothered to phone.

The rest of the disco was brilliant. Nesta, in her usual style of fancying older boys, got off with some Sixth Former and was last seen in the cafeteria snogging for Britain.

Then Tony turned up.

"I have to speak to you," he said urgently. "About Lucy."

"What about Lucy?" I asked, doing my best innocent face.

"Tell me what to do. You're one of her best mates. How can I get her back?"

"What does Nesta say?"

Tony laughed. "Nesta? Nesta's told me from the beginning to keep away from Lucy. But I don't want to. I *really* like her."

"She's over there," I said, pointing out Lucy to him. She was slow dancing with a good-looking boy who looked really keen.

Tony's face dropped. "I've blown it, haven't I?"

"Maybe," I said. "Maybe not. You never know until you've tried."

What an evening, I thought, as Tony went on to the dance floor to cut in on Lucy. Boys. Strange species. Don't want you when you want them and do want you when you're not interested. But I'm learning. Fast.

As the party started to wind down, I went to go and get my coat and Ben caught up with me.

"Izzie," he said. "Can I phone you? You know, about getting together to do some songs?"

I was about to give him my number when I stopped and laughed.

"What's so funny?" asked Ben.

"Nothing," I said, getting out my pen. "I'd love to do some songs with you. But you give me *your* number. *I'll* call you."

Mates, Dates, and Designer Divas

Chapter 1

Love Train

"Nesta, is that you?" said Lucy's voice at the other end of the phone. "You sound weird. Where are you?"

"In the loo, on the train from *hell*," I groaned.

I could hear her laughing. Why do people always think it's funny when my life turns into total disaster?

"No, *seriously*. It's a nightmare. We're stuck in the middle of nowhere. I should have been home hours ago."

"Sounds like you're in a bucket," said Lucy. "The phone's all echoey. Anyway, what are you doing in the loo? You're not stuck in there, are you?" She started laughing again.

"I am in here," I said primly, "to talk on my

mobile without the whole car listening in and hopefully to get some sympathy from someone who's *supposed* to be one of my best friends."

"I *am* sorry, Nesta. It'll get going again soon."

"What are you doing?"

"Watching telly. There's a repeat of *Dawson's Creek* on. Going to Izzie's later."

"Lucky thing. I wish I was there. I can't bear this much longer. I'm bored out of my mind."

"Haven't you got a book with you?"

"Read it."

"Magazine?"

"Read it."

"Call Izzie."

"She's out."

"Then go and chat to one of the passengers. That'll make the time go faster."

"Don't even go there. I've got the Family of Satan sitting behind me. Remind me never to have kids."

"I thought you liked kids?"

"Yeah. But I couldn't eat a whole one. Honestly, it's awful. This little boy behind me is driving me bonkers. Banging on my seat, arguing with his sister, playing some irritating computer game that makes a noise like a police siren. And his parents are just sitting there like he's the most adorable creature ever. I wish they'd tell him to zip it."

"So move. It's Saturday. Go into weekend first and pay the extra. Have you got enough?"

"Yeah. I moved already. Dad gave me the extra. But because it's Easter, the train's massively over-booked and there aren't enough seats, so they've moved *everyone* into first class. *And* the heating's broken. *And* there's no buffet car! I can't even get a Coke. Stop laughing. I don't see what's so funny."

"Sorry, Nesta," said Lucy. "It's just the thought of you hiding in the loo. You get to go to *all* the trendiest places."

"Yeah right. Hysterical. Phworr. It smells awful in here; I think someone's been having a cigarette. Just a mo, I'm going to spray."

I got out my CK1 and squirted into the air. "That's better. I'm *sooooo* bored, Lucy. Entertain me."

"Go and sit back down and try some of that meditation we did at school."

353

"Oh, gimme a break. That's Izzie's thing."

"So when will you be back?"

"Dunno. Never, by the looks of it. I'm clearly being punished. I've died and gone to hell and am going to be stuck on this train with all these mad people for eternity."

"You're such a drama queen, Nesta. You'll be back before you know it."

"I wish. Dad dropped me at Manchester at one o'clock and the journey's supposed to take *three* hours. We've already been on the train that long. And now we appear to have broken down. . . . Though there've been no announcements to tell us what's going on. What shall I do?"

"Er, I don't know. Put some makeup on."

"Good idea." I got out my makeup bag and began to put on some lipstick. "Oh, hold on a mo," I said as the train suddenly lurched forward causing me to smear my lipstick in a gash up my cheek. "Oops. I think we're off. Yep. We're moving again . . . Lucy, Lucy . . . ?"

My mobile cut out, so I checked my appearance in the mirror and gave my hair a quick brush. I wondered if I should spend some more time in

354

there plaiting it. Or maybe I should leave it loose. There was a boy who'd been checking me out the whole journey. He was quite good-looking. People say my hair's one of my best features: It's long right down to my waist. I decided I'd leave it loose. I wanted to look good for when Boy In The Corner made his move. It had to be only a matter of time.

Passengers were staring at me as I made my way back down the car. I'm used to it by now as people always look at me. Izzie says it's because I stand out in a crowd as *très* good-looking, but sometimes I think it's also because they can't make out where I'm from. I can see their brains are going tick-tick-tick trying to work out what nationality I am. Actually my dad's Italian and my mum's Jamaican. Sometimes I tell people I'm Jamalian or Italaican. That confuses them.

Being hard to identify comes in useful some days, though, like when I'm out with Lucy and Izzie and we're in a mad mood. We pretend that we're foreign students. I pretend I'm Spanish or Indian. I could be either. Lucy pretends to be Swedish, as she's got blond hair and high cheekbones and can do a really good accent. And Izzie, for some reason, always pretends to be Norwegian, though with her dark coloring and beautiful eyes she's a typical Corrs-type Irish colleen.

As I squeezed past various irate people sitting in the corridor on their suitcases, an announcement came over the loudspeaker.

"We apologize for the delay and lack of seats, but we are on our way again and will be arriving in Birmingham in a few minutes. However, due to a problem with the engine, we will be stationed there while the engineers rectify it. We will be arriving at Euston approximately two hours later than scheduled."

A moan went through the train, then a chorus of voices as people got out their mobile phones and began dialing.

"Martha, I'm outside Birmingham. Dunno what time we'll be back. I'll get a taxi."

"Tom. I'll be late as the train's stuck. I'll call when we're a bit closer."

"Gina. Damn train's late again. Call you later."

On and on it went through every car.

Then I realized I couldn't find my seat. I checked the other passengers, thinking that maybe I was in the wrong car. But no, there was the Family of Satan. Cute Boy In The Corner. Oh no. Someone was in my seat. An old dear with white hair and glasses. She'd made herself comfortable with a flask of tea and an egg sandwich. I couldn't possibly ask her to move. It would be mean.

I looked around the car, but there weren't any other seats. Oh well, I'll just have to stand, I thought. For two and a half hours. Whoopee. Not.

But the gods decided to take pity. A few minutes later, we pulled into Birmingham and, hallelujah, the man opposite Cute Boy got up to go. The boy looked at me and nodded his chin at the seat opposite him. Fabola, I thought, and made my way over.

As the train lurched to a stop, I lost my balance. Given the day I was having, the next bit seemed inevitable.

"Hi," grinned Cute Boy as I fell straight into his lap. "Actually, I was thinking of the seat opposite. But this is okay by me."

I could tell he expected me to leap up all

357

embarrassed, so I decided to outcool him. I stayed where I was for a moment like I was really comfortable and gave him one of my best seduction looks—the one with a smile and one raised eyebrow.

Then I got up.

"Yeah. Maybe later," I said as I took the seat opposite.

"Oh. Okay. Right. No prob," he said, looking flustered. "Er, I'm Simon. Hi."

"It was so romantic," I said to the girls later that day as I helped myself to a salt-and-vinegar Pringle round at Izzie's. "Like in a film. I just *fell* into his lap. If anyone ever makes our story, I think I'd like that guy who plays Angel on *Buffy* to play his part."

We were in Izzie's bedroom. The train had eventually got into London at six thirty. After Mum had picked me up and I'd dropped off my stuff, I begged her to let me go out. This was urgento. Not only had I not seen the girls for three whole days, but I had *so* much to tell them.

"Your story! But you've only just met him," said Lucy, taking a swig of Coke.

"And knowing you," said Izzie, "it was, like, fall accidentally on purpose."

"It was not," I said. "The train lurched."

Izzie pulled one of her yeah-right faces, but Lucy looked all ears, she's such a romantic herself.

"So tell us all about it," she said, settling on to the purple beanbag on Izzie's floor.

"Well, the rest of the journey whizzed by. We talked nonstop. Before we knew it, we were pulling into Euston. . . ."

"What's his name?" asked Lucy.

"Simon Peddington Lee. He lives in Holland Park and he's eighteen."

"What does he look like?" asked Izzie.

"Tall, dark, and handsome. Lovely brown eyes."

"What was he doing on the train?"

"He'd been up to have a look at Saint Andrews University, to see if he'd like to go there after A levels. I've decided I might go there as well after school. It really is *the* place now."

"That's where Prince William goes, isn't it?" said Lucy. "He'll be finished by the time you get there."

"Does Simon know him?" asked Izzie.

"No. But one of his cousins does. From Eton."

"Does Simon go to Eton?" asked Lucy.

"No, he goes to some other private school. I forget the name. In Hampshire somewhere. He's a boarder."

"So he's a posh boy?" said Izzie, then put on a silly snobby voice. "Peddington Lee."

"He's not snobby or stuck-up or anything," I said, ignoring her. "I told him I went to a private school as well."

"But, Nesta," said Lucy, "that's a lie."

"No, it isn't," I laughed. "Our school *is* open to the public. And I think I may change my name— you know, make it hyphenated as well. It could be Nesta Costello-Williams by using my dad's then my mum's name. Or should it be Nesta Williams-Costello?"

"Oh, don't even go there," said Izzie. "Just be yourself. Nesta Williams sounds just fine."

"Nesta Top Toff Totty," giggled Lucy.

"I thought you'd be pleased for me," I said, feeling hurt. "I've met someone I really like."

"I *am* pleased," said Lucy. "But are you sure you want to get involved with a boy who might be going away soon?"

360

"Not until autumn. It's only April. Then if we still like each other I can join him up in Scotland when I finish school."

"I thought you wanted to be an actress," said Izzie. "I bet they don't do drama at Saint Andrews."

I hadn't thought of that. "They might. And anyway, I think it's best to keep all your options open at our age."

Izzie burst out laughing. "You sound like my mum, Nesta. Did he ask to see you again?"

"Yeah. We're going riding."

"Riding! As in horses?"

"Yeah."

"Doh. Have you ever actually been on a horse?"

"No, but I'm sure I'll soon get the hang of it."

Lucy and Izzie exchanged worried looks.

"You did tell him you've never ridden, didn't you?" said Lucy.

"Course not. It can't be that difficult."

"Uhh, Nesta . . . ," Lucy started.

"No," interrupted Izzie. "She's going to have to find out for herself. . . ."

Nesta's Diary

Guess what? *J'ai un* boyfriend *nouveau. Il s'appelle* Simon Peddington Lee and he's lush. He's already sent me a text message. :-» Which means "a huge smile." And BCNU.

I sent him back one ☺)))) Then CUL8R.

I wish I could tell the future, as I think he may be The One. I haven't fancied anyone for ages. And I've never been in love. Not properly. He seems more grown up than all the rejects I've been out with in the last year and has nice legs, really long, and a *très* snoggable mouth.

Rejects since I came to *Londres*:

Robin: (1 week going out last Sept) Sweet but boring. Stares off into space in what he hopes is a cool way but I think makes him look like a right plonker.

Michael: (2 dates in October) A user and a bad snogger who likes to bite.

Nick: (1 date in December) Disgusting. Uses too much hair gel. Has strange habit of trying to lick girls' ears out. Not pleasant.

Steve: (Jan) Quite liked him but was juvenile and smaller than me.

Alan: (3 weeks in Feb) Half and half. He said he wants to be a doctor and tried to put his hands down my jumper to examine any problems. Pathetic.

My brother Tony has another new girlfriend and apparently he dislocated his jaw after a snogging session. How did he manage that? I don't know whether to tell Lucy or not. Must check out state of play with them now as they were an item last year. Girls always fancy Tone but he was v. hung up on Lucy.

Izzie's having a bit of a SOHF (sense of humor failure). I don't know why, as she is going out with Ben the lead singer from King Noz and is happier than ever.

Am v. v. tired. ZZZZzzzz

Chapter 2

Hard Times

Mum's been kind of quiet since I got back from Manchester. She usually sings in the morning. Badly, I have to say, but I don't tell her that. But today, she's sitting in the kitchen, reading the morning paper and not looking her usual self at all.

I pulled up a stool next to her at the breakfast bar. "Are you missing Dad?"

"Sure," she said. "Course I miss him, but I'm used to him working away. Why do you ask?"

I gave her my Inspector Morse you-don't-fool-me look. "You seem a bit low. Was it because I raced off to see Lucy and Iz last night and didn't stay to catch up with you?"

Mum laughed. "No, honey. I'm kind of used to that as well."

"Okay, then. Sure you're okay?"

"Sure," she smiled.

"Okay. Then can I have horse-riding lessons?"

"Horse-riding? Whatever for? You've never shown any interest in horses before."

At that moment my brother, Tony, trudged in. His hair was sticking up all over the place, and he was still wearing his robe and yawning sleepily. "Yeah. What do you want horse-riding lessons for? Who do you want to impress now?"

"Unlike some people present," I said, "I don't have to impress."

"Some boy, I expect," continued Tony.

"Actually I did meet a boy on the train back yesterday. . . ."

"I knew it," said Tony as he stuck his head in the fridge.

"Well, he's invited me to go riding," I said, trying to resist the urge to push the rest of Tony into the fridge and close the door behind him.

"Where?" said Mum.

"Somewhere down near Hyde Park. Kensington, I think. He gave me the address. I've got it upstairs."

"When?" said Tony, coming back out of the fridge with orange juice and croissants.

"Tomorrow."

Tony plastered his croissant with raspberry jam, then sat at the bar. "And you were like, going to learn how to ride in one afternoon? Get real."

I stuck my tongue out at him. "Thought you'd dislocated your jaw from snogging too much. How are you even going to chew?"

"Same way you're going to horse-ride," he said, grimacing as he took a bite. "With difficulty. Anyway, it's not dislocated. Just a bit sore."

"Serves you right. I can go, can't I, Mum?" I said. "Horse-riding?"

"Actually," said Mum, "I've been wanting to talk to both of you about something. I was going to wait until your dad was back, but this is as good a time as any."

Oh *NO*, I thought. Mum and Dad are splitting up. Please *no*. I remember Izzie telling Lucy and I about when her parents separated. It started exactly the same way. She noticed her mum was unhappy. Her dad hadn't been around for days. Then the conversation, "I've been

366

wanting to talk to you about something."

"No. *NO!*" I cried. "Have you tried Relate? Marriage counseling? You *mustn't* just give up. You have to work at relationships."

Mum and Tony stared at me as though I was mad.

"What are you going on about, Nesta?" said Mum.

"Divorce. Please, *please*, for me and Tony, give it another try."

Mum cracked up laughing. "I'm not going to get divorced, Nesta. I'm very happy with your father."

"So what is it, then?"

Mum's expression grew serious again. "Work. My contract is up for renewal at the beginning of next month and there's been talk of bringing in new blood at the station."

Tony thumped the breakfast bar angrily. "New as in younger?"

Mum nodded.

"Pathetic," said Tony. "How can they? You're the face of the evening news. They *can't* replace you."

Mum put her hand over Tony's. "Oh yes they can, honey. It happens all the time. Producers want

367

better ratings—they're always looking for ways to bring in more viewers."

"Well, I don't think it helps to get rid of some of their best people. You read the news really well," said Tony.

Mum smiled at him. "Thanks, kid. You wanna be my agent?"

"It wouldn't be the same if you didn't do the news," I said. "It's like, the next best thing to you being at home when I get back from school. I always switch on the telly when I'm having my tea and there you are in the corner to say hello to."

"When will you know?" asked Tony.

"In the next few weeks. But this is what I wanted to talk to you about. It means tightening the purse strings. We're going to have to economize."

"We'll be all right," I said. "Dad earns loads of money. And he's still working."

"That's why I was going to wait until he was here," said Mum. "You're right, he does earn good money *when* he's working. But, don't forget, he's a *freelance* director. That means if he's working, he gets paid. If he's not, he doesn't. And we did rather overextend ourselves buying this flat."

"But why is it different now?" I asked.

"Because *my* job is insecure, that's what I'm trying to tell you. He finishes his film in Manchester in the next few weeks, and so far he hasn't got anything else lined up. See, it didn't matter in the past as my regular income helped us ride those times. But now . . ."

"OhmyGod," I groaned. "We're *poor*. Oh, God."

My mind was swimming with images. *Poor? No* pocket money. *No* trips out to the movies. *No* more McDonald's. I'd be the one out in the rain with my nose pressed up against the window watching rich people in nice clothes eat nourishing meals in the warm. And I'd be outside in rags, cold . . . hungry . . .

Mum laughed again. "We're not poor yet, Nesta. We still have a roof over our heads. And food to eat. All I'm saying is that until things are more certain, there won't be any money for extras."

"So no horse-riding lessons?"

"Exactly. No horse-riding lessons," said Mum.

"But I can go and meet Simon?"

369

"As long as you're home for supper. Yes, you can go and meet this Simon."

"But won't you need money to go and meet Simon?" said Tony, trying to stir it as usual.

"No I won't, smartypants," I replied. "He's known the lady that owns the stables all his life. He told me all about her on the train. He teaches some of the young kids that go there at the weekend. In exchange, she lets him and his friends ride whenever they like. For free. So there."

"So why did you want horse-riding lessons if he could teach you?" asked Tony, doing one of his all-knowing smug faces. "Oh I see, you wanted to show off, like, yeah, I'm Nesta Williams and I've been riding all my life. . . ."

"I did not."

"Did."

"Didn't."

"Did."

"When will you two grow up?" asked Mum, putting her hands over her ears.

Chapter 3

Me and Robert Redford

I'd arranged to meet Simon at High Street Kensington tube as he said it was near the stables. I was really looking forward to it—a whole afternoon on my own with him. It would be a chance to get to know him better. And it wouldn't cost anything.

I got to Kensington station, ran up the stairs, past Prêt à Manger and the Sock Shop in the tube entrance, then out to the High Street—and there my heart sank. Simon was waiting with two tall, slim, blond girls. They were about the same age as me, maybe a year older, and both were slouching against the rails outside the station doing that pouty I'm-so-bored-*Vogue*-model look. They looked like experienced riders with their hair tied back, jodhpurs, and riding boots.

Both of them looked at me as if I was an alien.

I was wearing my Levis, Nike trainers, and my psycho babe top. It's really cool. On the front it has a picture of a trendy girl with psychedelic eyes that swirl about. On the back, is written "All stressed out and no one to choke."

"This is my sister, Tanya," said Simon. "And this is her friend, Cressida."

Tanya smiled, but Cressida did a sort of Posh Spice grimace and looked disdainfully at my T-shirt.

"So you're Nesta?" she drawled.

"The one and only," I grinned. "Hi."

Tanya looked nice, with an open friendly face like Simon's. Cressida, on the other hand, looked as though she had a bad smell under her nose. Shame, because she would have been quite pretty otherwise.

As we set off in the direction of the park, I felt in a really good mood. It was a lovely spring day, and the daffs and tulips were out in the park. And I was with Simon.

Cressida and Tanya trailed along beside us talking into their mobile phones and I could see Cressida watching my every move. When Simon reached out and took my hand, she looked positively horrified.

"You *did* say you'd ridden before, didn't you?" asked Simon.

"Yeah, I did, but to be honest, no, I haven't. I thought I could wing it. It can't be that hard, surely? You just get on the horse. Check your rear mirror and pull out into oncoming traffic."

Simon cracked up. "No prob. I'll show you. And actually, you're not that far from the truth. We do have to take the horses a short distance on the road from the stables to the park."

"On the road!" I wasn't sure I liked the sound of that. "But what about traffic?"

"Don't worry, the horses are used to the cars and most motorists know to go slow round here. And we'll find you a nice horse. One who won't give you a hard time."

"Oh, okay. Cool," I said, but I was beginning to feel a bit nervous.

"You mean you've *never* been on a horse *ever?*" sneered Cressida, catching us up.

I was about to say, "You. Off my planet," but I bit my tongue and shook my head in response to her question. I've met her type before and have little time for them, but she was a friend of Simon's and I didn't want to embarrass him.

The stables were tucked away from the main road down a cobbled mews. On the corner was a small stable block with horses looking out over the individual doors.

"Amazing to find this here," I said. "I never even knew you could ride in London. I thought you had to go to Devon or Cornwall."

"I know. Good, isn't it?" said Tanya. "We've been coming here since we were little, but loads of people don't know it's here."

"There's been riding in Hyde Park for three hundred years, so it's not new," said Simon.

"Wow. Three hundred years," I said. "Impressive."

Cressida did her snooty look for the nth time that day. "I prefer to ride in Richmond," she said. "My cousin has stables there and that's where all the real riders go. One's so aware that one's in town here, whereas in Richmond it's more coun-trified."

I felt like saying, Why don't you bog off there, then? (Or rather, in her language, why doesn't one bog orf there, then? Like yah spiffy bonce.) But again I bit my tongue.

A lady came out of what looked like an office and waved hello.

"The lady with the blond hair, that's the one I told you about, Mrs. Creighton," said Simon, waving back. "She'll sort you out a good horse. I'll just go and have a word. Come on, Tanya, you can help me saddle up."

They strode off, leaving me with Sour Puss.

"Aren't you going to change?" she asked.

"No. People tend to like me the way I am," I grinned.

"But you're not riding like *that*, are you?"

"Sure," I said. "Why not?"

"Well, it's not standard," said Cressida.

I glared at her. "And your point is?"

We stood there for a while in uncomfortable silence. I wished Lucy and Izzie were there, then we'd all have been beginners together and had a laugh.

Tanya came forward and gave me a hard riding hat. "Put this on, Nesta. You'll have to wear a hat in case you fall. It'll protect your head."

I put on the hat and turned to see Simon leading a chestnut brown horse with a white star on his forehead toward us.

"Here we go," he grinned. "Mrs. Creighton says this is the boy for you."

Cressida snorted with laughter. "Heddie! You're putting Nesta on Heddie! But he's *ancient*!"

"It's her first time," said Simon, patting Heddie on the neck. "We don't want to put her on a horse that will take off with her."

Cressida looked as if that's *exactly* what she wanted.

"Come on, Nesta, let's get you up. Then we'll take it real slow," said Simon.

As I took a step toward the horse, my oh-I-can-wing-it philosophy changed to if-you-can't-beat-'em-make-a-run-for-it. I felt *really* nervous. Heddie looked enormous. I mean, I'm tall for my age, but my head only came up above Heddie's legs. How was I ever going to get up on him? I made myself breathe deeply like we do in drama to calm our nerves and took another step toward him. He blew dust and shuffled back.

376

Out of the corner of my eye, I could see Cressida enjoying every minute of my discomfort. I'll show you, I thought. I may not have ridden a horse before, but I *have* read Izzie's copy of *Feel the Fear and Do It Anyway*—well, the first three pages. I decided that's exactly what I'd do. I stood tall, felt the fear, and strode toward the horse with every ounce of confidence I could muster.

"Okay," said Simon, smiling at me reassuringly. "Take it real slow. Put your foot in the stirrup. Good. Lift yourself up over Heddie, then, when you're ready, lift your other leg over."

I did as he told me, but didn't feel I could haul myself over. I got my right foot in the stirrup, but couldn't get a grip to pull the rest of me up so I was sort of hopping around on one leg like a total prat. Luckily Simon came to the rescue and gave me a push up. And guess what? Suddenly I was on the horse. High off the ground. Scary. But, once I got my balance, brilliant.

Tanya came out of the stables with two horses, a gray one and a black one, and Cressida disappeared, presumably to get hers.

Simon took the reins of the gray horse. "Stay

where you are, Nesta. I'll get on Prince then we'll go."

No problem, I thought as Simon mounted his horse gracefully. I ain't going nowhere.

Whooaghhhh.

Apparently I was.

Heddie had taken it into his head to have a drink of water and wandered over to a trough outside the stable in the mews.

Whoooooah.

He bent his head down to drink and I started to slide forward. I thought I was going to go over his shoulders and held on for dear life. Of course Cressida came out at that moment, looking fab on a stunning white horse. She looked at me with disapproval, then nodded to Tanya, and the two of them trotted off and disappeared down the mews to the road leading into the park.

"Wait for us," called Simon, trotting over to me. "You're doing really well, Nesta. Just pull on the rein gently and he'll come up."

I did what he said but Heddie took no notice. I pulled again. Still no reaction. Simon took the reins from me and up Heddie came.

"Sometimes they can tell if someone's a bit nervous," he said.

"Me? Nervous? Nah," I said. "Born to ride."

Inside I was shaking.

Mrs. Creighton came over a moment later and looked at me kindly. "I'll lead you until you get into the park," she asked. "It can be a bit nerve-racking going alongside traffic your first time."

Thank God. I hadn't been sure how long I could have kept up the bravado act.

It felt weird being high above the cars as we walked toward the park, but I felt safe with Mrs. Creighton leading Heddie and Simon just in front. Once we got through the park gates, she let go.

"We never let a beginner out without an instructor," she said. "And Simon's taught a lot of my pupils, so you're in safe hands."

"Don't even think of getting up any speed today," he said after she'd gone. "Just try to get comfortable with the feel of the horse."

"No prob," I said. "I think Heddie's okay with me now."

"If you're sure you're okay for a second," said Simon, "I'm just going to ride ahead, only for a

379

minute or two, to check on Tanya. I promised Mum I'd keep an eye on her, and she does tend to get carried away, especially when she's with Cressida. Cress does a lot of competition riding and likes to show off a bit."

"Fine," I said. "You go ahead."

"Don't go anywhere," he insisted.

As he cantered off and disappeared round a corner, I imagined myself playing the part of a country heroine in a period drama. I could be Tess of the d'Urbevilles. Or Jane Eyre. Or maybe in a modern drama. I could be in *The Horse Whisperer* with Robert Redford. I could be the daughter who learns to ride again after her horrible accident.

Suddenly Heddie swung to the left, bent over and started chewing grass by the side of the track. Once again, I almost slid off his shoulders, this time into a rhododendron bush. I gripped my knees and pulled hard on the reins. "Come on, Heddie. This isn't in the script. Come on, there's a good boy. Up you come."

Heddie took no notice. I pulled again. He pulled against me.

I knew from watching *The Horse Whisperer*

380

that it's best not to get aggressive. Horses respond to kindness. Clearly I'd have to do some horse-whispering.

I bent forward and stroked Heddie's neck. "Come on, boy. Lovely boy. Handsome boy," I whispered. "Up you come."

No response. Maybe he didn't speak English.

"Hoopla," I whispered. "Aley oop. Venez upwardos. Muchos gratios stoppee eatee grassee."

I heard someone laughing behind me. It was Simon.

"What on earth are you doing?"

"Durrh. Horse-whispering. What else?"

He burst out laughing. "Honestly, Nesta, you crack me up. Is he giving you a hard time?"

"Sort of. He thinks it's lunchtime."

Once again, Simon pulled the reins and up Heddie came.

"Hold on to the reins and we'll try a bit of trotting," said Simon. "Sit straight. Give a gentle dig with your heels and then try to rise and fall in time with the horse as he goes along."

Off we went. After a few bumps, I found the rhythm. Up and down I went. I was doing okay.

As we turned a corner, I saw a tree about ten meters ahead and slightly to the left of us with its branches sticking out into the path. Simon rode to the right to avoid it and I tried to steer Heddie to do the same. But no, he wasn't having any of it. He was heading straight for the branch, or rather, *he* was heading straight under the branch. I tried to duck but it was too low. It was going to hit me straight in the tummy.

Next thing I knew, I was in midair, hanging on to the branch as Heddie trotted off without me.

"Simon!" I cried.

Simon turned and gasped.

As I hung there, I suddenly got a fit of giggles. "I think I've really got the hang of it now," I said.

Simon got off his horse and came toward me. "Here, let me help you down." Then he got the giggles as well. "Oh, I wish I had a camera," he said. "I could put a photo of you dangling there in my album with the caption: *Nesta goes horse-riding.*"

"Or *Nesta branches out from horse-riding,*" I laughed as he helped me to the ground and took a leaf out of my hair.

"Or *Nesta takes a leaf out of her book when it comes to horse-riding*," I said.

We were bent over laughing as Cressida trotted up to join us.

"We were wondering where you'd got to," she said, looking very disgruntled that we were having a good time. "What are you doing?"

"Oh, just hanging out," I said, and that started us laughing again.

Simon quickly told Cressida what had happened and she laughed as well. But at me, not *with* me.

I felt hurt. I mean, she'd obviously been riding for years. I reckoned she could have been a bit kinder seeing as I was a beginner.

Then the penny dropped. Oh I get it, I thought. There's some history between them. Either she fancies Simon or they've been out together in the past. I wonder what happened?

Nesta's Diary

Went horse-riding today. Fabola. Simon was a brill rider and looked incredibly sexy in his riding boots. After we'd finished we went and had a cappuccino at the Dome by High Street Kensington. By now his sister and her Pedigree Chum Cressida (I think I'll call her Watercress) had got the message and cleared orf. The way they talk is hysterical. Simon and Tanya aren't too bad but Cressida talks like she's got a ping-pong ball stuck in her gobbette.

Me and Simon had our first snog at the tube. *Très bien*. Gentle. He's a good kisser, eight out of ten. Not bad for a start. We didn't want to get too carried away because there was a crowd of tourists staring at us and one even took a photograph. Cheek. Of course that will be worth money in a few years' time when I'm famous.

Chapter 4

Pedigree Chums

"But, Mum . . ."

"No buts, Nesta. I thought I'd made it clear to you . . ."

"Yeah, but you don't understand. It's really important to have the right gear. I have to look the part. This is more important than *anything* I've ever done in my life before."

Mum laughed and said, "N. O. No."

"*Please*, Mum. Just this and then I promise I'll never ask for anything else. Ever. *And* I'll clear up." I rolled up my sleeves, cleared some dishes, and started loading the dishwasher.

Mum sighed and cleared away the remaining dishes from the table. "No, Nesta. I know it's hard, but until things are more settled, the answer's no.

You'll be fine riding in a pair of chinos and a T-shirt."

"It's not fair. Why do we have to run out of money just at the exact time I make friends with people who have loads of it?"

"Welcome to the world, kid," said Mum. "Sometimes life isn't fair."

"Mum doesn't even try to understand," I said to Lucy and Izzie later when we met at Lucy's house. "She could easily sell something. The car or something."

Lucy gasped. "Nesta!"

"What? *What?*" I said. "I was only joking. Not the car. But I'm sure there's something we could sell so I can get kitted out. You *have* to have the right gear to be taken seriously."

"Says who?" said Izzie's voice from behind the sofa. "I think all this right-gear-or-you're-not-a-serious-rider stuff is pants. Who *says* you have to wear this or you're a reject? People like Cressida, that's who. And she sounds like a right snotty cow."

"What are you doing, Iz?" I asked, looking over the sofa.

386

In the gap between the sofa and the wall, Izzie was standing on her head. "Headstand."

"Yeah. I can see that."

"Yoga," said Iz. "Supposed to do ten minutes a day to let the blood flow to my brain. It's to aid relaxation."

Looks like it does exactly the opposite, I thought as I settled on the sofa to do my nails like a sensible person.

Yoga is Izzie's new thing. Personally I think it's a bit antisocial. Like, you'll be in the middle of a conversation and suddenly she'll start wrapping her leg round the back of her neck. Or she'll lie on the floor and roll up on to her shoulders and you find yourself talking to her butt.

"I think I've seen a pair of jodhpurs in the spare room," came The Voice From Behind The Sofa. "One of the Ugly Sisters' castoffs. Want me to check when I get home?"

The Ugly Sisters are Izzie's stepsisters Claudia and Amelia. They're in their twenties so don't live at Izzie's anymore, but both of them seem to have left clothes there for when they visit.

"Does Robbie Williams have a tattoo? Course I

do," I said. "Thanks. It really is awful being poor, you know."

For some reason this made Izzie laugh, and she lost her balance and came up from behind the sofa. "You don't get it sometimes, Nesta. Poor is having no food. No home. No clothes."

"Exactly," I replied. "No clothes."

Izzie tossed her hair impatiently. "Not designer clothes, dummy."

"Easy to say, but you know what it's like at school. If you don't have the right trainers you get slagged off."

"So what?" said Izzie. "The people who slag you off for something so stupid as what brand of trainers you have or haven't are total morons."

"And you don't let people like that get to you, do you?" asked Lucy.

I shrugged. Sometimes I acted braver than I felt. "How do you manage, Lucy?"

"Don't look at me," she said, looking taken aback. "We may not be rich, but we're not poor."

"Nesta! Sometimes you should think before you open that big mouth of yours," said Izzie.

Iz and Lucy have known each other since junior

school, longer than I've known them both as I only joined their school last September. Izzie always confronts anyone she thinks might hurt Lucy. Even me. Even me when I'm *completely* innocent.

"But . . . ," I started.

"It's okay," said Lucy. "I'm not offended."

"I wasn't being insulting, Izzie. I was asking advice. What's wrong with that? We all know that Lucy gets less pocket money than us. And she hasn't as much money for clothes."

"Yeah, but Lucy might not want it broadcasted to the whole world."

"Excuse *me*, but I am actually *here*," said Lucy, "like, in person. And it's cool. I don't mind you two knowing that my parents aren't as well off as yours or, sorry Nesta, yours *were*. And you know how I manage. I make my own clothes. And sometimes I baby-sit. Why not try that?"

"Oh, get real," I said. "I need a lot more money than I could earn baby-sitting."

This time Lucy did look offended, and Izzie gave me one of her mess-with-my-mate-and-you're-dead looks.

"What? *What?*" I asked.

389

"So you're clearly not *that* desperate, then," said Izzie. "Really poor people take what work they can. And for your information, you can earn quite a lot baby-sitting."

Eek. The atmosphere was starting to feel really uncomfortable. There's only one way out of this, I thought. When the going gets tough, the tough resort to being silly.

"Oh, come orf it," I said, doing my best impression of the Queen. "One is only trying to say that one *must* have other options."

Thank God, both of them laughed.

"Look, I know it's hard," said Lucy, "when you really want something badly and you can't have it. You're not the first to discover horse-riding, you know. A couple of years ago, I wanted lessons, but they cost thirty quid a time. No way Mum and Dad could pay for that."

"So what did you do?"

"I had to forget about it."

"When I'm rich and famous," I said, "*I'll* pay for you to have lessons."

"At least Simon can help you with that side of things," said Izzie, settling on the floor and crisscrossing her legs into the lotus position. "You don't have to worry about lessons."

"I know, he was fab. I was more nervous than I let on and, to tell the truth, I felt like crying when I couldn't get on the horse and Watercress was laughing at me hopping about with one foot stuck in the stirrup. I didn't let her see I was upset though."

"Why are you bothered about impressing a creep like her? Sounds like Simon couldn't care less whether you turned up barefoot or in Gucci gumboots—and he's the one that matters."

"I just want to show her that she can't intimidate me. That I'm as good as she is."

"Why?" said Iz. "You don't even like her."

"Yeah," said Lucy. "Remember that quote on one of Mum's Angel Cards last year. 'No one can make you feel inferior without your permission.' Saying you want to prove that you're as good as Cressida means that you think she's better than you. It's like you've given her permission to make you feel inferior."

I was getting confused. I didn't want to talk about it anymore. I thought they'd understand how I felt, but they didn't. And to tell the truth, neither did I.

"Oh, let's watch the video," I said, hoping to change the subject. "You're both way too deep for me."

We spent the next half hour watching Lucy's video about a man called Monty Roberts. He's the guy that the character Robert Redford played in *The Horse Whisperer* is based on, only Monty does it for real. Lucy got it as a Christmas present when she was going through her horse-mad phase.

"So the general idea is not look the horse in the eyes, as that's seen as a challenge," I said after watching the video.

"Yeah. And to let him know that you're not a threat," said Lucy.

"Be friendly but confident," said Izzie as she tried to come out of her lotus position. Sadly, her legs had gone numb from sitting in such a strange position for so long and she couldn't stand up. She sank back on to the carpet with her legs and arms in the air.

"And what position is that in yoga?" I asked. "The dead dog?"

"If you're afraid, horses pick up on it," continued Lucy as Izzie lay on the floor moaning, "and it makes them afraid. So the trick is to be cool."

"Cool," I said. "Confident. That's me."

"Cool," cried Izzie. "Oh *God*. Aghhh. Now I've got pins and needles. Help. *I'm in agony!*"

So much for yoga for relaxation, I thought.

"Shall we get another vid?" asked Lucy.

"Can't," I said. "Got a date."

"Where are you going?" asked Izzie.

"Movie. I said I'd meet Simon at the cinema on the King's Road at six thirty."

Izzie looked at her watch. "Six *thirty*! Nesta, it's five fifteen."

"Oh pants! I lost track of time watching that video. Now I won't have time to go home and get changed!"

"You'd better get going now," said Lucy, helping Iz up on to the sofa, "or you'll never make it. It'll take you at least an hour to get there."

Outside it was raining. I looked at Izzie and Lucy curled up all cozily on the sofa and felt really tempted to call off my date. A night here with the girls suddenly looked like a better option. Plus

393

Lucy's brothers would be back later and they're a real laugh.

I quickly dialed Simon's mobile number. "Pants. It's on answer service."

"You'd better go," said Lucy. "You don't want to stand him up."

"Come with me," I asked. "In case the Pedigree Chums are there as well."

"Pedigree Chums?" asked Lucy.

"Tanya and her horrid mate."

Izzie looked out of the window at the rain and pulled a face.

"We'll walk you to the tube," said Lucy. "It's on the way to the pizza shop. Come on, Iz. Get the brollies. Do you want to borrow a jacket, Nesta? You'll freeze in only a T-shirt."

She held out her silver jacket for me, but it was way too small.

"Or you could borrow one of Steve or Lal's?" she said, offering me a choice of two hideously naff anoraks.

"As if," I said. "I'm not turning up looking like a total plonker."

Izzie put on Lal's jacket and Lucy put on Steve's,

and we set off for the tube. After only five minutes I was soaked.

"You have to borrow a jacket," said Lucy. "You'll freeze. Do you want the maroon or the orange?"

I had no choice. "Maroon," I said miserably. "*Maroon!* My life as a style queen is over."

I hope Simon realizes the sacrifices I'm making for him, I thought as I emerged at Sloane Street tube about an hour later. Trust me to go and fall for someone who lives on the other side of the planet.

I asked the man outside the tube selling the *Evening Standard* where the cinema was, and he pointed to the left of the square.

"Down the King's Road, duck," he said. "Best get a bus in this rain."

As I ran in the direction of the bus stop, I tried to think of an appropriate film that I could imagine I was starring in. I find that pretending to be someone else helps me to get through difficult situations sometimes, but I couldn't think of any film where the heroine trawls over London in the rain in the anorak from hell.

The bus came after a few minutes, and as I got on,

I asked the driver to give me a shout when we got to the cinema. I took a seat and soon we were whizzing past shops and cafés down the King's Road.

Living in London is still new to me. We came to live here last summer when Mum got a job reading the news on Cable. Before that we lived in Bristol, which was okay, but nothing like this. I keep discovering more and more of it—different areas, and each one has its own atmosphere. It's brillopad.

"Cinema!" shouted the bus driver.

As I got off the bus, I couldn't see Simon or the Pedigree Chums. I quickly took off the naff jacket as I didn't want them to see me in it.

A few more minutes went by. I hope I haven't missed them, I thought. I checked my watch. I was ten minutes late. Surely they'd have waited? We'd only have missed the commercials.

Another five minutes passed. Then another five. I was freezing. So much for the coming spring; it had turned back into winter. Well, this afternoon's been a total waste of makeup, I thought, as I put Lal's jacket back on and started to walk back to the bus stop.

"Nesta!" Simon's voice called.

I looked across the road and there he was, waving frantically. He ran across to join me.

"So sorry we're late," he panted. "Traffic. Couldn't park anywhere."

"Been waiting long?" said Cressida, coming up behind him and looking like she couldn't care less how long I'd been waiting.

"No, I just got here," I said, then turned to Simon. "Hey, this place is great. I haven't been down here before."

I could see Cressida sneering again. One of these days I really must ask her what the bad smell is that seems to be perpetually under her nose.

"It *used* to be great," she said, "but Notting Hill is the place to shop now." She looked disdainfully at Lal's jacket. "But then I don't expect you've been there either, have you?"

She did look amazing, I have to say. She had a cropped white leather jacket on and the most amazing pair of black patent ankle boots—really high with peep toes. My soggy trainers looked so unglamorous beside them.

"I only moved to London last summer," I said.

397

"We were in Los Angeles before, so it's all very new to me." She doesn't need to know it was only for a week's holiday, I thought.

For a second Cressida looked impressed. "How come you lived there?"

"My dad's a film director," I said.

"Has he made anything we'd know?" asked Tanya, who'd been off getting the tickets. She looked fab as well in a leather mini and DKNY T-shirt. I was starting to feel way underdressed.

"Oh, loads. Course, it helps having Spielberg as an uncle."

Now Cressida did look impressed. And it wasn't a lie. I just didn't mention I meant Leister Spielberg not Steven. He's married to my aunt and runs a dry cleaner's over there.

"How did you get here?" asked Simon.

"Tube then bus. Took ages."

"You came by *bus*?" sneered Cressida.

Oh, here we go, I thought. "Well, how else from North London?"

"Taxi, of course."

I wasn't in the mood. "Dahling," I said in my best posh voice, "anyone who's *anyone* knows that buses

398

are the new taxi. Taxis are so *nineties*. Buses are the thing, the new cool way to travel."

Simon hooted with laughter and joined in. "Absolutely, dahling. In fact, the number eighty-eight is my favorite."

Even Tanya laughed, but old Watercress scowled and pulled Tanya away to queue for popcorn.

"That's one of the things I really like about you," said Simon.

"What?" I asked.

"Your attitude. You're so confident. It's brilliant."

Just as well he couldn't see what was going on in my head. It was far from confident. For some reason Cressida really bugged me. It was weird. What Lucy said was true; I gave Cressida permission to make me feel inferior. That confident attitude Simon saw? It was acting.

Nesta's Diary

Simon gave me a lift home after he'd dropped the Pedigree Chums off. He lives in Holland Park in a white house behind some black railings. It looked v. posh. He asked if I wanted to go in, but I wasn't up for meeting his mum or dad when I was dressed in my jeans and wearing Lal's jacket.

Simon says they also have another house in Wiltshire where they keep horses. I told him we used to keep hamsters up until a few years ago. He completely cracked up laughing. I don't think he realized I was serious about the hamsters.

He's got a fab car. A black Volkswagon. He put the Manic Street Preachers on really loud, and when we got to my street we sat and snogged for ages until Tony came past and knocked on the window, giving both of us the shock of our lives.

I have decided to shorten Cressida's nickname from Watercress to WC. Tanya is much nicer than WC, much more friendly. I asked her where they got their clothes from and she said all over really, sometimes Selfridges, sometimes Gucci on Bond Street,

400

sometimes DKNY, but mostly from the designer shops around Portobello Road.

I'm going to Notting Hill tomorrow with Iz and Lucy. I'm looking forward to it as it's another bit of London I've never been to and I know there's a famous song about Portobello Road. Saturrrdayee morning. That's it.

I wish I could afford to buy some new gear.

Chapter 5

Portobello Princesses

The next day, I drew thirty pounds out of my savings account and set off for Notting Hill with the girls. We got off at Ladbroke Grove tube and headed up behind the market. Tanya had told me that's where the good boutiques were.

"Doesn't look as posh as Knightsbridge, does it?" said Lucy, staring at the white terraced houses on the way.

"No," said Izzie, "but it is. Loads of celebrities live here, like Robbie Williams, Geri Halliwell, Chris Evans."

"My mum says that houses can go for as much as four million," said Izzie.

"You'd have to win the Lottery to live here, then," said Lucy.

After roads of terraced houses, we passed some amazing antique shops, full of enormous gold frames and mirrors big enough to fill a whole wall.

"Bit different from Homebase," said Izzie, gazing in at one window crammed with chandeliers made from molded glass flames and wrought iron.

"And—*wow*—look at these shoes," I said as we came across a shop called Emma Hope on the corner of one street. "They're so pretty, like made for fairytale princesses."

"Portobello Princesses," said Izzie, looking at a shop further down. "You need to be royalty to afford the prices."

"Portobello Princesses," I laughed. "I like that. That describes Cressida and Tanya *exactly*."

We spent the first ten minutes window shopping, looking in a shop called Joseph and another called Rikki, then at the end of the row, a window display caught my eye. "Now *this* looks interesting."

"No," said Lucy. "I don't want to go in."

"Why not?"

"Doesn't look friendly. And there's no one else in there."

"Oh, don't be silly," I said, and dragged her up the steps to the shop. I pushed the door, but it was closed. Inside, a stick-thin assistant looked up and indicated we should ring the bell.

I rang the bell and the door bleeped open.

"I'm going to wander down toward the market," said Lucy, pulling away. "I'll meet you later."

"Lucy," I whispered to her as I shoved her into the shop, "what was it you were saying to me about people only being able to make you feel inferior if you give them permission? You belong here as much as the next person. In fact you'll probably run a place like this when you're up and running as a designer."

"I doubt it," said Lucy, looking around. "*I'm* going to make my customers feel welcome."

Inside it was all concrete and chrome with lilac tube lighting, sort of minimal, so it did look a bit cold. And the assistant was eyeing us suspiciously. But the clothes on the rails looked the biz boz. We rummaged around and there were loads of things I liked. I really wanted to get something special to wear on my next date with Simon. So far, he'd only seen me in jeans and trainers. Next time, I was determined to make an impression.

"Oh, *chulo chulo*. Look at this," I said, pulling out an amazing orange chain-mail sleeveless tank top. "*Got* to have it."

I quickly glanced at the price. Twenty-three pounds fifty. I could afford it *and* have some money left over.

I went into the changing room and tried it on. It did look fantastic. The fabric was stunning: little silky cubes all sewn together.

"Let's see," said Lucy, sticking her head in the cubicle. "*Très* sexy."

"Must have," I said.

"Musto must have," agreed Lucy.

I got changed into my own clothes and took the top over to the cash desk.

The assistant took it from me and looked at the label.

"Cash or card?"

"Cash," I said, getting out my money and handing her three ten-pound notes.

405

She took them but seemed to be waiting for something.

"What?" I said.

"I need another two hundred and five pounds," she said, as she showed me the label. It said two hundred and thirty-five pounds. Not twenty-three pounds fifty.

I wanted to die.

"Er, bit more than I thought," I stuttered, and quickly put the top back on the racks, before joining Izzie at the other end of the shop.

"What a rip-off," said Izzie, picking out a skirt. "This is *only* a bit of cotton, and it's a *hundred* and eighty-five pounds."

"Perhaps you'd like to look at our sale rack," said the assistant, coming up behind us.

We trooped over to the sale rail where Izzie proceeded to embarrass me further.

"*Blimey*. Come and look at this, Lucy," she exclaimed as she held up a strapless pink dress. "You could make one better than this. This is eighty-five quid and that's on *sale!*"

Honestly. Izzie goes on about me and my big mouth, but she can be worse than me if she wants to.

I wandered to the back of the shop to look at the shoes and boots. There was a pair there just like the ones WC had on the night before. I picked them up and gulped. Four hundred and ninety-five pounds! That's like, almost a *year's* pocket money! And that was only WC's *boots*. Lord knows what the rest of her outfit cost.

The assistant was watching us like we were kids on the nick, and I suddenly remembered that scene in *Pretty Woman*. The film where Julia Roberts is shopping in posh dress shops and the assistants give her a hard time and she gets intimidated. Then she goes back with Richard Gere and shows them what's what as he buys up half the shop for her.

That's my film for today, I thought, and tossed my hair back.

"Not really our style, is it?" I said loudly. "Let's get a cab home and see if Daddy will fly us over to Paris in the helicopter."

Izzie and Lucy gawped at me. Then Iz caught on.

"Yah. *Super* idea, dahling," she said. "This place is so, so . . ."

And we both wrinkled our noses and said, "*Nineties.*"

With that, Izzie and I flounced out of the door, followed by Lucy who looked like she wanted to die. Poor Lucy. She isn't the coolest cube in the ice tray at the best of times and she'd gone a brighter red than usual.

We ran round the corner and bent over laughing.

"Did you *see* the assistant's face?" I said.

"Yes, I did," said Lucy, punching me. "Honestly, you show me up sometimes."

"We were only having a laugh," said Iz. "But what a rip-off, eh?"

"Yeah," I agreed, "but the clothes are something else, you have to admit."

"They might make you feel good for a moment," said Izzie as we set off toward the market, "but they don't give lasting happiness."

"What *are* you going on about, Izzie?" I asked.

"Buddhism," explained Lucy. "Izzie's become a Buddhist like Ben. She told me all about it when you went off to the cinema last night."

I laughed. "You should do a single, you know, like Bob the Builder? You could sing Ben the Buddhist to the same tune only with windchimes and chanting as well and maybe dolphins in the background. It'd probably go straight to number one." I started singing, "Ben the Buddhist, Ben the Buddhist," then did my dolphin impersonation, "dwoink, *bverk*, squeak."

Lucy giggled and even Izzie cracked after a minute's trying to keep a straight face.

"Okay, then," I asked. "So why would being a Buddhist mean you can't wear nice clothes?"

"It doesn't," said Izzie. "You can wear what you like to be a Buddhist. But it *does* teach that the root of all unhappiness is desire. And, mostly, desire is never-ending. Like, you get one thing, it makes you happy for a moment, then up comes another desire and you're dissatisfied again until *that* desire is satisfied and so on."

"Yeah, I suppose," I said. "But so what?"

Izzie sighed impatiently. "Ben says that in the West, we're all lost in desire, drowning in materialism."

"Yeah. *Top*, isn't it?" I said as I spied another interesting boutique and went to look in the window. "Drown *me* in it anytime."

"Let's go and look at the market," pleaded Lucy. "I don't think I could face another of those stuck-up shops."

She pulled me away and we headed off in the direction of Portobello Road. On the way, we passed a health shop and of course Izzie had to stop and look.

Health shops aren't really my thing, but she'd come to my shop and fair's only fair, so we trooped in the door. Once inside, we found there were three floors selling every variety of health food ever made. The place was so Izzie. She was in heaven, but try as I might, organic turnips just don't do it for me. There was fruit, vegetables, grains, nuts, a floor with books and aromatherapy oils and soaps and lotions, then another floor with fresh juices and healthy-type meals. I was bored after five minutes. I mean, who wants to look at millet when you can look at makeup?

"I wish we had a place like this near us," said Iz, after we'd had a good look round. "It's wonderful."

"Yeah, right," I said. "Let's go."

"See, places like this are what it's all about," continued Izzie as she picked some organic chocolate off the shelf and took it to the pay counter. "Feeds your soul as well as your body."

"Seven pounds fifty," said the girl at the till.

Izzie's jaw dropped open in shock as she counted out the coins from her purse.

"*Most* of the stuff in there is a bargain," she said sheepishly when we got back out on the pavement.

I shook my head sadly. "Wot a reep-off," I said in my best Indian guru accent. "That sweetie thing will only give you temporary happiness. You are lost in chocolatey desire but in an hour, oh deary me, desire will rise again. Probably for a burger. With extra onion. Or a milkshake. With big fat flakey things. Such is the nature of Western man who is drowning in illusion."

"Then you won't be wanting any, will you, Barmy Swami?" said Izzie, handing Lucy a piece of the chocolate, then running off down the road.

We spent the next couple of hours cruising Portobello Road and having the most brilliant time. The street was literally jammed with people eagerly looking at what was on sale at the many colorful stalls there. Here, there really were bargains. Pashminas, jewelry, picture frames, antiques, clothes, CDs, *everything*.

Lucy bought a fab 1940s dress from a stall selling

vintage clothes. It was a soft cream voile, and she said she could use the material for an idea she had. Lucy wants to be a dress designer when she leaves school. She's mega-talented. She gets old clothes and sews them together with bits of new to make really original things. Already you can see her individual style, and I'm sure in years to come, people will know exactly what a Lucy Lovering creation looks like.

Izzie bought some pink flip-flops with beads and sequins from a hippie-dippie Indian stall, and I bought an amazing little transparent handbag with a pink feather trim—fluffy and girlie and only four pounds ninety-nine.

"It's the way you wear 'em," I said as I posed down the street with my new bag, doing my Marilyn Monroe wiggle.

By four o'clock we'd pretty well done the market, so we decided to walk down to look at the big shops on Kensington High Street. After an hour there even I, Queen Shopaholic, was starting to feel exhausted.

"One more stop before home," I said, leading

the girls down a side street behind the tube. "There's a shop that sells riding gear down here somewhere. Simon told me about it."

"Well, don't get jodhpurs," said Izzie. "I found that pair of Claudia's. I'll bring them over to you later."

We found the shop behind a square with super-posh houses built round a park-type garden blooming with magnolia trees.

"Bet it costs a packet to live here," said Izzie, staring in the window of one of the houses next to the riding shop. The room looked like a film set, with oak-paneled walls, old paintings, and heavy red curtains.

The smell of leather hit us as soon as we entered the shop. It was crammed from floor to ceiling with everything you could imagine to do with horses—riding gear, boots, hats, stirrups, saddles, reins, books, magazines.

What I really wanted was one of the tweedy riding jackets, but as I scanned the rails, I soon discovered that they were way out of my price range at over two hundred pounds. I was about to try one on to see what it looked like, when the door chimed open and I heard a voice I recognized. Luckily we were at the back of the shop and hidden by racks full of clothes, so she didn't see us.

"Hi," said Cressida. "I've come to pick up my outfit for next week's competition."

"Miss Dudley-Smythe," gushed the shop owner. "How are you? And Lady Dudley-Smythe? Not with you today?"

I wasn't in the mood for bumping into WC. After having had such a nice day with the girls, I didn't want to ruin it.

"That's WC," I whispered. "I'm not up for saying hello. Let's try and get out without her seeing us."

Of course Izzie wanted to have a peek at her, so she sauntered up to the front of one the aisles and pretended to have a look at some riding boots. She came back after a second.

"What's she doing?" I whispered.

"Chatting to the owners."

"Can we sneak past?"

"Well, not all three of us," said Izzie. "But she doesn't know me and Lucy, so we could walk out easily. But what about you?"

414

She had another quick look at what was happening at the front of the shop. "Okay," she said, coming back. "This is the plan. They're on the right and look quite busy with clothes and stuff. So, Nesta, you walk to the left of us with your head turned away. Me and Lucy will be like a shield. Come on."

We set off down the aisle nearest to the door with Lucy and Izzie on the right and me walking kind of sideways behind them. I had to bend my knees as I'm taller than both of them.

"Just go slow," urged Izzie, "kind of casual."

As I half bounced, half slid along, I felt like John Cleese in the Monty Python shows when he was doing the Ministry of Silly Walks. We'd almost made it to the door when Lucy got the giggles. She tried to hold it in but her shoulders began shaking up and down in silent laughter. That started Izzie off. Then, of course, me. Then Lucy couldn't hold it in a moment longer.

"Hooo, hoo, HOOO," she exploded.

The shop owners and Cressida looked around immediately.

"Nesta, is that you?" asked Cressida.

I was bent over the book section, heaving with laughter.

"Sneuck, yeah, bffff," I said, trying to stop. "Er, Cressida, this is Izzie and Lucy."

"Hi, nnya, whey . . . ," spluttered Izzie, who dove for the door quickly followed by Lucy.

"Do you know these girls?" said the shop owner, looking mystified by our behavior.

"Yeah, sort of," said Cressida disdainfully. "What's so funny, Nesta?"

I coughed. "Nothing. Er, private joke. Nothing." I was just managing to get my face straight when I looked over Cressida's shoulder and out of the window.

Izzie and Lucy were outside pressing their faces up against the glass so that their features were all squashed. Both of them were doing mad faces and had made their eyes go cross-eyed.

I exploded laughing again.

"*Ummphh.* Gotta go, Cressida. See ya laters," I stuttered.

As I ran for the door I could hear her saying, "Honestly, some people are *so* juvenile."

Nesta's Diary

Simon sent me loads of text messages today:
:-<   Missed U today.

I sent him back:
 *^_^*   I had a good time with the girls.

He sent me back:
⊗ because I wasn't there with U.

(He wants to meet Lucy and Iz so I hope WC doesn't fill him in about bumping into us in the riding gear shop as I can just imagine her version.)

I sent him back:
 :->>> because I'll see U in a few days.

Then he sent me this:
   (*_*)

I had to text Izzie immediately to check it meant what I thought it did. It did. It does! It means I'm in love!!!!!
   Treat 'em mean to keep 'em keen is my brother Tony's motto, or at least it was until he met Lucy who

I still don't think he's quite gotten over. Anyway, I'm not going to be mean to Simon, but I'm not going to tell him I love him back. Not yet. Even though I do.

Instead I sent him this: (OvO) It means I am a night owl.

He sent back < ^ O ^ > which means I am laughing loudly.

Me and the girls had a brill time today. Notting Hill is the biz and I saw loads of things I wanted in the shops there. I felt a bit down about it after though, because our family is financially challenged at the moment. Tony came up with that term: He says it's a politically correct way of saying poor. He's mad. He's doing politics as one of his A levels and is always coming out with rubbish like that. Anyway, after feeling rotten about being financially challenged, I decided I ought to do something about it. Sink or swim time. I decided to swim and made A PLAN.

Chapter 6

Power Brekkie

The next morning I got up early—well nine thirty, early for a weekend day—and checked my e-mails. I wanted to see if Lucy and Iz had replied to the invite I'd sent the night before:

```
Dear Ms. Foster and Ms. Lovering
Time: Sunday 10 A.M.
Place: Kitchen at Ms. Williams's flat.
Event: Power breakfast.
Be there. Or be square.
Signed: Ms. Nesta Williams. Esquire.
HRH
```

Excellent. Both of them had replied that they'd come so I got dressed and went to buy the morning papers and croissants from the corner shop. When I got back, I began my preparations in the kitchen. Pens, writing pads, pencils, juice, fruit, tea, cereal, coffee, milk.

Then it was time to say hi to Mum.

I switched on the TV and flicked to the news station.

"Morning," I said, as her face appeared on screen. Then I changed channels to MTV. Destiny's Child was on. Most excellent, I thought. They're my favorite band. I closed the kitchen door as I didn't want the music to wake Tony who was still in bed.

Lucy arrived first.

"I brought some blueberry muffins," she said, handing over a bag. "What's so important we have to get out of bed for?"

"I'll tell you when Iz arrives. Now. Orange juice, tea, or coffee?"

"Juice," said Lucy, looking at me suspiciously.

"What? *What?*" I laughed.

"You're up to something. . . ."

Just at that moment, the doorbell rang.

"Lerrus in," came Izzie's voice through the letterbox.

I went out into the hallway, knelt down, and yelled back through the letterbox. "Only if you know the secret password."

Izzie started posting bananas through the door. "Bananas," she called. I love Izzie, but there's no doubt, she is a Strange Friend.

I opened the door and burst out laughing. Izzie was wearing jeans and a purple T-shirt, but she was also wearing the most enormous pair of knobbly shoulder pads, which made her look like an American football player.

"Power breakfast needs power dressing," she laughed as she took two oranges out of her T-shirt and handed them to me along with a carrier bag. "Needs *big* shoulders."

"What are you like?" I laughed as I looked in the bag.

"Claudia's jodhpurs," said Izzie.

"Cool. Thanks. I'll try them later."

"So what's all this about?" she said, following me through to the kitchen.

"I read this article last night," I explained, "in one of Mum's magazines. It was about what businessmen do to begin their day. A power breakfast.

It gets them revved up to go out and do their best."

"Like motivates them?" asked Lucy, who had made a start on the croissants.

"Yeah."

"But this is the Easter holidays, Nesta," said Izzie, sitting at the breakfast bar and biting into one of Lucy's muffins. "What's to get motivated for? It's time for"—she went into her American accent—"rest and recuperation."

"Only for slackers," I said. "High achievers never rest. They only stop for power breakfasts."

"Yeah but at six A.M.," remarked Lucy, looking at her watch, "not ten fifteen after a lie-in."

"Ah well. It *is* Sunday."

"So why?" said Izzie. "*Why* am I here when I could have been tucked up under my duvet for at least another half hour?"

I picked up Mum's copy of *Woman Today* and read the list. "Define goals. Identify negativity. Prioritize needs. And make up a game plan."

"Oh," said Lucy. "That all?"

"Sounds impressive," said Izzie.

"Yeah," I said. "Cool, huh? It was just that

when I got home last night I started feeling a bit of in-built free-floating depression. . . ."

Izzie cracked up laughing. "Some *what*?"

"In-built free-floating depression," I repeated. That was the term used in the article I'd read for when people couldn't get what they wanted and felt bad about it.

Izzie shook her head and gave Lucy one of her Nesta's-a-nutter looks. "What're you like?" she said. "Everyone else gets a bit low from time to time. Oh, but not Nesta. Nesta has in-built free-floating depression."

"Go on, laugh. Mock. I thought that you, of all people, would understand. I *do* have days when I'm down, you know."

"Sorry, Nesta. I didn't mean to mock. You know that. It's just it . . . ," she started sniggering again, "it *is* a bit of a fancy term."

"Everybody has their gray days, even me. And that's what got me thinking. You can either go down and be miserable or fight."

"Sink or swim," said Lucy.

"Yeah. I reckon that's what life is all about. Choices. You can go for what you want or watch everybody else get it and feel rotten."

"Yeah," said Lucy. "She's right, Izzie."

"You have to really focus on what you want," I said.

"That's true," said Izzie thoughtfully. "All those people in that *Popstars* audition program, the ones that got to the final band, Hear'Say, they'd all been going for it for years."

"Yeah. So I thought we could have our power breakfast and talk about strategy, game plans . . ."

"But first breakfast," said Lucy eagerly. "Shall I put the kettle on?"

"And I'll squeeze some fresh orange juice," said Izzie.

At that moment, Tony staggered in in his usual morning disarray. He was half asleep and only wearing his boxer shorts. He woke up quickly when he saw Lucy.

"Hi, oh, whoops," he said, covering his crotch with his hands and sort of dancing backward out of the room. "*Nesta*. Why didn't you *tell* me you had guests?"

Hysterical, I thought. It really was. Tony was usually Mr. Cool but he had a real thing about

Lucy. I think it's because she's the only girl who's ever dumped him. And what a turn around, from her being all shy and in awe of him when she first met him—now she calls the shots. He's all gaga and she's all, Oh hi, Tony, you want to go on a date? Yeah . . . maybe. I'll call you sometime.

"You still cool about him these days, Luce?" I asked.

"Yeah. *Très* cool. I mean, he'll always be a bit special to me having been my first snog and that, but that's all."

"Doesn't look like he's very cool," remarked Izzie. "In fact, I think he still fancies you."

"Good," smiled Lucy. "It's nice to be admired. I just don't want to get into a heavy relationship at the moment. Now, who wants what?"

"You have learned well, oh Lucy Skywalker," I said, doing my Obi-Wan Kenobi voice. She has. Lucy used to be mega-uncool about boys, thinking she was lucky if one even looked at her. But she's got so much more confident in the last few months and now knows she doesn't have to say yes to the first one who looks her way. She's learned the golden rule: Boys run

425

from desperate but run toward cool.

We spent the next half hour stuffing ourselves with toast and peanut butter and honey and cappuccinos made on Dad's machine. Then it was time to begin.

"So," I said, wiping the last crumbs from the breakfast bar surface. "The game plan. We each make our own. We have to write down the top three things we'd really like to achieve. Then what's holding us back."

I pointed to the pens and paper I'd set out.

"Achieve like when?" asked Lucy. "In the next few weeks or ten years?"

"Either or both. You can choose."

Izzie chuckled. "Okay," she said. "Give us a pen."

I scribbled my ideas quickly:

1) Be an actress (future)
2) Have lots of money (now)
3) Be very popular with everyone (now and future)

"I think we should be very specific," said Izzie. "You know, like, with details. Like if you're going

426

to write, 'I want a boy to fall in love with me,' you should specify that it's a decent-looking boy with a good personality or else you may get a boy to fall in love with you but he'll be a total plonker with knobbly knees and spots. Then we should put these notes in a secret wish box in a special place in our bedrooms."

"Right," me and Lucy chorused.

I added "earning at least ten million a picture" to number one on my list and smiled to myself. I *knew* Izzie would get going in the end. In fact she's usually the one who starts things like this. She's into all sorts of alternative therapies and self-help books and Lucy told me that she's even tried some witchcraft spells.

"Right, ready," said Izzie after ten minutes.

"Yep, so am I," said Lucy.

"Okay, you go first, Izzie," I said.

"One," read Izzie, "be a very successful and popular singer-songwriter. Two, get my own fabulous three-bedroomed flat—that's so you two can stay over. Three, travel the world first class and stay in fab locations."

"Okay," I said. "Lucy?"

"One. Career goal. Be a dress designer, success-

427

ful. Two. Love goal. Meet my soulmate before I'm thirty. Fall in love with each other. Three. Home goal. To have a cottage in the country with dogs and cats and lots of animals."

I quickly read mine then said, "Right, now part two. The next thing to think about is how are you going to achieve this and what's holding you back."

After another ten minutes of scribbling, we'd finished.

"I'll go first this time," I said. "Okay. To get lots of money. Only solution is to get a job."

"I thought you said baby-sitting didn't pay enough?" said Lucy.

"Doesn't." I indicated all my newspapers on a chair by the door. "I'm getting a proper job."

"Have you found anything?" asked Lucy.

"I'm going to look later."

"And what about the 'being popular' bit?" asked Izzie.

"Easy. Just carry on being my natural charming self."

"And modesty is your middle name," laughed Izzie.

"So what's holding you back, then?" said Lucy. "Sounds like you've got it all sorted."

"I know what I want, but some days, with the acting bit, it's hard. I look at myself and think, what makes you so special? There are thousands of people out there all trying to make it."

"My mum says there are two mistakes you can make in life," said Lucy. "The first is to think you're special. The other is to think that you're not."

"Good quote," said Izzie. "But, Nesta, I'm sure you'd be a fabulous actress, and you're easily the best-looking girl in our school. All the boys swarm round you like bees round a honeypot. I wouldn't worry. Everybody has days when they doubt themselves. Days when they"—she grinned—"feel in-built free-floating depression. You have nothing to worry about—you stand out in a crowd. People always do double-takes when they see you."

"Yeah," I said. "But is that because they think I'm pretty or because I'm mixed race?"

"What difference would that make?" said Izzie, looking surprised.

"It's because you're pretty," said Lucy. "Course it is."

"I'm not so sure," I said. "That's probably why a part of me wants the right gear, you know, to fit in."

"*Course* you fit in," said Izzie. "Doesn't matter what you wear."

"I remember once when I was little," I said. "I was with my mum away for a weekend by the sea. Dad had gone off to get some ice creams and me and Mum were walking along the pier. This man passed us and did a double take. He was really staring, then he came up to Mum and said, 'Oi you, go back to your own country.' He definitely wasn't staring because we were pretty. To him, we didn't fit in."

"You're kidding?" said Izzie angrily. "Where was this? Would you know him again if you saw him? I'll give him a piece of my mind. What was his name? How *dare* he?"

I had to laugh. Izzie looked like she was about to get on the next bus, go and find the man, and challenge him to a fight. "It was years ago, Iz. Mum told me to close my ears. But it was after that I noticed people staring at Mum. And staring at me."

"I *hate* that," said Izzie. "More than anything. I can't stand people that are racist. It's so narrow-minded. It's what you're like on the inside that counts."

"I think more often than not," said Lucy, "people stare at both you and your mum because you're both so glam. Not because of the color of your skin."

"Maybe," I said, "but I'll never know, will I? I remember another day when I was about six, at school, there was a kid in the playground talking about colored people. I remember thinking, how wonderful—a colored person: purple legs, a green face, turquoise arms. I wanted to paint one in art. But then the kids started sniggering and pointing to me, saying that I was one. I hadn't really realized I was different until then. Then later, that man by the seaside—I decided no one was ever going to see if they had upset me. That's why I act confident. It doesn't mean I always am. I've just got good at the act."

"I feel a bit like that with my height," said Lucy. "I know people think I'm just a kid because I'm so small. But, small, tall, fat, thin, black, white, you

431

can't judge what people are like only by their appearance."

"Well said," said Izzie. "We all have our hang-ups. And there will always be people who'll judge us."

"What's your hang-up, then?" I asked.

"It's *exactly* what's getting in the way of me achieving what I want."

"What do you mean?" asked Lucy.

Izzie looked worried. "Well, you know Ben's been putting some of my lyrics to music?"

We both nodded.

"Well," she continued, "he's asked if I'll sing at the next gig with his band."

"OhmyGod," said Lucy. "How brillopad is that? When?"

"Next week. Friday. But that's it. I don't mind singing in front of Ben. But at the thought of performing in public, I go cold. What if I dry up on the night? Just stand there with my mouth open and no words coming out? I'll look such a fool. I have nightmares about it."

"Do what I do," I said. "On days I don't feel brave, I pretend I'm a character in a film and I think, okay, what would she do?"

432

"Oh God," laughed Izzie, clamping her hands over her ears. "You're going to sing that song from *The Sound of Music*. The one sung by Mother Superior. 'Climb Every Mountain.' Any minute. Aggghhh. Tell me when it's over."

"I am not! And what a cheek," I said, punching Izzie's arm. "Nuns, I *don't* do."

"Yeah, we'll be 'aving nun of that! But it's a good idea to think of a character," said Lucy. "It doesn't even have to be a film, does it, Nesta? She could just pretend to be some singer."

"Who's the most confident singer you can think of?" I asked.

"Um, Madonna, I guess."

"Right," I said. "Pretend you're Madonna."

"And," said Lucy, "there's no time like the present. You can start by singing in front of us."

"Oh no, *no*, I couldn't."

Lucy put a tea towel on her head like a nun's wimple, joined her hands in prayer and started singing, completely out of key, "Climb every mountain, ford every stream, er . . . follow every rainbow trout till you find your dream. . . ."

"Aggggh," said Izzie, putting her hands over her

ears again. "I give in. Mercy. Mercy."

"If you can't sing in front of us, your best mates," I said, "you'll never do it. Now go outside and take a deep breath. Imagine Madonna in your head. Madonna who's going to sing one of your songs the best she's ever done."

"Do I *have* to?" said Izzie.

"YES!" said me and Lucy.

"Or else I'll sing again," said Lucy.

Izzie sighed and got down off her stool. "Bossy pair. But I guess it is now or never."

She went outside then returned a moment later.

"Can I sing facing the window?" she said.

"If that's how Madonna would do it, sure," I said.

"Yeah, she's feeling a bit shy today," said Izzie as she turned away from us. "It's a song I wrote about stage fright."

There was a moment's silence, then she started singing:

"You say I got what it takes
And you say I know what makes the world go round,
But I don't know what I'm going to do about you.
I still can't go on.

434

You say I should leave the shadows
And run for the sun,
Stand in the spotlight and have some fun.
Your faith is my strength but I'm afraid I'll still fall."

Lucy and I started cheering madly as Izzie turned round and bowed. She was good, really good. A deep velvety voice. Assured.

"Izzie, I never knew you could sing like that," I said. "That was really top."

"Yeah," said Lucy. "With a voice like that, you've got nothing to worry about."

"You think so?" she said, blushing red.

"Who was that singing?" said Tony, poking his head round the corner. He was dressed in his best pulling outfit. Black jeans and black T-shirt, and he had his hair slicked back and reeked of Dad's Armani aftershave. It was so obvious he'd done it to impress Lucy. Poor boy. He's really got it bad.

"Our knight in shining Armani," I laughed as he came in.

"It was Izzie," said Lucy.

"Wow," he said, looking at her with admiration. "You've got a good voice."

Izzie looked really chuffed. "Thanks. And thanks, Nesta. This power brekkie was a brillopad idea. Now, where are those papers? Let's find *you* a job."

We spent the next hour looking for jobs for me but soon discovered I am unemployable. There's not a lot around for fourteen-year-olds.

There were jobs for drivers, but I can't drive.

Household interviewers, but car essential.

Cleaners needed, but have to have references. I doubt if Mum would give me one as it's not my best skill.

And finally, jobs for receptionists, but only the over-fifties need apply.

"There's nothing in here for you, Nesta," said Izzie as she put the last paper down. "You found anything?"

"Almost finished," I said. I was looking through a local paper and something had caught my eye. I jotted down the number on a bit of paper. £100–£1000 a day? I could help Mum and Dad

> Earn between £100–£1000 a day as a full-time or part-time model.

out on that kind of money. Do it full-time in the holidays and part-time when I was at school. Hurrah! A solution.

I was about to tell the girls, but Tony kept popping in, pretending that he needed stuff in the kitchen. It was *so* transparent that he wanted to be near Lucy. I decided not to say anything about the ad to the girls while he was there as he knew what Mum and Dad had already said about me modeling—that I couldn't even think about it until I had finished school.

I was dying to ask the girls what they thought, but Tone wouldn't go away. He kept asking if we wanted cappuccinos or toast or a bagel. Iz and I kept saying thanks, no and no, thanks. Lucy, on the other hand, was acting as if he wasn't even there.

Finally, though, I think he'd had enough. He came and stood right in front of her and grinned cheekily.

"I suppose a snog's out of the question?" he asked.

Even Lucy couldn't resist that and she burst out laughing.

437

Nesta's Diary

☺☻☺☹ (An up and down day)

Major disaster after a good start. Discovered I am unemployable. ☹ ☹ ☹

Then I found a solution!!! ☺ ☺ ☺

Then I realized I was missing Simon so I messaged him:

RsQMe :-[[[[(rescue me, I am unhappy)

He wrote back IRLEWan2CU

So I sent :-D))(I'm very happy)

Then he sent :-)~ (I am drooling)

I sent (O-O) (I am shocked)

He sent (((H))) (a big hug)

So I sent <3 (love heart)

I know it's not exactly poetry, but then this is the twenty-first century.

My power breakfast was excellent. Iz sang in front of us and was really fab. She's got something special. She and Lucy are top friends

Then I saw an ad for a model agency. People always tell me that I look like a model, so I'm going to phone and check it out tomorrow.

Hurrah! Hurrah! ☺☺☺

Soon I will be wearing Gucci and earning loadsa£££££!

Chapter 7

Trustafarians

First thing the next day, I picked up the phone and dialed the number of the agency I'd seen in the paper.

"Morgan Elliot models," said a voice at the other end.

"Good morgan, I mean morning," I said, putting on my professional voice. "I read your ad in the paper for models and wanted to know what to do next."

"How old are you?"

I crossed my fingers. "Sixteen," I fibbed.

"Well, first you need to come in and let us see if you have potential, then, if we think you do, you have to register. That costs sixty pounds and you should bring two hundred pounds for your portfolio as we'll need pictures of you to send out to clients and we want to make you look the best you can. Now, would you like to arrange a time to come in and see Mr. Elliot?"

Two hundred and sixty pounds? I thought. Where was I going to get *that* from? I only had thirty pounds left in my savings. Maybe I could borrow some.

"Er, I'll think it over," I said. "I've had a few offers and want to consider my options."

"What offers?" called Tony from the sitting room.

"Er, none," I said, putting down the phone and hoping that he hadn't overheard everything I'd said. "Just going horse riding again this afternoon, maybe . . . probably. . . . That's one of my options."

"With the trustafarians?"

"Durrhhh? The *what*?"

"Trustafarians. You know, kids whose parents put lots of dosh in trust for them, until they're twenty-one or something."

"Oh, yeah, with them."

"Down Hyde Park again?"

"Yeah," I said, going in to join him flopped out

441

on the sofa where he was watching a video of *The Matrix* for the third time.

"Can I come with you?" he said, flicking off the TV. "I'm not doing anything and I'm *soooo* bored. All my mates have gone down to the West End but . . . you know, with us being financially challenged . . . no dosh for Tone to play with. A day out on the horses sounds a laugh."

Simon was cool about Tony coming too. As we made our way over to Kensington, he called on my mobile to say he'd meet us in the park as he was giving a little boy a lesson there before seeing us.

I spotted Simon waiting on the track by Alexandra Gate as soon as we arrived in the park. He had three horses with him and I felt myself smile inside as we got closer. Looking gorgeous in jeans and a Barbour jacket, he seemed to get better-looking every time I saw him.

"Hi," he said, striding forward and shaking Tony's hand. "You must be Nesta's brother?"

Tony grinned, nodded, and pointed to the horses. "One of these for me?"

"Certainly," said Simon. "Nesta said you'd never

ridden before so I thought you might like to have a go. Here, put these on."

As he handed us riding hats, the Portobello Princesses cantered by. WC was wearing her usual sour expression and was about to ride on. But then she saw Tony. I could see her say something to Tanya, then the two of them turned round, rode up to us, and dismounted.

Off came her riding hat, *out* came her hair band as she shook her blond hair and flicked it back, looking up at Tony flirtatiously. "It's just *so* constricting," she said, smiling widely at him, "wearing your hair back all the time."

I had to laugh to myself, as I've seen girls react to Tony like this a million times.

Tony ran his fingers through his hair and kind of shook his head like in a shampoo commercial. "Ooooh. I know just what you mean. . . ." He grinned back at her, giving her his killer charm look.

She snorted with laughter. Woah, Neddie, I thought. He's not *that* funny.

"Cressida, Tanya, this is Nesta's brother, Tony," said Simon.

443

As always, when Tony's introduced as my brother, the girls looked puzzled.

"Same dad, different mothers," I said, going into the old familiar routine to explain our different color skins.

"Oh, yah," said Cressida, swishing her hair around, flick, flick, and not taking her eyes off Tony. "My parents are divorced as well."

"His mum's dead, actually," I said flatly. How dare she assume that they'd got divorced?

Instead of looking embarrassed, WC linked her arm through Tony's. "Oh, you poor darling," she cooed. "So you need a bit of looking after."

"Yeah," said Tony, who was loving every minute of it. "So Cress," he said. "Gonna show me how to horse-ride?"

Cress(!!!?) giggled.

"It's his first time," said Simon. "Put him on Heddie."

"Yes, my first time," whispered Tony seductively and looking at Cressida meaningfully. "I hope you'll be gentle with me."

She shrieked with laughter again, then turned to Simon. "Oh, don't put him on Heddie, Si. Let him go on Prince. I promise I'll take care of him."

"Well I was going to put Nesta on Prince this time, but . . ."

"Oh, I don't mind," I said. "I don't mind Heddie. At least I know him from last time."

As Tanya led the gray horse over to Tony, Cressida looked over at me and made eye contact for the first time.

Like *yeah*, I thought, I *am* here too.

The "smell under her nose" look returned as she saw what I was wearing. "*Cream* jodhpurs!" she snorted. "Nesta darling, *no one* wears cream jodhpurs."

Luckily for her, Tony didn't hear as he was chatting to Tanya. Tony can be a flirt, but he's still my big brother and won't let anyone bully me or be horrid.

"Er, no, Cress *darling*, I think I do," I said, smoothing the jodhpurs over my thighs. "Not the sharpest knife in the drawer, are you?"

"No, really, sweetheart, it's you who's not the brightest crayon in the box," cooed Cressida. "Proper riders wear *dark* colors."

I leaned forward so only she could hear me.

"Actually, Cressida, most people wear dark colors to disguise their fat thighs. Very few people can wear cream. You have to be very slim to get away with it."

She blushed angrily. I knew I'd hit a sore spot. She may have fabulous hair and a pretty face when she lightens up and she may be slimmish, but her build is pear-shape, with a slightly big bottom and thighs.

I went over to join the others. I noticed Cressida hadn't said anything about Tony not wearing the right gear. He was dressed in khaki combats and a fleece, but Cressida didn't seem bothered about what he was dressed in, only that he paid her some attention. Tony was trying to get up on the horse, and, a bit like me when I tried the other day, he was all over the place.

Cressida was straight in to help.

"Put your hand on my shoulder," she said, diving in beside him. "Foot in the stirrup, then lift yourself up."

Tony milked it for all he was worth. First he managed to get his foot stuck in the stirrup so he had to hang on to Cressida to hold him up. Unlike my first time when she'd laughed at me, this time she was all kindness and understanding.

Luckily for Tony, Prince was a patient horse and didn't seem to mind his antics as he attempted to get up into the saddle but kept falling back into Cressida's waiting arms. Hah, I thought. If only you knew what he was really like. Tony's one of those rare boys who can fool girls into thinking she's the only one there and *so* special. I'd seen him do it so many times. He may be gorgeous to look at, but I know what a love rat he really is.

Simon helped me up onto Heddie and when we were all ready, we began to trot up the track. Cressida gave me a filthy look as she passed me so I grinned back at her and turned my riding hat round backward like some people wear their baseball caps.

"You have to wear the proper gear to be a serious rider," I called to Tony who was behind me. He gave me the thumbs-up and promptly turned his hat round backward as well.

Simon cracked up and immediately did the same.

Cressida turned back and was about to scowl when she saw what I had done. Then she saw Tony and Simon's hats and looked like she was going to be sick as she tried to change the scowl to a smile.

"Cool, huh, Cress?" called Tony.

"Er, yah," she said. But she couldn't bring herself to turn her hat round.

Nesta's Diary

Had a brillopad day riding today. Looked fab in cream jodhpurs. WC was sniffy about them. Later on Simon explained that serious riders only wear dark jodhpurs because they have to muck out their horse's stable after riding. Poo. I can't imagine owning my own horse. Must be top.

It was cool having Tony along today. WC made an effort to be more pleasant to me because he was there. Well, at least when he was around. Must make use of this and take him along more often. We had a real laugh wearing our hats backward, but of course WC was suffering her usual sense of humor failure and was not amused.

Phoned model agency. They want £260 to register and do a portfolio. Am seriously considering it so that I can be mega-rich and buy a whole stable of horses.

Am getting the hang of horse-riding. Be cool. Be unafraid. Be gentle. Don't try to run before you can walk. Ha ha.

I got on a lot better with Heddie today. I didn't feel so frightened and I think the feeling was mutual.

I don't think it must be very nice to have a leathery bit thing in the mouth that people pull on. No wonder he wouldn't do what I wanted the first time, when he wanted to eat grass and I kept yanking him up. It must have hurt. Now I have decided to be very gentle and just nudge him a little when I want to go off instead of kicking him. It seemed to work better. I think he knew I was trying to be nice. Also, it's common sense that if you treat anyone—human or animal—nicely, they will be nice back (except WC).

Maybe if I don't become an actress I will be the English Horse Whisperer. Maybe not, as that would probably mean mucking out, which I don't fancy the sound of at all.

Chapter 8

Strange but Healthy Meal

Sometimes holidays can seem like eternity, I thought, as I mooched around our empty flat the following morning. All the world seemed to be busy except me.

Simon was going to lunch with his dad at some hotel called the Connaught. They were going to discuss His Future.

Izzie was rehearsing with Ben the Buddhist and his band King Noz. She'd decided at the power breakfast that she's going to go for it and sing at the next gig. It's a really big deal for her as she's never shown anyone her songs, never mind performed live in front of an audience. She is very brave.

Lucy was being all secretive and said she was doing a "sewing project."

Tony had gone to Hampstead Heath with yet another girlfriend. He's been going through them like hot cakes lately. One a week. The phone's always going with girls on the other end wanting to speak to him. He says it's the only way to help him get over Lucy. I know he's hoping that I'll pass this on and make Lucy jealous, but I don't. Lucy seems to be doing just fine without him, unlike some other girl I could name. It was hysterical when we went horse-riding—Cressida was all over him like a rash and dropped humongous hints that she didn't have a boyfriend at the moment and was free in the week. But Tony was doing his cooler than cool act and didn't ask her out. He said he prefers Tanya anyway.

Mum was working the sunrise shift again. She still hasn't heard if her contract is to be renewed and has been spending loads of time these days scouring newspapers looking for alternative jobs.

Dad isn't due back from Manchester until Friday night. I'll probably be in bed when he arrives. I'll leave a nice welcome home note for him.

And me? Not busy. Unoccupied.

I picked up the papers I'd bought a couple of days before and was about to put them in the recycling bin. Should I try the modeling agency again, I wondered? Maybe I could just go down there and check the place out? I wouldn't have to commit. Should I? Shouldn't I?

I picked up the telephone and dialed.

"Can I come over?" I asked when Lucy answered the phone. "I know you're sewing, but I promise I'll sit in the corner and won't make a sound. You won't even know I'm there."

"Sure," said Lucy. "In *fact*, I may have a surprise for you."

Lucy's bedroom floor was knee-deep in bits of assorted fabric.

"Careful," she said from her desk where she was sitting in front of her mum's sewing machine. "Stand on the bits of carpet in between."

"What are you making?" I said as I tiptoed my way through bits of lace, silk and crêpe to the bed.

"I'm experimenting. See"—she pointed to a newspaper by her bed— "have a look in there. A few pages in. I nicked it from one of your papers on Sunday. Look at the page about fashion week. There's a designer called Elspeth Gibson, got it? Read what it says about her."

I turned to the page she said and scanned the many designers featured on the page: Ben de Lisi, Ronit Zilkha, Ghost, then in the bottom right, Elspeth Gibson.

"Wow. Lucy. These are lush," I said, looking at the designs.

"Yeah, but read what it says about Elspeth Gibson," insisted Lucy.

"Jodhpurs are topped with fragile Edwardian-style blouses, and a hacking jacket goes over a flirt's skirt of frothy chiffon. . . ."

"Exactly," interrupted Lucy, indicating the floor with her arms. "We've got frothy, we've got chiffon. It says what's in is a mixture of new and vintage. Like tweed with organza, a bit of lace against chiffon, velvet and Lycra."

"You're really into all this, aren't you?" I asked. She looked so animated. Enthusiastic.

Lucy nodded. "I've really found my thing. I love making clothes. And seeing those designs in the paper, I thought that's exactly what I like doing. Mixing old and new. Vintage clothing is so in. Especially since Julia Roberts wore that ancient Valentino dress to get her Oscar." She pointed to the wardrobe. "Have a look in there, Nesta, at the bottom."

I did as I was told, being careful not to stand on the bits of material on the floor. I reached into the wardrobe and pulled out the bin bag. It was full of bits of material and old clothes.

"What am I looking for?" I asked, sifting through more cut-up blouses on the top.

"A jacket down the bottom somewhere. That's the bag of stuff that belonged to my grandmother."

"Ah," I said. "The treasure trove."

I knew all about this bag. In the autumn term, Lucy had found it in the cupboard under the stairs where her mum had stashed it years ago with a load of junk. It was full of clothes from the forties and fifties. Lucy used bits of the old fabric to do some of her early designs, two of which were fab tops for Izzie and me.

"It's at the bottom," said Lucy, watching me rummage around.

In the end, I emptied all the clothes out on the floor, adding to the mess.

"There," said Lucy, pointing to a jacket.

I picked it up. "OhmyGod."

"Try it on," beamed Lucy.

It was the most perfect riding jacket.

"I know," grinned Lucy. "It was after we'd been to that riding gear shop the other day. I thought, I'm *sure* I've seen a jacket like that somewhere, but I didn't say at the time as I didn't want to get your hopes up."

The label inside said HARRIS TWEED and it was brown with little fudge- and cream-colored flecks. It was far nicer than any of the ones we'd seen in the shop. I put it on. It fit perfectly and was beautifully cut, nipping in at the waist.

"Sleeves are a bit short," said Lucy, getting up and examining the arms, "but I can let them down a little."

"Lucy, I *love* it. Can I wear it? Really?"

"Yeah, course. It's yours," said Lucy. "And that's not all." She held up a floaty cream voile blouse with a ruffle down the front.

"Try it on with this," she said. "I made it from

that dress that I got from Portobello."

"But you bought it for you," I said. "For the material."

"Loads of material left in the skirt," said Lucy. "And anyway, all good designers have models that take their collections out into the public. You can be my live mannequin. Come on, try it on."

I stripped and put on the blouse, then the jacket.

"Wear those with your cream jodhpurs and I reckon you'll look like you stepped straight out of *Vogue*."

I looked at my reflection in the mirror. She was right. The outfit looked just like one of those from the fashion week.

"And if I borrow Mum's knee-high boots, it'll look amazing," I said. "Lucy, you really are a top friend."

Lucy blushed. "No prob," she said. "Now let's let those sleeves down."

After Lucy finished her sewing, I gave her a manicure and pedicure as a thank you. And I did it really properly. I got a bowl from the kitchen and filled it with hot water. Then we put in some of the magnolia bubble bath that Lucy got for Christmas and she soaked her feet. Then I did a bit of a massage on her feet and hands with vanilla body lotion before painting her nails the pale blue color that she's into at the moment.

Around six o'clock, Izzie turned up from her rehearsal and Lucy's mum said we could all stay and have supper if we didn't mind eating on our knees in front of the TV.

"I can't be bothered doing a big number at the table," she said.

She's so cool, Mrs. Lovering—really laid-back and easy.

I love being at their house. All of them have made me feel like one of the family ever since I arrived in London. *However,* when it came to eating there, I wasn't so sure. They eat some very weird stuff at the Loverings'. Even Lucy would agree. Her dad runs the local health food shop and sells all the health foods that Izzie is into but I've never heard of.

After half an hour or so, Mrs. Lovering brought through plates of food.

"Mmm, smells good," said Izzie.

"What is it?" I asked.

457

"Quinoa, steamed vegetables, and soy sauce," said Mrs. Lovering. "And to make it a bit more interesting, I've chopped in some nori."

Lucy and I exchanged looks.

"Mmm, my *favorite*," I said as Lucy and I both burst out laughing. She knew I hadn't got a clue what quinoa or nori were.

Izzie raised her eyes to heaven. "Nori is seaweed. And quinoa is like a grain. It's really good for you."

I took a forkful and put it in my mouth as I do believe in trying everything once. It tasted like rice mixed with freshly mown grass and lemon. "Yeah. Suppose it's okay."

"Yeah," said Lucy, chewing a bit of hers then going into her best Shakespearian actor luvvie voice. "But *ohhh* how I *lonnngggg* for egg and chips and *beeeeans* some *niiiights*."

"How was rehearsal?" I asked Izzie after we'd finished our Strange But Healthy Meal.

"Tough," she said. "But fun. They're well pleased that I'm going to sing. At first I was soooo nervous, but then we went over and over it to the point where I just wanted to get it right and stopped thinking about my knocking knees."

"What are you going to wear?" asked Lucy.

"Ah. Not sure. I had thought maybe my velvet—"

"Where's the gig?" I interrupted.

"Somewhere in Kentish Town."

"Then *not* your velvet. It's too nice-girl-who-lives-in-Hampstead," I said. "You need to look dangerous, like you've got an edge."

"That's exactly what Ben said," said Izzie. "In fact, he's working at this place his cousin owns in Camden Lock, just for the hols, to get some dosh so we can hire a studio to do a demo tape. He says he thinks I should go down there and have a look before deciding on anything."

"If Ben's a Buddhist, he might kit you out in Eastern robes," I said.

"Nah. He says this shop is mega, like nothing he's ever seen before."

"When shall we all go?" said Lucy. "Next week?"

"Yeah," said Izzie. "Brillopad. And you'll come to the gig as well, won't you? To see me sing?"

"Wouldn't miss it for the world," said Lucy. "But how are things with you and Ben apart from the singing?"

459

Izzie grinned. "Most excellent. He's so cool and—oh, he says that there are some people coming to check out the band from a record agency. We need as many people there in the audience as possible, so it looks like the band's really popular."

"I'll bring Simon and the Princesses," I said. "It's about time they came north of the river."

Chapter 9

Prada 'n' Prejudice

"Nesta! You look totally amazing," said Tanya as she opened the door to their house in Holland Park. "Where did you get that fab gear?"

"Oh, a little designer I know in North London," I said casually as I stepped into a vast marble hallway.

Lucy *is* little. In fact, she's only four foot eight.

I knew I looked good. I'd spent ages getting ready, as I'd decided to show Simon exactly how I could look if I tried. He'd only ever seen me in my scruffs. This time, I'd washed and conditioned my hair in camomile rinse so it looked really silky. Then I'd painted my nails with Mum's Chanel

461

Rouge Noir. After that, I'd put on some Mac kohl and Bobbi Brown lipstick and a little blusher. Then on with my Lucy Lovering designer extraordinaire outfit—that is, the blouse and jacket were from Lucy, but I wore them with a ra-ra skirt, not jodhpurs, as we weren't riding. I got the skirt at Christmas from Morgan; it's made of a bronze swishy material that flares out in a little frill just above my knees. Looked great with the blouse. And to complete it all, I'd borrowed a pair of Mum's sexy Jimmy Choos.

"I wish I could wear shoes like that," said Tanya, "but they kill my feet. You walk in them so easily."

"Just takes practice," I said. Hah! If only she'd seen me round the corner a few minutes ago. I'd worn my Nikes most of the way and changed into the killer heels at the last minute so I wouldn't have to walk far.

"Simon's in the library," said Tanya. "Come through."

"With Miss Scarlet and the rope?" I joked as I took in the luxurious surroundings, but Tanya looked blank.

"Clue," I explained. "Have you never played it?

Who did the murder? Professor Plum in the hall with the dagger or Mrs. White in the library . . . oh never mind."

I tried not to look too gobsmacked when Tanya opened the door to the library. There's serious money in these here walls, I thought, as I took in the airy elegant room. Heavy ivory silk curtains hung at windows that must have been at least ten meters high. Plush pale sofas were arranged opposite each other in front of the most stunning fireplace I have ever seen. It was white marble. A man's torso was carved out on each side with fruit and grapes and leaves winding round him. From floor to ceiling were shelves lined with endless books. Even the flower arrangement on the piano looked like it had cost a small fortune. No simple daffs for this household, here were lilies, white roses, and orchids. Shame about the rugs though, I thought, as I walked over to the sofas. They were beautiful, but looked a bit faded round the edges.

Simon looked like he was asleep, and Cressida was jabbering on her mobile phone while flicking through a copy of *Tatler* which lay on top of a pile of glossy magazines. *Country Life*.

Vogue. Harpers & Queen. Vanity Fair.

"Nesta's here," announced Tanya.

Cressida ignored me and turned her knees toward the fireplace whilst continuing her phone conversation. Simon opened his eyes, looked up sleepily, then his face lit up. "I was just thinking about you," he said, getting up to greet me. "You look beautiful." Then he turned to Tanya. "Aren't you two off somewhere?"

"Yeah, yeah, ballet," said Tanya. "And I think I can safely guess what you two will be up to. Come on, Cressida, or we'll be late."

Cressida gave me a cursory glance, then did a double take and checked out my outfit. She raised her eyebrows slightly, but didn't say anything.

Some people find it hard to give compliments, I thought, and some people find it hard to receive them. Me, I'm good at both and decided maybe it was time she learned from the Master.

"You're looking good today," I said to Cressida as she picked up a little handbag from the coffee table. "Cool bag."

Before she could stop herself, she smiled. "Thanks. It's Prada."

Then, before I could stop myself, I blurted, "Oh. Like in that book by Jane Austen?"

"What book?" asked Cressida, taking the bait like a dream.

"*Prada 'n' Prejudice*," I said.

Simon and Tanya burst out laughing. "Oh very good," said Tanya. "In fact, we're doing *Pride and Prejudice* at school next term."

Cressida didn't laugh. I was waiting for one of her eyebrows to go up or down. She had quite a range of eyebrow expressions. Left one up for an "I'm superior" look. Right one up for disdain. Both up for bored interest. Both down and pulled together for disapproval.

"Actually, before you go, I wanted to ask you both something," I said.

They stopped at the door.

"My friend Izzie is singing at a gig on Friday night and I wanted to know if you'd like to go."

"Yah, okay," said Tanya. "I don't think we're doing anything."

"Is she one of the girls who was in the shop the other day?" asked Cressida. Aley-oop. Eyebrow up.

"Yeah. Dark-haired one," I said. "She has an

amazing voice and sings with a band called King Noz. They're getting a really good name for themselves round North London."

"Well I'm in," said Simon.

"Where exactly will this gig be?" drawled Cressida.

"Kentish Town somewhere. I'll let you know nearer the time."

"*Kentish* Town? Where's that?" asked Cressida. Smell under nose and both eyebrows down.

Stuck-up cow, I thought. I was about to tell her that there is life outside West London, but then I remembered Izzie wanted loads of people at the gig to impress the talent scouts.

Then inspiration struck. I *know* how to get you there, I thought.

"There's a whole crowd of us going," I said. "Lucy, her brothers, *Tony*."

Suddenly Cressida looked interested, but I looked directly at Tanya. "I know he'd like to see you again."

Of course, Cressida thought I meant her.

"I suppose we could go," she said. "In fact, why not? It'll be a hoot."

After they'd gone, I settled in with Simon on the sofa. Even though it was spring, there was a real fire burning and the atmosphere was so cozy I thought we could stay there all afternoon. It was the first time I'd been alone with him properly since I'd met him, and I didn't fancy trawling round the pavements in Mum's shoes. They look good but they're clearly not for walking.

"Shall we stay here?" I said, snuggling up to Simon.

He put his arm round me. "Yeah. Mum's around somewhere. In fact, I want to introduce you but she's upstairs with one of the slave team in at the moment."

"Slave team?"

"Yeah. She has a whole load of people who look after her."

"Is she ill?"

Simon laughed. "No. She's an interior designer. She's quite famous." He indicated the fabulous flowers. "Our home is her showcase, so she has a florist who comes in to make sure the place looks good. A nutritionist to make sure she eats right. A manicurist and pedicurist to make sure her nails look good. A hairdresser . . . then she has her PA and her reflexologist and her aromatherapist and beautician . . ."

"We also have people who come to the house," I said. "The milkman, the postman, the garbage-men . . ."

Simon laughed, but I felt sad for a minute because there was my mum worrying about work and money and telling us to economize and here was I sitting in this mega-posh place surrounded by dosh. Eight people to look after one! His mum must earn a fortune, I thought. Life's a funny busi-ness. Why are some people so rich and others have nothing? I must ask Izzie later. She's bound to have some kind of answer.

"I think Mum's having a massage," said Simon, putting his arm around me, "so that means she won't be around for a while."

"Cool," I said and took his other hand in mine. Simon stroked my fingers and sort of massaged my palm. It was heavenly. Holding hands can be so nice if you do it properly I've discovered. Almost as good as kissing.

"Actually, I was going to ask you something," he

said when we came up for air after a divine sno-gathon. "There's a whole gang of us going away next week, for a few days. Skiing. At Courchevel. There were six of us, but my friend Marcus has dropped out and I wondered . . . do you think you might be able to come?"

"God, I'd love to . . . ," I began, but I realized this was the time to come clean. My family couldn't begin to keep up with his. No doubt about it, especially now that I had seen where he lived. Izzie's words of encouragement echoed in my mind and gave me the strength to say what I knew I must.

He likes you no matter what, she'd said.

I had to tell him I couldn't possibly ask my mum. It wasn't only the trip away, there would be the gear to buy, and pocket money. Mum had enough stress as it was without me laying more on her. She'd been looking tired lately. And even Dad sounded strained when I talked to him on the phone. It's *them* that needed the holiday break, never mind me.

"You know what I really admire about you?" said Simon just as I opened my mouth to explain.

"What?"

"Your amazing attitude. You don't let *anything* faze you. It's the kind of attitude that we're always being encouraged to have at school. Even my dad was on about it the other day at lunch. But *you* don't have to learn it. It's natural with you. You're one of life's winners. Other people give up before they've even begun but not you. You go for it."

Gulp. How can I possibly tell him now? I thought. Shatter his illusions that I am a tip-top winner-type person? Tell him I can't go to Courchevel. That my family's broke?

Er. I don't *think* so.

Nesta's Diary

Très interesting day.

Simon's house is out of this world. Stunning. Classy. Going to the loo there is a spiritual experience as everything is so beautiful.

Lovely sandalwood soaps by Floris. Air freshener by Czech and Speake.

The sink and faucets were a work of art.

I took notes of everything for when I am rich and famous.

Piles of white towels. Izzie's mum would think she'd died and gone to heaven. (She's big on white towels as well.)

Met Simon's mum briefly. She looks expensive. Blonde with not a hair out of place. Dressed in cashmere. Looks like she sweats French perfume.

Big dilemna though. I said I'd go to Courchevel. Tony told me it's a super fab ski resort and loads of the boys from his school go there.

V. expensive.

I thought again about contacting the model agency, but even with them, I wouldn't have the money in time. So. I'm drawing out my £30 savings and I'm going to gamble. Scratchcards.

Chapter 10

Cyberdog

"You're mad," said Izzie, when I met her on the corner of our road. "Do you know what the chances are of you actually winning? It's like, millions to one."

"So? Someone's got to win. Why not me?"

"Well, why exactly do we have to go to East Finchley High Road?"

"In case anyone sees us. I can't risk running into Mum or Tony or someone in Highgate."

"Are we meeting Lucy?"

I shook my head. "Nah. You have to be sixteen to buy Instant cards. Someone might suss that I'm not old enough if she was with us."

"God, you've really got this all worked out, haven't you?"

"You bet," I said, then laughed. "I mean *I* bet."

"Well as long as you know I don't approve," said Izzie. "And I did promise Lucy I'd take her with me to Cyberdog today."

"Cyberdog?"

"The shop where Ben's working. The manager is his cousin. He said I could borrow an outfit for the gig as it will be publicity for the shop."

"Cool. Maybe I could buy something there with my winnings. I've got thirty quid left in the world and I reckon that will give me a good chance."

"Okay," she said doubtfully. "But don't blame me if you lose it all."

"I'm feeling lucky. And my horoscope said I may get a windfall this week."

That shut her up. Izzie's *well* into astrology.

"It's like, sometimes in life, you have to gamble. Someone has to win. If you're not in, you can't win."

"Yeah. Maybe. Whatever," said Iz.

We came across a newsagent in the High Road with a lottery sign outside, and I quickly looked up and down the road to make sure that no one

473

I knew was about. Like Mrs. Allen the head-mistress, or Tony.

I felt like a spy on a mission. "Just call me Bond. James Bond. Double-oh-seven," I said.

"You'll be more like double-oh-zero when you've no money left," laughed Izzie.

"Coast clear," I said as I opened the door and stepped inside.

Now. Which to choose? There were about eight varieties.

Now how much do I want to win? I thought. One thousand pounds. Five thousand pounds, twenty thousand, or the big one, one hundred thousand pounds.

"Are you going to get one of each?" asked Izzie, looking at the cards.

I shook my head. "No. I read somewhere that they only put a winning card in every now and again so I reckon I have a better chance of winning if I buy a few of one type from the same roll."

I decided to go for the big one.

"Can I have five of those instant scratchcards?" I asked the lady behind the counter. "The ones for one hundred thousand."

May as well aim high, I thought, as a thrill of anticipation ran through me.

"There may be more winners on the smaller amounts," said Izzie, eyeing the chocolate on display.

"No. Final decision," I said. As I handed over my money I spotted something I knew Izzie would like. "Er, and a bar of Greene and Blacks."

I handed Izzie the bar of organic chocolate and we went and sat on a bench in the High Road outside Budgens. I pulled out my purse and got out a coin.

"What would you do if you won?" asked Izzie, popping a piece of chocolate in her mouth.

Ah, my favorite fantasy, I thought. "I'd have a party with all our friends. . . . Buy some new clothes. . . . Get a car. . . ."

"But you can't drive yet."

"Yeah, but for when I can. Then I'd get presents for you and Lucy and Tony and Mum and Dad. I'd go on holiday with you and Lucy. I'd take you to Saint Kitts in the Caribbean where Mum's from. You'd love it: sand like talcum powder and the colors are to die for—turquoise, aquamarine

475

. . . gorgeous. Then to Ravello in Italy, where Dad was born. It's high on the Amalfi Coast. Amazing. Then I'd buy a flat. Get horse-riding lessons for Lucy and me. Buy you a studio. . . ."

Izzie laughed. "Er, Nesta . . . you'll only have *one* hundred thousand if you win. . . ."

"Money makes money. Isn't your mum always saying that? Anyway . . . what would you do?"

"Travel. Goa. Los Angeles. Phuket. Save some. Get a band together and a demo tape. Stuff like that."

I began scraping the cards. "Okay, here goes."

First one. Nothing.

Second one and my heart began to beat as I saw £100,000 appear. Then *another* £100,000.

"OhmyGod . . ." I held my breath as I scraped off the rest of the card.

Then my heart sank. £6. £10. £25.

Ah well, three more cards to go.

I could see Izzie having to bite her tongue as I finished scraping the last one. She was dying to say, "I told you so."

I waved the last one in her face. "I've *won*!!!"

"*Really*!" she gasped. "How much?"

"A *pound*," I said. "Whoo*pee*. Let's go and collect our winnings."

After we'd picked up the pound coin from the newsagents, we walked a bit farther down to a garage. The man at the till hardly even glanced up at me so I bought ten cards. Once again, a thrill of anticipation ran through me. This was serious fun. It was really exciting as each time I got a handful of cards, I felt full of hope. Possibilities. Until I scratched the cards, there was a chance I might win. Change my life. Change Mum and Dad's lives.

We sat on the brick wall by the road and I scraped five and Izzie did five. This time I won two pounds. Never mind, I told myself, I still had fifteen pounds left.

"Oh, let's go," said Izzie. "You've lost half your money. I can't bear it. Maybe your horoscope was right, and you've got your windfall—three pounds. Let's buy some chips with the winnings and go and collect Lucy."

There was *no way* I was giving up then. It was far too exciting and it wasn't over yet. And I hadn't lost *all* my money. Only half of it.

And I'd won three pounds.

And what *if*? What if I did give up and the *very* next card I was going to buy was the *one*? *The winning card?*

I couldn't back down now.

But which shop was the winning card in? The newsagents? The corner shop?

"Let's try the Post Office," I said, and set off eagerly.

"I'm going to Lucy's," said Izzie. "Are you coming with me?"

"No way," I said. "I'll only be another ten minutes. Why won't you stay?"

"Because this is a total waste of your money and it's painful to watch."

Killjoy, I thought. There was no way I going to stop now. I *had* to carry on. I couldn't even *think* about stopping.

"I'll meet you at Lucy's when I've finished," I said. "Be prepared to celebrate."

"Yeah, whatever," said Izzie, heading for the bus stop. "Later."

Honestly, I thought, as I puffed my way back

up the High Road. She's got no sense of adventure, that girl.

I saw another sign for the lottery outside the Post Office. I bet that's where the winning card is, I thought. I can just feel it in my bones. I was just about to go in when I saw one of our teachers, Miss Watkins, in the queue. I did a quick turn around. She was the last person I wanted to bump into.

I walked a bit farther up and found a corner shop that sold scratchcards, and there I bought seven. I decided to buy some of the ones with lesser prizes of two thousand five hundred, just in case Izzie had been right and you stood a better chance of winning.

I put them in my bag then went back to the Post Office.

I quickly checked that Miss Watkins had gone then, seeing that all was clear, I joined the queue. I was feeling really elated. I was sure the winning card was here.

An old woman in front of me bought some writing paper and when I saw she'd finished at the counter, I stepped forward.

But then the woman turned back. She looked at the scratchcards. "Oh, go on," she said to the lady behind the counter. "I'll have three." Then she saw me. "Oh, sorry love," she said. "Do you want to go? I'm in no hurry."

Oh *no*, I thought, panicking. *Decisions*. Should I let her have the next cards or should *I* buy them? Should I wait and let her go before me or should I butt in and take the next cards? What if the very next card is *The One* and I let her buy it? *Aaaghhhh*!

"No, you go ahead," I said.

She bought her cards and I stepped forward again.

"Eight of the hundred thousand pound cards," I said, laying my money out on the counter.

The lady behind the till smiled. "Feeling lucky?" she asked as she ripped eight cards off the roll.

"Yeah," I said. But I wasn't so sure any more.

On the bus to Lucy's, I sat at the back and got busy scraping the cards from the Post Office. One, two, three, four, five, six, seven, eight. Nothing. Not even a pound.

Then I got out the seven cards from the newsagents'. Maybe I'd have to settle for one of the smaller prizes. Scrape, scrape. One, two, three, four, five, six. Nothing.

The feeling of anticipation had now been replaced by disappointment. And horror. I'd spent all my money. I had nothing left to last me through the rest of the holidays.

I had one card left. I was about to start scraping but stopped myself and put it back in my purse for later. As long as I didn't look at it or scrape it, there was still a chance, some hope that it was a winner. I'd do it when I got to Lucy's.

But already there was a sinking feeling in the pit of my stomach. I had no money left at all now. That hadn't been part of the plan.

When I reached Lucy's, she took the card I handed her and scraped off the last bits of silver.

She looked up at me sadly. "I *am* sorry, Nesta," she said. "Nothing."

I sighed. "Do you think I need to go to Gamblers Anonymous?" I asked. "Now that I'm an addict."

Izzie laughed. "Not yet. But I do think that the

only kind of 'instant' you should stick to in the future is the mashed potato variety."

Lucy's dad dropped us in Camden. He drove us there in their hippie-dippie car and as always people stared at us when we drove by. The car does make quite a statement. It's an old Volkswagon Beetle and it's bright turquoise with a big lilac flower painted on the boot. No one batted an eyelid when we got to the Lock. The hippie-dippie look has come back in fashion there along with flares and tie-dye T-shirts.

"Ben says the shop is under the arches in the stable part of the market," said Izzie, leading us through a gate behind the main market.

The courtyard was heaving with people who looked like they were either at a fancy dress party or a meeting of different tribespeople. There were skinheads, goths, hippies, and punks. And wandering round in the middle, looking amazed by the sights, were little groups of tourists all dressed neatly in their Benetton best. Music of every variety pounded out from different stalls: techno, Latin, garage, turbo, trance, hip-hop, sixties, seventies, heavy metal. Every way you turned there were sounds. And smells.

The delicious aroma of garlic, spices, and onions hit us as we pushed our way through the crowds.

"You like some noodles, pretty lady?" called a Thai girl from behind an enormous steaming wok.

"I'd give *anything* for noodles," I said. "But I have no money."

The girl pulled a sad face, then called to a crowd of goth girls behind me.

"Wow," I said, pulling Lucy's arm. "Look, *look*, behind, a posse of death-cult zombie girls."

Lucy giggled as a group of teenagers dressed in goth black drifted by. Their faces were plastered in white makeup and their hair was black with purple streaks and so lank it looked like it hadn't been washed. Ever.

"I can't imagine what there is here," I whispered to Lucy. "I mean, most people we've seen are either retro, goths, or punks—nothing really new."

"Ben says it's the most happening place in London at the moment," said Izzie.

"And I'm hoping I can pick up some tips for my design work," said Lucy. "All the papers say that what's happening is vintage mixed with new. I need to check out if that's right."

The seductive smell of caramel hit my nostrils as we passed a stall selling roasted nuts. I groaned. "Oh. I'm hungry," I wailed.

Izzie raised an eyebrow. "You've only yourself to blame," she said.

I stuck my tongue out at her back as I hurried along behind her into a passageway. Soon the smell of food was replaced by a strong smell of joss sticks.

Loud music was pulsating from an entrance under one of the arches in a corner.

"Here it is," said Izzie, pointing up to the sign. "Cyberdog."

As we stepped inside, the music was throbbing and the ground shaking with the base.

It was like we'd walked into a spaceship. Brick walls were painted silver, orange, and turquoise. Tables lined the walls where people were seated playing on iMac computers and sipping cappuccinos. Dry ice was being pumped up from the floor, giving the place an other-worldly look.

Izzie disappeared off to look for Ben, and Lucy and I went through an archway into what looked like a clothes shop.

The clothes on the rails looked like they'd been stolen from the set of *Star Trek*. One top was made of rows of red ridges made to look like ribs. And the shop assistants looked like alien mutants. They were all dancing wildly to the music.

Lucy and I stood and stared. One girl in front of me had her head shaved except for a pink fluorescent ponytail at the back. She was wearing head-to-foot canary yellow. On her calves she had huge yellow furry leggings. Through her earlobes, she had about twelve rings, a stud through her nose, and another through her mouth.

"I feel sorry for whoever has to snog her," I said.

"Oh, wow. Look at these," said Lucy, pulling me over to look at the racks displaying jewelry. Most of it was made out of transparent plasticky stuff. Chokers and gauntlets, with metal studs and spikes. "I've seen this stuff. It glows in the dark in clubs."

"Cool. And definitely different," I said. "Cressida may say it's all happening in Notting Hill, but this takes some beating."

"Yeah, it's like galaxy princess meets Olive Oyle," said Lucy as an assistant wearing a tiny black dress and striped tights walked past in knee-high lace-up boots with four-inch rubber soles.

"New rock," said Ben, appearing behind us and pointing at the boots. "Everyone's wearing them."

Even Ben had made some concession to the style of the place. He'd replaced his usual John Lennon glasses with silver goggles and wore white overalls and silver space boots.

"Where's Iz?" asked Lucy.

"Getting changed."

At that moment Izzie appeared at the end of the aisle.

"Like it?" she asked, looking shyly at Ben.

She looked *amazing*. Transformed.

She had on a short black dress with no sleeves and a scoop neck, but the skirt was extraordinary. It stuck out, as if someone had lined the hem with coat hanger wire. Like crinoline skirts from ages gone by. On her legs she wore a pair of the furry leggings like the assistant was wearing, only Izzie's were blue. On her arms she had a pair of turquoise gauntlets and round her neck a turquoise choker with metal spikes.

"You look like an alien rock singer," I said.

"Rock chickerama," said Lucy.

"I thought I'd get some electric blue eyelashes," said Izzie. "And maybe some blue hair extensions, you know, the ones that look like dreadlocks. What do you think, Lucy?"

Lucy's eyes were shining. "I think," she said, "that this place is the biz boz. I mean, why look like your mum when you can look like an alien borg babe? This stuff is trekkie heaven."

Nesta's Diary

Dear Diary

Had an awful day. I went gambling and lost all my money. Then I went to Camden with the girls and saw a million things I wanted but couldn't afford. I couldn't even buy a cappuccino and felt very miserable. Ben bought me one and I was very glad that Izzie didn't let on to him about me being a hopeless gambler drowning in materialism. Although I wouldn't mind drowning in it a bit.

I think I have learned a BIG lesson today. If I hadn't lost all that money I could have had a really nice time at Camden. I could have had Thai noodles and roasted nuts and even bought one of the galaxy princess chokers that are out-of-this-world fab.

I tried not to let on, but actually I was v. fed up.

Chapter 11

Mobile Sloanes

The hall where the gig was to be held looked like a Boy Scout's hut. There was a tatty plywood stage at one end, battered plastic tables and chairs lining the walls, and threadbare curtains at windows that looked like they hadn't been cleaned in a decade.

"Good turnout," said Lucy, looking round at the people already gathered. There were to be three bands on and it looked like everyone had brought friends and family along for support.

"I can't wait to see Cressida's face when she sees this joint," I said.

"Shabby chic is not a look to be sniffed at," said Lucy. "It can take years to perfect."

A few moments later I saw Simon appear at the

back door with the Portobello Princesses. Predictably Cressida's face fell.

"Oh, here's WC," said Lucy. "Looks like she has a bad smell under her nose."

"What else is new?" I said. "Oh *do* let me introduce you properly."

Simon was as sweet as Cressida was sour. Immediately after the introductions, he asked who wanted what to drink and went off to the bar in the adjoining pub. I went with him to use the ladies'.

I fixed my lipstick, then went into a stall, and not long after I heard the door open and footsteps.

"What a dive," said a voice I recognized. It was Cressida. "And *erlack*, this place stinks. I would never have come if Tony wasn't going to be here."

"So does this interest in him mean that you've finally got over Simon?" Tanya's voice.

Very slowly and quietly, I lifted my feet up in case either of them decided to check under the stall doors. I wanted to hear what they had to say.

"Oh, yah. Though one can't see why he's going out with the zebra."

"The zebra?" asked Tanya.

"Nesta. Half black, half white," sniggered Cressida.

Inside my cubicle, I gasped.

"That's *really* mean," said Tanya. "You're jealous because she's stunning and Simon fancies her and not you."

You tell her, Tanya, I thought. I was tempted to yell out, "Earth is full. Go home!" But I bit my tongue. I wanted to hear what else they had to say.

"Nah. He doesn't fancy her, not *really*. He's only doing it to be different," said Cressida. "He's far too good for her. He probably wants to upset your parents. Going out with a middle-class mixed-race girl is his way of rebeling. It's a phase."

Agghhh. I thought. *Aaaghhhh*.

Tanya was silent for a moment. "You know what, Cressida? You can be a total witch sometimes."

"You say that as if it's a bad thing," laughed Cressida.

I heard someone open the door then slam it behind her. Tanya, I presume.

Then I heard some rustling and the hiss of a

491

spray, then a scent of vanilla. I heard the door open and close again. Then it was quiet.

I waited a few seconds before lowering my feet back on to the floor. It felt like someone had hit me in the stomach and I bent over in pain. I *wished* I hadn't heard.

It couldn't be true, could it? Simon was only going out with me because I was like, a *novelty*? He wanted to appear *different*? My eyes pricked with tears. I thought Simon really liked me. And his mum seemed very nice when I met her the other day. She hadn't seemed unduly upset, but had she just been acting polite and was secretly appalled?

It felt like someone had taken my breath away and I gasped for air. Then, suddenly, the flood gates opened and tears started running down my face.

Graffiti scrawled on the back of the loo door stared harshly back at me. "Life's a bitch," it said, "and then you die." Life *is* a bitch, I thought. My boyfriend's using me to upset his parents. My parents haven't got jobs. All I seem to do these days is want things I can't have. I've become really shallow. And I don't know anything any more.

Suddenly there was a timid knock on the door.

"Are you all right in there?" It was Izzie's voice. I unlocked the door. "It's *me*," I sobbed.

"Oh, Nesta," she cried, pushing the door open properly. "What's the matter?"

I took great gulps of air and tried to get out what I'd overheard. Izzie listened quietly, but by the time I'd finished she looked angry.

"What a *cow*," she said. She handed me a bit of loo paper and put her arm round me. "I'd like to sock her in her stupid snotty face. I saw them just now, standing at the back of the room like, so superior. Like they're so above the rest of us."

"Tanya's okay," I said. "She stuck up for me."

"Then I don't know why she hangs round with Cressida. She should dump her. And have you seen them? It's like they're both stuck to their mobiles. They haven't had them off their ears since they arrived."

"They're always like that," I said.

"We should call them Mobile Sloanes," said Izzie, referring to their favorite section of town. "I might even write a song about them. Mobile Sloanes. Ice-blonde clones . . . Yeah, I'll work on it," she said, smiling wickedly.

I was beginning to feel a bit better.

"Mobile Sloanes," I laughed and blew my nose. Then, for the first time, I noticed what Izzie was wearing. She had on the gear from Cyberdog but she'd done her makeup bright silver with electric blue eyelashes and glittery blue nail polish. Her hair was gelled back into a high ponytail and she had a blue lightning symbol painted on her forehead like a cosmic third eye.

"Wow, Izzie, you look totally amazing."

"You think? Not too much?"

"Yeah, *yeah*, too much. That's why it's so *cool*. You look *really* beautiful. Like a galaxy princess. I feel so boring beside you."

"You look great as well," said Izzie. "That biker-babe look really suits you." I'd worn my old favorites—black leather trousers and jacket. "You look a ton better than those two Sloane clones out there. At least you have your own style."

She gave me a hug and looked at me seriously. "You mustn't let WC upset you. She's not worth it. You've been acting really oddly ever since you met her. Like you have to prove something. And, believe me, you don't, not to people like her. Me

494

and Lucy have been really worried. It's not like you. So, come on, splash your face and let's get out of here."

I did as I was told and reapplied my makeup, most of which had run down my face.

"We'll do a deal," said Izzie, applying some bright blue lipstick. "You go out there and show them how to have a good time. Get out on the floor and dance. And I'll get up on stage and show them just how cool us Norf London girls can be."

"Deal," I said and we shook hands. "How are you feeling?"

Izzie stood up straight and put her shoulders back. Then she sank forward and leaned against the wall. "I'm terrified, Nesta. Absolutely terrified."

Then she got out a little bottle of something and swigged it back.

"*Izzie?* You turning to drink?"

"It's larch," she said. "A Bach flower remedy for confidence."

I love Izzie, I thought. Mad witch that she is.

As we went back into the hall, we saw that the first band had started up. Izzie disappeared backstage, so

I went to join Lucy, who was talking to Simon.

"Is everything all right?" asked Simon, scrutinizing me.

"Yeah, cool," I said, then pulled him aside for a minute. "I have to ask you something."

"Looks serious," he said. "Shoot."

"Are you going out with me to upset your parents?"

Simon looked horrified. "Course not. Mum really liked you when you met her the other day. Why should it upset them?"

"With me being, you know . . ."

"What? Being *what*?" he asked, then he stopped and looked at me closely. "Oh, I get it. Well actually, if I'm totally honest, I think Mum may be a bit upset. In fact, probably a lot. . . . And so will Dad be when he meets you. . . ."

Oh *no*, I thought. Cressida was right.

"See, Dad's going to be *insanely* jealous," continued Simon, "that I'm going out with the best-looking girl in London and he's far too old to get a look-in. And Mum, for the same reason. Jealous. You're naturally gorgeous and no matter how many facials or makeovers she has, she'll never look as good as you."

He wrapped me in his arms and gave me a huge bear hug. "Okay?"

"Okay," I said. I could see Cressida out of the corner of my eye, looking daggers at me. Then she spotted Tony who had just walked in and was making a beeline for Lucy.

She came over and hovered near us, hoping Tony'd notice her, but he only had eyes for Lucy.

I almost felt sorry for her as she desperately tried to get his attention and failed. She was standing all on her own. It was clear that Tanya wasn't speaking to her either, as she stood a distance away with her back turned.

After a while, Tony and Lucy went on to the dance floor to dance and Cressida came over.

"Who's that girl all over Tony?" she asked.

"That *girl* is Lucy," I replied. "One of my best friends. I introduced you earlier. And if you look closely you'll see that she's not all over him. In fact, it's the other way round."

"I seriously doubt *that*," said Cressida. "She looks like she's hardly out of kindergarten."

"Like Tony, do you?" I asked innocently.

"He's okay," she said, looking round. "Does he ever say anything about me?"

"You're *kidding*?" I said. "He hasn't stopped talking about you since he met you." It was true. He hadn't stopped going on about how stuck-up he thought she was. I could see Cressida was dying to ask me more, but at that moment Tanya waved at me and indicated to meet her outside.

I followed her out into the alleyway down the side of the pub. She had a huge Mulberry bag with her out of which she drew a bottle of champagne, a carton of orange and some plastic cups.

"Supplies," she grinned. "I brought it for me and Cress but, well, she's a pain and I thought you might like some. Ever had a Bellini?"

"No. What is it?"

"Champagne and orange juice. Actually it should be peach juice but they didn't have any at the store. Want one?"

"Sure," I said. I'd only ever had sips of wine before and I hadn't liked it at all. It was like drinking vinegar. But I didn't want to say no to Tanya when she was clearly making an effort to be friendly. And she *had* stood up for me before in the ladies. A few sips would probably be okay, I decided. Specially if diluted with orange.

Tanya poured a cup and handed it to me, then poured another for herself.

"To new friendships," she said as we slammed plastic cups and drank. Actually it was nice. Much better than the sour-ink taste of wine. The orange juice made it sweet and the champagne made nice bubbles that went up my nose.

"Want another?" asked Tanya.

I was beginning to feel game for anything. "Go on," I said and knocked back the second one.

A lovely giggly feeling came over me. I felt like the champagne, all bubbly and light.

"Iz will be on soon," I said. "We'd better go back in."

"Right," said Tanya, slugging back her drink. "Lessgo."

On the way back into the hall, I felt giddy and giggly.

"Amazing," I said to Tanya as we walked back into the hall with linked arms. "Life can go up and down all in the space of half an hour. From misery to fun."

499

Tanya hiccupped. "Yah. Know watchya mean. Water to champagne kindathing."

King Noz had just started up their set so I went to join Simon and Tony where they were standing at the back of the hall.

"Where's Lucy?" I asked.

"Gone to check on Izzie, I think," said Tony.

Lucy reappeared a few minutes later. She came straight over to me. "Izzie told me what WC said about you. Honestly, what a cow."

"A cow who's after Tony." I said, then giggled. "She's a cow and I'm a zebra. I told her that Tone fancied you and she was like, er, I doubt it. Like, not when he could have me."

"Oh, *really*," said Lucy, looking over at Cressida. "Okay. Just watch this, then."

Lucy walked over to Tony, who was talking to Cressida again. She was doing the flick-flicky thing with her hair and looking deeply into his eyes. Tony, on the other hand, looked like he wanted to escape. Lucy went over and slipped her hand in his and his face lit up like a Christmas tree.

"Want to dance?" she asked as King Noz started

playing a slow number. Tony nodded happily and went on to the floor with her. She snuggled into him, put her arms round his neck and whispered something in his ear. He replied by giving her a huge smoochy snog. It went on and *on*. A real Oscar winner.

Cressida's jaw dropped open.

"What was that you were saying about seriously doubting that Tony fancied my friend?" I said casually.

Cressida turned on her heel and stomped over to Simon.

He looked over at me apologetically as she hauled him out on to the dance floor. Tanya came to stand next to me and when she saw no one was looking, she slipped me another beaker of Bellini.

"Thanks," I said and knocked it back before anyone noticed.

Tee hee, I thought. It felt really good to be bad.

I watched Simon and Cressida on the dance floor. Neither of them were very good dancers. Simon was doing his best, which was a bit jerky, but Cressida—she was awful. She had no sense of rhythm at all.

"Immobile Sloane," I said to Tanya, who looked at me quizzically.

"Mobile Sloanes," I slurred, then remembered it had been Izzie who'd coined the phrase, not Tanya. Everything was a bit blurry.

"I mean Porobello Prin . . . princess. Thassit. Pincesses."

"Are you okay?" asked Tanya.

"Never been better," I said. "Wanna dance?"

If there was one thing I could do well, it was dance. I'd show these Mobile Sloanes how it was done, I thought.

After the band finished the slow number, I saw Ben go and take the microphone.

"And now, ladies and gents, I'd like to introduce a new member of the band singing with us tonight for the first time. I'd like to introduce you all to the very lovely Miss Izzie Foster."

He stood back to applaud as Izzie walked onstage. She looked fabulous and I cheered loudly along with everyone else. I felt so proud of her. S'my pal, I thought. Myverybestpal. Then the band started up and Izzie began to sing. Ben joined in with her for the choruses. They sounded wonderful. Really really great harmonies.

But no one was dancing.

People *oughta* be dancin', I thought. Makes the band look berra for the recor' company people. S'really important.

I decided *I'd* start them off. I'd do it for Izzie.

I made my way on to the dance floor, took off my shoes, and began to sway in time to the music. My head felt like it was spinning a bit, but if I listened closely to the beat, I could flow with it. I felt so light on my feet.

After a while, I noticed that everyone was watching me. It was my moment in the spotlight so I really went for it. Spinning. Hopping. Moving with the grooving. I was Madonna. Geri. Britney.

Then I noticed Izzie up on the stage. She was still singing but she was looking at me kind of strange.

Then I noticed Lucy. She was looking at me, kind of *mad*.

She walked on to the dance floor and hissed at me. "Nesta. Go and sit down."

"Why? Tryin' to gereveryone dancin . . . ," I slurred.

"Everyone's *looking* at you," said Lucy.

"S'all right," I said, "Un showin en how isdone."

"It's *Izzie*'s moment," whispered Lucy urgently. "Not yours."

She grabbed my wrist firmly and pulled me to the side of the dance floor.

"Woz happening?" I said. Everything seemed blurred and my mouth felt dry. I had a sudden urge to crawl under the table and fall asleep. "Whezevybudy?"

"What's the matter with you?" asked Lucy.

"Ballooni," I said. "Snice. Tanyanme. Owange juice and champy-ain."

"Oh *no*," said Lucy. "You're *drunk*. Wait here. I'll get Tony."

I leaned on my arm for a while and I must have dropped off as the next thing I knew Tony was nudging me. "Time to go home, kiddo." I looked over at the stage. King Noz were no longer playing.

I felt dreadful. I looked over to see where the others were and I could see Izzie, Ben and Lucy standing in the corner. They had their backs turned to me.

"Oops . . . ," I said as I remembered Izzie's face up on the stage.

Tony helped me to my feet. "Come on, let's get some fresh air."

"Where's Simon?" I asked as Tony put his arm round me and hauled me out to the pavement in front of the pub.

"Last time I saw him, he was desperately pouring water down Tanya's throat in an attempt to sober her up before their mum sees her and he gets the blame."

"Oh, dear," I said. "We had Balloonees. Sorrysorry."

The cool night air woke me up a little and my head began pounding. A sudden thought made me panic. "Is our mum here?"

Tony shook his head. "No. She phoned to say Mrs. Lovering is coming to get us."

"Oh *no*," I groaned. "It will make Cressida's night to see us all getting in that old jalopy of theirs."

"What does it matter what she thinks?" said Tony as a brand-new black Mercedes drove by and stopped a hundred meters past the pub.

A short distance behind it, at the traffic lights, I could see Lucy's mum's Beetle. I swear it was glowing in the dark like a giant turquoise insect. Oops!

I thought. Those balloonees really *were* strong.

At that moment, Izzie came out and turned away when she saw me. She was followed by Lucy.

"Sorry, sorry . . . ," I began.

"Tonight wasn't meant to be about you, Nesta," said Lucy, turning on me. "It was Izzie's big night, but somehow you managed to get all the attention as usual."

As *usual*? Suddenly I felt like I wanted to sit on the pavement and cry. It *wasn't fair*. It *wasn't* my fault I'd drank the Balloonees. I was only trying to be friendly to Tanya who had stood up for me when WC had called me a zebra. *Then* she said Simon was too good for me.

I looked up the road at the dilapidated old banger approaching, then I looked at Cressida who was walking toward the black Mercedes with her nose in the air.

It was all too much.

I wanted to cry.

I wanted Simon.

But he only liked me when I was fun, *didn't* he?

He was always saying how much he liked my attitude. My winning attitude.

He liked Fun Nesta. All Singing, All Dancing Nesta. He wouldn't like All Crying Nesta, so I couldn't let him see me *now*.

Tears were queuing up at the back of my eyes. I could feel them. I had to get away.

"Tell Tony I've made my own way home, will you?" I called to Lucy, who was standing with her arm around Izzie.

And with that I ran off toward the tube station as fast as I could.

Chapter 12

%*@:-(
(Hungover)

The next morning, when I woke up, I felt like someone had glued my eyelids shut in the night. Heavy, ukky. Finally I pulled them open and turned over to look at the clock by my bed.

Eleven thirty. I groaned as the room began to spin and I remembered The Night Before. Pants, I thought. Oh, *pants*.

How did I get home?

And *who's* Riverdancing on my brain?

I could remember running away. I'd got round the corner away from the pub, and I'd stood by a brick wall to catch my breath. I remember that. I remember feeling dreadful. All mixed up. I felt sick and I had to get home. Wanted Mum.

In the distance I could see a taxi with its light on. I was about to stick my hand out, when I remembered I hadn't enough money. I'd spent my last holiday money on stupid scratchcards and couldn't be sure that anyone was home to pick up the fare.

I looked in my purse. A pound coin, three twenty pences and one five pence. Enough to get the tube at least.

I quickly made my way over to the tube station and past three disheveled men swigging back cans of beer in a doorway. They stared at me as I hurried past.

"Wanna play out, little girl?" laughed one of them.

I kept my head down. This was the first time I'd been out so late on my own and I tried to remember what Miss Watkins had told us at school about traveling alone at night. That was it. Walk confidently and don't make eye contact with anyone.

As I reached the tube entrance, I almost fell over a huddle by the ticket office. It was a boy all wrapped up in a sleeping bag. He couldn't have been much older than me. In front of him was a handwritten sign that read, HUNGRY AND HOMELESS. CAN YOU HELP? Next to him was a black dog. The two of them appeared so pathetic, as they looked up at me hopefully.

I went and got my ticket then put the rest of my change in the boy's can.

"Sorry," I blurted. "S'all I got."

Then I made my way down to the platform. Luckily I didn't have to wait long for a train. Remembering rule two, don't get into an empty car, I made for the center of the train, which was full of people. I sat down and stared at the floor.

Some lads were sitting a couple of seats away. They were stuffing down hamburgers and the smell of onions and ketchup was inescapable. I felt like I was going to throw up.

"Wanna bite of my hot dog?" called one. All his friends started sniggering.

I kept looking at the floor. I wanted to cry. I wanted my mum.

I was out like a shot when we reached Highgate, and I ran up the stairs and out into the lane outside the station. It was so dark. Black.

Shadowy. What had *possessed* me to make my own way home? As I ran along the lane, I felt really frightened.

I maneuvered my bag so that it was over my shoulder diagonally. (Third rule of traveling alone, as it's hard to snatch a bag from that position.) Then I found my house keys and put them in my jacket pocket (fourth rule, so that if your bag is snatched, at least you can get in your front door). Miss Watkins would be pleased I'd managed to remember so much of her lesson.

Then I legged it as fast as I could.

Everywhere looked menacing. The trees, cars going by, people in the street, they all looked shifty. My heart was thumping in my chest as I hurtled along the street and into our road and up the steps to our flat. I fumbled with the locks, then, at last, the welcome sight of house lights, the sound of the TV.

I was home.

Dad came out of the living room. "Nesta," he said.

"Dad," I said. "Brilliant."

Then I threw up all over the hall.

* * *

Ah yes, it was all coming back to me as I lay under the duvet. I wondered how long I could stay there hiding. Somehow, I didn't want to go downstairs. What a mess. Was there a way to turn back the clock? I wondered. Twenty-four hours? A week?

Everyone was mad with me. Dad. Tony. Lucy. Izzie.

And myself.

I looked around my bedroom and remembered the face of the homeless boy in the tube station. His eyes were so empty. He had nothing and I had everything. CDs, books, clothes, perfume, makeup, a computer, my own TV, a mobile—but most of all a home. A safe place to return to.

And what had I done for the last few weeks?

Think about myself nonstop and all the things I hadn't got. All of it stuff I didn't even really need. And where had it got me? Nowhere.

I had never felt so miserable in all my life. Izzie was right with her Ben the Buddhist stuff. Desire makes you miserable.

I won't give in to another desire as long as I live.

I winced when I thought about Izzie. I'd *ruined* her big special night. She'd looked so beautiful and had been so brave getting up there, facing her private fear and singing and . . .

I started crying again.

I am the most *horrid* person that ever lived, I thought. *Bad. Selfiiiiiiish. Self-obsesseeeed.* And *God . . . starv . . . ing!!*

The aroma of frying bacon was wafting up the stairs.

Feed me. Feed me *now*! My film for the day was the *Little Shop of Horrors* and my role was that ever-hungry alien plant that demands food. Images of toast, coffee, muffins, and peanut butter sailed in front of my eyes.

My stomach was growling and all farther thoughts of contrition disappeared as I tried to think of a way of sneaking into the kitchen before the inevitable confrontation with Those Who Shall Be Obeyed. Parents.

I slipped into my robe and made my way into the kitchen. Mum, Dad, and Tony were sitting like High Court judges on stools at the breakfast bar, staring at me as I crept in. No getting out of this, I thought.

"Er, morning," I said as I tried to gauge the atmosphere. Something was going on, as Mum and Dad looked surprisingly cheerful considering that I'd done the technicolor yawn all over the hall the previous night. There was a bottle of what looked remarkably like champagne in an ice bucket. And a carton of orange juice! In front of Mum and Dad were two crystal glasses.

I went and sniffed a glass and the smell made me retch as it brought back last night.

"Are you drinking Balloonis?" I demanded.

"No, Mimosas," said Mum.

"Erlack, how *could* you? You'll get an awful headache, you know!"

Dad laughed. "Actually, the word is Bellini. It's champagne with peach juice—a Mimosa is with orange."

"Whatever," I said. "But first thing in the *morning*? Gross."

"And good morning to you, sunshine," said Dad.

"Actually, we're celebrating," said Mum. "I

would have told you last night but you'd already gone to bed by the time I was back. See the reason I couldn't pick you up last night was because I was having dinner with the studio boss and . . ."

"And?" I asked.

"*And* my contract has been renewed for another three years," grinned Mum. "Plus, they've given me a raise."

I went over and gave her a hug. "That's brilliant, Mum! Well done. So does that mean that everything's going to be all right?"

"For a while," said Dad, raising his glass. "Life goes on."

Tony hadn't said a word through all this. He was eating a bacon toastie and glowering at me through slit eyes.

Finally he couldn't hold it in any longer. "What the *hell* did you think you were doing going off on your own last night? Me and Simon spent ages looking for you up and down Kentish Town Road. Anything could have happened. . . ."

Oh God. *Simon*. I hadn't even said good-bye to him. Might as well add his name to the ever-growing list of people who were mad with me.

"I got the tube home," I said, eyeing up the pile of toast on the bar.

"Well *we* didn't know that. You said to Lucy that you were making your own way home. You weren't answering your mobile. *We* didn't know whether you'd tried to walk or get a bus or what. . . ."

Mum and Dad nodded along with Tony. It was like he was the strict parent, not them.

"It was far too late for someone of your age to be out on your own," continued Tony. "There are some real nutters on the streets."

I decided not to argue. "Sorry," I muttered, and I reached out for a piece of toast.

"Sore head?" asked Dad.

I nodded. "Tanya gave me one of those things you're drinking. I didn't realize they were so strong."

"How many did you have?"

"Er . . . three. And *never again*, I double promise," I said, turning to Tony. "Did Lucy or Izzie say anything? Are they speaking to me?"

"Dunno," said Tony. "They went home with Lucy's mum while Simon and I looked for you. You really don't think, do you? That people might be worried."

"Bet Lucy and Izzie weren't worried."

"Yeah. They did seem kind of mad," said Tony. "Specially Lucy."

I poured a cup of coffee from the coffeemaker.

"I'll text message them right away," I said.

"Chicken. Why don't you ring or go round?" asked Tony. "I think you owe them a face-to-face apology."

I couldn't. Not yet. I knew I couldn't face them being mad, not today.

Later that afternoon, Dad came and tapped on my bedroom door.

I was still feeling icky and my head hurt, so I'd gone for a lie-down. He came in and sat at the end of the bed.

"How's my princess?"

"Not great," I said. "Feels like a family of goblins in hobnailed boots are jumping about in my head."

"Do you want anything?"

"No." I still wasn't sure if I was going to get more of a telling-off, so I decided that, if there was one coming, it was best to get it over with. "Aren't you mad at me?"

Dad shook his head. "No, not mad, Nesta." Then he grinned. "Tony gave you enough of a roasting at breakfast. And I think you learned your lesson as far as drinking goes."

"First and last," I said.

"I doubt it," said Dad. "But maybe wait until you're a bit older before you go knocking back half a bottle of champagne, even if it *is* diluted with orange. Lesson one about drinking—champagne gives a killer hangover to even the most hardy of drinkers. So lesson learned. No, I'm not mad at you. More concerned than anything. Mum says you've been a bit down lately. And you sure looked bad last night."

Dad was looking at me with such kindness that I felt tears well up in my eyes. His reaction was so unexpected. I thought I was in for a major grounding. Suddenly it all came pouring out and I told him all about the journey home and how scared I was and . . .

". . . and I've got this new boyfriend. But I think he only likes me because I'm a laugh. And sometimes I don't *feel* like being a laugh. It's exhausting, being the entertainment *all* the time. . . ."

"So be yourself," said Dad. "If he's worth it he'll

stick around for the highs *and* the lows. Everyone has days when they feel a bit blue. It's okay. It's called being human. And if you're going to have a relationship with someone, it's important to feel comfortable enough to be real with them. Have you let this boy know how you feel?"

I shook my head. "No. He's going to Courchevel soon. Skiing. And there was a spare place and he asked if I wanted to go. . . . Oh, Dad, it's been *awful*. He's really rich and I haven't been able to keep up."

"It sounds to me like you and he have some talking to do. Tell him who you are. How you feel. And if he stays around, great. If he doesn't, he wasn't worth it."

He got up and walked over to my desk in the corner. I thought he was going to say something else, but he'd spotted the paper with the model agency ad circled. Oh *no*, I thought, don't let him look at that. Too late. He sat down at my desk chair and read the ad.

I put my head under the pillow.

"Oh, Nesta," he said. "You haven't contacted these people, have you?"

I nodded my head under the pillow.

"Did they ask for money?" he asked slowly.

I gave a small nod.

"Come out of there," he said. "I'll tell you something about these agencies. They make their money by exploiting young girls like you. Believe me, I know. I've worked with model agencies for over two decades and the good ones won't ask you for money for registration or a portfolio. The good ones will see it as an investment in your future. These other places tell all sorts of kids they've got potential, but only to get their money out of them. They never get you real work."

"Sorry," I whispered.

"Look, if modeling is so important to you, we'll look into it when you're sixteen."

"But I don't want to be a model," I said. "I want to be an actress."

"So what's with the ad in the paper?"

"I wanted to earn some money. To help you and Mum out. . . . And buy some clothes and stuff."

Dad laughed. "Oh, Nesta. You don't have to worry about us yet. Maybe when we're old and dribbling, but . . ."

"But you haven't got a film to work on, have you?"

"There are a few possibilities around. I just don't want to take the first thing that comes along," said Dad. "Plus I'd like to work closer to home for a while, keep an eye on my wayward daughter. We'll see. Nothing is ever certain in the film industry, and if you want to be an actress, you'd better get used to that fact. Actors, like directors, aren't always in work and you're only ever as good as your last job. There's an awful lot of talent out there that is, as we say, 'resting' or in between jobs."

"You mean unemployed?"

"Exactly."

"I hope something comes up for you, Dad."

"It will. It always has up until now," he smiled, "and in the meantime, there's a certain young man I think you ought to talk to."

After Dad had gone, I dialed Simon's mobile number. The answering service was on.

I tried his home number.

"He's gone down to Wiltshire," said a voice I didn't recognize.

Course. I'd forgotten. He'd told me on the night of the gig that he was going down to the country house for a few days.

I decided I'd send him an e-mail.

Hi Simon,

I'm writing this to you to say good-bye forever.

Also to apologize for last night. Tony told me that you were looking for me. I am sorry if you were worried, but I got home safe then threw up all over the hall. Mum and Dad were really chill about it.

I can't come to Courchevel. My family isn't as rich as yours and at the moment we can't afford extras like skiing trips.

That's why I think it's best if we say good-bye. I can't keep up with all the things you do, like skiing and horse-riding. Not on the pocket money I get.

And not being able to keep up makes me miserable. Speaking of which, I do. Get miserable sometimes, that is. In fact, some days I can be grumpy and horrid. Downright repugnant. In the weeks I've known you, I don't think you have seen the real me. You said you liked me because I was so confident and funny. Well now you know the truth. I'm not like that all the time.

Sorry about everything. And maybe we can still text message sometimes.

Lots of love and, as Ali G. says, keep it real.

Nesta.

Before I could change my mind, I pressed the send button and off it went.

Nesta's Diary

After breakfast, I sent both Izzie and Lucy the same
message:

RUStlFrnds?

No reply

So I sent:

%*@: -(hungover

:-I   unhappy

SrySrySry

No reply

So *then* I sent:

:-C   really unhappy

:-/   confused

:"-(crying

IluvU

SrySrySry

No reply.

E-mailed Simon to say good-bye. Kind of hoped that he'd
do something extraordinary like abseil down the side of
our flat with a box of Black Magic chocolate and declare
his undying love and say that he'll never let me go. Or
stand outside my window with a guitar singing a love
song.

But no such luck.

No reply from Simon. No reply from Lucy or Izzie.

So that's it. No girlfriends. No boyfriend.

My life is over.

Chapter 13

SrySrySry

"For heaven's sake, go round," said Mum after two days of me moping about the flat. "When does term start again? I can't wait. *Go.* Apologize. Make up."

"I will," I said. "I was just hoping that, well, they might have replied to one of my text messages or something."

"And what about Simon? Any word from him?"

I shook my head. "No. I don't expect I'll ever hear from him again either."

"But I thought you liked him?"

"I did. I *do.* But . . . I don't think he'd like me if he really knew me."

"Have you given him a chance?"

"Sort of. I was really honest in my e-mail. But he hasn't replied. Nobody likes me any more."

Mum came and gave me a big hug. "I do," she said. "In fact, I love you. Now, go on, phone your friends."

I took a deep breath and went to the phone. I dialed Izzie's number first.

"She's gone to Camden Lock with Lucy," said Mrs. Foster.

"Thanks," I said and put down the phone. Out having fun without me. It was too much. I couldn't let it go on.

"Mum. They're at the Lock," I called from the hall. "I'm going to look for them."

"Good for you," said Mum, getting her purse. "And here's a little spending money. Get yourself something you like while you're down there."

Twenty quid! I gave Mum a hug. Happiness is some dosh in your pocket and permission to spend, I thought, as I set off for the tube.

As usual, the Lock was heaving with people. I decided to try Cyberdog first as Izzie and Lucy might be visiting Ben.

527

"Ben? Nah, he's not in today," said one of the alien mutants who worked there.

I had a quick look round to see if the girls were there anyway, but there was no sign of them. May as well have a quick look at the clothes while I'm here, I thought, as I saw the rails of clothes and jewelry. On display there was a choker like the one Ben had borrowed for Izzie. Transparent turquoise with studs on it. I tried it on and it looked stunning. Then a little voice in my head said, buy it for Izzie. That's it! I realized. I'll use the money from Mum to buy something for Iz and Lucy. Then, if I don't find them, I'll go round and beg forgiveness.

I quickly bought the choker for Izzie, then went to look for something for Lucy. I wasn't sure Cyberdog was her style so I went to look at some of the stalls in the main courtyard. There were some brilliant T-shirts for sale. I flicked through the rails trying to decide which one Lucy might like.

One read, IF YOU THINK I'M A BITCH, WAIT UNTIL YOU MEET MY MOTHER.

Another, WWW.WHASSUP.COM.

Another said, MAD COW. Probably not appropriate to give to a friend who I'm trying to make up with, I thought. Nor was the next one. That said, I HATE EVERYONE AND YOU'RE NEXT.

Then I saw one that was perfect for Lucy. It had two inky hands positioned right over the boobs. She has a hang-up about being flat-chested and this would make her laugh.

I paid the stall owner and made my way through the rest of the stalls. I spent over an hour looking everywhere for Lucy and Izzie but there was no sign. I looked in the indoor *and* outdoor market.

By the entrance to the indoor market was a stall selling T-shirts and a huge sign saying that you could make up your own slogan. Five pounds.

A current trend going round school was to have the name of an opponent or rival written on your chest. I could have Jennifer Lopez written on one for Izzie and Stella McCartney for Lucy. I looked in my purse, but didn't have enough left. Another time, I thought.

I had four pounds fifty left, so I went and bought an Easter egg instead, then took a deep breath and phoned Lucy's.

Her brother Steve answered. "Er, is Lucy back yet?"

"Yeah," he said. "Just a—"

"No, no Steve, don't call her. Is Izzie there as well?"

"Yeah."

"Okay, don't tell them I called, okay?"

"Okay."

Half an hour later, I rang the doorbell at Lucy's house and Steve let me in. "They're in the bedroom," he said.

"Thanks," I said and crept up the stairs.

Should I knock or just burst in? I stood at the top of the stairs wondering what was the best plan of action. Maybe I should listen at the door for a moment? No. Bad idea, I thought. Last time I eavesdropped I heard Cressida calling me a zebra. No, there was only one way forward. I must think of a character from a film that I can be. Someone who needs to grovel . . .

Got it! I thought, and got down on my knees. I opened the door and crawled in.

"I'm not worthy. I'm not worthy," I said, prostrating myself at their feet. My film for today was *Wayne's World*. In it, Wayne and his mate Garth kneel and bow in front of their rock idol, Alice Cooper.

Lucy and Izzie looked very surprised to see me and exchanged looks.

"What on earth are you doing, Nesta?" asked Izzie.

Maybe she hasn't seen *Wayne's World*, I thought, as I got up off the floor. "Er, throwing myself on your mercy," I said. "Admitting that I am the lowest of the low, an amoeba. The slime on an amoeba. The slime on the slime of an amoeba. Please guys. I miss you so much. And I know I blew it. And the way I behaved at the gig was unforgivable. I'm so sorry. Please be my friends again. I brought presents and everything . . ."

I handed them the choker, the T-shirt and the Easter egg.

"Please. Sorry," I continued. "Buddhists are into forgiveness, aren't they? Izzie. Huh? Guys? I know I am the worst friend in the whole world. Truly horrid and I *beg* you to have mercy on me and . . ."

Izzie and Lucy burst out laughing. "We were just about to call you," said Izzie. "We miss you too."

"And we know it wasn't all your fault," said Lucy. "You were upset after those things WC said

531

about you. And then the champagne . . ."

"But that was such a show you just put on," laughed Izzie. "We couldn't *possibly* have interrupted."

I sank on to the bed. Happy happy.

"And we have a pressie for you," said Izzie, grinning wickedly. "We were down the Lock and saw this T-shirt stall that does slogans."

"I saw it," I gasped. "I was going to have some done but I'd run out of money. . . ."

"Well we had one done for you," said Izzie, pulling out a bag and handing it to me.

Lucy was grinning like a maniac.

I pulled out the T-shirt and burst out laughing when I saw what they'd had written on the front.

"Brilliant," I said.

They'd had a name printed in a red heart.

CRESSIDA.

We spent a top afternoon catching up. So much had happened. Lucy's thinking about getting back with Tony, though she hasn't let on to him yet.

"Going to keep him guessing a bit longer," she said.

"Serves him right," I laughed. "It's *usually* his motto, 'treat 'em mean to keep 'em keen.'"

"Exactly," grinned Lucy.

Izzie also had news. The talent scout had turned up to watch the bands and he'd liked what he heard.

"Early days," she said. "But he's asked us to send a demo tape in. Fingers crossed."

"And what about you?" asked Lucy. "You and Simon?"

"Over," I said. "It wasn't right. I haven't heard from him since the gig."

"Oh, I am sorry," said Izzie. "I liked him."

"So did I," I said.

Later that afternoon, we all went down to watch *As If* on TV. It was a really good episode and I felt over the moon to be with my friends again.

About ten minutes into the show my mobile rang.

I leaped up and answered it. I put one hand over the receiver and pointed at the phone with the other. "*Simon* . . . ," I whispered.

I went into the hall so I could have some privacy.

If I was going to have to grovel, then I wanted to do it without an audience.

"Hey," he said.

"Hey," I replied, thinking I really must work on my conversation skills. I realized I was very nervous.

"I've just got your e-mail," he said. "I'm sorry I didn't get in touch sooner—I left my laptop and mobile at the London house. I did try and ring you from Wiltshire, but your number's unlisted."

"Yeah," I said. Oh for God's sake, get a grip, Nesta, I thought. But I couldn't think of anything riveting to say.

"I've got a few things I want to tell you," continued Simon, sounding very serious. "Three things, in fact."

Here we go, I thought. I'm going to be dumped.

I went and sat on the stairs.

"First. Sorry about my sister. I don't know what she was thinking about, giving you all that champagne. Second, even more sorry about Cressida. Tanya told me what she said about you. Apparently you'd overheard. Lucy told Tony and Tony told me. Very very sorry about that. Personally I'm never going to speak to her again and I think

Tanya's dropping her as a friend as well. And thirdly, I'd like to keep seeing you even if you are horrid, grumpy, and downright repugnant. I have days when I feel crap too. I agree that being real is all part of a relationship. Accepting the package, not just the good bits."

"But what about . . . you know?" I said. "Your world, my world."

"*No*," said Simon. "It's *not* like that. There *is* no my world, your world. I'm so against that stuff."

"Cressida didn't see it that way."

"Just because we're from the same background doesn't mean we think the same way, Nesta. To think we do is as insulting as me thinking all Italians are the same. Or all Australians. Or all North Londoners. There's good and bad everywhere. Open- and narrow-minded. Generous and mean. It hasn't got anything to do with where someone grew up or what their mum or dad earns."

I felt like I'd had another telling-off. Point taken, I thought, as the words of John Lennon's "Imagine" popped into my head and I had to resist a sudden urge to sing.

535

"Cressida is a snobby pain and always has been," continued Simon. "That's why I finished with her in the first place. She doesn't get it. It's what's inside a person that counts. Whether they're nice or not. So . . . ?"

"So?" I asked.

"Er. So, can I see you when I come back from skiing?"

"Mmm. I'll have to think carefully about everything you've said. I'll text you," I said. "Sometime."

"Oh. Okay," he said, sounding very disappointed.

I waited thirty seconds after he'd hung up, then sent my message:

GetYaCoatUvePuld   CUL8R XXXXXXXXX (H) (H) (H)

He sent back:

☺☺☺☺☺☺☺☺☺☺☺☺☺☺☺☺☺☺☺ <3<3<3<3<3<3<3<3<3<3<3<3<3<3<3<3<3<3

Mates, Dates, and Sleepover Secrets

Chapter 1

Noola the Alien Girl

"'We are the champions, *we are the champions,*'" sang some Stupid Boy outside the window of the girls' locker room.

"How sad is that?" asked Melanie Jones as she rubbed strawberry-scented body lotion onto her legs. "We beat them three weeks running and they win *once* and think they're it."

"Yeah," I said as I pulled my hair back and plaited it. "Today," I said, raising my voice so that Stupid Boy could hear outside, "was a mere blip in our team's otherwise excellent performance."

"Yay," chorused the rest of our team, who were in various states of undress after the soccer match.

"You woz rubbish," shouted Stupid Boy.

I shoved my stuff into my sports bag and stepped outside into the dazzling June sunshine. There was Stupid Boy—namely Will Evans, goalie from the boys' team.

"You talking to me?" I asked.

Will tried to square up to me, which was difficult, seeing as I'm five feet seven and he's a squirt at five feet four.

"Yeah," he said to my nose.

"In that case, would you mind using the correct grammar? It's you *were* rubbish, not you *woz*."

Will went red as the group of guys around him sniggered.

He stuck his tongue out at me.

"Oh," I yawned. "Like I'm *really* scared now."

By now, most of the girls' team had finished changing and had come out to see what was happening. It was always the same. Every Saturday, after the match, the games continued off the pitch—often with the girls bombing the boys with balloons swollen with water from the locker room taps.

I picked up my bag to go home. I'd got bored with it all in the last few weeks. I was sure there had to be a better way to get a boy's attention than splattering him with water.

Anyway, it was Saturday and that meant lunch with Mum and Dad. Dad insists that we eat together as "a family" on the rare occasions that he's not working. What family? I think. It's not like I have hundreds of brothers and sisters. Only Marie who's twenty-six and left home to live in Southampton years ago and Paul who's twenty-one and been away studying in Bristol.

"Oi, Watts," called Will.

"The name's T. J., actually," I said, turning back.

"T. J.? What kind of name is that?" sniggered Mark, one of the other boys on the team. "T. J. *T. J.*"

I tried to think of something clever to say. "It's *my* kind of name," I said, for want of anything better.

I didn't want to get into the real reason. I'd never hear the end of it. My full name is Theresa Joanne Watts. Like, yeah. How dull and girlie is that? But Paul has called me T.J. since I was a baby and it stuck. Much better than Theresa Joanne. But

I wasn't going to explain all this to the nerdie boys from St Joseph's High. If they knew I hated my real name, then that's what I'd be called for ever.

"Okay then, *T. J.* You and me," said Will, pointing at a picnic table by the football pitch. "Over there. Arm wrestling."

Now this was tempting. Arm wrestling was my major talent.

I took a quick look at my watch. I had time.

"Okay, Evans. Prepare to die."

We took up our positions opposite each other at the table and both put our arms out, elbows down. A small crowd soon gathered round as we grasped hands.

"Ready," said Mark, "steady, GO."

I strained to keep my lower arm upright as we began to arm-wrestle.

"Come *on*, T. J.," cried the girls.

"Come *on*, Will," cried the boys.

"Hey, T. J., there's a guy looking for you outside the boys' locker room," said Dave, the boys' team captain as he came out to join us.

"Nice try," I said, not looking up. I wasn't going to break my concentration for the oldest trick in the book. Plus, Dave was A Bit Of A Hunk and I usually said or did something stupid when one of his super species was around. I made myself focus. The crowd around was beginning to get excited as I kept my arm firm and Will's started to weaken.

"Show him, T. J.," said one of the girls.

I could feel my strength wavering as Will fought back and my arm wobbled. Then I summoned every ounce of energy and *slam*, Will's arm was on the table.

"Hurrah," cheered the girls, then they began singing. "*We* are the champions. *We* are the champions. Champions, the champions, champions of Europe."

"*Stupid* girls," said Will, rubbing his hand and going to unlock his bike. "Anyway, we won the footie and that's what really counts. So there."

"Oh, grow up," I called as I walked away.

"There really is someone looking for you, T. J.," said Dave, catching up with me and putting his hand on my shoulder.

As I turned and looked into his denim-blue eyes, my stomach went all fluttery.

"I didn't say it to distract you. Over there, see?"

543

he continued. "Hippie guy with dark hair and an earring."

I looked to where he pointed and there was my brother Paul, a short distance away.

"*Nihingyah,*" I said to Dave, who looked at me quizzically.

I shrugged and turned back toward my brother, who gave me a wave. No point in explaining, I thought, as I made my way over to Paul. Dave would never understand how I get taken over by Noola the Alien Girl when confronted by Boy Babes. She doesn't know many words. Mainly ones like *uhyuh, yunewee,* and *nihingyah*, which I think means, "oh, yeah," and "thanks," in alien-speak.

"Hey, T. J.," said Paul, giving me a hug.

"Hey," I said, and hugged him back.

"Bit old for you, isn't he?" taunted Will as he rode past on his bike.

"Get a life, you perv," I said as I linked with Paul and drew him away from the crowds. "He's my *brother.*"

Paul grinned and looked back at Will. "Looks like I'm interrupting something."

"As if."

"Come on, you can tell me. Someone special?"

"Only the local pond-life," I said. "You home for lunch?"

"Yeah," sighed Paul, and ran his fingers through his hair. "Bad vibes. Thought I'd escape awhile and come and find you."

"Scary Dad still mad with you?"

Paul nodded. "And some. The way he goes on, anyone would think I'd committed a murder rather than dropped out of university. But you know how he is."

Boy, did I know! Night and day, me and Mum had to listen to him going on . . . and on: Paul has ruined his life. Paul has spoiled the opportunity of a lifetime. Paul has wasted his talent. If only Paul were more like Marie. He was always a dreamer. He had it too easy. What's to become of him? Where did we go wrong?

On and on and *on*.

See, Dad's a bigwig hospital consultant. Mum's a GP. Even my sister, Marie, is a doctor. Plan was, Paul was to join the club, follow in the family footsteps sort of thing. Only he never wanted to.

He wanted to be a musician. He went along with the doctor bit. Got good grades. Got into medical school. Did a year. Did a self-awareness type weekend in London. Saw the light or something. Dropped out of college. Grew his hair. Started spouting self-help jargon. Got into alternative medicine and rejected pretty much everything Dad stands for. Oops.

Dad mad.

Mum sad.

Me, though, I'm glad. Not that he's having a hard time, of course. I feel sorry for him getting all the stick from Dad, but Dad's got me lined up to be a doctor as well. Ew, no thanks. Way too much blood. I want to be a writer, so I'm hoping all this with Paul will pave the way for my eventual fall from grace.

"Seriously though. Looks like you had a lot of admirers there," said Paul, pointing back to the football pitch.

"Nah," I said. "Boys are never interested in me."

"Looked to me like they were *very* interested."

"Only because I'm the arm wrestling champ," I grinned. "I had to show them what's what after

546

we lost at footie this morning."

Paul gave me a look and sighed. "T. J., you're impossible. Wake up and smell the hormones, kiddo. You're easily the prettiest girl on the team."

"Me, pretty? Yeah, right. Get real."

"I am," he said and pulled on my plait.

"You're only saying that because you're my brother."

"No," he said. "You're always doing yourself down. Like you can't see that you're gorgeous."

"Now I know you're kidding. I couldn't get a boy if I tried."

"Have you tried?"

I shrugged. "Er, dunno. Not really. But . . . it's like, I either talk alien or go into my Miss Strop bossy act and start correcting their grammar. I mean. D'oh. How flirty is that? Or else, I terrify them with my super-human strength. You know, humiliate them by winning at arm wrestling. Very girlie. Not. It just never seems to come out right."

"It will, T. J.," said Paul gently.

"But *when*? Most girls in my year have sore lips from snogging. Me? The only sore bits I've got are bruises from where some boy has kicked me in a

547

soccer game. I'm hopeless. Hannah was so good at the boy thing. They used to really like her."

Paul looked at me with concern. "Sorry about Hannah. Mum told me. When did she go?"

"Fortnight ago," I said as my eyes stung with tears. I was still feeling raw about her leaving, but I was determined not to cry like a baby in front of Paul. Hannah was my best friend. And she'd just gone to live in South Africa. Yeah, in South Africa. Not exactly the kind of place you can hop on a bus to when you fancy a chat. I was missing her like mad.

"You'll soon find new friends," said Paul.

Arghhh. If another person says that to me, I think I will scream. In fact if Paul wasn't my brother, I'd have socked him. People don't understand. *"You'll soon find other friends,"* like you can go out and buy one in the supermarket.

"I don't *want* new friends," I said. "I want Hannah back."

Hannah was a riot. A real laugh. I knew I'd never meet anyone like her ever again. It was her that came up with the nickname Scary Dad for my father. And with her around, boys never noticed I was tongue-tied or awkward—she babbled enough for both of us. I could hide behind her and they never realized that my cool was actually frozen shy.

As we turned into our road, we almost ran into Mr. Kershaw on the pavement in front of us. He was walking his dog, Drule. Or rather Drule was walking him. Drule is a big black Alsatian and Mr. Kershaw was having a hard time holding on to the lead.

"He can't wait to get to the park." He grinned as Drule yanked him forward.

I laughed and turned to go in our gate but Paul stopped me.

"Actually, T. J., don't go in yet. I didn't just come to walk you home. I've got something to tell you."

"What?"

As he shifted about on his feet, something told me that I wasn't going to like what he had to say.

Chapter 2

Giggling
Girlies

"Hey, T. J.," called Scott Harris from his bedroom window. "Hang on, I'm coming down."

Before I could answer, his head disappeared and the window closed, so I sat on the front step outside our house and waited for him. The Harris family has lived next door to us ever since we moved here when I was seven, so Scott is the next best thing I have to a brother besides Paul. Scott's two years older than me and lately has discovered girls. Or rather, girls have discovered him. He's cute in that Richie from Five kind of way and there's often a group of giggling girlies outside his gate. Scott liked to talk his latest conquests over with me and no doubt that's what he wanted to do now.

"T. J.," called Mum from inside. "Lunch'll be on the table in five minutes."

"Coming," I called back. "Just got to see Scott for a mo."

I was glad Scott was coming over, as I badly needed someone to talk to. I was hoping he'd distract me from the sinking feeling in the pit of my stomach. Paul had just told me that he was going traveling with his girlfriend, Saskia. For a year, maybe two. Starting with Goa, then maybe Australia and Tahiti. First Hannah, now Paul. What was going on? My two favorite people disappearing out of my life in less than ten days.

"Where've you been?" said Scott, appearing round the rhododendron bush in our front garden.

I opened my mouth to say "football," but he was off again before I had time.

"Been looking everywhere for you."

"Good," I said. "Because *I* want to talk to you."

"Why? What's happening?"

"Oh, everything," I began. "You know Paul dropped out and everything, well, now he's off traveling. Hannah's gone. I—"

551

"Really? Cool," said Scott, looking at his watch.

D'oh? I thought. No. Not cool. "Scott, are you listening?"

"Yeah. Course. But I need to ask a favor first."

I sighed. "What?"

"Hot date," said Scott, with a grin. "I need to borrow a fiver. Just for today. I'll give it back to you next week when I get my allowance."

Yeah, I thought, you said that last week when I lent you two quid. But then I didn't want him to think I was a cheapskate. No one likes a cheapskate. I was sure he'd give it back to me in the end.

I rummaged around in my sports bag, found my purse, and pulled out the fiver pocket money that Mum had given me that morning.

"Thanks," said Scott. "You're a pal."

"So who's the sad victim this afternoon?" I asked.

"Jessica Hartley. She's from your school."

I nodded. I knew Jessica all right. She was hard to miss. Just Scott's type, glam and girlie with long blond hair.

"Yeah. She's in the year above me. In Year Ten. Anyway, as I was saying, Paul's leaving tomorrow,

Hannah's gone and it feels like . . ."

"Actually," interrupted Scott, "talking about your school. Do you know Nesta Williams?"

"Yes," I said. "She's in my class."

Scott looked as though he'd won the lottery. "Wow. You're kidding. How *fantastic*. She's like, a five-star babe. Could you put in a word for me?"

For some reason this irked me. Who did he think I was? First the bank that likes to say yes, now a dating agency?

"What about Jessica?" I asked.

"What about Jessica?"

"Well, if she's your girlfriend, would she like you asking about Nesta?"

"Hey. Not my fault," said Scott with a wide smile. "So many girls, only one me."

My jaw dropped open, but then I realized he was joking. At least, I *think* he was joking. Sometimes he acted as though he believed he really was God's gift to women.

"Oh, poor you having to share yourself around us miserable impoverished girls," I said.

Scott laughed. "You know, you're really cool, T. J. You're so easy to talk to. Like one of the boys."

"Thanks," I said, feeling chuffed with the compliment. Easy to talk to? Maybe that was it. I didn't need to worry about being tongue-tied or saying the wrong thing. I don't need to talk, only listen. Maybe there was hope for me after all.

"Anyway—Nesta. What's she like?"

It was out before I could stop myself. "Oh—a complete airhead."

I felt a bit rotten saying that, as I don't really know Nesta beyond the fact that she's the prettiest girl in the whole school. I've never spent any time with her.

"Airhead's okay," grinned Scott. "It's not like I want her to *talk* to."

"Yeah, right," I said, suddenly feeling miffed. Maybe it *wasn't* such a compliment that I was easy to talk to? Oh, I don't know. Boys. They confuse me.

"Wanna arm wrestle?" I asked.

Scott looked at me as if I was out of my mind. *"What?"*

"Arm . . . oh, nothing," I said as I saw Jessica tottering up the road in strappy high heels. "Your date's here."

Jessica appeared at the gate and looked surprised to see me. She looked fantastic in a tiny white tank top and white jeans with diamante bits sewn up the seams.

"Hey," said Scott, leaping up and going over to her. "You look good."

Jessica was staring at me as though I'd just crawled out from under a stone.

"Thanks," she said and jerked her thumb at me. "Sister?"

"Next-door neighbor," said Scott. "You know each other from school, right?"

I smiled at Jessica, but she didn't smile back. "Can't say I've noticed her," she said. Then, flicking her hair as if dismissing me, she turned away.

"See you later," winked Scott. He put his arm round Jessica, snuggled into her and whispered something in her ear.

Jessica giggled and they disappeared off down the road.

"Er . . . nice to meet you, too," I called after them.

Huh, I thought. You can act as superior as you like, Jessica Hartley, but I know Scott's got his eye on someone else. One week and you'll be history. So there. Stick that in your diet yogurt and eat it.

I sat out for a bit longer. So much for my heart-to-heart with Scott. Paul was leaving and I felt miserable. Who could I talk to? Scott was a waste of time.

"T. J.," called Mum's voice. "Lunch. On the table. *Now.*"

As I got up to go in, I saw Mr. Kershaw and Drule go past again. Mr. Kershaw was jabbering away to Drule and the dog was looking up at him as if he understood every word.

That's it, I thought. I'm going to ask Mum for a dog. She said I could have a pet ages ago. A best friend of the furry kind. One who won't leave the country.

Why didn't I think of it before?

```
e-mail:      Outbox (1)
From:        goody2shoes@psnet.co.uk
To:          hannahnutter@fastmail.com
Date:        9 June
Subject:     Norf London blues
```

Hi Hannah

Miss you loads.

Idea: Why don't we run away to L.A.? I can write film scripts and you can be a dancer?

Bad news: Our team lost at footie. But then, you were our best player so I guess it's to be expected. Don't your parents realize the devastation it has caused nationally by removing you from the country?

My bro, Paul, is leaving. Off to Goa. With Saskia.

Ag. Agh. *Agherama*. I'm losing all my friends.

Scary Dad is in v bad mood. It's not *my* fault Paul wants to play the bass guitar and be a hippie instead of being a doctor. Atmosphere at home awful.

Good news: Beat that scab Evans at arm wrestling. Hahahaha.

Mum says I can have a dog. Suggest you get one too if your mum will allow until you settle in at school. Dog—man's best friend etc, etc. We're going to go next weekend to look for one.

Paul is staying the night. Hurrah. And for Sunday lunch. After that he's off and I will be All On My Own.

And guess what? Jessica Hartley from Year Ten is going out with Scott. But he fancies Nesta Williams. Hahahaha.

If another person says, "You'll soon make new friends," I vill 'ave to keell them.

I am starting a collection of made-up books by made-up authors. For example:

Medical Hosiery by Serge Icklestockings

Modern Giants by Hugh Mungous

Please send contributions.

Tata for now

T. J.

PS: Confucius say: Man with no front garden look forlorn.

---

e-mail:	Inbox (1)
From:	hannahnutter@fastmail.com
To:	goody2shoes@psnet.co.uk
Date:	9 June
Subject:	Cape cool

Hasta banana baby

Miss you too, megalooney.

Keep your chinola up. It's hard for me too. Everything's so differentio here. It's supposed to be winter but it's hot hot HOT. Cape Town is mega. You must come and visit. So far been up Table Mountain. Pretty cool. Though hot. Haha. And to the beach. Pretty hot though cool. Haha. There are loads of beaches here, everyone hangs out there. Boys here look more healthy than back home. All suntans and white teeth. Still stupid though if the one next door is anything to go by. His name's Mark. He's okay but he asked me to a barbie at his house and he eats with his mouth open and you can see all his food. Ew. Gross. He'll never get off with anyone if he doesn't learn to eat properly.

Book titles. Hmmm. Let me think.

Okay.

Pain In the Neck by Lauren Gitis

Hahahahahaha.

Chow bambino

Love you muchomucho

Hannah

Confucius say: Who say I say all those things they say I say?

Arf. Arf.

Chapter 3

The Wrinklies

"Stand close," said Mum as she pointed the camera at us in the back garden. "Put your hand on Paul's shoulder, Richard. And *try* and look as though you like him a bit."

Dad shuffled about behind us then finally put his hand on Paul's shoulder. "Might be more appropriate if Paul put *his* hand in *my* pocket," he muttered.

"Oh, for heaven's sake," said Mum. "Enough now. You made your point over lunch. This is our last day together as a family before Paul leaves for Goa. Try and act like a grown-up."

Paul and I tried not to laugh as Dad looked at the lawn like a naughty schoolboy. Quite an achievement seeing as he's in his sixties, but Mum can be Scary Mum to his Scary Dad when she likes. She gets a look in her eye and you know she's not to be messed with. Hannah used to call my parents the Wrinklies because they're so ancient. Mum had me when she was forty-five and Dad was fifty-three. They thought they'd finished having children with Paul. Then seven years later, along came yours truly. I think I was what is commonly known in birth terms as A Surprise. Or A Mistake. Whatever. All I know is that I have the oldest parents of anyone in school. I used to get embarrassed when there'd be all these young mums in T-shirts and jeans waiting after school, then along would come my mum or dad in their "comfy clothes" looking more like my grandparents. I started telling people that Mum and Dad were actually the same age as normal parents but they'd been captured by aliens one summer and kept as an experiment on their spaceship for two days. The trauma made their hair grow white and they grew old before their time. One girl in my class actually believed me.

Mum took her picture and Dad headed for the car.

So much for our last day together as a family before Paul's trip, I thought, as I watched Dad reverse his Mercedes down the driveway and zoom off toward his golf club.

The rest of us trooped back inside, and Paul and I began to clear the table. Lunch had been a strained affair with Dad giving me a lecture about "the importance of qualifications" and "a good career meaning a good start in life." It was so obvious it was aimed at Paul, but I tried to look as if I agreed with everything Dad said. Anything to keep the peace.

Then he started on about how much Paul going to college had cost him. What a waste it all was.

"I will pay you back," said Paul. "I really will."

"It's not the money," said Dad. "I want you to be happy."

"I will be," said Paul. "I *am*. I want to see the world. Experience life. It's going to be brilliant."

"Well, at least let me give you some decent medical supplies for the journey," said Dad.

Paul sighed. "It's sorted, Dad. Don't worry."

Dad didn't look convinced and, for a moment, I felt sorry for him. He doesn't normally look his age, but today he did. He looked sad and a touch weary. Sometimes he can't accept that people have their own plans for their lives. He's so used to people obeying his every word at the hospital, he thinks it's going to be the same at home. Poor Scary Dad. I think he means well.

After loading the dishwasher, Mum went to water the pots on the patio and Paul and I went through to the living room. Paul flopped on the sofa and began flicking through the Sunday papers. At the bottom of the pile was our school newspaper, which he began to read.

"There are loads of things you can do in here," he said after a while. "Art, drama, choir. Getting a hobby would be a good way of making new friends."

"You sound like Dad," I said, sitting next to him and stretching my legs out onto the coffee table, "organizing my life. Anyway, I have loads of hobbies. Tennis. Football. Karate."

"Sounds like you'll meet lots of boys doing that stuff, not girls."

"Don't be sexist. Girls do all that stuff as well."

"Oh, *sorry*. Didn't realize you're a feminist," he teased.

"I'm not. I just believe women are the superior race," I teased back.

"Oh, look, there's you," pointed Paul as he came across our class photo. "And Hannah."

"It was taken just after Easter," I said, looking over his shoulder. "I look awful."

"No, you don't. What are the other girls like?"

"Oh, God. All sorts." I pointed to some of the girls in the photo. "That's Melanie and Lottie. I get on okay with them. They were at footie yesterday. Those three are the brainboxes, those two are the computer nerds, Jade and Candice are the bad girls that like to bunk off, Mary and Emma are the sporty girls, Wendy's a bit of a pain."

"So, who do you hang with?"

"Well, Hannah before she went, obviously. And now I suppose Melanie and Lottie a bit, but they're a twosome really. I'm lumped in with the brainboxes seeing as I'm usually first in the class at everything. Except math. I hate math."

Paul continued to study the photo.

"Now, she looks nice," he said. "Who's she?"

"God, typical," I said when I saw who he was pointing at. "She's Nesta Williams. Only the best-looking girl in our school."

"She looks like that girl in Destiny's Child."

"Beyoncé."

"Yeah. So who are her friends?"

I pointed out Lucy Lovering and Izzie Foster.

"They look like fun. Tell me about them."

"Not much to tell. I don't know them that well outside school. They don't do football or any of the stuff I do. Inside school, they're sort of in the middle. Popular. Not too swotty, not too disruptive, though Izzie does ask a lot of questions in class sometimes. One teacher called her Izzie 'Why?' Foster. But *everyone* fancies Nesta, that I *do* know. Even Scott next door. She's in the drama group and I think she wants to be an actress. She's probably completely self-obsessed. Anyone as gorgeous as her has to be."

"Not necessarily," grinned Paul. "I'm gorgeous and I'm not self-obsessed."

"And *I'm* gorgeous and I'm not self-obsessed," said Mum, coming back in with a

565

bunch of white roses she'd cut. "So why don't you get in with this crowd?"

"Oh, you don't understand, Mum. They hang by themselves. They'd never let anyone as boring as me in with them."

"You're not boring," said Mum, taking the newspaper from Paul and scanning the back page.

"Don't bother to read that," I said. "It's completely out of touch and dull."

"Well, here's your chance to change it," said Mum, handing it back to me.

"What do you mean?"

"There, back page. I saw it the other day when I had a look through. I thought you might be interested. It says that they're looking for a new editor, seeing as the old one will be moving on at the end of the year. And they want to make it more of a magazine than a newspaper. Applications open to everyone from Year Nine upward. You only have to do eight pages or so as an example."

"Not interested," I said, putting the newspaper back on the pile of papers.

"But you want to be a writer," said Paul. "You

should go for it. It would be good practice."

"Nah, people think I'm a swot as it is. If I went for that, they'd only hate me more."

"Suit yourself," said Mum and began to root around in the cupboards for a vase. "But I see that Sam Denham is doing a talk for all those interested."

"Sam Denham? Where does it say that?"

"Ah, so suddenly it's not so boring." Mum picked up the newspaper and read from the back. "Monday, eleven June, four thirty in the main assembly hall. That's tomorrow. He's going to talk about journalism. It says he got started on his school magazine."

Sam Denham is a celebrity journalist and though he's old, at least in his thirties, he's still cute in that Ricky Martin kind of way. They always have him on the news when they want an opinion about anything. He always has something interesting or funny to say.

And he's coming to our school?

"Maybe I *will* go to the talk," I said. "But only to listen."

e-mail: Outbox (1)
From: goody2shoes@psnet.co.uk
To: hannahnutter@fastmail.com
Date: 10 June
Subject: Night night

Hi Hannah

Feeling mis. Bro Paul gone. He and Saskia are booked on the overnight flight to Goa tomorrow. Boo hoo. Everyone I care about is going away.

Gotta go, school A.M.

T. J.

By the way, our crapola newspaper is looking for a new editor, and Sam Denham is coming to school tomorrow to do a talk. Apparently he got started on his school mag.

---

e-mail: Inbox (1)
From: hannahnutter@fastmail.com
To: goody2shoes@psnet.co.uk
Date: 10 June
Subject: Sam the Man

WAAAAKE UP.

  Exscooth me? Did you say Sam Denham as in Sam

568

Denham from the telly? He's a top babe. V V jealous. Wish never left U.K. Be sure to wear something short that reveals your legs as they are one of your best features. And sit on the front row.

T. J., you *must* go for editor. You'd be brilliant at it. And it would take your mind off missing me and Paul. I've read all about this kind of thing in Mum's mags. The agony aunts are always telling people to "keep busy" and "throw yourself into your work." I think this is a godsend. Your destiny.

And you think you're miserablahblah? Try being me. In a new country. With no friends at all. Not even Melanie and Lottie. No, young lady, you don't know you're born, as Dad would say.

Yours truly,

Your Agony Aunt Hannah

P.S. Few more for the book collection
Over the Cliff by Hugo First
The Cat's Revenge by Claude Bottom
Arf arf arf arf arf arf!

569

Chapter 4

A Lonely Little petunia

"I'm just a lonely little petunia in an onion patch, an onion patch, an onion patch," sang the record in my head. It was going round and round, louder and louder, as I sat eating my lunch in the school playground the next day.

I was on my own because Melanie suffers from awful hay fever and thought that sitting outside would make it worse. Course Lottie had to stay in with her to keep her company and hand her tissues. I was going to explain that as pollen is airborne, it could get anywhere, so it wouldn't make much difference where she was, but I didn't want her to think I was a Norma Know-It-All. Too many people thought that already. In fact lately I've found myself holding back when I know the answers to things in class. Let someone else be the one who always gets it right. It doesn't win you any prizes in the popularity stakes.

Perhaps I should have stayed in with them, I wondered, as I looked around at all the groups of friends. It is definitely possible to feel lonelier in the middle of a crowd than when on your own.

Most of the school was out making the most of the heat wave. Everyone in pairs or three or fours. All busy talking, laughing, having a good time. I always used to sit with Hannah at lunch, and I felt really self-conscious sitting on my tod. Like, everyone must be staring, going, "Oh, poor T. J., she's got no mates."

I continued munching my peanut-butter-and-honey sandwich like I didn't care, but I did care. I didn't like this feeling of being the odd one out.

"Hey, T. J.," called a voice near the bike shed.

I turned round to see Wendy Roberts. "Hey."

"You heard from Hannah?" she asked as she

perched herself on the bench next to me and lowered the straps of her top so the sun could get to her.

I nodded. "Yeah. I've had a few e-mails. I think she's missing England."

"You must miss her, too," she said.

"Yeah, I do," I replied, wondering what was going on. Wendy never normally gave me the time of day, so why this sudden interest in Hannah? Sensitive and caring are not words that come to mind when I think of Wendy. Mean and self-centered more like. But no one else had asked about Hannah or how I was, so maybe I'd got her wrong.

"You going to the talk tonight?" she asked. "Sam Denham?"

I nodded.

"He is gorgeous, isn't he? I saw him on morning telly last week. He was so funny. I wonder if he's got a girlfriend. Are you going to go for editor?"

I shook my head. I wasn't going to tell her, but Hannah's e-mail had made me think. Maybe I *should* go for editor. It would be perfect to take my mind off things, plus, as Paul had said, good practice for when I'm older. But I didn't want to tell

Wendy. I didn't want her thinking I was getting ideas above my station, and anyway, I might not even get the job.

Wendy got out her mirror and applied some lipstick from her bag. "Great color, isn't it?" she said. "Natural with a hint of gloss. Good for us brunettes. Want to try some?"

"No, thanks." Us *brunettes*? What is all this matey, let's-bond-over-a-lipstick act, I wondered. What *does* she want?

"Er, T. J. . . ."

"Yeah . . ."

"You know that exercise we had to do for math . . . ?"

Ah. So that was it. I felt my face drop. I couldn't help it. For a split second I thought someone was being friendly because they might have cared about me. Obviously not.

"Well I meant to . . . ," Wendy continued.

"You want to copy my homework?" I interrupted.

"Oh, T. J., *could* I? You'd be doing me the most *enormous* favor and you know what Mr. Potts can be like if anyone hasn't done it. . . ."

"Actually math isn't my best subject . . ."

Wendy stiffened. "It comes so easily to you but if you're going to be precious . . ."

"I'm not. Here take it," I said and got my book out of my bag. I couldn't be bothered arguing. Math didn't come easily. I had to really work at it and the last bit of homework had taken hours after lunch yesterday and I still wasn't sure I'd got it right. But I wanted friends not enemies, and Wendy could be really nasty when she wanted to be.

Just at that moment I caught Izzie Foster watching me from the bench to my right. She raised her eyebrows and half-smiled at me.

"Thanks. You're a doll, T. J.," said Wendy, grabbing my math book out of my hand. Off she went, leaving me sitting on my own again.

Izzie was still staring. She was sitting with her mates Lucy and Nesta and, like most of the other groups of girls dotted around the playground, they looked like they were having a good time, just relaxing in the sun. Nesta was at one end of the bench rubbing lotion onto her legs and Lucy was at the other with her skirt hiked high and her legs stretched out to get the sun. Izzie said something to them and they both looked over, then Izzie got up and came to join me.

"Hey, T. J. I was just thinking. You heard from Hannah?"

"Wendy's already borrowed my homework," I said.

"What homework?" asked Izzie, looking puzzled. "I saw you sitting on your own and suddenly remembered that Hannah'd gone. I wondered how you were doing?"

So people *had* noticed me sitting on my own. Well, I didn't need anyone's pity.

"I'm fine," I said, getting up and putting my half-eaten sandwich in the litter bin. "Got to go."

I was going to go and sit and read in a cubicle in the loo for the rest of the lunch break. That way no one would see me on my own and feel sorry for me.

"So, to sum up," said Sam Denham from the stage later that day, "you've got five main rules, and if you stick to them, you won't go wrong."

I turned the page of my book to write more notes.

"Rule one," he said. "Your job is to stop people just flicking through the magazine. You have to draw them in to actually read what's on the page. You do this by having hooks on the page. These are pictures, titles, words under the picture that give an idea what the feature is about, a quote and the picture captions. Now, if people scan your page, they can quickly access what it's about. So, the title and the captions should be . . . what?"

He looked around as a few hands went up in the hall, including Nesta Williams' who was sitting next to me. Sam pointed at her to answer.

"*Interesting*," she said, and gave him a flirty smile.

"Right," said Sam, flashing a big smile back at her and keeping his eyes on her for a few moments. "*Interesting*. Or funny. These hooks are as important, if not more so, than the copy."

I was scribbling furiously to get it all down when I noticed Nesta hadn't written a thing. "Do you need paper?" I whispered to her, ready to rip out a page for her.

She grinned and shook her head. "No, thanks. I'm just here for the view."

You and half the school, I thought. I don't think

a talk had ever been so well attended, not only by the girls but also by the teachers. But then, most of the teachers are aspiring writers, according to Hannah's mum. She was a headteacher before she left for South Africa. She told us that half her staff were secretly working on novels and planning to get out of teaching.

"Rule two," Sam continued. "Make sure your picture or photograph is appropriate to the copy. You don't want a big smiley picture of someone next to a tragic piece. Rule three. Use your pictures and captions in a creative way. For instance, you're doing a sports page and have a feature about tennis coaching. Any ideas?"

Wendy Roberts put up her hand. "You could have a photo of some kids playing, with the caption *Learn to play tennis.*"

Sam nodded. "You could. It's apt, but not very inspiring. Any other ideas?"

I had one, but I didn't want to look a prat in front of everyone. Wendy was blushing like mad after Sam had squashed her idea. I went over in my mind what I'd say if I could only pluck up the courage.

Sam pointed at a girl at the back.

It was Izzie Foster. "How about a picture of Pete Sampras in full flight going after a ball, saying something like, 'Are you the next Sampras?'"

"Now we're cooking," said Sam. "That's more like it. Only it might be a bit intimidating, as most people know they'll *never* be the next Sampras. So, it might put them off going. But, good idea. Any more?"

Me *me*, I thought, trying to summon up the courage to put my hand up.

"Come on," said Sam, looking round at the rows of silent girls. "Part of being a pro is throwing ideas into the pot and not feeling bad when someone knocks them down. It doesn't matter. We learn as much by our mistakes as our successes, if not more. Come on, who's going to stick their neck out?"

I could feel myself going red as I put my hand up, but I was bursting to see what he thought of my idea.

"You," said Sam, looking in my direction. "Lara Croft on the front row."

I looked behind me. He couldn't mean me, could he? *Lara Croft?* But no one else had their hand up.

578

He pointed at me again. "You. Come on. Girl with the plait?"

Oh, he *did* mean me! I could feel myself going redder than ever. I took a deep breath. "What if you use a picture of, say, Tim Henman?" I finally managed to get out, "on his backside with the ball bouncing past and a caption saying something like, 'Even the best needs a little extra help'?"

"Love it," beamed Sam. "It may not make you want to play tennis, but it will make you stop long enough to read what's going on."

"Well done, Lara," whispered Nesta as the red from my face spread to the tips of my ears.

"Rule four. Never be afraid to try new things. Rule five. In your layout, make sure the reader always knows where to go next. And make sure the information is accessible, especially in a magazine. Know your market. And not too many long paragraphs. Break some of it up. You know, ten tips about this, five ways to do that, and so on. . . ."

At the end, he took some questions from the floor, but I hardly took in what was going on. I spent the last ten minutes of his talk in a daze at having spoken to him. I was well chuffed that he'd liked my idea. Loved it, in fact. I couldn't wait to tell Hannah later.

As everyone got up to leave, I noticed Sam making his way over to where I was sitting. I froze to the chair. Ohmigod. He was coming over to speak to me. I could feel myself going red again and breathless as I planned what I'd say. I tried my best to look natural and smile as he approached, but I had a feeling I looked like a grinning hyena, I was so thrilled.

As he reached the front row, he knelt down next to me and turned his back.

"So, did you enjoy the talk?" he asked Nesta.

"Oh, yes," beamed Nesta. "Fascinating."

That wiped the smile off my face. Literally. *Fool*, I thought, you utter *utter* fool. He had no intention of coming to talk to you.

I had a quick look round and prayed that no one had witnessed it, but too late, I noticed Lucy Lovering hovering at the side. She'd seen it all. Me perking up with a stupid grin, then Sam turning his back on me to talk to Nesta. God, how humiliating.

I looked away from Lucy and got up to walk

out the back door. Sam slipped into my vacant chair as though I'd never been there and continued chatting to Nesta.

"Hey, T. J.," called Lucy, as I reached the school gates and turned into the street. "Wait up."

Oh, no. I wanted to get out. Get home and hide. What did she want? I pretended I hadn't heard and carried on walking.

"T. J.," said Lucy, catching up.

"Yeah?"

"That was a great answer you gave in there."

"Thanks," I muttered and carried on walking. It didn't feel so great anymore. "Bye, Lucy."

"What bus you getting?" she persisted.

"102."

"Me too. We can go together."

"Aren't you going to wait for Nesta and Izzie?"

"Nah. Izzie's gone off to band practice. And Nesta. Well . . ."

"Probably hoping she'll get a ride from Sam Denham," I said bitterly. I couldn't help it. I felt miffed. Nesta wasn't even interested in writing or going for editor and yet she was the one Sam had picked out for special attention afterward.

"A ride from Sam?" Lucy giggled. "That I'd like to see. He came on a bike."

"Really? I thought he'd come in a flash car or something."

"I know," said Lucy. "But it *is* a flash bike. I saw him arrive on it in a helmet and clips and everything." Then she added, "People aren't always how you think they are."

I felt awkward then and a bit rotten about what I'd thought about Nesta. She can't help being a man magnet.

We stood in silence for a few minutes, then Lucy turned to me. "I hope you don't mind me saying, but . . . back there, I saw . . . you know . . ."

I shrugged and tried to pretend I didn't care. "Well, Nesta *is* gorgeous. She has everything any boy could ever want."

"What? A hairy chest and big muscles?" asked Lucy.

I burst out laughing. "I thought he was coming to talk to me. Or both of us at least."

"I know," said Lucy gently. "I saw."

"I felt a right idiot. Like I was invisible or something."

"I've been there, believe me. I used to feel like that a *lot* when Nesta first arrived," said Lucy. "I mean, I know she's my mate, but she is stunning, so people always look at her before anyone else. And she's funny, so people like her. It's easy to feel left out sometimes. I thought she was going to steal Izzie from me when she first began to hang out with us. I thought she didn't want to be my friend, only Izzie's. It was like I wasn't even there. So, yeah, I know *all* about feeling invisible."

"What did you do?"

"Oh, took a very grown-up approach. Sulked. Acted like a baby. Felt *very* sorry for myself. *Hated* Nesta. Then I got to know her. And discovered that she's really nice. In fact she had been feeling the same way. She thought *I* hated *her* and didn't want to be her friend."

Just at that moment, Sam Denham cycled past on his bike and jolted as he went over a bump in the road.

"If you think about it," said Lucy with a wicked grin, "men really ought to ride sidesaddle."

I burst out laughing as I watched Sam wobble down the road and disappear round a corner.

"And he did call you Lara Croft," said Lucy.

"Yeah, he did, didn't he?" I said. I'd forgotten that. "I thought he meant someone else at first. I guess it's because of my plait."

"Maybe. But you do have a look of her. So, yeah," teased Lucy. "T. J. Watts—invisible? Hardly. Only mistaken for the most sexy woman in cyber-space."

"*Yeah*," I said. "Don't mess with me. . . ."

I liked Lucy. She was a laugh, like Hannah. She had a way of turning things round and making it all seem okay.

Somehow it didn't seem to matter anymore that Sam Denham had snubbed me. He probably didn't even realize he'd done it.

The rest of the journey home flew by as Lucy and I chatted away. As I let myself into the house later, I realized it was the first time in weeks that I'd actually felt happy.

Things were looking up.

e-mail: Outbox (1)
From: goody2shoes@psnet.co.uk
To: hannahnutter@fastmail.com
Date: 11 June
Subject: Wham Bam thanku Sam

Hi H

Excellent talk by Sam Denham. He fancied Nesta, he made a beeline straight for her after the talk.

I am definitely going to go for editor. Hurrah. And thx for the advice.

Got bus home with Lucy Lovering. She's a real laugh and easy to talk to. She has invited me to her house after school on Friday. Brill. Can't wait.

Scott came over to borrow my *Buffy* vid. He wants to show it to Jessica. He sends his love. He seems to have forgotten he said he'd give me back the money I lent him. I know I should say something, but I can't face it. . . .

Got piles of hwk so better go.

Miss you loads

Spik soon

Love,

T. J.

e-mail: Inbox (1)
From: hannahnutter@fastmail.com
To: goody2shoes@psnet.co.uk
Date: 11 June
Subject: School

T. J.

Help. Am mis. Don't like it here. I WANNA come HOME. And now you're going to be best friends with Lucy Lovering and you'll forget me. Started school today. Lots of geeky boys in our class. They have their own language over here. And accent. Like if someone's invited somewhere they say, "Like, yah, rock up when you like man." Or "I rocked up to Jine ee's (Janie's) about farve (five)." And they say "och shame" a lot. And a girlfriend is called a "cherry." It's going to take me ages to learn it all.

Gudnight ma cherry

Spik spox spoooon

Your v sad friend Hannah. Och shame Hannah.

Mark next door has some book titles for you. As he is a boy, they are all rude or stupid.

Rusty Bedsprings by I. P. Nightly

Chicken Dishes by Nora Drumstick

And *The Revelations of St. John* by Armageddin Outtahere

Chapter 5

For Real

"Make yourself at home," said Lucy, flinging her bag down and opening the fridge.

I pulled a chair out at one end of the pine dining table that took up half the kitchen. Before I could sit, I was accosted by a golden Labrador who appeared from under the table. He put his paws up on my chest and began to lick my face with great enthusiasm.

"*Down*, Jerry," said Lucy as another dog appeared next to him and joined in the let's-wash-the-guest's-face game.

"How many are there?" I asked, wiping my face with my sleeve.

"Two," said Lucy, opening the French doors. "Ben! Jerry!" she called as she ran out into the garden. The dogs jumped down and ran after her, tails wagging. Once they were out, Lucy stepped back inside and shut the door. The two dogs looked in through the glass with bemused faces as if to say, "That was a *really* mean trick."

"I didn't mind them," I said. "I like dogs."

"So do I. They're my best friends as much as Iz and Nesta, but they can be a bit much sometimes," said Lucy, then added with a grin, "And so can the dogs."

She held up two cartons of juice. "Cranberry or apple?"

"Cranberry, please," I said, settling into my chair. I liked Lucy's house immediately. It looked like the kind of place you could relax in. "Lived in," as my mum would say. Every surface was covered with books, papers, and magazines, the walls were plastered with paintings and drawings, and there was a lovely old dresser against one wall with colorful bits of mismatched crockery.

"Hi," I said to the boy who was sitting at the other end of the table and reading the latest John Irving novel.

"Uh," he said. Or, at least, that's what it sounded like.

"Steve, this is T. J. T. J., this is my charmer of a brother."

Steve barely looked up. He only grimaced at what his sister had said.

"Oh, hi, T. J.," said Lucy. "I'm Steve. So *pleased* to meet you. I *would* look at you, but then you are my *younger* sister's friend, so why bother? You're too young for me and probably stupid. Nothing you have to say will be of the slightest interest to me. I am your superior in every respect, and everything I say—no, *think*—will be over your head."

Steve's mouth twitched. He almost laughed.

"Good book that," I said, pointing at what he was reading. "I've read all of his, but I liked *The World According to Garp* best."

Then he did look at me. A strange look as though he was considering something unsavory that a cat might have brought in. I met his gaze and tried to look friendly.

"New, are you?" he asked.

"Ohmigod, it speaks," said Lucy, putting a glass of juice beside me. "Sorry about the juice. It's organic, but it tastes okay when you get used to it. My parents are both health freaks, so . . ."

589

"We have to go out of the house to keep our toxin levels up," said Steve.

"In answer to your question, no, I'm not new," I said. "New here, I guess. But I've been in the same class as Lucy since we began secondary."

"T. J.'s a brainbox like you," said Lucy. "She's going to go for editor of our school newspaper."

"Really," said Steve, looking totally unimpressed.

A brainbox? Was that really how people saw me? How boring.

It got worse.

"She's arm wrestling champion as well," continued Lucy, who was oblivious to the fact that I was squirming in my seat. D'oh. Thanks for the great introduction, Lucy, I thought. Like hi, I'm T. J. Watts, brainbox with muscles. How sexy is that? Not.

Steve put down his book and did what all boys did when my arm wrestling talent was mentioned. He put his hand out.

At that moment, the back door opened and another boy burst in and flung his bag on the table. Blond like Lucy, he looked younger than Steve, maybe fifteen or so, whereas Steve looked like he was in sixth form.

"Excellent," said the boy, plonking himself down next to me. "Arm wrestling. I'll play the winner."

"T. J., other brother, Lal," said Lucy.

We nodded at each other as Steve and I locked hands and put our elbows down. Steve tried to test my strength before we began. I let my hand go limp in his, so he'd think I was weak. This was going to be easy.

"Ready, steady, GO," said Lal.

It was all over in two seconds.

"I wasn't ready," objected Steve, as his lower arm hit the table. "You called GO too soon."

"Rubbish," said Lal, pushing Steve out of his chair and sitting in his place. "You're a puny weakling. Right. Now me."

We locked hands and this time Steve called.

"Ready, steady, GO."

Lal was more of a challenge. Ten seconds.

"Wow. You're pretty good for a girl. Do anything else this well?" he said, picking up my hand and this time stroking it and looking at my mouth with what I can only describe as longing.

Lucy whacked the back of his head. "Take no

notice, T. J. Lal thinks he's Casanova."

Lal dropped my hand and Steve did a kind of smirk. "Don't suppose you can mend computers as well as you arm wrestle, can you?"

"Maybe . . . ," I said.

The rest of the evening went brilliantly.

I fixed Steve's computer no problem. He had one the same make as mine, complete with same operating system. He was well impressed when I pressed a few keys and, hey presto, it worked. He dropped his superior act after that and we got chatting about books. The shelves in his half of the bedroom were heavy with them.

"So who's your favorite author?" he asked.

"God, so many. Can I do top three?"

He nodded.

"Okay, I know that they're kids' books but I still love the Narnia books by C. S. Lewis."

"Yeah. They're cool," he said.

"And I like Bill Bryson."

"Yeah," said Steve, pointing to his shelf. "I've got all of his."

"And I loved *Alias Grace* by Margaret Atwood."

"How's the computer?" called Lucy from the corridor.

"Mended," Steve called back.

"Then stop hogging T. J. She's *my* friend," said Lucy, bursting in the door. "Come and look at my bedroom."

I got up to follow her, feeling well chuffed. She'd called me her friend. I hoped I would be. Steve and Lal, too. They were all really easy to be with and, for once, I hadn't been tongue-tied when meeting boys.

"Wow," I said as Lucy opened the door to her room. "It's like a princess's room. An Indian princess."

"Thanks," said Lucy, looking pleased. "Me and Mum did it last year. The curtain material is from a sari. I got it in the East End."

On one of her walls were cut-outs of people from magazines. Not the usual pop bands and actors—I didn't recognize any of them.

"Who are all these?"

"Dress designers. Gaultier. Armani. Stella McCartney. I want to do design when I leave school."

"Well, I can see already that you have a good eye for color, Lucy. This blue, lilac, and silver looks gorgeous. I wish you'd come and do my room. It's so boring. I think the paint Mum used was called Death by Magnolia."

"I'll show you some clothes I've made," said Lucy, opening the wardrobe and pulling out a selection of skirts and tops.

She held some of them up against her and they looked good, even to me, someone who doesn't know a lot about clothes.

"Maybe you could do a fashion piece for my newspaper. Like, what's in for the summer."

"Sort of five top tips?"

"Yeah. Summer sizzlers," I laughed.

"Love to," said Lucy. "And are you going to change the name of the newspaper? *Freemont News* sounds *sooo* boring."

"Exactly what I thought. I *was* going to change it. What do you think of calling it *For Real*?"

"Brilliant," said Lucy, "because that's exactly what it isn't at the moment and it's *exactly* what everyone wants. You're going to be so good at this, T. J. I can tell already that you're going to win."

I shrugged. "I'll give it a go. But I was amazed to find out how many others are going for it after Sam's talk."

"I know," said Lucy. "Even stinky Wendy Roberts, though she was mega-miffed after Sam didn't go for her answer. I saw her face at the back. She was livid. Even more so when he loved yours."

"She's even more angry with me today. She borrowed my math homework and I'd got most of it wrong. Not my fault if it's my worst subject."

"Serves her right," said Lucy as the doorbell rang downstairs. "Don't worry, one of the boys will get it. Probably Nesta, she said she'd come over."

Sure enough, Nesta appeared moments later.

"Hey," she smiled at both of us and flopped on the bed. She looked slightly surprised that I was there, but not unduly bothered. The whole evening was going so well. Maybe I could be friends with her too?

"We were just discussing the newspaper," said Lucy.

"Cool," said Nesta. "So, you going to go for it?"

595

I nodded. "And Lucy's agreed to do a fashion piece."

"Excellent," said Nesta. "And I tell you what readers like more than *anything*. A makeover. You know, before-and-after sort of thing."

"Good idea," said Lucy.

Nesta was staring at me. "And you know who we should do?"

I shook my head.

"*You*, of course. You could look *fabulous* if you wanted to."

Lucy looked shocked. "Nesta. T. J. *does* look fabulous. Honestly, you and your big mouth. You don't think before you open it, do you?"

"What? *What?*" said Nesta, looking flustered. "I didn't mean anything. . . . I only meant . . ."

I tried to smile but I wanted to die. She thought I looked awful. I knew I didn't wear all the latest fashions, but she didn't have to rub it in. I got up to leave.

"Oh, don't go, T. J.," said Lucy.

I looked at my watch and made for the door. "I have karate at seven and it's the last one before the summer hols, so I can't miss it. Honest, really, it's okay." I did my best to look cheerful, but Lucy didn't look convinced.

"T. J., I hope I didn't . . . ," started Nesta. "Oh, hell. I mean . . . I was only trying to say, I don't think you make . . ."

"Nesta. Button it," said Lucy, linking my arm. "Come on, I'll show you out."

When we got to the front door, Lucy made me promise I'd come again. "You sure you're okay?" she asked.

I nodded. I wanted to get away. And I did have karate that night, not that I was in the mood anymore. I really wanted to go home and talk to Hannah on e-mail.

I looked back at Lucy's house after she shut the front door. No way was I going to go there again for Nesta to point out how awful I look. It's all right for her, she'd look fab in a trash bag.

```
e-mail:    Outbox (2)
From:      goody2shoes@psnet.co.uk
To:        hannahnutter@fastmail.com
Date:      15 June
Subject:   Best friends


To Hannahnutter
I was so wrong about thinking I could be mates
with Lucy. Not in a million years. Not while she's
friends with Nesta Williams. You won't believe what
she just said . . . that I need a makeover. So every-
one at school pities me. And thinks I'm a swot.
And ugly. Everything over here is awful.
    I called Scott to ask if he could think of anything
I could do to improve my appearance. He laughed
and said, you could wear blue more often, it will go
with your veins. He thought it was really funny. I
said I was upset and needed cheering up and he
said he'd phone me back after watching Friends.
He hasn't phoned back yet.
    I miss you loooooaaaaads. Spik spoon.
    T. J.
```

From: goody2shoes@psnet.co.uk
To: hannahnutter@fastmail.com
Date: 15 June
Subject: Where are you?

Hannah. *Where* are you?

Even Scott hasn't phoned me back and he promised.

And Paul will be on the other side of the world now. Probably on some amazing island like in *The Beach*.

I feel so alone.

Love, T. J.

Oh, I met Lucy's bros tonight. They're sweet and the eldest one Steve is okay when he drops his snotty act. He gave me some brill book titles and suggested I put them at the back of the school magazine as a sort of silly fun page.

Bubbles in the Bath by Ivor Windybottom

A Stitch in Time by Justin Case

Chest Pain Remedies by I Coffedalot

Skin Rash Remedies by Ivan Offleitch

WHERE ARE YOU? I have to go to sleep now as it's late.

Chapter 6

Furry Friends

I woke up the next morning feeling better. It was the weekend and Mum had promised to take me to Battersea Dogs' Home. Who needed girl-friends? I was going to get my new best friend of the furry kind.

I got dressed and hurtled down the stairs. Nobody in the kitchen. No one in Dad's study. No one in the living room.

"Where's Mum?" I asked, on finding Dad sitting out on the patio reading the paper and having a cup of coffee.

"She got called out on a case. Good morning, T. J."

"Oh, yeah. Morning. Good. When will she be back?"

"She couldn't say. . . ."

"Oh, *no!*" I wailed. "We were going to go to the

dogs' home. And I have football this afternoon . . . We won't have time if she's not back soon."

"I've got the day off," said Dad. "Ready when you are."

"School all right?" asked Dad, as he drove down Edgware Road toward Hyde Park.

"Yeah."

"Not long until the summer holidays?"

"No. Not long."

"Feeling all right?"

"Yeah. You, Dad?"

"Yes. Fine, thank you."

I could see that he was trying, but I wasn't in the mood for telling him how I was really feeling. He'd never understand how much I missed Paul and Hannah and what it was like to be the only girl in Year Nine without a best friend. Plus, I didn't want to get him started on Paul and how he's wasted his opportunities. The last thing I wanted was a lecture on how I must focus on school and my career and get good grades.

I felt relieved when he gave up and switched the

radio on, even if it was to listen to classical music. He means well, Dad does, but sometimes, he's so busy offering his solutions that he doesn't realize that he hasn't really listened to the problem. It's much easier to talk to Mum. She understands better that sometimes people don't want to be told what to do, they just want someone to listen and give a bit of sympathy.

I spent the rest of the journey looking out of the window as we drove down Park Lane, toward Victoria then over the Chelsea Bridge.

"I've always wanted to come here," said Dad as we parked the car near Battersea Park. "I've been wanting a dog for *ages*."

"Really?" I said as we got out and walked round the corner to the home. "I never knew that. Have you ever had a dog before?"

Dad nodded. "When I was a lad. Best friend I ever had. Being an only child, he was my constant companion."

"What was his name?"

"Rex."

"What happened to him?"

"He died after I left for university. I was heart-broken. I thought it was my fault, you know, because I'd gone away and left him. But my mother said it wasn't like that. She said it was his time to go and that he'd waited until I'd gone so as not to upset me."

We walked into the reception area at the home and I watched Dad as he found his wallet to pay our entrance fee. I swear his eyes misted over when he'd talked about Rex. It made me see him in a new light. Dad clearly had a soft side when it came to animals.

"Pound for you," said the lady behind a counter. "And fifty pence for the young lady. Have you come to look or to buy a dog or cat?"

"Buy a dog," I said.

"Then you need to have an interview with a Rehomer first. Follow the red paws on the ground and someone will come and talk to you. See what sort you want and so on. Then you follow the blue paws and go and have a look."

I couldn't wait and felt really excited. I could see Dad did as well. He'd turned from Scary Dad into Smiley Dad.

We followed the red paws and went to sit in the waiting room with a group of other people. A sign on the wall told us that it cost £70 for a dog and £40 for a cat. After a short wait, a man in a red tracksuit came out and called us into a room where he asked loads of questions about where we lived and whether there were other children or cats and if was there a garden.

It was funny because he was stern like a headmaster and Dad had to really sell the fact that we would be good owners.

"Our chief concern," said the man, finally relaxing, "is that the dogs go to a permanent home where they will be happy and well cared for—for the rest of their lives. Hence the interrogation. Many of our dogs are here because their previous owners couldn't or wouldn't care for them. Last thing we want is for a dog to have another bad experience."

"Quite right," said Dad. "I can assure you that we'll take very good care of whomever we get today."

"Okay, then. Let's go and look at the dogs," said the man.

Dad looked at me and winked as we followed the man along the path of blue paws through a courtyard to a building at the back.

Inside it was like a hospital with long sloping corridors leading up to different floors. Each corridor had a different name: Oxford Street on the ground floor where the clinic was; Bond Street and Bow Street on the first floor where the dogs were kept; Regent Street and Baker Street on the second with dogs and cats and a private floor, Fleet Street and Pall Mall on the top.

"Here we go," said our Rehomer, opening a door to a side ward. "I'll leave you to look around. Take your time, then, when you've decided, we'll bring the dog to you for an introduction and see if you get on. Takes about fifteen minutes. Then, if all parties are happy, you can go."

Two things hit us as soon as we entered the ward. The sound of barking. And the smell. Not a bad smell, but distinctive nonetheless. Like wet hay mixed with dog food.

"*Phworr,*" I said.

"Aromatherapy of the canine kind," laughed

Dad as we looked in to see the first hopeful face looking out at us from behind bars.

"It's like they're in a prison cell," I said as a Jack Russell poked a paw through at us and barked in friendly greeting.

We spent the next hour walking through all the ward on every floor. We must have seen about fifty dogs. Each one had a little room in which was a blanket, water, a toy, and outside access to a corridor at the back.

There were all sorts of characters to choose from. Collies, beagles, Jack Russells, muts of every color, even a Samoyed, which Dad told me was a rare breed. He looked like a big white teddy. At the side of each cage was a report with the dog's details: the breed, name, age, history, and whether they liked cats or children. Whether they needed an experienced owner and whether they were destructive or not!

At the end of their report was a comment as though written by the dog. "I make a good companion." Or "I need commitment." Or one big dog whose comment said, "I am a majestic individual!"

"That one sounds like you, Dad," I said, pointing at the last one. With his tall stature and silver-white hair, Dad did have a majestic air.

"I don't know what you mean," he laughed, then pointed at one that said, "And there's one that sounds like you: 'I have a strong will and need a lot of training.'"

On one ward, a black mut called Woodie was doing everything he could to get people's attention. All sorts of mad antics—bouncing off the walls, paws up against the bars. It was as though he was saying "pick me, *pick me*, look what I can *do* . . . back flips, jumping, bouncing!!!! Pick me. *Pick me.*"

Another old brown-and-white collie sat looking at us with pleading eyes. She looked as though she had a bad wig on.

"This is heartbreaking," said Dad, reading her report. "She's called Kiki. She's thirteen."

Kiki put her paw through the cage and even though there was a big sign saying not to touch the dogs, Dad took her paw and stroked it. "Hello, girl." Then he turned to me and I swear his eyes were misting over again. "Poor thing. At her age,

607

she's probably here because her owner died or something. She looks as though she's been well looked after though. Shame, because a lot of people come here and only want the young dogs. They see 'thirteen years' and see the expense of vet's bills."

I was finding it excruciatingly difficult. I wanted all of them. Every ward we went into, the dogs would perk up and start wagging their tails as though Dad and I were their best and oldest friends. So pleased to see us. It was like they were saying, "Oh *there* you are, hold on a mo, I'll just get my stuff and we can go." Then, as we walked past their cages, their faces would fall and their tails would go down as if thinking, "Come back. Hey, where are you going? I thought we were outta here?"

"Can't we hire a coach, Dad, and come back with it and say right, everyone in? And then go and buy a big house in the country . . ."

"I wish," said Dad. "But, sadly, we can only have one. Have you made up your mind?"

I shook my head. I'd fallen in love with about six of them. Woodie and the Samoyed and Kiki the old collie, a mut that looked like an old teddy, a beautiful black Alsatian, and a cheeky Jack Russell.

Some had to be overlooked as it said clearly on their report that they could be destructive and didn't like children, even teens. Others, I knew, were too big, like the Alsatian. Arm wrestling champion that I am, I knew I wouldn't be able to keep him on a lead.

It was then that I turned a corner and saw Mojo. He was sitting quietly in his room, a medium-size black dog with a white patch over one eye. He gazed up at us with the saddest eyes I've ever seen. You look how I felt last night, I thought. Sad, lonely, and badly in need of a friend. "Mojo is four years old and a stray," said his report. "He has a very gentle nature and likes people. He is very distressed at finding himself here and would like a good home as soon as possible."

Mojo looked up at me with hopeful eyes.

I glanced over at Dad.

"He's The One, isn't he?" said Dad.

I nodded.

Dad and I didn't stop talking all the way home. He told me all about how he had wanted to be a vet, but didn't think he could cope with having to put people's pets down as you sometimes had to do.

609

We even talked about Paul.

"At least this fella won't get on a plane and leave us," said Dad, looking at Mojo, who was sitting happily in the back, looking out the window. "Unlike some people I could mention."

"Paul, you mean?"

Dad nodded. "I hope he's all right, wherever he's got to. He may be grown-up, but you never stop worrying. And I know you and Mum think I go on, but I know my own son and he can be naive at the best of times. Even as a young lad, he was a dreamer, too trusting of people. . . . You have to have your wits about you when you're traveling."

"He'll be okay," I said. "He's with Saskia."

"Hmmmph," said Dad. "And she's as daft as he is. Still, I guess he's not alone. You're right."

I was glad it had been Dad who'd come with me to the home. I felt I'd got to know him better. And discovered he was missing Paul as much as I was.

When we got home, Mojo ran around sniffing everything. Tail wagging happily, he seemed more than pleased when Dad opened the French doors to the garden. He ran out and sniffed the air as if he couldn't get enough of it.

"I think he likes it here," said Mum, watching him from the kitchen. As he ran about familiarizing himself with the smells, the phone rang.

"Oh, that will be someone called Lucy again. She's phoned a few times since I've been back and so has someone called Nesta."

I went to answer the call. Mum was right. It was Lucy.

"About Nesta last night," she said. "She really didn't mean to upset you. What she meant to say was that with your potential you could look totally amazing. She wasn't saying you looked awful or anything."

I'd forgotten all about the incident the night before. And it didn't seem so bad in the light of a new day.

"I suppose I *was* being a bit oversensitive," I admitted. "Overreacted a bit."

"We all have days like that," said Lucy. "Like my mum says, only the wearer of the shoe knows where it rubs. You know, sometimes we don't know where each other's sensitive spots are and tread on them by mistake. Nesta treads on people's sensitive spots with hobnailed boots on. But she doesn't mean to. We all want to be friends. Honest. We all agreed. That's why Nesta came to sit next to you at Sam's talk the other afternoon."

"Really? I thought that was just coincidence."

"No. It was so you had someone to sit with."

"Really?"

We chatted on for about ten minutes and I told her my news about Mojo. She wants to come over on Monday to meet him.

After I put the phone down, I had plenty to think about. It looked like I had misjudged the whole situation and I decided I should give Nesta another chance. I watched Mojo as he ran about. He looked a different dog already. His tail was wagging madly, his tongue out.

Mum had her radio on in the kitchen and an old song was blasting out. How true, I thought, as I listened to the lyrics. "What a difference a day makes, twenty-four little hours . . ."

We're all going to be good friends, I thought, going out into the garden to Mojo and doing what

I'd wanted to do ever since I'd set eyes on him.

I gave him a big hug.

---

e-mail: Inbox (1)
From: hannahnutter@fastmail.com
To: goody2shoes@psnet.co.uk
Date: 16 June
Subject: Asta la vista

Ola bamboo baby.
Me velly sollee no e-mail back last night.

Sollee you had bad time. Wish I was there to make it all better. Confucius, he say all things will pass. Particularly if you eat plennee fiber. Arf, arf.

Had brill time. Went for a grand beano feast and drinky drunky woos at a girl from school's. She's new like me only she's come here from Johannesburg (known over here as Jo'burg). I think we might be friends. Her name's Rachel.

Am getting bronzed and beautiful. It may be okay here after all.

She has two book titles for you. Bit rude.

Poo on the Wall by Hoo Flung Dung

Dog Bites by R. Stornaway

Love you loads,

Hannah

---

e-mail:	Outbox (1)
From:	goody2shoes@psnet.com
To:	hannahnutter@fastmail.com
Date:	16 June
Subject:	Illo mysterio of lifeio

Great to hear from you. All changed from last night. V happy. Have new furry friend called Mojo. He's adorable and Mum says he can sleep in my room. I think Dad is jealous. He was so sweet today at the dogs' home. I realized I don't know my dad as well as I thought. He's v worried because Paul said he'd call when he got to Goa but nothing so far. Hope he's okay. I think it's just Paul and he'll call when he remembers.

Also, Lucy called and apologized about Nesta. May be okay after all, but no one will ever replace you. I am glad you met this new girl though as I don't want you to be lonely. Lucy said her bro Steve liked me and thought it was unusual to meet a girl who had half a brain and was good to talk to. Not sure if this is a good thing as boys seem to view me as "one of the lads" and I would like to have a boyfriend some day. Maybe Nesta was right. Maybe I do need a makeover. Anyway, I told Mum I want to change my appearance and maybe try and look a bit more like a girl. She was v pleased and said I can have a new dress.

Scott came over to meet Mojo. He has ditched Jessica already. He was looking mucho cute and was very sweet with Mojo.

Funny business, life, isn't it? Just when you think everything's rotten and life stinks, it can all change. Love you.

T. J.

Books:

Rhythm of the Night by Mark Time

Bad Falls by Eileen Dover

---

e-mail: Inbox (1)

From: paulwatts@worldnet.com

To: goody2shoes@psnet.co.uk

Date: 17 June

Subject: Goa

Hey T. J.

In Goa, it's awesome. We sleep under the stars and look out over the sea. We met some amazing people (travelers mostly—Brits and Irish and a large number of Dutchies) and the locals here are very kind. I have bought an amazing crystal, and every time I hold it, it is like there are enormous

615

beams of light pulsating through my head via my temples, brow and crown chakra, but it gives Saskia a headache. I have been having real funky lucid dreams lately and been feeling like a million dollars with this quartz.

Rock on.

Paul

P.S. Please let Ma and Pa know I am okay. Tried to ring but lost wallet soon after we arrived. Have got job in a bar though. So all okay. Please ask Ma to send some dosh. Tell her I'll pay her back, promise, promise. Don't mention to Dad. Saskia got some nasty insect bites. Please ask Ma to send some more homeopathic stuff—arnica and apis and citronella and lavender oil.

Chapter 7

Dog
of the Week

Our class was in a mad mood the next week at school. I think the heat wave had affected everyone's brain.

It started in science, when Mr. Dixon asked if anyone knew the formula for water.

Gabby Jones put her hand up. "HIJKLMNO," she said proudly.

"Er, can you tell me why?" he asked.

"Yesterday, sir," said Gabby, "you said H to O was the formula for water."

"H *two* O." He sighed, then wrote on the board. "H two, as in the *number*, O. Okay, last question about water. What can we do to save water in a water shortage?"

"Put less in the kettle, sir," said Lucy.

"Excellent. Anyone else?"

"Don't use the hose," I said.

"Another good one. Any others to help our water supply go further?"

Jade Wilcocks' hand shot up. "Dilute it, sir," she said.

Mr. Dixon shook his head, but I could see he was trying not to laugh.

Then it was into the school hall for a film about the cosmos and all the planets and stars. Afterward, Miss Watkins asked us questions to see if we'd been paying attention, as I think some girls used the hour in the dark as an excuse to have a kip.

"What is a comet?" asked Miss Watkins.

I knew the answer to this and put my hand up.

"Star with a tail, miss."

"Correct. And can anyone name one?"

Candice Carter, who was one of those I saw nodding off, stuck her hand up. "Mickey Mouse, miss," she said as everyone cracked up.

★ ★ ★

But the best was in RE. Again, it was poor Miss Watkins taking the class and she asked if anyone knew what God's name was.

This time it was Mo Harrison who put her hand up.

"Andy, miss."

"Andy? Why on earth would Andy be the name of God?"

"It's in all the hymns, miss," said Mo. "Andy walks with me. Andy talks with me . . . There are loads of examples."

"No, Mo," Miss Watkins said, turning to Nesta who was crying with laughter. "Nesta Williams, seeing as you clearly find it so funny. What do *you* think the name of God might be?"

"Er, not sure," said Nesta, looking caught out. "What do you think?"

"I don't think," said Miss Watkins. "I *know*."

"I don't think I know either," giggled Nesta.

The whole class got detention, but it was worth it. I felt like I'd spent the whole morning laughing my head off.

We never did get to know what God's name was.

★ ★ ★

"How are you getting on with the mag?" asked Izzie as we sat doing our lines in detention in the lunch break.

"So-so. I've got some ideas, but need to get them down on paper," I replied.

"Come over to ours at the weekend," said Lucy. "I'm sure Steve would like to see you again, and he can help. And so could me and Izzie and Nesta."

The offer of help was tempting. Less than two weeks to go until the entries were due in and there was going to be a lot of competition. Intense discussions and hushed conversations were going on everywhere.

"I could do a horoscope page for you, if you like," said Izzie.

"That would be brilliant," I said. "And I may do a piece about Battersea Dogs' Home."

I showed Lucy and Izzie the Polaroids of Mojo. Soon, everyone wanted to look, so they got passed round the class. Everyone ooed and aahed until it got to Wendy Roberts.

"Arrr, *sweet*," she said loudly. "T. J.'s new boyfriend. Hey, T. J. Is this *all* you can pull? He needs a bit of a shave."

A few girls giggled half-heartedly, but as though they felt they had to rather than because they thought Wendy was hilarious. Why was she being so horrid to me? Was it because Sam had liked my answer and not hers? Or because she'd got a low mark after copying my homework? It wasn't my fault I was crapola at math. I racked my brains for something funny to say back so it would look like I didn't care, but I couldn't think of anything quick enough. Bummer and bananas, as Hannah used to say. Why can I never come up with the right words when I need them?

After detention, we all trooped out to the playground for the last ten minutes of lunch. I ate my sandwiches and stretched out in the sun, but I couldn't help but notice that some girls were passing a piece of paper round, then staring at me and giggling in a nervous way.

Oh, what now? I thought as Izzie came out to join me on the bench.

"What's going on?" I asked.

"Oh, Wendy. You know she's running for editor as well. She's just jealous. . . ."

"Take no notice," said Lucy, coming to join us.

"You don't need to know, T. J. She's a sad cow and you should ignore her."

"No, I want to see," I said, and got up and went over to a group of girls who were standing round Wendy looking at the piece of paper. I glanced over Wendy's shoulder. There was a picture of a dog with its head cut out and mine stuck on instead. She'd cut out the photo of me from the group shot in last month's newspaper. Underneath Wendy had written "Dog of the Week."

"What do you think, T. J.?" giggled Wendy. "You getting your dog gave me the idea. Each month in the newspaper, we pick someone to be Dog of the Week. What do you think?"

As I searched for the right put-down, a voice behind me got in first. "I think, Wendy, that if you were any more stupid, you'd have to be watered."

I turned round and there was Nesta. She looked mad.

She took the paper and, much to Wendy's astonishment, she ripped it up. "This is not remotely funny, Wendy. And you know it's not. It's not journalism. It's just nastiness. Come on, T. J. Don't lower yourself by breathing the same air as this lowlife."

I was as gobsmacked as Wendy, but I turned away with Nesta and followed her to a bench where Lucy and Izzie were sitting.

"Thanks, Nesta," I said, "but I was okay. I can handle Wendy Roberts."

"I know. But I've been waiting for a chance to show you that I'm on your side. I'm sorry about the other day. Sometimes words come out the wrong way."

"Not just then," I grinned. "That was brilliant. I wish I could come out with stuff like that. I always think of good things to say later, like when I'm falling asleep or something. . . ."

"Nesta's special talent is fighting for her mates," teased Lucy. "Her special downfall is her big gob."

"Well, I know what it's like to have some saddo like Wendy have it in for you," said Nesta.

"I don't know why. I never did anything to her."

"With her sort you don't have to," said Nesta. "She's probably jealous."

"Of me? Don't be mad."

"Looks and brains," said Nesta. "Lethal combination."

I felt really chuffed. Maybe she didn't think I looked too bad after all.

Then I looked over at Wendy who was glowering at us from the other side of the playground. I hoped this wasn't going to be the start of something.

Then I looked at Lucy, Izzie, and Nesta glowering back at her like they were my best mates. And I hoped that this *was* going to be the start of something.

```
e-mail:      Outbox (1)
From:        goody2shoes@psnet.co.uk
To:          hannahnutter@fastmail.com
Date:        18 June
Subject:     notalot

Dear H

Weather is lovely. Wish you were here.

T. J.
```

e-mail: Inbox (2)
From: hannahnutter@fastmail.com
To: goody2shoes@psnet.co.uk
Date: 18 June
Subject: notalot either

Dear T. J.

Weather is here. Wish you were lovely. Arf arf.
Must dash. Going to movie, i.e., Drive-in.
Bigola hugs and heeheehasta la vista baby.
Hannah

Book title:
Chest Complaints by Ivor Tickliecoff

From: nestahotbabe@retro.co.uk
To: goody2shoes@psnet.co.uk
Date: 18 June
Subject: Friday night

Hey, Lara Croft
Wanna come to a sleepover Friday night? Iz and
Lucy are coming. About 7?
Nesta

Chapter 8

Sleepover Secrets

"T. J. T. J.!" called Mum excitedly as she came in the door. "Where are you?"

"Here," I called from upstairs, where I was straining to get started on some ideas for the school magazine. So far, I'd written one word. Aggh.

It was Friday night and I was going to the sleepover at Nesta's in half an hour. An evening of culture had been planned. *The Simpsons* and *Buffy* on Sky, then *EastEnders*, *Friends*, and *South Park*.

Mum came in carrying a large carrier bag and plonked herself on the bed. She looked *very* pleased with herself.

"I couldn't resist," she said, getting something wrapped in tissue out of the bag. She pulled out a calf-length dress with swirly rust, maroon, and orange-colored flowers on it.

"What do you think?" she asked.

The word *disgusting* came to mind, though I suppose it was pretty in that cottage-chintzy-curtain-fabric way.

"Not your *usual* taste, Mum," I said, thinking I was being diplomatic. Mum isn't fashion-conscious at the best of times, but her style is more plain than flowery. Jaeger and Country Casuals for work and sloppy tracksuits for the weekend. And her idea of making an effort to dress up is to wear a blue glass bead necklace. Even if it's with the tracksuit.

"Not for me, silly," said Mum. "It's for *you*."

Whaaat? Aggggh. No. *Buuuut it's horrid*, I thought.

"It's lovely, isn't it? I saw it in a little boutique opposite the surgery and remembered what you'd said about wanting to look more like a girl. Perfect, I thought. I described you to the lady in the shop, said you had dark hair and hazel eyes and

627

she said you'd be an Autumn according to her Color Me Beautiful chart and would suit the brown rusty colors," said Mum, not drawing breath. "Cost a fortune but we won't tell Dad. It's about time you had something nice. So what do you think?"

She was so delighted with her purchase that I didn't have the heart to hurt her feelings.

"There aren't words," I said truthfully.

"I *knew* you'd love it. You can wear it to your new friend's house, can't you? Try it on, try it on."

I smiled weakly as I desperately searched for something to say. Hmm? *How* do I get out of this one?

Ten minutes later, I was in the kitchen wearing the dress and still wondering, literally, how to get out of this. Course, that had to be the very moment Scott banged on the back door.

"Evenin' all," he said, letting himself in and stroking Mojo, who jumped up in greeting. Then he saw me. "Yuk. You going to a fancy dress?"

"*Shhh,*" I said. "Mum's upstairs. She bought it for me."

"What, to wear?"

"No. To scare off burglars. *Yes*, to wear."

Scott pulled a face. "You look weird. Like you're in *The Waltons*."

"Thanks a bunch. So how do I get out of it?"

Scott went round to my back, put his hands on my waist and nuzzled into my neck. "Now *that's* one thing I'm good at, helping girls out of their dresses." He started to stroke my hair then play with my zip. "Now, Miss Watts," he whispered. "I really don't think this is your style. Let me help you out of it and into something . . . more . . . comfortable."

I giggled and slapped him, hoping he didn't see me blushing. Him nibbling my neck made me feel all fluttery inside. Nice.

"*Uhyuh yunnawee*," I started to say, then took a deep breath and made myself remember this was Scott *for heaven's sake*. "Seriously though," I said, turning so he couldn't see my red face. "I'm going to a sleepover tonight at a new mate's house and I can't possibly wear this. She'll think it's so naff."

"What new mate?"

"*Oh*," I suddenly remembered he fancied Nesta. "Er . . . Nesta Williams new mate."

"You're kidding. *Nesta?* Why didn't you tell me? When did this all happen? I thought you said she was an airhead."

"Well, I was wrong. She's actually very nice."

Scott punched the air. "*Yes*. Will you promise, promise, *promise* to put a word in for me? Or even better, you could bring her here and I could kind of casually drop in and you could introduce us?"

I *could* I suppose, I thought, watching Scott as he went into the hall and checked himself in the mirror. I just wish that a boy would feel that enthusiastic about me one day. And even more to my surprise, I found myself thinking, I wish *Scott* would feel that enthusiastic about me.

By the time I was due to go, I had a plan.

I went down into the kitchen wearing my usual tracksuit and trainers to find Mum chopping peppers and onions on the counter.

"I can't wear the dress tonight, Mum. I'm going via Lucy's house and they've got two huge dogs. Labradors. *Very* hairy. *Always* moulting. The kind of dogs who jump up on you. With *enormous* claws and muddy paws and they like to chew

630

everything. They'd *ruin* my dress. Do you mind if I put it away for a special occasion?" (Special occasion like Bonfire Night and I put it on a guy to be burned, I thought.)

"Sure," said Mum. "And are you *sure* you like it?"

Was she giving me a get out? I was about to open my mouth and say *nooooo*, I hate it . . .

"Because they had it in pink," she said.

Ag. Agh. Agherama.

Later, I thought, as I made for the door. I will sort this later.

"Got your jimjams?" asked Nesta, closing the front door behind us. She looked fab in a lilac cami set with the words *Groovy Chick* across the top.

I nodded as she led me through into a living room with high ceilings, deep-red walls, and plush brown velvet sofas. Impressive, I thought, as I took in the mix of dark wood and Turkish and Moroccan-looking rugs.

Izzie and Lucy were already there, curled up for our telly night, and both gave me a wave. Izzie was wearing red flannel pajamas with fluffy sheep on them, and Lucy had blue ones with stars and moons all over. I waved back and hoped that they couldn't see how nervous I was feeling. Nesta's flat was so glam, I hoped they wouldn't think my house was mega-dull when they came to visit me.

"You can change in there," said Nesta, showing me a cloakroom off the hall. "No one's here. Tony's staying over at a mate's, and Mum and Dad have gone out to eat. Mum said we can order pizza. What's your fave?"

"Four cheese. Please," I said as I closed the cloakroom door behind me.

"Coming up," called Nesta. "*Quattro formaggi.*"

My pajamas looked so boring as I got them out of my bag. A pale grey vestie thing for the top and bottoms to match. Ah well. What you see is what you get, I thought, as I pulled them on, then went back into the living room and pulled a cushion onto the floor.

"Let the viewing commence," said Izzie, passing me the Pringles.

After we'd finished watching *South Park* and munching our way through crisps, pizza, chocolate, and ice cream, the real fun began. Nesta put on a *Riverdance* video. After we'd danced our socks off for fifteen minutes, we all collapsed on the sofa and they talked about *everything*—music, clothes, mags, school gossip, horoscopes, and, finally, boys.

As they chatted, we painted each other's toenails. I did Nesta's dark purple and then she did mine the same color. Izzie did Lucy's pale blue and she did Iz's red. None of them seemed to mind that I didn't say a lot. I was happy to sit back and take it all in.

Nesta was a hoot and seemed to be *very* experienced with boys. She's had loads of boyfriends. At least eight. Maybe more, I lost count. And she seems to be an expert on snogging.

Izzie is just fab. She's into loads of interesting stuff, not just horoscopes but alternative health, food, nutrition, aromatherapy, crystals, and witchcraft. And she's *also* in a band with her boyfriend. His name's Ben and the band's called King Noz. She sang a song for us that she'd written herself. She has the most amazing voice.

And Lucy. Lucy's sweet. And kind. She kept checking on me to see I had enough to drink and eat. And was I comfortable. Did I need another cushion?

They all made me feel so welcome I suppose it was inevitable that, in the end, they'd turn the spotlight on me.

"So T. J., is there anyone you fancy?"

I shook my head. "Not really."

"So why've you gone red?" asked Nesta.

"Nesta!" said Lucy.

"What? *What?*"

"Let her tell in her own time," said Izzie.

I decided to plunge in. They'd all been so open with me, I felt I should be the same with them.

"Well, I suppose there *is* one boy," I said. "I've known him all my life, but he treats me more like one of the lads than a girl."

"Does he know you fancy him?" asked Lucy.

"*Noooo*. In fact," I said, looking at Nesta, "he fancies you."

"*Me?*"

"Yeah, he's seen you at the Hollywood Bowl and asked if I'd put a word in."

Nesta looked surprised. "What's his name?"

"Scott Harris."

"Don't know him," said Nesta. "And anyway, I have a boyfriend."

"Posh boy," teased Lucy.

"Simon Peddington Lee," said Izzie in a voice like the Queen's.

"He's away at school at the mo," said Nesta, "but we speak or text most days. He'll be back soon for the summer hols. And, *anyway*, I don't steal other girl's boyfriends."

"He's not my boyfriend."

"Not *yet*," said Nesta. "Anyway, you saw him first ,so in my book that means he's yours whether he knows it or not."

"Maybe you should let him know you like him," said Iz.

"*Noooo*. Can't. *No.* You don't understand. That would ruin everything. See, he's one of the few boys I can talk to. I have known him so long I don't get all tongue-tied like I do around boys I fancy."

"You got on with my brothers okay," said Lucy.

"Yeah. But that was different."

"Ah, you don't fancy Steve. Is that it?"

"No. Yes. I don't know. I didn't think about it. It felt so natural round your house, I kind of forgot he was a boy. And, well . . . it's just, we got off on the right foot. I won at arm wrestling and we were away."

"Got off on the right arm then," grinned Lucy. "Not foot."

I decided to tell them everything. "See, I can karate-chop a boy to the floor and stand on his neck easy peasy, but the thought of having to kiss one and I'm terrified."

"*Ah . . . ,*" said Lucy. "I get it."

"You have to be like Buffy," said Izzie. "Like, one minute she's snogging Angel, the next, she's out vaporizing vampires. It's a question of balance."

"Right," I said, feeling more confused than ever.

I could see Nesta was bursting to say something.

"What?" I said.

"Nothing," she said, but she was holding her stomach as though keeping something in.

"Spill. I can take it."

"No. Nothing. Well. What if . . . ? No . . . nothing . . ."

"Oh, for God's sake, Nesta. Spit it out," said Izzie.

"Well," said Nesta. "How about you don't tell

Scott you fancy him? How about we get him to fancy *you*?"

"Ah," I said. "And how do you propose to do that?"

I knew exactly what she had in mind, but felt like teasing her.

"Er . . . ," she looked anxiously at Lucy. "Dunno really."

I decided to help her out. "You still want to do a makeover, don't you?"

"Er, *no*," she said with a quick glance at Lucy.

"You think I look like a bag lady, don't you?"

"*NO*. I never said *that*!" Now Nesta looked really worried. Lucy may be small in height but she's clearly big in Nesta's books. "No. *No*. I think you look fab. Oh, all right. . . . I think you could look fabber. With a makeover. That's all. And now you're going to hate me. And think I'm mean because I want to help. And Lucy's going to go on about my big gob. And how I never know when to stop. . . ."

I laughed. "I'm only teasing you. No, please, do it. To tell the truth, I took a look at myself in the mirror this evening in the dress from hell that my mum bought me and I thought, T. J., you need

637

help. I'd love it if you gave me a makeover. I'll use it in the magazine. And . . . anyone got a pen? I've had an idea for a feature for the mag. A Sleepover Special Report."

Nesta handed me a pen and paper from the drawer in the desk behind the sofa. Then she took my face in her hands and turned it to profile and back. Then she clapped her hands and went into drama luvvie persona, "A mi-vake over. Oh, *daaahlling*, ve're going to mi-vake you look *faaaabulouse.*"

D'oh, I thought. What've I let myself in for?

Sleepover Special Report

Ever wondered what makes the perfect sleepover? *For Real* asked four teenagers for their top tips and fave ingredients. Here's what they came up with.

Five main ingredients
1) Nosh for the munchies
2) Drinks

---

3) Videos
4) Music
5) Makeup for makeovers
6) Mags

Special Spot Report
Izzie Foster. 14. Aquarius. Finchley. London
Fave thing to do at sleepovers? Goss. Listen to music. Nosh.
Fave music for sleepover? Anastacia. Christina Aguilera.
Fave video? *Austin Powers 2*. Yeah baby yeah.
Top nosh? Choc-chip cookies. Doritos.
Top drink? Organic elderflower juice.

Nesta Williams. 14. Leo. Highgate. London
Fave thing to do at sleepovers? Dance. Read problem page in mags and have a good laugh. Makeovers.
Fave music for sleepover? Destiny's Child. Craig David.
Fave video? *Charlie's Angels* or *Scream*.
Top nosh? Nettuno pizza with extra cheese. Häagen Dazs.
Top drink? Coke.

Lucy Lovering. 14. Gemini. Muswell Hill. London
Fave thing to do at sleepovers? Talk about snogging and boys.
Fave music for sleepover? Robbieeee.
Fave video? *Titanic*. I'm King of the Wooooorld.
Top nosh? Chinese take-away. Yum. Pecan nut Häagen Dazs.
Top drink? Hot chocolate made with milk and marshmallows.

T. J. Watts. 14. Sagittarius. Muswell Hill. London
Fave thing to do at sleepovers? Chill. Laugh my head off.
Fave music for sleepover? *Top of the Pops* summer CD.
Fave video? *South Park Christmas Special* starring Mr. Stinky the Christmas Poo.
Top nosh? Burger and chips. Toffee popcorn.
Top drink? Banana milk shake with vanilla ice cream on top.

Chapter 9

American Pie

"So The Plan is," said Nesta, through a mouthful of toast, "we all go to T. J.'s and sift through her wardrobe."

It was Saturday morning and we were still in our jimjams, sitting round in the kitchen, eating toast, and drinking milky coffees.

I wondered if I could get out of The Plan. Not that I was bothered about the makeover anymore, no, I was worried what the girls were going to make of the Wrinklies. Izzie, Lucy, and Nesta's parents were normal ages. And Nesta's are so *glamorous*. I met them this morning while I was waiting for the bathroom. Her mum's a newsreader on cable television and her dad's a film director and both *très* good looking and stylish as far as grown-ups go.

Mainly though, I was worried what the Wrinklies might make of the girls. Dad in particular. He can turn into Scary Dad at the slightest bit of noise or disturbance. Our house was never one to throw its doors open and welcome in the neighborhood. I always used go to Hannah's house rather than the other way round. Dad likes his privacy, the fewer people he sees when he's not working, the better. Radio 4 and peace and quiet and he's happy. Last thing I wanted was him showing me up in front of new friends by asking them pointed questions like, "What time's your bus home?"

I thought I'd better warn the girls.

"Okay, er, about my parents, well my dad . . . ," I said, and explained the situation.

"Same at our house," said Izzie. "My mum doesn't exactly encourage me to bring my mates back. Some parents are like that. It's easy to hang at Lucy's or here where no one's running round cleaning up after you all the time."

"So, no problemo, T.J.," said Nesta. "We will be the perfect example of quiet refined teenagers."

"Well behaved and demure," said Izzie.

"And *very* mature," said Lucy.

I breathed a sigh of relief. I could trust them to be cool. At that moment, the back door opened and Leonardo DiCaprio's younger Italian brother walked in. I mean, this boy was *seriously* handsome.

"T. J., Tony. Tony, T. J. My brother," said Nesta as if I hadn't realized.

"Hi, T.J.," said The Vision.

"Hi, Tony," said a friendly voice inside my head. However, what came out of my mouth was, *"uhyuh."* Oh, *noooo*, I thought. Alien Girl from the Planet Zog is back to haunt me.

Tony looked at the croissant I was about to eat, then looked right into my eyes and did a half-smile that made him look even more gorgeous. "So, T. J., what do virgins eat for breakfast?"

"Dunno," I replied, breaking his gaze and staring at the floor.

"Thought so," he said and laughed.

"Take no notice of Tony, he's a dingbat," said Nesta. "So. Aren't you going to ask?"

"Ask what?"

"How come Tony is my brother?"

"No."

"Why not?" asked Nesta. "*Everyone* asks. He's light-skinned, I'm dark-skinned, how come?"

"Obvious," I said. "Same father, different mothers."

"Hmmm," said Nesta. "Smart cookie."

Not really, the voice in my head said. I met your mum and dad this morning. I know she's Jamaican and your dad looks Italian. Tony looks like your dad so I reckon he must have had a different mother. Elementary, my dear Williams. However, Noola the Alien Girl is a person of few words and all that came out was, "*uh*." Smart cookie indeed. Why did this *always* happen when boys I fancied were around?

"My real mum died before I knew her. I was six months old," explained Tony, coming over and laying his head on my shoulder. "Really, I'm an orphan. An orphan prince who needs *love* and *affection*."

"*Uhyuh*," I stuttered, hoping that by some strange quirk of fate, Tony might be fluent in Zoganese.

I could see Lucy giving me a strange look then giving Tony a *filthy* look. Hmm? Something going on there, methinks. Must ask later.

Tony went over to the fridge and opened the door. "What's to eat?" He got out a half-eaten apple pie, put it on the breakfast bar, and cut himself a huge slice.

"Apple pie for breakfast?" said Iz. "Ew. Gross."

He turned and grinned at her. "Would you prefer I did something else with it?"

"Like what?" said Iz.

"You seen that film *American Pie*?"

"Yeah," said Izzie, then pulled a face. "*Ew*, double gross."

"What are you on about?" I asked.

Nesta looked at Tony wearily and sighed. "Sorry about my disgusting brother, T. J. In *American Pie*, a boy asks what it's like to have sex. His mate says it's like putting your thingee in a warm apple pie."

I blushed furiously as Tony watched me closely to see my reaction.

"Apparently some guy in Australia tried it," said Lucy, getting down from her stool at the breakfast bar and refilling the kettle. "Steve read about it in the paper. This guy didn't wait for the pie to cool when it came out of the oven. He was taken to the local hospital and treated for burns."

"*Aggghhh*," said Tony, putting his hands over his crotch as the rest of us laughed. "I wonder how he explained *that* to the nurse on duty."

Lucy looked at the apple pie and I saw a wicked twinkle appear in her eye. "Would you like me to warm that up for you, Tony?" she asked sweetly. "I could put it in the microwave. On high?"

Tony went over to her and put his arm round her. "And how *is* the love of my life?"

"Dunno. How is she?" said Lucy as she took his arm away from her shoulder.

"You know you want me really," said Tony.

Lucy began to walk out of the kitchen. "Yeah. Right. It's *agony* keeping my hands off you. Not."

"That girl . . ." Tony sighed as he watched her go out of the room. "So what are you lot doing today?"

"Makeover," said Nesta.

"Who's the poor victim this time?"

Nesta looked at me. I looked back at the floor.

Tony got up and started dancing in front of me. "'Don't go changing, tryin' to please me . . .'"

"Go and see Mum, Tony," said Nesta. "It's time for your medication."

"So what was all that about?" I asked Lucy. The four of us were sitting on the bus on our way over to my house later that morning. "You know, Tony?"

Lucy shrugged. "We used to go out. Then we finished. Then we got back together. I don't know where we are now."

"Muswell Hill," teased Nesta as the bus went up the Broadway past Marks & Spencer.

"He adores you," said Izzie.

"That's part of the problem," said Lucy. "See, we're just getting on great, then he starts again"— she caressed the air with her hands—"with wandering hands. I'm not ready for all that yet. I want it to be special when I go further with a boy. I don't want to do it because I feel pressured that if I don't, he'll dump me for someone who puts out more easily. You know?"

I nodded. No, I didn't know. I hadn't even been *snogged* yet.

"And you saw what he's like,' said Lucy. "Flirting with you . . ."

"Oh, I never . . . ," I started. "I would never . . . I mean he *is* gorgeous, there's no denying that, but . . ."

"Oh, don't worry, T. J., he's like that with all girls. That's another reason why I don't give in to

647

the wandering hands. I'd never feel as if I could trust him."

"Well, no reason to worry about me. You saw what I was like back there. Always the same when there are decent boys around. I told you, I go *stupid*. You know there's that book *Men are from Mars, Women are from Venus*. Well, I want to write one, *Men are from Mars, Women are from Venus, Teenagers are from Planet Zog*."

"Good idea," said Lucy.

"It's mad," I continued, "because, I want to be a writer but, well, I told you my problem with finding the right words at the right time. Why do they always come after, like when I'm falling asleep or something?"

"That's good, it means your subconscious mind is working on it," said Izzie. "I find that with my lyrics. You have to consider the words. Play with them until you've got them right. Let them come to you sometimes. It can happen in the middle of the night. I'd say that is the sign that you *will* be a writer."

"And if you're from Planet Zog," said Lucy, "you can always write science fiction."

I laughed and punched her arm. "I wish I could be more like you, Nesta. I wish I could come out with great one-liners or put-downs."

"*We* all wish she'd be more like *you*," said Lucy with a grin. "Think before she speaks, sometimes."

"It does get me in trouble," said Nesta. "Sometimes."

"So, at last," said Lucy as we got to our gate. "We get to meet the man of the moment."

"Who? Scott?" I said, glancing up at his bedroom window to see if he'd seen us. "He usually goes out Saturday mornings."

"No, silly. Not Scott," said Lucy, pointing at the downstairs window next to our front door where a furry face was looking out. "Mojo."

I laughed as I unlocked the door and was almost knocked over as he leaped up to say hello.

"I've only been away a night," I said as he licked my face then ran round the girls, sniffing then rolling on the floor, his tail wagging madly.

After they'd all made a huge fuss over him, we all trooped up to my bedroom.

"Fab garden," said Nesta, looking out of the

649

window. "It's huge and *wow*, a hammock. How cool. You've got visitors though. On the patio, your gran and grandad are here."

I went over to look out.

"Er, no," I said, pulling back. "That's my mum and dad."

Nesta looked like she wanted to die.

"Mum had me late, when she was in her mid-forties."

"Oh, *très* Cherie Blair," said Izzie, going for a look.

"No," said Nesta. "*Très* Jerry Hall. Much more glam. Now let's look in your wardrobe."

And that was it. No problem. *Très* Jerry Hall and show us your clothes. I needn't have worried at all.

"I hope I didn't offend," said Nesta as she held up baggy tracksuit bottoms and put them on the reject pile. "You know, calling them your grandparents."

"No prob. I know they're ancient. In fact I call them the Wrinklies."

"I nicknamed my step-father The Lodger when he first arrived," said Izzie, flopping on the bed next to Mojo. "I couldn't relate to him any other way, although we get on better now. But the

650

thought of him sharing a bed with Mum, you know, *eew.* . . ."

"Huh," said Lucy. "You think you've got problem parents? Mine get the prize. Why can't they be normal instead of mad hippies? They're so embarrassing sometimes."

"My brother's a hippie. You know, the one who's abroad. I could introduce him to your mum and dad when he's back."

"Yeah," said Lucy. "They could have a soy bean party or something and talk about vegan shoes."

"Vegan shoes?" I asked.

"Plastic. No leather. Dad sells them at the shop."

"I think your mum and dad are great," said Izzie. "I really like them."

"Well that's because you are a *very* strange person," said Lucy.

Izzie retaliated by throwing a cushion at her.

Not wanting to be left out, Nesta grabbed one of my pillows and bashed both of them over the head with it. "Oh, be*have*," she said in her best Mike Myers voice.

Both of them picked up cushions and began pelting her.

If you can't beat them, join them, I thought as I reached for a second pillow.

It was hysterical. Even Mojo joined in, jumping on whomever he could and barking his head off.

Five minutes later Lucy was face down on the floor with Izzie sitting on her back. Izzie was tickling her under her arms. "Repent, repent. Say I am the most fab fabster in the world, no, the *universe*."

"Never," cried Lucy into the carpet.

Whilst they battled it out on the floor, Nesta and I were using my bed as a trampoline.

"I'm Xena, Warrior Princess," cried Nesta as she leaped in the air and whacked me over the head with a pillow.

"And *I'm* Buffy the Vampire Slayer," I yelled as I delivered a nifty whack to her knees. "*Die*, you pathetic imbecile."

Just at that second, my bedroom door opened.

"What in *heaven's* name is that din?" shouted Dad above the racket. "It sounds as if someone's being murdered."

We all froze on the spot as if playing a game of statues.

Dad was definitely in Scary Dad mode and I

prayed he wasn't going to make a scene.

"Aren't you a bit old for this tomfoolery?" he asked.

Nesta and I got off the bed and Lucy and Izzie got up off the floor. We stood in line, looking sheepish and not knowing what to do next. Lucy was staring at the floor, Izzie was grinning at my father like an idiot, and Nesta was looking at her nails, trying to pretend that she wasn't there.

Then I noticed Lucy's shoulders going up and down in silent laughter. This set me off. Then Izzie. Then Nesta, as all of us exploded into a fit of laughing.

Dad looked to the heavens in exasperation. "*Fourteen*, T.J. Isn't it about time you started acting like a young woman?'

I nodded furiously, but tears were falling down my cheeks.

"I'm going to my club for a bit of *peace*," said Dad, going out and slamming the door behind him.

"Oops," I said, then started sniggering. "Iz, Lucy, Nesta meet my dad. Oh dear . . ."

"Sorrysorry," said Nesta. Then she picked up one of my bras from a pile of ironing on the desk and put it on over her T-shirt.

"Guess we're going to have to work on our

653

refined and well-behaved bit, huh?" she said, sticking her chest out.

I nodded. "Demure and wotsit," I said, picking a pair of knickers from the pile and putting them on my head.

"And vewee vewee mature," said Lucy in a little girlie voice as she sprang up on my bed and jumped up as high as she could.

---

e-mail:	Inbox (4)
From:	hannahnutter@fastmail.com
To:	goody2shoes@psnet.co.uk
Date:	22 June
Subject:	Cape Town boy babe

Mambo bandana baby. Bin bisy bee. Fabola barbie last night and I have neeews. I met a boy. I seriously think he may be the One. I may even have to phone you for a yabayaba. He is Drop Dead Divine. A bronzed Adonis. His name is Luke. We had devine tucker and deep talk.

H X

P.S. Luke (swoon swoon) has a book title for you. *Romantic Fantasies* by Everly Night. Heehee. Double arf.

From: hannahnutter@fastmail.com
To: goody2shoes@psnet.co.uk
Date: 22 June
Subject: Scary Dad

Where are you? I phoned and got Scary Dad who said you were at a sleepover. Then he grilled me about whether my mum and dad knew I was phoning. Don't dare phone again. Get thine holy finger out and e-mail me as SOOON as you get in. Loooooooooaaaaaaaaaaads to tell you.

Hx

From: hannahnutter@fastmail.com
To: goody2shoes@psnet.co.uk
Date: 23 June
Subject: Alert alert. Lost T. J. Watts.

Okela. Ista no joke no more. *Ou est* you? *Ou Ou OU?*

Hx

From: paulwatts@worldnet.com
To: goody2shoes@psnet.co.uk
Date: 23 June
Subject: hols

Hey, little sis. Hope it's all going well and Scary Dad not giving you too hard a time. Life here is truly wonderful. Did a day with a holy man, amazing as he is out here in India, but is really from Kilburn. Lots of stuff happening with my third eye. Plus he's re-energized my chakras.

Did two-day meditation session with holy man. Nice group. All gelled well. Fairy-story landscapes and sunsets. Friendly people but Saskia has got amoebic dysentery.

Rock on. Stay true.

Paul

PS Please can you ask Ma to go to the Embassy and get me a new passport. Mine was nicked when I slept on the beach the other night. Ta. Plus some peppermint oil and sulphur and pulsatilla homeopathic stuff for the runs.

e-mail: Outbox (1)
From: goody2shoes@psnet.co.uk
To: hannahnutter@fastmail.com
Date: 23 June
Subject: Friday night

Hey H

Glad you met boy. Luke. I want *details*. Height? Weight? Snogged yet? Level of snogging? Marks out of ten for snogging? etc.

Me had fabola time at sleepover with Nesta, Izzie, and Lucy. Nesta's bro is divine, but taken by Lucy. Sort of. He has wandering hands apparently, which Nesta says is a disease a lot of boys in North London suffer from. She's going to do a makeover on me for the magazine. Before/after kind of thing. They all came over to go through my wardrobe but couldn't find anything. *Quelle* surprise. Oh and Mum bought me the dress from hell. Lucy said I had to be honest with Mum so I was and she's given me the receipt so I can change it. Thank de Lord. After we'd been through my wardrobe, we went into the garden as we are having uno heat wave here. It was nice and relaxed as Dad had gone to his club for A BIT OF PEACE. (He caught us being *un peu* silly and making a lot of noise and well, you know what he can be like.) Nesta had a go on the hammock under the cherry trees. Scott came running over the minute he

657

spotted her from his bedroom window. He leaped over the fence with a flower, trying to impress her, but he gave her the shock of her life and she fell out of the hammock. Then Mojo jumped all over her. It was very funny. Scott was all over her, all dopey with big cow eyes. I felt a bit jealous, although I know that she has a boyfriend and she said after that Scott wasn't her type. Still. I wish a boy would be all over me. I think I may be the only girl in our class who hasn't been snogged. Maybe I'll never get a boy ever. Maybe I'm just not the sort boys like.

T. J.

e-mail: Inbox (1)
From: hannahnutter@fastmail.com
To: goody2shoes@psnet.co.uk
Date: 23 June
Subject: you don't 'alf talk rubbish sometimes

T. J.

You're not the only girl who's never been snogged in Year Nine. I know for a fact that Joanne Richards and Mo Harrison haven't been and unless Mo sorts out her halitosis, she never will be.

Luke. Height 6ft at least. Blonde. Body like a god. Snogged, yes. Level 3. Okay, 4. Well, he is a god. Marks out of ten for snoggability? 9. But practice will make perfect.

I think it's great, those girls doing a makeover. You are gorgeous, but don't make the most of yourself. I've always said this. I like the sound of Nesta, Iz, and Lucy and often thought that if I hadn't been friends with you, I would like to have been friends with them.

Tata for now

Hannah. South African goddess of luurve

Books: Are you still doing this?

Run to the Loo by Willie Makeit

Chapter 10

My Fair Lady. Not

"You'll never do it," I said, beginning to feel desperate. "It's hopeless. I am Ugly Git from Uglygitland."

"Roma wasna builta in a day," said Nesta, tugging her way through my hair.

"The darkest hour is just before dawn," said Lucy, who was kneeling on the floor next to me, retouching my nails.

"Suppose," I said, looking gloomily at my reflection in the mirror in Nesta's bedroom. My hair was a frizzy mess. I had an aloe-vera face mask on that made me look like a ghost and a big spot threatening to erupt on my chin.

"Lack of self-esteem," said Izzie. "That's your problem, T. J. You are a babe, but you don't know it. Look, you have fabulous hair that you always scrape back in a plait, long *long* legs that you never show, a fab figure that you hide in baggy tracksuits, and a great mouth that all those thin-lipped models who have collagen injections would die for."

Always one to accept compliments graciously, I said, "Humphh. And you clearly have the observational skills of a brain-dead gnat."

We'd already done the "before" shot in the morning at Lucy's house. Steve had offered to be photographer with his new camera and it was hysterical. I'd worn the "dress from hell" that Mum had bought me, and Izzie had done my hair in two bunches high on either side of my head. Lucy had stuck dog hair from Ben and Jerry's brush onto my legs with Evostick so that I'd look like I had hairy legs. (I put my foot down when she got carried away and tried to stick some on my upper lip to give me a moustache though.) And Nesta had

661

given me some lessons in bad posture so I looked even more frumpy.

"All beautiful women have great posture," she'd said. "It's one of the first things they teach at modeling school. To stand up straight. So for these shots, stoop, like you have round shoulders."

Lucy raided her mum's jumble sale bargain bags and produced some seriously tasteless jewelry. Big dangly earrings and an Indian necklace.

"But they don't go with the dress," I'd said.

The girls had looked at me as if I was stupid.

"And the object of this exercise *is*?" said Nesta.

By the time they'd finished, I looked like a sack of old potatoes. With hairy legs.

"You look awful," Steve'd said approvingly when I came down the stairs, then walked across the hallway like a duck. A round-shouldered duck.

"Yeah, like Waynetta Slob from Harry Enfield's show," laughed Lal.

"I want to do the shots round the back garden near the trash cans," said Steve.

"What, like I'm on the scrap heap?" I asked.

Steve gave me a look as if to say "yeah", then he grinned. "You don't look that bad," he said. "It's only that dress that makes you look like a frump."

"But the trash cans in the background give a sort of subliminal message, like I'm a load of rubbish," I said.

"Yeah," said Steve. "Exactly. We've been doing it in film class, all about how surrounding images register with the subconscious and can reinforce what you're trying to say without people realizing."

"What are you on about?" said Lucy. She did an enormous yawn as though bored out of her mind, but I found what he was saying interesting.

We had a great laugh as Steve clicked away and I assumed the most unattractive positions and facial expressions I could.

At one point, Mr. and Mrs. Lovering came out to see what we were up to. They watched for a moment as I cavorted for the camera doing my sumo-wrestler position, then a bit of karate chopping. They looked very puzzled to hear Steve say in a French accent, "And look as miserable as you can. Like your durg 'as just died and gone to durgee 'eaven *avec les autres chiens.* That's it. *Eh bien. Marvelleuse, mon ooglee légume. . . . Diable* mon sooth, chins up, chins down. *Mais oui, bien sûr. Degoûtantamont.*"

Clearly languages were not his thing, I thought, as his parents both shrugged and went back into the house.

The second part of the makeover wasn't a laugh. Oh no-ho, not at all. The girls were taking it seriously. As in *mega*-seriously. They were on a blooming makeover mission.

I was plucked, waxed, massaged, moisturized, conditioned, manicured, pedicured, blow-dried, made up, made over, and dressed.

"Okay, you can look now," said Nesta, removing her dressing gown from the mirror where she'd draped it so I couldn't see.

The reflection of a brunette Barbie doll gazed back at me. I was wearing one of Nesta's dresses, a short pale blue number and her mum's Jimmy Choo gray strappy heels. Nesta had given me "big" hair, loose and flowing over my shoulders, and Lucy had made up my face with a little shadow, blusher, and rusty lipstick.

"You shall go to the ball, Cinders," said Nesta. "You look fab."

"Yeah, a top babe," said Lucy. "Do you like it?"

I wasn't sure. I did look good. And I had to admit that my legs looked really long. But I wasn't sure that looking like such a girlie girl was me. Mind you, I didn't know what *was* me.

"What do you think, Izzie?"

"Watch out boys," she sang. "There's a new kid in town."

Nesta's mum gave us a lift to Hampstead High Street where we were meeting Steve to do the "after" shots.

She dropped us halfway down Heath Street and as we got out of the car, someone did a long wolf whistle. I looked over to where it was coming from and there was Scott. He was with a bunch of his mates sitting at a table outside Café Nero.

"T. J. Watts. *Cor* bloody cor," he said as he looked me up and down and then up and down again, his eyes finally resting on my legs. "You're a *girl*."

"*Uhyuh*," I said as I noticed all the other boys round the table also ogling me. I felt exposed standing there in my shorter-than-short dress and I wasn't sure I liked the attention I was getting. Everyone was

665

staring and there was nowhere to hide. Even an old bloke in his forties was gawping as he went by. Served him right, I thought, when he walked smack into a woman with her dog and got all tangled up in the lead.

Scott took my hand and introduced us to his friends. He seemed to be enjoying himself immensely. Then he was all over Nesta and acting like he'd known her for ever. All his mates sniggered when she dismissed him saying, "In your dreams."

He didn't seem to mind though. In fact, I think he took it as a come-on.

Lucy spotted Steve coming down the street and waved. He waved back and, when he saw me, he did a slow whistle under his breath.

"See they've done a number," he said.

"Wow," I said to Izzie as we walked or rather they walked and I tottered. "Is it really this simple? A bit of lipstick, high heels, show your legs and boys turn to jelloid?"

Izzie nodded. "And even more so if you show a bit of cleavage. It's amazing to watch. Hysterical. You see boys' cheekbones twitching with the effort not to look at your chestie bits, but their eyes keep zinging back there as if pulled by an invisible magnet."

"Not a problem I have," said Lucy, "being a thirty-two triple A myself."

"Lucy's bros call her Nancy-No-Tits," confided Nesta.

"We can't all be Dolly Parton like you," laughed Lucy, punching her arm.

We went down to the bottom of Heath Street with Scott and his mates trailing after us and sat at a table outside House on the Hill. Nesta ordered drinks and Steve took some shots as he said he wanted them to look natural rather than posed. This time I didn't have to do much, he did all work. He was much quieter this time, not acting as loony mad as he had been in the morning. He wasn't as much fun. In fact he seemed to want to get it over with, as though he'd lost interest.

"Why did you choose Hampstead for the 'after' shots?" I asked, in an attempt to get him talking.

"Trendy place. It's glam. Rich," he said, then he clamped up again.

He didn't hang around after he'd got his photos

and muttered something about having to get back to finish homework.

Something had clearly upset him since this morning. He was really subdued. I must ask Lucy if she knows.

---

e-mail: Outbox (1)
From: goody2shoes@psnet.co.uk
To: hannahnutter@fastmail.com
Date: 24 June
Subject: The new *moi*

Hey Hannahlooloo

Had brill time today with makeover. Steve took photos on his new camera. Will send copies. Nesta made me look very girlie girl but not sure it's me. Felt uncomfortable for a few reasons. I never realized before that you can be invisible in big baggy clothes and no one takes too much notice. It's kind of safe. But going out in Hampstead today, everyone was staring. I felt exposed. Nesta said to "strut my stuff, girlfriend," but people act differently to you if you do. Girls can be bitchy. Boys disturbed. Scott went all googly-eyed at me. But mainly people stared. I wasn't sure if I liked it. Talking of

---

668

which, we bumped into Wendy Roberts coming out of Accessorize. She did a double take when she saw me and almost spat out her Magnum. Then she said that dressed like I was, I should go far, the further the better. I wasn't sure what to make of her reaction.

Spika soon

Love, T. J.

P.S. Yes, yes. More book titles, as I'm definitely going to put some in the mag. *Body Parts* by Anne Atomy

---

e-mail: Inbox (2)

From: hannahnutter@fastmail.com

To: goody2shoes@psnet.co.uk

Date: 24 June

Subject: The noo *vous*

Ole *le* noodley noodles baby

I think the word to describe Wendy's reaction is *envy*. God, I wish I'd been there to see her. And you. I do miss Hampstead and Highgate and hanging out. I bet you looked the business. Don't worry about looking girlie. You'll find your style. Today was just the beginning of T. J. as Sex Queen of North London. Remember Confucius he say, "Every journey start with first step. That is, unless step going sideways or backward."

Have been to Luke's posh pad *avec* pool this weekend. Some consolation for missing Ingerlandie.

May your flobbalots be mighty

HannahXXXXXXXXXXXXXXXXXXXXXXXXXXXXX

From: hannahnutter@fastmail.com
To: goody2shoes@psnet.co.uk
Date: 24 June
Subject: d'oh. Steve?????

Er ex*scooth* me?? But I just re-read your e-mail. Have you been holding out on me? More about Steve? Details? Height? Weight? Fanciability? Etc etc.

Immediatetment.

```
e-mail:     Outbox (1)
From:       goody2shoes@psnet.co.uk
To:         hannahnutter@fastmail.com
Date:       24 June
Subject:    d'oh. Steve?????
```

Gordy flobbalots. I told you already. *Lucy's* older brother. Fanciability. I guess he's nice-looking, but not in a drop-dead way like Scott, who I think I may be in love with. And at last he's noticed I am a girl. It's different with Steve. He's easy to talk to. I don't go peculiar when he's around. He's a mate.

T. J.

Book: *Strange Breasts* by Won Hung Low

```
e-mail:     Inbox (1)
From:       hannahnutter@fastmail.com
To:         goody2shoes@psnet.co.uk
Date:       24 June
Subject:    d'oh. Steve?????
```

Zoot allors. Snog him anyway and get in some practice!

HXXXX

Book: *Drink Problems* by Imorf Mihead

671

Chapter 11

Walking the Durg

"Don't go into the woods," said Mum as I got ready to take Mojo for a walk on Wednesday after school. "Stay on the roads where people can see you."

"I'm going to ask if Scott will come," I said. "Then it will be okay, won't it?"

"Yes, fine," said Mum. "But don't be too late back. You've still got homework to do."

I couldn't wait to call on Scott. I'm sure it wasn't my imagination that he'd been so flirty in Hampstead on Saturday. He'd seemed genuinely bowled over by my new look and at one point he'd held my hand and squeezed it. I'd got that lovely fluttery feeling again, like when he'd nuzzled my neck. I couldn't stop thinking about it and what it might be like to hold his hand again and even kiss him. My insides went all liquidy and peculiar just imagining it.

I combed my hair loose, put on a bit of lipstick, then put Mojo on his lead and went next door.

Mrs. Harris answered.

"Is Scott home?" I asked, trying my best not to give away the fact I was quaking. Mad really, as I'd been over to his house a million times and thought nothing of it.

She called up to him in his room and he emerged at the top of the stairs a few minutes later.

"Oh, hi, T. J."

"Er. Hi. Um. I'm taking Mojo for a walk. Do you want to come?"

He shook his head. "Watching *The Simpsons*," he said.

"Oh. Okay, cool. Another time," I said, hoping that I hadn't shown how disappointed I was. He didn't even come down to say good-bye.

As Mojo and I went up to Muswell Hill Broadway, I wondered if I'd misread the signals.

Had he ever held my hand before? Or squeezed it? I couldn't remember. Maybe I was reading too much into it. Maybe he hadn't liked my new look after all. But he seemed to at the time. He kept staring at me. I felt so confused.

I decided I'd look in a few shop windows in the hope of finding an alternative style to Barbie babe. Fat chance, I thought, as I looked at the various tops and skirts on display. I wasn't sure what I wanted to look like, though one thing I was certain about was that I didn't want to wear those high heel things again. Agony. They may have looked good, but there was only so far I was prepared to go in the have-to-suffer-to-be-beautiful game.

Mojo trotted alongside me happily as I pondered the great philosophical question of who was the real T. J. Watts.

Is she Noola the Alien girl?

Or Miss Strop-Bossy Prefect who likes to put boys straight?

Or Arm Wrestling Champion of North London?

Or Miss Goody 2 Shoes who always does her homework?

Or Norma Know-It-All?

674

Or Barbie's brunette sister?

Or on the other hand, is she a total nutter with loads of different characters living in her head?

"What do you think, Mojo?" I asked as we made our way past the cinema and down Muswell Hill High Road.

"Aha," said a voice behind me. "Talking to yourself, first sign of insanity."

I turned and there was Steve with Ben and Jerry.

"I was talking to Mojo," I said. "But you might be right about the insanity bit. In fact I was just thinking I might well be going bonkers."

He laughed. "You going to Highgate Woods?" he asked as Mojo, Ben, and Jerry got down to the dignified business of sniffing each other's bottoms.

"No," I said. "Mojo would love to, but Mum said I mustn't go on my own."

Steve checked his watch. "Well, we have just been, but I've no doubt these guys wouldn't object to a bit longer. Come on, I'll keep you company."

I gave Mum a quick ring on my mobile and, after giving me the third degree, she finally agreed.

We set off for the woods and once inside, let the dogs off their leads. They raced off excitedly, best of friends already. As they charged about, Steve and I chatted like old mates. It's so weird, I thought. Here's me, all great pals with Steve and nervous with Scott, whereas only a week ago, Scott was my pal and Steve was a complete stranger.

"So, what's with you and that guy?" asked Steve after a while.

"What guy?"

"One outside Café Nero. You seemed to like him."

"God, am I *that* obvious?" I was taken aback that he'd read my thoughts. "I hope he didn't notice."

"I don't think he did. Too busy ogling Nesta."

My heart sank. Maybe that was it. It was really Nesta he was interested in. And he'd been doing the flirty bit to get to her through me.

"I know," I said. "He lives next door to me. Has done for years and we've always been mates. Until lately. It's all changed. I found myself . . . you know, er, well, thinking about him a lot. I don't know what I feel, it's all so weird. And I certainly don't know what he thinks, but I don't think he rates me other than someone to talk to. Oh, I don't know. . . ."

"Any boy who doesn't fancy you must be mad," said Steve. "And I'll tell you one of the biggest secrets about boys. . . ."

I held my breath for the great revelation.

"They're exactly the same as girls in that they also feel shy and awkward that they don't always say the right thing or act the right way."

"Really?"

Steve looked at me closely. "Boys may act confident but can be just as nervous as you underneath. Everyone fears being turned down and looking a fool."

"I just don't think he's interested. . . ."

"How do you know who's interested or not?" said Steve. "Sometimes when a boy is acting disinterested, it's actually more frozen than cool. Frozen with fear as mostly girls call the shots. Boys fear rejection like anyone else."

Me calling the shots? That was a laugh. But boys being nervous too, that was obvious really. I'd never thought about it before. I'd been so caught up in my own ill-ease, I hadn't thought about theirs. Of course boys must feel that way too sometimes.

"For instance," said Steve, "you may think a boy doesn't want to know, but he may be too scared to say anything. I know I am sometimes, you know, if I like someone."

Maybe that's what Scott had been doing just now, I thought. Acting cool. Afraid I'd reject him. No. Not possible. Or was it? I felt more confused than ever.

"In fact . . . ," said Steve.

"How does anyone ever get together then?" I interrupted. "I think I'd need someone to make it *very* clear to me."

"How?"

"Dunno. Cards. Presents. Billboard in Piccadilly? Shout from the top of the rooftops I FANCY T. J. WATTS."

Steve laughed. "I'm sure there are loads of boys after you," he said. "You just don't know it."

"Really?"

"Well you saw the reaction you were getting yesterday."

"Yeah. But I wasn't sure if that girlie-girl look was really my style."

Steve nodded. "Yeah. Don't get me wrong, but

I thought Nesta had made you into a Nesta clone. That look suits her, but I see you more as Buffy than Barbie."

"Really?" Cool, I thought. I liked the sound of that. More Buffy than Barbie. I must make a note of what kind of clothes she wears.

"So how's the mag going?"

"Okay. But it's brought out the competitive side of everyone at school. And some of them can be pretty bitchy. Like there's this one girl, the one we saw in Hampstead. She's giving me a really hard time." I continued filling him in on the Dog of the Week stunt that Wendy had pulled. "Wendy Roberts."

Steve slapped his forehead. "The one outside Accessorize? I *knew* I knew her. Now you say the name . . . A mate of mine went out with her." Then he chuckled. "I could tell you some good goss about her."

"What?"

"No front teeth."

"How do you know?"

"My mate found out when he snogged her. One of them came loose. That's how I remember her name. She's waiting for implants, but the dentist won't do them until she's older. So she's got dentures. Real false teeth. Apparently she knocked both of them out in a riding accident. You could print a piece about dentists. And put in a picture of her as an example."

I laughed at the thought of it. "With a caption: All I want for Christmas is my two front teeth."

"Or instead of 'wide-eyed and legless,' you could write, 'wide-eyed and toothless.'"

"Don't tempt me," I said.

The time whizzed by as we chatted on about ideas for the school newspaper and Steve offered to do a piece on photography.

When I looked at my watch, it said eight o'clock.

"God, I'd better go," I said. "Mum'll kill me."

We rounded up the dogs, put them back on their leads, and Steve walked me to the top of our road.

"So, bye," he said as we reached our gate.

"Bye."

He went to go, then turned back.

"Er. Um. Do you . . . would you like to play tennis one day?"

"Sure," I said. I'd enjoyed the time we spent together and was beginning to think we could be good mates. "If you're prepared to be beaten."

```
e-mail:    Outbox (2)
From:      goody2shoes@psnet.co.uk
To:        paulwatts@worldnet.com
Date:      25 June
Subject:   runs


Dear Bro

Sorry to hear about the amoebic dysentery. Have
asked Mum to get you another passport and get it
sent to you. Haven't told Dad. Be careful.

   Love,

   T. J.
XXXXXXXXXXXXXXXXXXXXXXXXXXXXXXXXXXXXXXX
```

From: goody2shoes@psnet.co.uk
To: nestahotbabe@retro.co.uk
Date: 27 June
Subject: movie

Do you fancy the new Julia Roberts movie on Friday? It's on at the Hollywood Bowl. Lucy and Izzie are up for it. Hope you can come.

T. J.
XXXXXXXXXXXXXXXXXXXXXXXXXXXXXXXXXXXXXXX

---

e-mail: Inbox (1)
From: goody2shoes@psnet.co.uk
To: nestahotbabe@retro.co.uk
Date: 27 June
Subject: movie

Cool. I'll be dere.

Chapter 12

More Buffy than Barbie

To do:

1) Watch Buffy videos to note clothes.
2) Return Dress From Hell and swap for something the Buffster would wear.
3) Go to movie wearing new outfit.

It worked.

"T. J., you look wicked," said Izzie as we walked from the bus stop toward the Hollywood Bowl the following Friday. "Your hair looks so much better now you leave it loose, and I love the combats."

Lucy looked me up and down and nodded her approval. "Yeah. And I'm glad to see you haven't ruined the effect by hiding in a big baggy fleece. The tank top is great."

"Yeah. Bootylicious," said Nesta.

I *think* that means she approves.

We made our way through the car park to the cinema and it felt great. I could see groups of lads ogling us. And not just Nesta this time. Even I was getting a few looks.

When we got to the foyer, Izzie and Lucy went off to get the tickets while Nesta and I went upstairs and queued up for popcorn. As we were standing in line, I noticed Scott standing at the top of the escalator on his own. He kept checking his watch and looking down toward the entrance as if he was waiting for someone.

After we'd gotten our popcorn, Scott was still standing on his own, so we found Lucy and Izzie, then made our way over to him.

"Been stood up?" asked Nesta.

Lucy punched her arm. *"Nesta!"*

"What?" said Nesta. *"What?"*

"Actually," said Scott, his face brightening

immediately. "I was waiting for you."

"As *if*," said Nesta, tossing her hair.

Scott checked downstairs then, seeing no one was coming up, he linked his arm through hers. "Looks like my mate has been held up, so the honor of keeping me company is yours."

"Mate or *date* been held up?" asked Nesta. "Admit it. You've been stood up."

Lucy punched her arm again. "Excuse my *rude* friend," she said to Scott. "We don't often let her out at night."

Scott grinned. "So, you coming then?" he said to Nesta before turning to the rest of us. "Sorry, girls. Only got dosh for two tickets."

Nesta took his arm out of hers and came to stand behind us.

"Actually," she said. "I already have plans. With people who actually bother to turn up. Come on, girls. I'm going to the ladies'."

Scott looked taken aback as we walked off leaving him standing there. As I looked over my shoulder, I couldn't help but feel sorry for him. I know him well enough to recognize that what we'd just witnessed was a huge act of bravado.

Everything Steve said to me yesterday came flooding back. How hard it is for boys to take rejection even if they don't show it. It still hurts. His date hadn't shown and Nesta had made a fool of him on top of everything else.

As we stood in front of the mirrors doing our hair and lippie and stuff, I made up my mind.

"I'm going to ask if Scott would like me to go with him to a movie."

"No," chorused Izzie, Lucy and Nesta.

"Why not? He's been let down. He probably feels lousy."

"Who? Scott? Nah, he's well sure of himself," said Nesta. "He thinks he's God's gift and could probably do with being brought down a peg or two."

"No, he's really sweet underneath. It's all an act," I said.

"Ah," sighed Lucy. "Love is blind."

"Well, you don't want to be too easy if you really like him," said Iz. "You need to play hard to get. Boys like the chase."

"But I feel sorry for him," I said. "I'm going to go and ask him."

"How can someone with so many brains be so stupid?" asked Nesta as Lucy sighed in exasperation.

"You can think what you like," I said as I did a last check of my appearance. "But I've known him longer than you and this is something I have to do."

With that, I turned on my heel. As the loo door closed behind me, I could hear Lucy telling Nesta off for being insensitive.

"Yeah. Okay, then," said Scott when I told him that I'd keep him company. "But I'm not going to see the same movie as your mates."

"But Izzie already got me a ticket."

"I'm not sitting anywhere near that lesbian."

"Lesbian?"

"Nesta."

I laughed. Sour grapes, I thought, but I didn't say anything. He was just lashing out because she'd humiliated him in front of the rest of us.

There were five other films on at the complex so I let him pick what we were going to see. He chose a sci-fi film.

687

"I'm not mad on sci-fi," I said. "Are you sure you don't want to see the new comedy with Julia Roberts? I've heard it's a real laugh. And we can sit on the other side from the girls."

"No way," said Scott. "The sci-fi or I'm going home."

In the end, I gave in. I didn't mind. What I really wanted was a chance to spend some time with Scott alone and see what happened.

Scott loved the film, but I couldn't concentrate. As the screen filled with manic scenes from intergalactic wars, I was only aware of the proximity of Scott. Our knees and elbows touched a couple of times and I was hoping that he would hold my hand, but he just stuffed his face with popcorn.

Maybe real life isn't like the movies, I thought, as another alien got his three heads ripped off, squirting green blood all over the hero. Maybe in real life romance isn't beautiful sunsets and gentle kisses. Maybe in real life romance is sitting in the dark wondering if the boy you're with is *ever* going to make a move that isn't him merely shifting position in his seat. Maybe romance is all fantasy. For the last few days, that's all I'd done. Every night before I went to sleep, I imagined my first kiss with Scott. First he'd push a lock of hair behind my ear, then look deeply into my eyes, then softly press his lips on mine and . . .

A *phwt* noise beside me disturbed my thoughts. Scott had farted.

"Oops," he said with a grin. "Popcorn-flavored."

After the movie, we made our way out back into the foyer and Scott was a few steps in front of me. Suddenly he spotted a few of his mates who had been with him in Hampstead on the day of the photo shoot.

One of them came over.

"You're the girl who was having her photo taken the other day, aren't you?" he asked.

I nodded.

"You looked really good," he said.

"Thanks."

Suddenly Scott took my hand.

"Yeah, this is T. J.," he said as he introduced the group of boys.

Then he put his arm round me. "Just been to see *Alien Mutants in Cyberspace*," he said, then winked at them. "Didn't get to see much of the film, though, if ya know what I mean. . . ."

The boys sniggered knowingly.

"Anyway, got to go," said Scott and looked at me fondly. "The night is young."

"Yeah, right," said one of the boys as Scott pulled me away.

What was going on? I wondered. Did he fancy me after all and, as Steve said, had been acting cool? Or was this all a big act to make his mates think we were on a date? He still had hold of my hand as we went down the escalator and out the foyer but, unlike the day in Hampstead, I wasn't feeling all fluttery inside. I felt muddled. I didn't want to take my hand away though, as I remembered what he'd said about the night being young. Things could only get better.

When we got outside, I suggested we go and have a cappuccino.

"Got no money left," he said.

"No prob. My treat."

Scott shrugged. "Okay, then. And a hot dog?"

"Fine," I said.

"With onions."

"Fine."

For the next half hour, he talked. I listened.

He talked.

He talked.

I listened.

I was bursting to tell him all about my last few weeks. E-mails from Hannah and Paul. The magazine. My new mates. So much had happened, but I couldn't get a word in edgeways. He talked, I listened. That was the deal and always has been since I'd known him. I'd just never been bothered about it before. As I tried to appear interested, I thought that even Mojo was more interested in what I had to say. And he's a dog.

"So, enough about me. What about you?" he said, finally pausing for breath. "What do you think of me?"

Then he laughed like he'd said the funniest thing ever.

I couldn't help but think how easy Steve had been to talk to. We'd never shut up the other day in the park. But with him, it had been equal. I talked, he listened. He talked, I listened. He'd seemed interested in what I had to say and what my opinions were.

I took a long look at Scott. No doubt he was mucho cute to look at. A lovely curly mouth and deep-brown eyes. But as I stared into them, I thought, Scott Harris, I've never realized this before but you are boring. As in B. O. R. *iing*.

I had a sudden urge to go home, talk to Mojo, e-mail Hannah, and even maybe catch up with Steve. He had promised to start work on his article for the magazine and I could call to see how it was coming along.

We got the bus home together and when we got to our houses, Scott did a quick check up and down the street, then up at the windows. I was about to go in when he suddenly pushed me against the wall and the next thing I knew I was being snogged.

My first snog.

Ugh. Agh, I thought as his mouth crashed into mine. And erlack, onions. His mouth tasted ukky. It was a really wet, slimy kiss, not how I'd imagined it at all.

When he'd finished cleaning my teeth with his

tongue, he stood back, looking really pleased with himself.

"Catcha later," he said, pointing his index finger at me. Then he turned and went inside.

Not if I see you first, I thought as I wiped my mouth on my arm.

A couple of hours later, I was up in my room working on some ideas for the magazine when the phone went.

"T. J., it's Nesta."

"Oh, hi . . . Nes . . ."

"Listen," interrupted Nesta. "I've got something to say to you and I hope you won't take it the wrong way, but, well, that boy Scott . . . he's not the one for you. Don't ask me how I know, I just do. He thinks too much of himself and I know boys like that look pretty, but all they are interested in is themselves. You deserve better. You mustn't be a doormat. You can do better, believe me. It's just you're suffering from low self-esteem, but someone will come along who you'll have a better time with. Who really wants to be with you. Because you are a babe. With brains. Lethal combination as I've said before. And I know you like Scott, and now you're probably going to hate me and not speak to me, but as a friend I felt I had to tell you. T. J., are you there? Do you hate me now? Please say something? Oh, hell bells and poo. Lucy said I shouldn't phone but Izzie said I should. T. J., T. J. . . . ?"

I couldn't say anything because I was too busy laughing and I'd put my hand over the phone so she couldn't hear.

"Nesta. I agree."

"You . . . you *what*?"

"Yeah, you're right. Scott Harris. Cute but dull. Dull as dishwater. And . . . he's a bad snogger."

"He *snogged* you!" exclaimed Nesta. "*Ohmigod*. Details."

We spent the next half-hour yabbering about snogs and Nesta told me all about some of her early disasters.

"It's not always like that," she said in the end.

"Phewww," I said. "So there's hope."

"Mucho mucho," said Nesta. "It can be just how you imagined it and better."

When I put down the phone, I felt really happy.

That night, as I fell asleep, a different boy seemed to have taken Scott's place in my snogging fantasy.

```
e-mail:     Outbox (1)
From:       babewithbrains@psnet.co.uk
To:         nestahotbabe@retro.co.uk
Date:       29 June
Subject:    new e-mail


Note new e-mail address. Whatdoyathink?

T. J.
```

```
e-mail:     Inbox (2)
From:       nestahotbabe@retro.co.uk
To:         babewithbrains@psnet.co.uk
Date:       29 June
Subject:    new e-mail

Bootylicious. See you tomorrow P.M. at Lucy's for
the magazine finale.

  Nesta
```

From: paulwatts@worldnet.com
To: babewithbrains@psnet.co.uk
Date: 29 June
Subject: hol

Hi T. J.

Holiday really not going as planned. Monsoons have hit the resort. Torrential rain so impossible to sleep on beach. Am crashing in a hut with four other travelers, but caught head lice after I borrowed a sleeping bag (mine was nicked). Oh, and to top it all, Saskia has run away with the holy man from Kilburn. I have the runs and mosquito bites as big as golf balls.

Hope all well your end.

Love,

Paul

P.S. Please ask Dad to send very strong medical supplies. Anything and everything.

Chapter 13

The Mad House

The next afternoon, I had half of North London employed as my editorial staff.

At home, I'd asked Mum and Dad each to write something.

"We're theming the magazine toward summer," I said to Dad, "so I'd like you to do some handy hints for traveling abroad from a doctor's point of view. Make it relevant. A mini medical cabinet that you could pack in a suitcase. Stuff for sunburn, mosquitoes, the runs, and so on."

"Will do," he said with a grin.

I think he was really chuffed to have been asked.

And Mum was doing an article on how to deal with exam stress.

"Ten handy hints," I said. "It has to be accessible."

I left them listening to Radio 4 and sipping Earl Grey tea as they worked.

Over at Nesta's, Tony was working on a cartoon for a competition. We were going to invite readers to send in captions and print the best in the next edition. If there *was* a next edition.

At Lucy's, Steve and I worked on the computer in his and Lal's bedroom.

Lucy and Nesta were finishing their articles in the living room.

Izzie was on the computer in Lucy's bedroom, working out horoscopes for the coming month.

Mrs. Lovering kept bringing us herbie drinks with ginseng and some icky-tasting stuff called Guryana.

"Keeps you alert," she said.

And Mr. Lovering sat in the kitchen playing his guitar.

"Music to inspire the workers," he said when I went down to ask for a new ink cartridge for the printer. How a rendition of "You Ain't Nothing but a Hound Dog" was supposed to motivate us, I have no idea, but Ben and Jerry seemed to like it as they joined in, howling away with great gusto.

"This place is a *mad* house," said Lal, looking at his dad with disapproval. "I'm off somewhere normal. Where I can *think* in peace!"

"Go to my house, then," I said. "It's like a morgue."

No one's ever happy with their lot, I thought, as I watched him storm off in a huff. I'm sure Mum and Dad would agree with Lal if they came over, but I loved it. Mr. L. (as Izzie calls him) is a real laugh and as opposite to my dad as anyone you could meet. He's an old hippie who's losing his hair, yet has a ponytail. And he wears very bright Hawaiian shirts and Indian sandals. Mrs. L. is hippie-dippie too, today wearing a Peruvian skirt with mirrors round the hem and a rather strange crocheted top.

"You okay, T. J.?" asked Steve when I went back upstairs. "You're kind of quiet today."

"Yuh, yunewee," I muttered.

A *lot* had happened in the last twenty-four hours. Mainly in my head. I'd had my eyes opened to what a user Scott was, and I was experiencing an almighty twinge of conscience that I'd treated Steve the same way. Someone to earbash with my problems. Only last week I'd been on about how much I fancied Scott and how he never noticed me and treated me like a mate and nothing more. That was *exactly* how I'd treated Steve. And he'd been so sweet, reassuring me that I was fanciable and telling me how boys really felt about girls.

As I sat next to him at the desk, I felt the warmth of his arm against mine and caught the scent of soap on his skin. Back came the old fluttery feeling, only this time, I was with Steve, not Scott. How had I not noticed what nice eyes he had? Kind. Hazel-brown with honey flecks around the iris. And good hands, I thought, as he pressed keys on the computer keyboard—long fingers, elegant.

And it was too late. If I said anything, he'd think I was a complete airhead. Fickle and a half. In love with Scott one week, fancying him the next.

"So have you decided what to do about Wendy Roberts and her dentures?" asked Steve, leaning over me to see what I'd written.

"Er, *yu . . . nu . . . wee . . .* Wendy, yes. I've decided I'm not going to stoop to her level. I'll save stuff like that for my secret notebook and use it later when I write novels."

"Good for you," said Steve. "So do you reckon we'll be ready to hand the mag in on Monday?"

"Nih . . . ing . . . yah . . . ," I said, cursing Alien Girl who had taken over my vocal chords. "Umost. I mean, almost."

Steve was looking at me as though I had two heads.

"Gottask Luceand Nestasomething. Backin aminute," I said, jumping up.

I stumbled downstairs to find Lucy and Nesta. I needed help.

I sat on the floor and put my head in my hands. "Ag. Agh. Agherama."

"Hey, it'll be all right. We're almost there," said Nesta. "We'll do it on time."

"Do what?" I said, looking up.

"The mag."

"Oh it's not that. It's . . ." I looked at Lucy. Steve was her brother. What would *she* think if she knew I'd been fantasizing about him? She knew how I

701

felt about Scott. She'd think I was a complete tart for changing my mind so fast.

"So what is it?" asked Lucy.

"Nothing," I said.

"Yeah, looks like it," said Nesta. "Come on, spill."

I sighed. Then looked at the two of them waiting expectantly. Then I sighed again.

Nesta and Lucy started doing big sighs as well. Then really exaggerating them, heaving huge extended breaths until I had to laugh.

"Okay. Lie out on the sofa," said Lucy.

I did as I was told and Lucy sat at the other end.

"So Miss Vatts. Vat seems to be ze problem?"

I couldn't say. Silence. Big silence. It grew and filled the room.

"Ah. Boy trouble," said Lucy.

"But which boy?" said Nesta. "You're over Scott, *n'est-ce pas?*"

I nodded. "It's another boy who I've only just realized I like. Much nicer than Scott. And now I'm all tongue-tied and stupid around him. And I think I've blown it. And it's probably too late."

"Oh, you mean *Steve?*" asked Lucy.

"*How* did you know?"

"Kind of obvious from the start," said Lucy.

"*Obvious?* To *whom*? *I've* only just realized. And who knows what's going on in his head. If he likes *me*."

"Er, *hello*?" said Lucy. "What planet are you on exactly?"

"Planet Zog, actually," I said, and explained all about Noola and her ability to take over my head.

"Well, for your information, Steve hasn't stopped talking about you and asking about you ever since he met you," said Lucy. "And he was well miffed with the fact you fancied Scott. Didn't you notice how weirded out he was when we bumped into Scott in Hampstead?"

"Suppose he was kind of quiet that day. I thought I'd done something to upset him."

"D'oh. *Yeah*. You had," said Lucy. "Fancied someone else."

Izzie came down the stairs and flopped on the sofa.

"Whassup?" she asked.

"T. J.," said Nesta. "She turns into Noola the Alien Girl whenever she fancies a boy. Noola only knows three words. Tell her, T.J."

"*Uhyuh. Yunewee.* And *nihingyah.*"

Lucy started giggling and doing an alien robot impersonation like C-3PO in *Star Wars* up and down the room.

"*Uhyuh,*" she squeaked in a high voice. "*Yunewee. Nihingyaaaah.*"

We were laughing so hard that Steve came down to see what was going on. Of course, I went purple.

"So?" said Steve.

"So noth . . . nothing," chuckled Nesta.

"Just something Lucy said," said Izzie.

Steve looked up to the heavens, then turned to me. "You coming back to finish your editorial?"

"Uh . . . *uhyuh,*" I said, and Lucy exploded with laughter.

Steve heaved a sigh, which Lucy and Nesta copied.

Steve looked at us all as though we were stupid. "*When* you're ready, T. J.," he said, and went back to his room.

"See, do you *see* now?" I said. "I'm going to blow it. And we were getting on so well and now I'm going to act like an idiot around him and he'll think I'm Dork from Dorkland, Nerd from Nerdville, Airhead from . . ."

"Shut the door, Lucy," said Izzie. "We clearly have work to do."

We spent the next twenty minutes doing a visualization with Izzie. She's well into self-help stuff and had been reading in one of her books about positive thinking.

"It's all in the mind," she said. "You can get over this and put Noola the Alien Girl to rest. But you have to see yourself acting confidently. I've been reading all about it for when I do gigs."

"But I think you're either confident or not," I said. "Like Nesta. It's not something you can learn."

"Oh, yes it is," said Nesta. "We all have our own tricks. Sometimes I pretend I'm a character out of a film if I feel nervous. Then I act as I think they would. It really works."

"And I used to be hopeless about singing in public," said Izzie. "So bad I couldn't sleep at night. I used to be well terrified of looking a fool and this has really helped."

"So, you think I could learn to talk sense when I meet a boy I like?"

"Definitely," said Izzie. "In fact, my book says,

"'We are what we repeatedly do. Confidence is not an act but a habit.' You have to practice."

"Cool," said Lucy. "Sounds good to me. What do we do?"

Izzie made us all sit down and close our eyes. First we had to imagine the situation we felt nervous in, so I thought about being close to Steve upstairs. We had to imagine the room, the surroundings, what we were wearing, all the details.

Then Izzie said, "Imagine yourself being relaxed, calm, and completely in control. Imagine the other person's response to you. In your mind, see them laughing at your jokes, listening with interest to what you say, *liking* you."

She made us imagine the situation over and over again until in my imagination, Steve was gawping at me in open admiration, amazed at my witticisms. In *awe* at my brilliant conversation.

"Okay, open your eyes, everyone."

We did as we were told and looked around at each other.

"How do you feel now, T. J.?"

I stood up and went to the door. "Awesome. Noola. She dead." I put my hands on my hips

Arnold Schwarzeneggar style and said, "I'll be back. *Hasta la vista,* baby."

Nesta laughed. "Go get him, girlfriend."

I went back up the stairs. As I stood outside Steve's bedroom, my butterfly nerves came back, so I imagined Steve smiling at me and enjoying my company.

I went in, sat down next to him at the computer, did a quick visualization in my head, then turned and gave him a huge smile.

He turned to look at me. "Aaagjjhh. What's the matter with you *now*?"

"Nothing," I beamed, thinking, I am confident, I am great, stunning, brill, dazzling, fantabulous.

Steve looked at me as though I was totally bonkers.

"You're *really* weird, you know that, don't you?" he asked.

Just at that moment, my mobile went.

"'Scuse, Steve," I said as I put the phone to my ear.

"Hey, T. J.," said Scott's voice. "What you doing?"

"Magazine. Remember, I told you. Deadline Monday."

707

"Oh, that can wait," said Scott. "Wanna go out to the Heath?"

"Sorry, Scott," I said. "Busy. Later."

Then I hung up.

"That guy?" asked Steve.

"That guy."

"And . . .?"

"And . . . history," I said.

Now Steve had a huge grin across his face.

"What's the matter?" I asked.

"Nothing," he beamed.

"You're *really* weird," I said. "You know that, don't you?"

"Yeah," he nodded. "So that makes two of us."

For Real

Summer edition

Contents

Editorial by T. J. Watts	1
Coming events in the school calendar	1
Lucy Lovering's top fashion tips for a sizzling summer	2
Sleepover Secrets: a report by T. J. Watts	2

Dr. Watts' (Mum) ten tips for pre-exam stress 3

Dr. Watts' (Dad) handy hints
for holiday health abroad 3

Makeover madness: before and after
makeover with beauty tips for being
a top babe by Nesta Williams 4

Ten tips for taking good summer
holiday shots with an automatic
camera by Steve Lovering 5

It's a dog's life: an article on
Battersea Dogs' Home by T. J. Watts 6

Flirting dos and don'ts by Nesta Williams 6

Aromatherapy bath-time oils by Izzie Foster 7

Horoscopes by Mystic Iz 7

Wot a larf: strange book titles,
and their even stranger authors 8

And finally: a cartoon competition
by Tony Williams. Readers are invited
to write in with a caption 8

Chapter 14

Sabotage

The magazine looked great. We'd done the final layout on Steve's computer, eight full pages that looked fun and interesting.

Steve had found all sorts of visuals on the Internet to liven up the articles, pictures of dogs for the Battersea Dogs' Home article, stars for the horoscope page, herbs and flowers for Izzie's aromatherapy piece. Plus the mad "before" and "after" makeover photographs for the center spread.

It looked good. Very good. I reckoned I was in with a chance.

At assembly on Monday, Mrs. Allen asked that all entries were handed in to our form teacher.

"I know a lot of you have worked very hard on

this," she said, "so we won't keep you waiting. We hope to have an announcement about the winner by the end of the week."

Five minutes later we filed into class and I joined the group hovering around Miss Watkins' desk. I put my copy on the small pile of entries from our class.

"Quite a number getting it all finished on time, wasn't it?" I asked Wendy Roberts, who was standing behind me.

"Er, *no*," she said. "Unlike some saddos in this class, I didn't do one. See, I have a life."

"Oh, I thought you were into it."

"You thought wrong. Deadlines are for losers. And, by the way, Mrs. Allen said she wanted to see you. I saw her just now in the corridor. She wanted you to go to her office immediately."

That's strange, I thought as I hurried off down the corridor to Mrs. Allen's office. I hoped nothing was wrong.

"Mrs. Allen wants to see me," I said as her secretary looked up when I knocked on the office door.

"I don't think so, dear," she said. "Mrs. Allen's in with Mr. Parker. She said not to be disturbed. Must be some mistake."

No mistake, I thought as I went back to class. I suppose Wendy thought she was being funny.

Miss Watkins was at her desk flicking through the entries when I walked back into the class. "You're late, T. J.," she said.

"Er, sorry, miss," I said, going to my desk.

Luckily she didn't go on about it, as Wendy Roberts came in just behind me.

"And you, Roberts, what's your excuse?"

"Loo, miss," she said, breathlessly taking her place.

Miss Watkins continued flicking through the entries. "Well done girls, we have six entries from this class." Then she looked at me. "But I thought we'd have had one more. I thought you were going to enter, T. J."

"I *did*, Miss," I said. "I put it in the pile after assembly."

"Well, it's not here now," she said.

I looked round at Wendy Roberts. She was gazing out of the window, looking like butter wouldn't melt in her mouth.

"Are you sure, T. J.?" said Miss Watkins. "Check your bag."

I did as I was told, but I was sure I'd put it on the desk. "Not there, miss."

"So where is it?"

Suddenly I didn't know what to say. And I had no proof that Wendy had taken it.

"Maybe it's fallen on the floor?"

Miss Watkins had a quick look around, then faced the class.

"Has anyone taken T. J.'s entry?"

No one spoke.

"This is very serious. If T. J. says she put her entry on the pile then either she's lying or someone's taken it. Is anyone going to enlighten me?"

Again no one spoke.

"She *did* do an entry," said Lucy. "I saw it. Honest, miss."

Miss Watkins looked upset. "This is *very* unfortunate, girls. It's almost the end of term and next year, you'll be going into Year Ten. You're not beginners anymore and, frankly, I'm disappointed in this sort of behavior. However, I'm going to ask you to act like mature adults and sort this out amongst yourselves. Twelve thirty this lunchtime is the deadline for entries, so unless you find it, T. J., or

713

someone owns up, I'm afraid there's not a lot more I'm prepared to do."

"That cow," said Lucy, as we filed out at break-time. "I'm sure it was Wendy Roberts."

"Did anyone see anything?" I asked.

Nesta shook her head. "She must have taken it from Miss Watkins's desk when you went to see Mrs. Allen."

"There was a whole crowd round Miss Watkins' desk," said Izzie. "Anyone could have taken it. You know how competitive everyone's been."

"But Wendy did come in after you, T. J. You know, before lessons started. Remember?" said Izzie.

"To the loos," said Nesta. "Let's go."

We ran down the corridor to the cloakrooms. Lucy looked in the cubicles while Nesta searched in the trash can.

"Er*lack*," said Nesta, as she rummaged around amongst bits of old tissue and paper towels.

"Oh, *noooo*," I heard Lucy say, as she reached the third cubicle.

She came out holding a sopping wet pile of ripped paper. "I'm *so* sorry, T. J., it was in the trash can next to the loo."

714

Izzie took what was left of the magazine. "It looks like she ran it under the tap first."

"But *why*?" I said. "Why has she got it in for me?"

"Doesn't have to be a reason," sighed Nesta. "Some people are just very *very* sad. They can't stand to see anyone else doing well."

"I reckon she never got over being made to look an idiot when Sam Denham was here," said Izzie. "You know, when he praised your answer and dismissed hers."

"What are we going to do?" I said, leaning back against one of the sinks. "I can't hand it in like this."

"We could go to Mrs. Allen," said Nesta.

I was gutted. "We could, but what will that achieve? Only make Wendy hate me more. The main thing is, my entry's unreadable. *All* that work, wasted." I was near to tears. "And all your contributions."

Lucy got her mobile out of her bag. "What time is it?" she said.

"Eleven," I said.

She began dialing frantically.

"Who are you phoning?" I asked.

"Steve," she said. "His year's doing exams and stuff, so their schedule's all over the place.

He might be at home revising."

"Brill," said Izzie. "He's got the mag on his computer. It will only take a minute to print out."

"That's if he's there," said Nesta.

Lucy listened as the phone rang, then she grimaced. "Voicemail," she said. "He must be doing something."

"Leave a message anyway," said Izzie. "It's our only chance."

We went back into the next lesson, but I couldn't concentrate. And neither could Nesta, Izzie, or Lucy, by the looks of it.

"If you look at your watch one more time, T. J. Watts," said Mr. Dixon, "I'm going to take it off you. And Lucy Lovering, if whatever you're staring at outside the window is so fascinating, I suggest you go and stand there for the rest of the lesson."

I glanced across at Wendy Roberts. She looked up from her book and smiled smugly.

You just wait, Wendy Roberts, I thought. It's not over yet.

We flew out of the classroom at lunchtime and out into the playground toward the gates.

No one there.

Lucy got out her phone again. She dialed, then shook her head. "Still on voicemail."

I checked my watch. Ten past twelve.

Twelve fifteen.

Twelve twenty.

"Did you say what time the deadline was when you left the message?" asked Nesta, looking up and down the street anxiously.

"Yeah," said Lucy. "I said twelve thirty. I'll try ringing again."

She was about to dial when Izzie grabbed my arm.

"Here he is," she cried as Steve came flying round the corner on his bike.

He screeched to a stop and pulled an envelope out of his rucksack.

"Good luck," he said as he handed it over.

"Thanks," I called over my shoulder as I ran back inside.

This time I wasn't taking any chances.

I went straight to the staff room and asked for Miss Watkins. I wanted to put my magazine into her hands myself.

Chapter 15

Result

"And the new editor will be . . .," said Mrs. Allen, as we stood in assembly on Friday.

I held my breath as Nesta gave me the thumbs-up.

"Before I announce the winner, I must say it's been very difficult," continued Mrs. Allen. "The standard of entries was exceptionally high and I'm very proud of all of you. Ultimately there are no losers. We've had a very hard time deciding and . . ."

Izzie gave me a look as if to say, "I wish she'd get on with it."

"Finally we narrowed it down to two. We decided on a tie. Two winners. First, Emma Ford from Year Ten. And second, T. J. Watts from Year Nine."

There were cheers from Nesta, Izzie, and Lucy at the back of the class. But, best of all, Wendy Roberts' face was a picture. Her mouth literally dropped open.

I gave her a huge smile as I went up to join Emma on the stage with Mrs. Allen.

After school we all piled back to Lucy's for celebratory ice cream and cake. When the girls were settled chomping away, Steve beckoned me up to his room.

"I . . . I have something for you," he said shyly.

He went to a drawer in the cabinet next to his bed. He pulled out a small package wrapped in silver, with a gold bow and a card and handed them to me. "These are for you."

I opened the card first. On the front it had a black-and-white photograph of a man on a road, with a caption underneath saying, "Life shrinks or expands in proportion to one's courage." Inside he'd written, "Good Luck to the new Editor of *For Real*."

"Thanks. That's really . . ."

"Open the pressie," he said, smiling.

I ripped off the paper and found a beautiful pen inside. It was Indian-looking, shiny turquoise and silver with sequinny things on the side.

"*Yu . . . nu . . . wee,*" I said, slipping back into Zoganese for a moment.

"You're welcome," he said, as if he understood perfectly. "It's for writing your novels."

For a moment, we just stayed looking at each other. It was the most perfect feeling. Like time stopped still and we were somehow melting into each other.

Then Steve grinned. "So next . . . ?"

"Next?" I asked. "What do you mean? Next?"

"That day in the park, when you asked how does anyone ever get together and you said for you, they'd have to make it *really* obvious—pressies, cards, a billboard in Piccadilly . . ."

I looked at my card and my present and smiled. "Oh. But please, no, not a billboard in Piccadilly, I'd *die. . . .*"

Steve laughed, then leaned toward me, pushed a lock of hair away from my face, looked deeply into my eyes and . . .

"We could go and see a movie next," he said.

"Love to," I said. "As long as it's not *Alien Mutants in Cyberspace*. And you don't spend the whole movie eating popcorn."

"Deal. Anyway, I hate popcorn."

We sort of grinned stupidly at each other, then I remembered what he'd said that day in the park. That he sometimes felt scared when he liked a girl.

No time like the present, I thought, as I leaned in and kissed him softly on the lips.

```
e-mail:      Inbox (1)
From:        paulwatts@worldnet.com
To:          babewithbrains@psnet.co.uk
Date:        5 July
Subject:     hol


Dear T. J.

New passport received this morning.
Coming home.

Paul
```

```
e-mail:      Outbox (1)
To:          hannahnutter@fastmail.com
From:        babewithbrains@psnet.co.uk
Date:        5 July
Subject:     mates, dates
```

Hey Hannahnutter

Whassup? Sorry I haven't been in touch; it's been mad here. So much has been happening. Paul's coming home. Scott is history. Got a date with Steve. Realized boys can be mates as well as dates. Der. Took me a while!

Velly happy. Hope you are.

And I won the competition with Emma Ford from Year Ten. I am now the new joint-editor of the school magazine. Hurrah.

T. J.
XXXXXXXXXXXXXXXXXXXXXXXXXXXXXXXXXXXXXXX

```
e-mail:      Inbox (1)
From:        hannahnutter@fastmail.com
To:          babewithbrains@psnet.co.uk
Date:        5 July
Subject:     Goody flobbalots
```

Velly solly me no been in touch either.

Goody flobbalots and hurrah about mag thing. I knew you'd get it.

And coolerooney about Steve. I could tell even from a zillion trillion miles away that something was going to 'appen zere. Hasta la banana and many jolly jollities to him. He soundeth superbio. A mate and a date. Best kind.

Mad here too. Replaced ze Luke with ze Ryan. So many boys, so little time etc, etc. Most excellent fun here. Loadsa big bashes and barbies, though I truly miss you and your strange angle on life and SOH.

Send me photos of your new look. And new boy. And new mag.

At last le T. J. has recognized she is ze babe *avec* ze brain.

Keep buzy and yabberyabber spoon.

Lurve and keesses

Your friend for ever and ever and ever and ever and ever and ever and . . . (oh, shutup H)

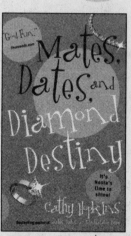

BY THE BESTSELLING AUTHOR OF THE MATES, DATES SERIES CATHY HOPKINS

Mates, Dates Guide To Life, Love, and Looking Luscious

WHAT HAPPENS WHEN LUCY, NESTA, IZZIE, AND T J GET TOGETHER AND START TALKING?

THEY COME UP WITH ALL SORTS OF SOLUTIONS FOR LIFE'S LITTLE DILEMMAS. . . .

Like boys for a start: what they want, where to find them, how to be a great kisser—everything you really need to know. They also share loads of lifestyle tips, from achieving the essential wardrobe to how to deal with a bad hair day.

From Simon Pulse
Published by
Simon & Schuster

The Mates, Dates girls are dishing all their secrets . . . just for you!

truth or dare

By the bestselling author of the Mates, Dates series,

Cathy Hopkins

Meet Cat, Becca, Squidge, Mac, and Lia. These girls and guys are totally tight—and totally obsessed with the game of truth or dare . . . even when it reveals too much!

Every book is a different dare . . . and a fun new adventure.

Read them all:

White Lies and Barefaced Truths
The Princess of Pop
Teen Queens and Has-Beens
Starstruck
Double Dare
Midsummer Meltdown

From Simon Pulse
Published by Simon & Schuster